Blade of
Redemption
by

Lee Roland

Guardians of the Blades, Book 1

Blade of Redemption

COPYRIGHT © 2021 by Lee Roland

Cover Art by *Debbie Taylor*

The Wild Rose Press, Inc.
PO Box 708
Adams Basin, NY 14410-0708
Visit us at www.thewildrosepress.com

Publishing History
First Edition, 2021
Trade Paperback ISBN 978-1-5092-3561-2
Digital ISBN 978-1-5092-3562-9

Guardians of the Blades, Book 1
Published in the United States of America

Dedication

For Woody. Still miss you, babe.

Boston, Massachusetts

My wonderous magic knife had disappeared again. Not that it could save me. My broken fingers wouldn't curl around the hilt. Being beaten and kicked to death hurts. Each breath brings more shrieking agony. But it's almost over. I barely see the last boot coming. I don't feel my ribs break. I hear them. They snap like small limbs on dying trees. Blood gushes into my throat from a punctured lung. I choke, drowning.

Hands lift me, drag me across the floor. I'm hurled, naked, shattered, onto the frozen parking lot. Oh, the light. Blinding daylight. Bitter, burning cold. I land half on the asphalt and half on the dirt at the edge. No pain now. My body, in shock, has raced past that sensation. Not long now. This atrocious existence would end. My fingertips, missing nails, drag across polluted, oil-soaked soil. Tiny slivers of ice crumble under them.

A man hovered over me. Through my one open eye I see an angelic face. McKay. My lover. My killer. His merciless smile mocks me. He slowly shakes his head. I hear the melodic voice that had once thrilled and aroused me. "Well, baby girl, it's been fun. See you in another life."

Another life? Okay. I'd finished with this one. Ah, the fireflies have come. That's what I called them, those tiny magical dancing lights that so delighted me as a child. I was the only one who could see them, so they were mine alone. How long had it been? What's that noise? Someone screaming? Not me. My mouth is full of blood.

The fireflies' radiance grows brighter. Glowing warmth cradles me as they whirl and turn. Their bright trails weaving delicate patterns. I hear the song now, the delicate melody. It rises from the earth and flows softly through my mind. It whispers of love and carries boundless magic. I fall into darkness, certain that enchantment will welcome me when I wake.

Chapter One

The future doesn't look promising when you get off the bus and the first person to greet you has a uniform, badge, and gun.

The bus slowed to a jerky, squawking stop.

"Garnet," the bus driver shouted over his shoulder. He pronounced it Garrrr-net, stretching the "r" a preposterous distance. I rose from my seat. Muscles protested at the movement, inactive far too long. Road Rash Transport was not among the major passenger carriers in Arizona. No one would ever accuse them of speeding, and as far as I could tell, they had no time schedule other than a probable day of the week. Ride for three days and three nights across the country to Flagstaff, sit in the bus terminal for nine ass and mind-numbing hours, connect with a local carrier—a.k.a. Road Rash—and then head…which way? I'd lost my sense of direction. In keeping with the current events of my life, the call of the open road was more a sour brass bellow than a song of seduction. I didn't bother to wonder how my life had come to this lonely, uncomfortable journey. It would be a waste of time. But I guess it's better than the times when I wondered why I was alive.

The bus had rolled across the long miles into what had to be the driest, most unpopulated part of Arizona—or the entire country. Absolutely flat in places, then between the low hills and onward west toward the distant mountains. North of the Grand Canyon, between reservations, Garnet wasn't on any map. Dry, red and gold land stretched under the current noonday sun. A high-elevation desert of unyielding uniformity, it spread for miles upon endless miles. Widely scattered and unpretentious juniper trees fought with sparse gray-green shrubs for any drops of water that might fall. A starkly scenic place, but big, open, and empty.

My fellow Road Rash travelers consisted of a cluster of tired looking people going God knows where. Most had deep copper skin, raven black hair, and spoke in a language I couldn't identify. I didn't stand out too much since I have caramel skin and my hair is long, thick, and deep, earthy brown. Only my gray eyes set me apart. Once upon a time people had called me beautiful or gorgeous. Those words flattered me then. They mean nothing now. The face staring back at me from a mirror hadn't changed, but that mirror didn't show everything. That I was twenty-nine pushing thirty meant nothing either. Of course, as a woman standing five-eleven, I'm noticeable.

My Aunt Lo had sent me tickets for this luxurious passage from Boston. She had called it a fresh start. I told her it was simply an evasion of the inevitable. I'm a long-term captive at the mercy of other people's whims and desires.

I walked the aisle to the front of the bus. Right before I got there, a bony hand, rough with calluses, grasped my own. I turned to look down into the face of a woman so old it amazed me that she lived. Her eyes, alert and deep gold like the desert, had a faint shine.

She spoke a few words in that unidentifiable language, then grinned. She had no teeth. I nodded, returned the smile, and she released me. I *think* she meant well. She might have blessed me—or cursed me—for all I knew. I walked on and stepped onto the concrete tarmac of a gas station, the official bus depot in Garnet.

I had the letter Aunt Lo sent me.

Well, Lilly Girl, Garnet has four retail stores, a gas station, one semi-retired doctor who is also the pharmacist, a sheriff, and deputy. A couple hundred people live scattered around here and there. Officially that many. Might be more, might be less. Everyone knows everyone and no one minds their own business. Don't miss the bus. It only comes once a week.

Lilly Girl, that's what Aunt Lo had always called me as a kid. She'd kept in touch with me and my brother Frank over the years, occasionally visiting, trying to help us, keep us alive. Each time we made one of our sudden moves we let her know where we'd landed.

The badge, uniform, and gun standing on the Garnet tarmac most certainly waited for me. No surprise. The inevitable jolt of anxiety punched my guts before I punched back, refusing to let it rule me. I'd had challenging experiences with law enforcement. Violence and its consequences had been a part of my life for a long time. The stain of that brutality would never go away.

I carefully ignored the uniform until the driver retrieved my one bag from the compartment under the bus and handed it to me. It wasn't full or heavy, just a medium sized duffel bag decorated with multiple pockets. That bag, my threadbare jeans, T-shirt, and the denim jacket on my back were everything I owned in this world. You don't carry much while you're on the run—or when you've lost so much you have absolutely nothing else worth losing. I hoisted it to my shoulder and waited for the bus to roar away in a cloud of dense, black, carbon smoke.

When the air cleared, I turned my attention to the man. He was too big to ignore. Not that his size mattered. Lesser men could hurt a woman just as easy as any other. Tall, six-five or so, broad shoulders, he wore a crisp tan uniform appropriate for the desert land around us. He had short jet-black hair and eyes deep and dark enough a woman could lose her way in their depths. Thirty to thirty-five, his skin, a little darker than mine, said he spent time in the sun. A full mouth, but tight and disapproving. He could be considered handsome, but only if you liked hard-ass authority figures. His focused gaze raked over me for what seemed like a long time. I fought the urge to shrink away. This had to be the sheriff Lo mentioned in her letter.

"Ms. Dusalte." Such an impersonal voice, deep and hard. This sheriff knew who I was and didn't want me in his town.

I nodded. *When unsure what to say, keep your mouth shut.*

"I'd like to look in your bag."

Whoa. He had no cause for a search, but I'd learned to pick my battles. Two men now stood at the gas station bays to watch us—a real, old fashioned gas station, not one connected to a convenience store. Ah, small towns. You had to love them. In a couple of hours, I'd be the subject of conversation everywhere.

My arrival might be the entertainment for the month—or year.

"Sure." I dropped the bag to the concrete.

He picked it up. "Come with me."

Obviously, the sheriff had performed due diligence and examined every piece of information available about my sordid life. He turned and walked away leaving me to follow him and my meager possessions. Since he'd offered me his back, the man obviously didn't consider me an immediate threat.

It was no major journey. Only a wide yellow dirt alley separated the sheriff's office and gas station. According to Aunt Lo, the whole town was less than an eighth of a mile long. Three cars and two pickups parked up and down the street, but no foot traffic around. I spied my ultimate destination a hundred yards away. Aunt Lo's Garnet Tavern. She'd sent me pictures over the years, so I recognized its distinctive appearance.

Garnet teetered on a fine line between worn and worn out. Traditional landscaping that might soften bleak, boxy architecture didn't exist. Water would be precious in this land, and not wasted on frivolous aesthetic features. Aunt Lo said the dry, high-elevation, Colorado Plateau wasn't as hot as the lower deserts. It snowed sporadically in the winter, but today, just past noon, a comfortable seventy-five degrees made me want to remove my jacket. A layer of thin, omnipresent sand triggered tiny crunching sounds beneath my shoes.

The sheriff's office, brick and covered with a layer of dust, was fifty feet wide and twice as long. Words painted in white on the window identified it as such—Sheriff's Office, City of Garnet. In much smaller letters, *Paxton J. Harrow, Sheriff.* Two patrol cars were parked at the side inside the alley. SUV type patrol cars that could crawl across rough terrain in pursuit of…whom? Why would anyone misbehave with such a fierce lawman on guard?

The sheriff opened the door and to my surprise, gestured for me to enter first. His sheer presence washed over me as I passed close to him. Was I intimidated? Oh, yes.

I walked into a single front room that held two desks, bulletin boards, and file cabinets, all sitting behind glass-fronted wood counters. The place might have been a retail store in a former life. Several pine scented air fresheners scattered around the room couldn't quite mask the odor of age.

There was a door in the back wall I presumed led to the jail cells. I didn't know how sturdy those cells might be since significant cracks in the exposed brick wall would undoubtedly give way to a solid boot. An old fashioned, cast-iron, wood-burning stove nestled in one corner. *How quaint. Wonder how far they had to go to find wood to burn.*

Another uniform stood in the middle of the room. Ah, the deputy. Young, like barely out of college, he looked so new and innocent it made me wonder how he'd ever deal with a real criminal. My former companions would eat him alive in less than a minute.

Not as sizable as the sheriff, he had bright blue eyes, sand colored hair, and a pretty, boyish face. His healthy lean body would make schoolgirls yearn to grow up and married women wish they were single, at least for a few hours. *Not my type, but my friend Julia…ah, don't think about Julia, Lilly. Don't think about her.*

The sheriff dropped my duffel bag on the counter. The deputy frowned, as if unsure of what was happening. He came closer, obviously interested.

"Hi," I said. I gave the deputy my best smile, simply because he wasn't glaring at me with the sheriff's cold fury. "I'm Lilly Dusalte."

I offered my hand across the counter, and he accepted it. Hands tell much about a person. Calluses covered his. He had worked extremely hard at physical labor and had a thickness on the trigger finger, too. He could shoot. He practiced often.

"Ben Rico," the deputy said. "Lo told us you were coming." He grinned and held my hand a little too long before he let go. "Welcome to Garnet."

I stared pointedly to where Sheriff Harrow continued *his* warm welcome by dragging stuff out of my bag. The deputy, Ben, gave me an apologetic look. He wouldn't interfere, of course. The sheriff was alpha here, and Benny-boy would follow his lead.

The sheriff inspected my limited clothing, searching every pocket. Jeans, T-shirts, plain utilitarian underwear. He did a thorough examination of the bag that carried soap and shampoo. I had a box of tampons I kept for rare periods. He even opened those. What was he looking for? Drugs? Weapons? My cheap cell phone only rated a single cursory glance.

He turned to me. "ID?"

I handed him the small wallet from my pocket. I had a Massachusetts driver's license, twenty-two dollars, and a small stack of business cards with my probation officer's name, title, and phone number. He pulled one of the cards, then tossed the wallet on the

9

counter by my clothes. Obviously finished, he stalked away and sat behind the larger desk. That left me to fold and repack my things. Relief washed over me. He hadn't performed a body search.

The sheriff stuck my probation officer's card under a desk mat. "Why did you come here, Ms. Dusalte?"

He already knew the answer to his question. I played the game, though. "Needed a place to stay. My Aunt Lo offered."

"You mean you need a place to hide." Oh, such a deep, hard, stone voice. Its owner was certain I planned vile, evil deeds. This stern sheriff had thoroughly checked me out before I arrived. He knew everything inscribed in official files, and I'm sure he'd sought information from the underground criminal sources. I guess a small-town lawman had more time to be proactive about crime and not wait until someone acted. He obviously expected extensive unlawful conduct from me.

"Hide?" I shook my head. "No. Not hide. He *will* come for me eventually. Fewer people here, though. Line of sight is better, too. Maybe I'll see him coming."

He, of course, was McKay, my ex-lover who had gone on the run after the FBI sting took down his lucrative criminal organization. I was McKay's girlfriend, and unfortunately, his bookkeeper. I knew where he'd hidden the loot.

The FBI watched, scooped me up, and used the knowledge against me. I'd agreed to testify to get probation. By that time, I was terrified and desperate to get away from McKay and his violent life before it killed me. Everything was okay until he found me. He hurt me first, then he tossed me to his gang.

The only thing that saved me that day was the fire that brought people to the scene. *A mysterious warehouse fire*. McKay escaped, but most of his gang, trapped inside the building, burned.

McKay is out there. I don't know what he's waiting on. Hide? Wrong word. He could get to me whenever he wanted. The son of a bitch sent me flowers once—and a single bullet on my hospital dinner tray. Did it mean he'd kill me next time instead of torturing me again? Or did it mean I should kill myself to avoid more pain.

When I finished my year in rehab, the FBI picked me up and let me sit in jail to remind me that they still owned me. Aunt Lo, a fortress of determination, had somehow managed to convince them to let me come here to Garnet. She said I'd be safe. I had no money, no job, nowhere else to go. I didn't want anyone, including people I cared about, to be around when McKay came for me.

The dour sheriff raised his head and stared at me as if looking for something. "You don't carry?"

"A gun? No. Probation, remember. If McKay shows up, I'm supposed to call *you*."

"Yes. You most certainly are. Remember that. *Call me*." He dismissed me and turned his attention to the papers on his desk. I'm sure he thought he could deal with McKay.

I'd seen reports, written by law enforcement, that grossly underestimated McKay's cunning. With his genius mind and well-earned street smarts, the man was resourceful and unbelievably cruel. His strength and vitality were the things that had drawn me to him in the first place. Even now, after all the pain, I remembered the passion, the intensity.

After I repacked, a smiling Ben came and lifted my bag onto his shoulder.

He winked at me. "Come on. I'll walk with you."

Such a pretty boy. I glanced at Harrow. He didn't look up. Deputy Ben followed orders but didn't seem overly intimidated by his boss.

When we walked outside and the door closed behind us, Ben said, "Don't mind Pax. He's not that bad." He hesitated and glanced over his shoulder. Did he think someone followed, that someone was listening?

"Pax worries about…everything," Ben continued. "It's the job. It's home. And it's always personal. He was born and grew up here, knows everyone."

"So was I, Ben. Born in Garnet. I don't know anyone because my Mama took me away as a baby." I didn't know why. Mama's judgment was always dubious and frequently bizarre. She made bad choices in her life. I paid for them because she always blamed me when the shit came down.

Ben was silent for a moment, then… "This man, the one that's after you—"

"McKay? I don't want to talk about him now. Maybe later." Had the sheriff not given Ben the details of my sordid past?

We didn't walk far. From what I could see, other than the sheriff's office, the buildings of Garnet consisted of pathetic concrete and steel boxes. The largest, Garnet Grocery and Mercantile, looked like one of those *little bits of everything* stores. A few block houses and storefronts lined the road, but most appeared uninhabited. No sidewalks, just the worn asphalt road and dirt. A massive, aged log cabin, the Garnet Tavern, stood out of place and out of time.

According to Aunt Lo, my great grandfather had built it from logs he had shipped in from Oregon. Significant trees had not graced the barren land under my feet since the last Ice Age. A single sign carved with the word *Tavern* hung over the door. The requisite neon beer signs shone in the windows. It had a wide front porch, which was unusual. Since I'm a magnet for trouble, it also had the requisite bully who slammed out the front door as we were going up the steps.

Oh, he was a beast of a man. So stereotypical I'd laugh—if he didn't look so dangerous. Big gut, tattoos, shaved head, dirty leathers—and thick arms that ended in massive fists. One of those fists punched out lightning fast and collided with Deputy Ben's face. His jaw cracked like a ball hitting a bat. Ben flew straight back, arms wide, sprawling onto the dirt.

I was inclined to step out of the way and let the big bastard pass, then see to Ben. Nothing was that easy. The brute lifted a massive boot back to kick…oh, no.

"Hey, asshole!"

As he turned to face me, I bent down and grabbed both hands full of dirt and gravel. I flung it in his eyes. He roared with rage, clawed at his face, stumbled, and cursed with words too obscene for the dictionary. I needed a better weapon. There. A football sized rock beside the porch steps.

Ben moved, struggling to rise. Okay, a diversion. "Ben! Damn it. Shoot him!"

The brute immediately whirled back to what he thought would be the real danger. The lawman with the gun—who unfortunately remained helpless on the ground. I snatched up the rock. A solid grip, using both hands, I lifted the makeshift weapon high and smacked it down on the Big Brute's head. A solid strike, right at the base of his thick skull. It sounded like hitting a ripe melon. He staggered two piddling steps sideways.

Barely dazed, the man grunted and twisted back toward me. Could I outrun him? At least get him away from Ben? I backpedaled, but my legs, tight from the bus ride, failed me. I smacked down on my ass. With him standing over me, memory engulfed my mind. *Fists hurt. Hands hurt. Burning, holding sharp...*

My assailant made one step, then froze, rigid as a statue. What the hell? His eyes bugged out. His mouth opened, and he panted like a dog. I scrambled to my feet.

Aunt Lo stood on the tavern porch. She wasn't looking at me. She wasn't looking at the brute. She stared at Sheriff Harrow. He knelt by his deputy. He had arrived, watched, and made no effort to help me. No pointed gun, no shout to halt? Oh, damn. He'd turn the other way when McKay arrived. Or stand back and enjoy the show. I'd expected nothing in this place, and nothing is what I'd receive. The unbending thug standing in front of me slowly collapsed to his knees. He swayed and toppled over completely. I was on my feet by then and had to dance away to keep him from hitting me.

My Aunt Lo—Luella Love Dusalte—looks like my mother, Louise. Not a surprise since they're identical twins. She's a little taller than me, which made her at least six feet. We have the same deep brown hair, tan skin, gray eyes, and solid build. Lo can be hard as concrete at times, then instantly turn gentle as a warm soothing bath. Mama isn't like that. Mama is cold and bitter all the time. *And Mama is bat shit crazy.*

The sheriff helped Ben to his feet, but the boy swayed and staggered. Aunt Lo was suddenly in the sheriff's face and backing him away. I should have been able to hear what they were saying, but I couldn't. My, what a lively argument. I went to Ben and grabbed his arm.

"Hey, how are you?"

"Okay." I could barely hear him. And he most certainly wasn't okay. It had to hurt. Poor man. His rapidly swelling jaw meant he probably wouldn't be able to talk soon.

"What's going on?" I nodded at the sheriff and Aunt Lo.

"Don't know." The words came out in a mumble. He swayed again, so I guided him to sit on the edge of the porch. I sat by him and held his hand. He needed medical attention, and the people who could summon it for him stood squabbling in the street.

Finally, the sheriff turned his head and stared away into the distance. Lo seemed to have prevailed. She came to us. "Lilly, please go inside."

Fine by me. I could tell by that little twitch under her left eye she remained majorly pissed.

I glanced at Ben. His head drooped. He wouldn't stay up much longer. "He's hurt, Lo. He should have an x-ray or something. He got hit hard. Broke his jaw, maybe a concussion."

"Doc is coming. He'll take care of him."

I kissed Ben on the cheek. "Hope you're better soon."

His head bobbed a fraction. I grabbed my duffel

bag and went into the tavern. I had no curiosity about what would happen next, except for Ben. I had a mighty sympathy for a young man rewarded with violence and pain. Especially when his kind offer of friendship to a stranger put him in the direct path of an irate giant.

Chapter Two

Not bad, the Garnet Tavern. Way bigger than it looked from the outside. From the joints and uneven earth-colored logs, I'd say a caretaker had expanded the original building over the years. It had that beery smell of all such establishments, but there was no ceiling, so it wasn't claustrophobic. Exposed beams and rafters stained dark with age and smoke testified to a time when a person could light up in a bar. The massive rock fireplace against one wall ran floor to roof. It probably couldn't heat the whole place, but it was a masterpiece of stonework.

The tables and chairs, sturdy solid wood, hadn't been new since the seventies. Bandstand to the side, jukebox, large dance floor, the place would be lively when full. Could I dance? I loved dancing once. Physical therapy had given me the strength. There was no physical therapy that could repair the broken desire to do anything so lively.

The grand ornate bar with its rich wood design could grace a movie version of an old west saloon. Oh, there were two bars with two distinctive styles, both antiques from another era, probably the 1800s, when things, like people, were smaller. They were stuck end to end to make a long, beautiful, but oddly matched single piece of furniture.

My new job? Bartender. Lo had sent me a book of

drink recipes to memorize. No problem. I have what I'm told is eidetic memory, commonly called photographic memory. I never believed that the clinical definition was a perfect fit for my condition, but I didn't know anything else to call it. Unfortunately, it's sporadically debilitating. I can remember most of the scenes of my life, satisfactory and appalling, if I try. But under stress, a mob of memories can escape. In defense, my mind shuts down. I usually achieve control in seconds, but it's a fearsome battle.

To deal with the problem, I created compartments, little boxes in my mind. I stuff them full and locked them tight. My mental boxes are how I make order from chaos. The major flaw in control? A sudden, intense spike of stress pokes what feels like a thin silver hook into my brain. That hook usually tears open one or more of my constructed mental prisons. They could be memories of rare times of happiness, or every hour of shrieking pain, blinding sorrow, and substantial guilt I'd suffered in my life. My battle for control remains desperate and epic, at least in my own mind. Of course, no memory, no life lesson, had kept me from making monumentally bad decisions at times.

I had to have special permission to work here in the tavern because of probation. No alcohol beverages for me, but I could pour them in a glass and hand them to others. Lo had taken total responsibility to keep me a gainfully employed, alcohol free, law-abiding citizen of Garnet, Arizona. My probation officer, wanting to be rid of me and the chilling specter of McKay, wholeheartedly agreed.

Lo burst in, her face locked in an expression of wrath. She muttered under her breath, obviously cursing the sheriff. I hated that.

"I should leave, Lo. Your sheriff doesn't want me here. And I don't blame him. I told you I didn't want to be a problem."

I didn't want to go back to jail for violating probation either. I was certainly aware the sheriff could use his authority to set me up. That equaled a quick death sentence, instead of a delayed one. McKay had people in jail, too.

She ran her hands through her hair then rubbed them on her jeans. "This is your *home*, Lilly. Pax knows that. You belong here. What is wrong with that stubborn ass male? Just try to stay out of his way." Lo turned on the inevitable warmth and hugged me. "So glad you're okay, girl."

"Okay is a big word, but I'm physically healed and functioning now." I held her tight, wanting to cling to her, absorb her strength.

She'd been a regular visitor after McKay and his men enjoyed their monstrous beating and cutting party. Broken, smashed like an egg on concrete, I clinically died twice—once in the ambulance and again on the operating table. The minute she saw me, Lo had me transferred to a private hospital and rehab facility. Mega expensive, but I had the best care. I never asked how she paid for it all. I knew she owned and operated a tavern in a desert town. The dismal isolation of the business surprised me.

"Lo? Why did that asshole hit Ben? Do you know?"

"No. He came in, acted like an ass, and I kicked him out. I think he discharged his fury on the first person he came across. Come on, let me take you to your new home. No mansion, but it's clean. Has heat and AC, too."

She led me out the back door of the Tavern. We walked four hundred feet down a narrow path. The rough parched ground around the pathway, strewn with baseball and football size rocks, stood ready to trip the unwary trekker. My new home consisted of a long, low single-story motel, built at least sixty years ago. Lo had it fixed up and converted into apartments.

"My great uncle built this. It was originally twelve rooms," she said. "Now it's six apartments. I don't have time to do maintenance for all of them, so I don't rent them anymore. You have the place all to yourself."

The apartments had dividers on the long covered front walkway to create individual porch spaces. My porch space had a jungle of healthy green plants in pots. They might stay healthy if I could remember to water them. A small table and two metal chairs created a patio of sorts. The once white table, now speckled with rust, had a layer of sand where I could sign my name.

The apartment was neat, recently cleaned, with a small kitchen, a table and three chairs, and a comfortable looking couch, all perfect for me. Another room with a queen bed, dresser, and bathroom finished it off nicely. Very homey. A mix of colors, but after the unrelieved white and beige of the medical facilities and jail, I didn't care.

Lo gestured at the TV, a moderate sized flat screen. "You have access to satellite, and there's a cell tower down the road, so you have a signal for your phone. You can use my computer if you'd like. There's a new mattress, linens, towels, dishes, microwave, and a coffee maker." She pointed to the kitchen where the life-saving appliances covered half of the available counter space. Not that I'd need counter space. I have never cooked, nor ever desired the skill. Mama had an intense irrational fear that I would poison her. She put locks on every refrigerator and pantry we'd ever had to keep me away from food. And that one deed kept me starving half the time, too.

Lo leaned against the door frame. "Tavern's open Tuesday through Saturday five to two."

I dropped my bag on the couch. "The tavern does big business? Seems like there aren't enough people around here."

"More than you think. Mostly locals on Tuesday, Wednesday, and Thursday, but there's a big mining outfit, a couple of factories, and retail stores in Sioux Crossing. It's a small town about fifteen miles to the northwest. The kids here go to school there, too. I get a crowd on the weekends. Loud, rough, and rowdy." She frowned. "Do you have money for food?"

"Twenty dollars or so. But I don't eat much."

"Go over to the store and get groceries. Tell Ronnie, Ronnie Valentine, he's the owner, to put it on my tab. We'll settle at the end of the week. Keep a smile on that pretty face and you'll have plenty of tips in your jar. I'll pay you, too."

I'd never be able to truly settle with her. She had not only paid for my hospital and rehab, she also paid for the exclusive private asylum Mama had resided in for the last seven years. The asylum where Mama would stay, warm, fed, and prudently medicated, for the rest of her tormented life. Unless the money ran out. It was odd. At first, I figured money was why Lo sent me a cheaper bus ticket instead of an airline ticket. I would not question her about money or her generosity.

Lo pulled me into her arms again. I enjoyed her embrace so much. "May the goddess forgive me, Lilly, but I hate your mother at times."

"The goddess? Come on, Lo, don't let Father Frank hear you talking like that. You'll get a lecture on worshiping pagan deities."

Lo chuckled and patted my cheek before stepping back. "Your self-righteous brother can kiss my butt. He is a sweetheart, though. I do love him. How is he?"

"He's fine. Worried about my journey to Garnet, a.k.a., pagan deity central. Worried about McKay getting to me again."

My brother Frank, ten years my senior and my mother's pride and joy, had joined the Catholic priesthood after a stint in the army. He loved me, cared for me. He was the only reason I hadn't died from neglect and Mama's brutality as a kid. He protected me from Mama as much as he could and called child services when he couldn't.

Mama had taken both of us from Garnet right after I was born. Beautiful, intelligent, she could have had the world had her mind not disintegrated. I'd heard hours of her indecipherable ranting and raving over the years. Garnet was full of devil worshipers was the most common theme. How she had to save us kids. Frank said it was a small town in the desert from what he remembered, but he was only eleven when we left. Pagan was the word he used for Garnet after he joined the church.

"Lo, why did Mama take me and Frank away from here? What happened?"

"Disagreements, her instability, it's hard to be

certain. Please be patient. This will be your home for a while. I promise I'm going to make sure you learn all about us. There is so much that you've missed. Certainly, more than your mother ever told you. It will take time. Okay?"

I nodded. I could wait. My long and painfully exhausting physical recovery had taught me patience. Besides, I had little else to do. I did wonder, though, how there could be *so much* to learn in such a small place in the middle of this arid desolation.

She grabbed me again and held me in another fierce hug.

"Lo, Frank and I will never be able to repay you for everything you've done for us."

"Oh, goddess bless you, sweetheart. You and Frank are my only family. Who else would I take care of? But you're here with me now, and I'm going to keep you as long as I can."

Lo had made several attempts to get custody of Frank and me. Most of the time, Mama would turn on her best behavior act, con judges and social services. We'd go into foster homes occasionally, but she inevitably regained custody. Then we'd move and go into hiding again. Lo did her best to keep track of us, and Frank and I did our best to let her know our location.

I noticed that she hadn't included Mama in her *only family*. Mama had cried for home and family regularly and spewed vile curses in the next breath. She cursed me, too, but fawned over my brother. I was either a demon or I didn't exist. Nonexistence was a useful status for me then, much safer than being her demon. I'd only met my father once. His face burns bright in my memories. When I was eight years old, a man with pure white hair came to my room one night. He stayed only brief minutes. He told me he was my dad and said he was sorry. He didn't say what he was sorry for unless it was leaving me with Mama. When I asked Mama about him the next day, she beat me unconscious with a belt.

"You'll be safe here." Lo sounded sure of that. "You can sleep easy at night."

"Okay, I don't sleep much, though."

I lied. I don't sleep at all. An occasional ten to fifteen-minute half-assed nap when I was tired did it for me. The sleeplessness started after McKay's last beatings, the ones that should have killed me. A brain injury the doctors told me. Something about damaged neurotransmitters.

I don't miss sleep, don't seem to physically suffer. Except in jail. Not being able to sleep made for long days and longer nights there. I did, however, learn to meditate. My preference was for hard physical exercise, but one of the nurses at the rehab facility taught a class to help control the pain. If I thanked God, or Lo's goddess, it would be for that. Meditation brought me as much peace as my life would allow.

Lo left me and I made myself at home. I needed to shower and change the clothes I'd been wearing for five days. First though, I had to strip and peel away the tape securing my knife and sheath to my leg. The tape took a bit of hair and skin with it. I'd left it there too long.

The knife. So unbelievably beautiful. The amazing blue-white blade had swirling designs incised along the surface. Frank called them runes. They deeply alarmed him, so I kept it hidden. The carved bone hilt had a single black stone affixed to the end.

Beyond amazing, it is the strangest thing in my life—other than the fact that I'm still alive. My remarkable memory failed on how it came to me. I believe it arrived during adolescence, a particularly brutal time. It was a phenomenon that defied all logic, all reason. I don't like the word magic, because it connotes a slight of hand, a trick. What else? *Enchanted? Supernatural*? The eight-inch blade is always sharp and will cut almost any organic matter—except me. A butter knife is more dangerous to my body.

There was never anyone I'd trust to ask questions about the weapon. It would disappear at critical times, like when I was in jail. When things settled, I'd find it in an odd, but safe place. I hadn't seen it in over two years when I found it wrapped in a shirt as I packed my pitiful possessions for the trip to Garnet. *Magic or miracle, the knife was mine, irrevocably mine*.

I had a sheath that hooked to a belt, the most comfortable way to carry. Not here, though. Given the hostility, I didn't know how the sheriff would react. Thankfully, he hadn't done a body search. The knife would probably leave, but how would I explain the layers of tape around my leg. I swore I'd never be without a weapon, though. I couldn't buy a gun. I'd committed vile acts but never had the earnest desire to kill. I had told myself so often that I had not battled my way through recovery, through agony and sorrow, to give up. I will die fighting when McKay comes for me. My death will, I hope, be formidable enough to honor the memory of my beautiful friend and the two FBI agents who died trying to protect me from a monster.

That sounds so noble, Lilly. It's bullshit. Does it ease your guilt for your own crimes? Does it ease your fear?

After my shower, I shoved the knife and sheath in my jacket's roomy inside pocket and walked to Garnet Grocery and Mercantile which, like the tavern, was far bigger than it looked from the outside. But I suppose it had a captive clientele in this little…what? Town? Bus stop?

The store, a concrete box, carried boxed and canned food, various frozen items. Hardware, over the counter drugs, and a small post office in the back corner. The post office was only open on Mondays and Thursdays. It had a zip code, though I did wonder how large an area that zip covered.

I introduced myself to Ronnie Valentine, the owner. A lean, hard man, to look at him, I'd have guessed he was a construction worker, not a storekeeper. Salt and pepper hair, dark eyes, he wasn't openly hostile like the sheriff, but he gave me several cool stares. Forget Lo's account. I used my own money for my purchases. I could live on coffee, bread, peanut butter, and a couple of cans of soup until I earned my wages. At least the date on the bread hadn't expired. I did grab two used fifty-cent paperback books off a shelf in the corner by the post office.

When I got back to the apartment, I dug out my new cell phone, a gift from Frank. As I had promised, I made my first call to him. I had to leave a message.

"Okay, Father Franklin, I've arrived in wild pagan territory. I've not seen any rituals yet, no naked dancing in the meadow. I haven't even seen a meadow. It's mostly sand and rock. But don't despair. There is a full moon in a couple of weeks. Prime time for rituals and naked dancing. I'll keep you posted. Little sister loves you, Frank."

Chapter Three

I ate a couple of peanut butter sandwiches and decided I needed to go outside and stretch my legs. I'd been sitting for days. The sun barely touched the western mountain tops by then, poised as if uncertain whether to hide behind them or drop and set them ablaze. Given the low humidity to hold the heat, the temperature would make a steep plunge as the light faded.

A walk behind the motel would be good. I'd managed three or four hundred feet over rock and dry sand when I came to an old, abandoned roadway. Not covered wagon old, but old as in nothing had rolled over it since World War II. Way long enough for native weeds to sprout, their roots eagerly eating through crumbling asphalt cracks.

Utterly flat land surrounded Garnet itself, but it stretched only a short distance to low hills. I passed a deeper wash, a furrow gouged in the flat land. Twenty feet deep, a steep-sided thirty-foot wide crack broke the earth. Treacherous for cross country drivers. I'd read about them and other features on the internet when I knew I was coming here. The dry sandy ripples on the bottom were testament to equally treacherous flash floods. Rain, miles away in the mountains, would send a raging deluge of water roaring down the channel.

I liked the look of Garnet more, though. I had a

better sense of place. I could set aside the last hour's violence and find a surprising peace. It wouldn't last long, that peace, but for a few moments, it was mine.

I walked along the old roadway and spied the first stone. It flashed a tiny spark in the last light before the sun dropped completely behind the mountains. A clear crystal. I brushed the sand off and held it to the light. The internet said I might find turquoise, topaz, or the town's namesake, garnets. I doubted I'd find them lying around here, beside a road like this. Builders usually hauled roadside fill from off the site during construction. Surprisingly, I picked up several pretty stones and had a decent handful.

"What are you doing?"

I whirled at the words. My collection of stones escaped. They bounced and clattered on broken asphalt, striking with the sound of thin ice cracking in the spring thaw.

The sheriff stood behind me. Straight as a tall pine, stern as a hanging judge, he'd made absolutely no sound as he'd approached. I drew a deep stuttering breath, then let it out. My racing heart slowed. "I'm collecting rocks. Is that against the law here?"

"No, but if you're running from someone, I suggest you pay more attention to what's around you. Or who's behind you." His voice was cold as sleet, a near impossible moisture in this desert.

He, however, was right about paying better attention.

I knelt to pick up my treasures.

The sheriff knelt beside me. What…? He pulled a neatly folded handkerchief out of his pocket. Did men still carry those? He unfolded the cloth, laid it across

29

his palm, and offered the material to me to use as a basket. He waited patiently as I picked up my treasures and dropped them in his hand. He folded the handkerchief and handed it to me. How very strange.

When we stood, he asked, "Why do you collect stones?"

I drew the bundle close to my chest. "They're pretty. I like to look at them."

I shivered and hoped he hadn't seen my reaction. Twilight had fallen and to my surprise, he walked with me as I headed back to the motel. He had a natural grace rare in a man his size, but he gave the impression of absolute authority, absolute control. He wouldn't hesitate or waver in action. A valuable trait for a cop, I guess. But could he stand up to McKay? My mind, my experience said no. Sheriff Harrow would be no match for the deceit and treachery of McKay's schemes.

"How's Deputy Ben?" I had to ask.

"Resting. Doc fixed him."

The sheriff stepped away to a low pile of desert rubble, knelt and scratched at it with his fingers. He picked something out, rose, and came back. He offered me a pea sized red stone. An actual garnet. I placed it with the rest of my treasures. This man had a formidable presence that made me want to lean closer and run away at the same time.

"Thank you." I did have a few manners.

He didn't speak again until we got back to the motel. At my front door, I said, "Thank you again." I held up my bundle of stones. "I'll get your handkerchief back to you, minus the dirt."

"Ms. Dusalte."

"Yes, Sheriff."

"I received a call from the FBI. An informant spotted McKay in Los Angeles. You think that's coincidence?"

So that's what the lawman had come to me for. The dread, the oppressive knot in my guts tightened. The rare moments of peace were gone for the day. My hands curled around my bundle of stones, and I held them to my heart as if they could offer protection.

"No, Sheriff, I don't believe in coincidence. Not with him, anyway. I'm quite certain McKay knows where I am. As for LA, money and power are the focus of his life, and that's the place for it, I suppose. He'll get around to me eventually."

"So, you haven't heard from him?" He scowled, fierce and angry. Angry at whom? Me?

And didn't this sheriff have the darkest, most beautiful eyes. What? Now where did that thought come from?

"Sheriff, the last time I heard from McKay was a note on my dinner tray at rehab. It said, 'get well soon' and that he'd see me again." Rehab where I cried and screamed every day. My broken bones and torn muscles healed, but the pure hell of making them function was the most difficult memory I had to keep locked away.

"The man who attacked Ben was asking for you. Did you know him?"

"No. Never saw him before." Why hadn't Lo told me that? Wanting to protect me?

"You don't seem surprised, though."

"Why should I be? McKay might have sent him. I left Boston fast, once they cut me loose. He might have lost me."

The sheriff stood motionless. How did he do that?

Most people fidgeted, moved their hands, and nodded heads.

"Ms. Dusalte, you do understand, don't you? The FBI is using you. You're here as bait on a hook. Damn the consequences."

Consequences as in damage to the sheriff's town, his people, not consequences of damage to me. The sheriff had classified me as a criminal, right along with McKay. He wasn't the first and was justified in doing so. My sins are not as numerous and profound as McKay's, but I had much to atone for.

I fought to keep my misery, fear, and resentment from showing. "Yes. I know what the FBI is doing, Sheriff. I can't change it." Bait? Of course I was. The FBI would continue to use me if they could. That's why they greeted me when I walked out of rehab. They'd locked me up to humiliate me and show me how bad it could be. Lo's demand that they allow me to come to her was merely a lucky convenience for them. The city's masses could swallow me. Not so easy in this flat empty land. I clutched my stones tighter.

The sheriff's expression remained hard and unyielding. "Garnet is quiet most times. Gets crowded on weekends. Ben and Chuck, our part time deputy, will watch for anyone suspicious. Lo said she'd walk you to your place after closing. Or one of us will."

Because of Lo. He was offering me protection for her sake. No, no. I didn't want that. Make someone else a target for trying to help me? Absolutely not. "Sheriff, that isn't necessary."

"Yes, it is." He turned to leave.

"Sheriff?"

He faced me again.

"McKay is smart and treacherous. I swear, if he catches me, I'll jump into his arms, beg him to forgive me, and if he does, I can try to kill him later. Did you read about him, Sheriff? Do you know what he's capable of?"

He stared at me, once again, his expression grew cold and angry. But he did speak. "James Alton McKay, forty-three years old, former Army Special Forces. He had a high-level organization. Murder, major theft, money laundering, and large-scale drug deals. And you produced the evidence that broke him. The FBI took his organization apart two years ago." Disgust seeped into his voice. "They let him get away."

"Please understand, Sheriff. He's charismatic. Hypnotic…like a cult leader. He always has followers, and they worship him, make personal sacrifices. They believe in him." So, had I—for a while. An unparalleled lover with a wonderful face and body that drew me in and kept me for three years. I had adored him too.

The sheriff stepped closer. When he spoke, his voice was thick and deep with revulsion. I'd heard it before, that tone of abhorrence telling me exactly how vile, how evil I was, how I was no better than the man I'd served.

"Tell me, Ms. Dusalte, exactly what did he see in you before you turned him in? What made *you* so important to him? *Obsessed.* That's the word used most often in the reports. Many of the reports."

"I don't know. I lived with that obsession, and I don't understand it either."

Yes, lived with McKay's obsession, his jealous, dangerous rage from the day I met him. I'm attractive yes, but even after he stopped loving me, McKay wouldn't let me go. His torture, his attempt at killing me spoke to the depth of that obsession, too. I had no idea of how my escape from death had affected him.

The sheriff slowly shook his head. "I don't like it when people lie to me."

"I haven't…" I stopped, then shrugged. What he liked, disliked, or believed was beyond my control. He turned, and I watched his tight ass until he rounded the corner of the tavern and disappeared. Damn, I should have asked him what happened to the guy who hit Ben. Why he froze and passed out. A seizure? Did my hasty whack with a rock cause it? Did I care? No, but it was so unusual my curiosity remained.

I went inside to soak and clean my new-found treasures. The red stone the sheriff had given me. A garnet the size of a pea. Nothing spectacular, but with a suitable deep color. I might find more lying around.

I washed the handkerchief, hung it to dry, then quickly went back out. Wood was scarce around this arid land, but I'd passed a couple of low Juniper type trees. High altitude, slow growing, these beauties had branches that twisted like twine. I soon found what I'd seen earlier. I picked up a broken branch half buried in the sand.

A touch of sound whispered above me. An owl perched on a low limb. Petite, beautifully speckled brown and white, he blinked those big eyes that embodied the bird's reputation of wisdom. Frank had told me that some Native American cultures considered owls ill omens. I liked them.

"Sorry if I disturbed you, oh wise one. I'll leave now." I walked away. When I glanced back, the owl had turned to watch my progress.

Sheriff Harrow had missed the small items I'd hidden in the seams of my bag. Not that they were dangerous. Two cheap multi-blade folding knives and three tightly rolled pieces of sandpaper. I'd found them exploring a Flagstaff hardware store during the tedious hours I waited for Road Rash.

I started carving wood when I was nine. I used a pocketknife to shape a crude little cat from a fallen branch. When I showed it to Mama she screamed and hit me so hard, she knocked me unconscious. Thank God, Frank was there. He carried me to the emergency room.

Not the first time she'd knocked me out, but someone had been counting. My third ER visit triggered child services to take over. That meant a foster home. Life after that consisted of a rollercoaster. Mama crying and begging forgiveness, pleading with a judge to give her another chance, then back to foster care when she beat me again. If anyone was obsessed with me, it was Mama. Frank did what he could, but the hateful court wouldn't give custody of a girl to a young, unmarried man, even her own brother. He gave up years of his life to remain home until I turned thirteen and was able to stay out of reach when necessary. Frank and I growing up and leaving seemed to have triggered Mama's final descent into pure madness.

One of my kinder foster fathers was a carpenter. He gave me the tools and taught me the basics of building solid furniture and wood carving as a hobby. Lots of how-to books helped too. It used to fascinate McKay. He would sit and watch me shape wood. Back when I cared, he did pleasant things. I won't presume the psychopath ever genuinely loved me.

I made a pot of dark coffee, turned on the light over the table, and went to work. When you have beautifully shaped wood, you let it tell you what to carve. This piece was not ideal, but I could make something. It had a twisted L shape, so, with a little trimming, it would stand on its own. A subject came to me immediately. One thing about never sleeping. You can be super productive.

I picked up the knife and began to whittle, gouge, and scrape an image. When I had the basic shape, I turned the light off. I did the final carving by touch. I finished in the pale beginning of a new morning. The face and shoulders of the little owl perched in the juniper tree worked beautifully. I'd managed fine detail and expression. A modest piece, barely a foot tall, but it felt right. Then I had to choose a stone from the ones I picked up on the roadway. I always added a natural uncut stone or crystal to any piece I created. My artistic signature.

The red garnet the sheriff found would do. I cut a small spot at the base of the wood and forced the stone into the groove. It had to be tight—I didn't use things like glue. I rubbed my fingers over the finished wood. Not a masterpiece, diminutive, but a respectable bit of art.

Now, who should I give it to? I never keep the pieces I make. For an unfathomable reason, I'm compelled to give them away. I'd starve as a professional artist. I made my decision by sunrise. After more coffee, I would carry my piece to the sheriff's office. I'd give it to Deputy Ben.

Chapter Four

I went out a little after eight in the morning. The sun, a distant angel hanging above the horizon, offered brilliant light. Too bad it had a halo that promised a change in the weather. Tuesday had dawned, and later I would spend my first night working the bar for Aunt Lo.

I genuinely disliked bars. For some people, they're pleasant places to sip alcohol and talk with friends. Others take part in mini soap operas played out each night. Looking for love, desperate for those brief highs when they think everything might turn out okay. Then the inevitable downward slide when they realize nothing was going to change. But another beer, a song on the jukebox, maybe a quickie in the backseat, made it tolerable.

I paced the short distance to the Sheriff's Office and went in. The sense of the building's age struck me again. When was it new? The wild west 1800s? Sheriff Harrow sat behind his desk. There was no sign of Deputy Ben, but I hadn't expected him so soon after such injuries.

The sheriff stared.

"I came to check on Deputy Ben. See how he is."

"Why?"

Ah, there was that familiar arrogant authority. His renewed disapproval of my presence made the air thick and hard to breathe. I shrugged but managed to keep a straight face. "Because he was kind and helping me when he got hurt."

Damn him. Was he going to question my every move? Did he need my bathroom schedule?

I'd stopped at the glass display counter that divided the room. He rose and came to me. I held out the owl carving. "Would you give this to him? I made him a little get-well present." The sheriff accepted the gift and turned it over in his hands.

"You made this." His voice sounded a tiny bit surprised.

"Yes, I did. That stone is the one you found and gave me." I dug in my pocket. "Here's your handkerchief—washed and dried. Thank you again." I laid the smooth folded white cloth on the counter.

He placed the owl on a desk beside his own. He didn't look at me. No eye-contact at all. "He'll be in at eleven."

I'd been dismissed. I guess I was lucky that he didn't ask what kind of blade I'd used.

I left and walked back toward my apartment. I did shiver. The promised change in the weather had arrived way too soon. High thin clouds skated across the sky, pushed by a sharp wind. Summer had barely begun, but once the sun fell, this high elevation desert would grow cold. I'd have to replace my only well-worn jacket. It was far too thin to fight back the chill.

Lo surprised me in the tavern parking lot. She beckoned, and I climbed in her older but well-maintained pickup truck, a substantial four-wheel drive. Did that mean she crossed the desert sometimes? I'd like to try that. See how far I could go. I didn't expect anything new or different, but who knows, a surprise might be lurking behind a bush somewhere. If I could find an actual bush.

She examined me and frowned. "Are those the best clothes you have?"

"I have a new pair of jeans to wear to work tonight."

"Come to my trailer later. I have several shirts that would look nice on you. Right now, we're going to the valley."

We were going to the valley. She spoke with reverence, like a deeply religious person would say, *we're going to church.* As if this valley was the only one that existed in the high mesas and mountains surrounding us. When I laughed and asked her, she simply said, "Well, it's the only one that matters in our lives."

And yet, this so important valley had no formal name. I started to ask her to define *us*, but let it go and leaned back to enjoy the ride.

She drove east a quarter mile then made a sharp turn off the asphalt and onto a wide, solid packed, red clay road. Ruts and wash outs along the edges were testament to an occasional serious rain. A mile or so into the parched land, rolling between two high barren hills, up another incline, and there it was below. The valley. It embodied the red and gold high desert. It surprised me because it had features instead of monotonous waste.

A sharp, narrow line of bright green vegetation wandered across the empty expanse like a piece of loose string tossed on a plain red and yellow cloth. A couple of lesser lines broke away from the main string, but they didn't go far. In the distance, a tiny glint of water flashed. A lake or river? It couldn't be large. Electrical power invaded the valley via a single line of power poles. They stuck up along the road like giant black toothpicks.

Lo pointed to her left where another rocky cliff loomed. "There's a creek. See those green lines. Water comes out of a rock cave back there in Oro Canyon. There's a river farther down. It's wide and super shallow, but spring and mountain fed. I'll take you there later." The road leveled out and the vista opened.

My aunt made a sharp right onto what looked like a long unused lane. Desperate, low growing shrubs clawed and scratched at the truck doors as if trying to hold us back. She drove to a house made of precisely fitted, stacked red, brown, and yellow stones. No roof, but it had walls. Concrete lintels braced the window and door openings. Lonely, abandoned, it was losing the battle against time and weather. That battle would be a long one here in the arid desert. Behind it, I spied two more stone buildings, far smaller. Lo pulled closer, stopped the truck, and climbed out. I followed her.

We walked through the doorway of the windowless, roofless house. The floor felt like stone, but time had covered it with a layer of sand and dried crackling vegetation.

"You were born in this house." Lo held out her hands and turned. She grinned at me. "So was Frank. Our family midwife, Matoma, delivered both of you."

"Did it have a roof then?"

"Oh, yes. It was a home."

Lo continued to smile. This place meant something to her. I guess she wanted it to have significance for me, but it didn't. For her sake I smiled at the empty pile of meticulously stacked rocks in the desert. Born at home delivered by a midwife, that was news. Curious news. My birth certificate says I entered this world in a Flagstaff hospital. So did Frank's. All my life Mama had spun a myriad of contradicting stories, pure lies, and for some unfathomable reason, despite proof to the contrary, people would magically believe them. Particularly social workers and judges.

My aunt stared at the floor for a few moments, then abruptly marched out. Nothing broke the silence around us until she moved. I followed her across the dirt yard toward a small line of green. A tiny, shallow creek, barely a trickle, branched off the larger ones cutting across the valley. Reeds and low water plants crept up the bank two or three feet but ventured no farther into the desert land. The sharp thin line, the contrast of dry red earth and living green, captivated me. A tiny trickle of water sustained a meager but distinct portion of life.

Lo, still in a sentimental mood, said, "Frank used to hide here so he could read his books."

Hide I understood. Mama hated books. Unnecessary reading was the only thing she chastised her precious son for. "Frank is so amazing, Lo. He's learned a bunch of ancient languages that nobody in the world speaks now. He translates books, old books. Scrolls. He travels to Rome, Greece, Istanbul, places like that. And he teaches, too."

She laughed. "I'm not surprised. There was never enough learning here for Frank. The old Garnet school is gone. Busses are more reliable, so kids go to Sioux Crossing now. Back then I'd buy him books when I could. I have them, his books. Packed away when he left." She dragged me into another fierce hug. I guess she thought if she could hold me often enough it would erase certain vileness in my life—or prepare me for more to come. "Ask Frank if he wants them when you talk to him again. I'll ship them."

"I will." I'd promised him I'd call him at a specific time once a week.

Back in the truck we continued down the main road. We passed other side roads, and I could see houses, widely spaced on acreage. Well maintained, neither massive nor tiny, they would fit into any middle-class subdivision. Random, older, doublewide mobile homes made up the mix too. Numerous homes had substantial barns and metal buildings behind them, often larger than the houses themselves—surprising since I could see no agriculture, no fences, no animals.

Lo started to speak, stopped, and cleared her throat. Her mouth made a funny little twist, and her brows scrunched together. What was wrong with her? I'd never heard her speak in less than a confident, take-charge manner. Another deep sigh. *Like her multiple hugs, Lo had expressed emotions in many sighs since I'd arrived.*

"Okay." She leaned forward as if bracing herself for a crash. "I'm going to start your lessons. History and culture of your family. Your mother threatened to never let me see you and Frank if I told you any of this. I didn't want that, so I agreed. Not sure how you're going to take this. It's wild, and you need to suspend logic and judgement for a while. The truth is vast, complex, and filled with things that will surprise you and yes, shock you."

Her speech sounded like a schoolteacher's lesson. I

glanced over at the woman who wore my mother's face. She and Frank were the anchors that kept me sane, kept me from suicide until I escaped Mama. I owed her debts I could never repay. Judgement? I could back off that. *But, damn, what could be so wild I needed to suspend logic? Oh, wait. There was the knife secured inside my jacket. I'd be a hypocrite if I denied anything she told me.*

"I'll listen, Lo. I love you, and I trust you. But I got to warn you, I'm not gullible. I've heard too many lies from too many people—especially Mama. Please forgive me if I don't react the way you expect or want me to."

She slowed the truck to a crawl and began. "The town of Garnet, this valley, and thousands of acres around it is a restricted, exclusive community. There's no land for sale to outsiders. Those of us who live here refer to ourselves as a tribe."

"Tribe? Like the Indians that used to own this place?"

"Yes. But more than one group of people calls itself a tribe. Everyone allowed to live here, including you, is related by blood—or by marriage. Marriage—who you marry—is incredibly important. We're clannish, insular, and virtually always marry within family." She winced and shook her head. "I mean we do track lineages to keep all marriages at a healthy distance. And we let the occasional stranger in. For new genes. To prevent mutations."

I choked trying not to laugh, but… "Mutations? Lo…?"

"Mutation of hereditary DNA. Genetic health. We're not incestuous. Wow, that does sound weird."

She chuckled under her breath. "I've never had to explain it before. And by we, I mean, there are ten related tribes, including the one here in Garnet. Open mind, Lilly, open mind. Please."

I winced. "Sorry. I'll shut up."

She stared straight ahead, not at me. "Bastet is your, our tribe's name. The tribe's history goes back to 2,000 BC, and the mountains near the Black Sea. At our origin, we were a single tribe that served a powerful goddess. Populations increased, and the split came gradually over the years to the ten-tribe structure we have now. But the tribes remain cohesive as a people. We serve our goddess to this day."

Wow, this speech was wild. Maybe Frank's assertions of Pagan activity had some validity. *Served a goddess?* I'd heard her invoke the goddess before but thought it unlikely that everyone in Garnet felt the same. Again, I laid my hand against my jacket. I wouldn't speak of the knife, not yet.

"Lo, I'm not sure my suspension of belief can go back that far. Thousands of years?"

"Our actual origins are older. Our tribal historians have a hereditary version of a perfect memory and keep our oral and written history. You're not the only one in the family with that little gift."

Memory was, of course, always a sensitive subject given its power over my mind.

Lo grunted as the truck hit a rut and bounced. "Frank would make the perfect historian, because he loves such stuff and always has."

"Frank's not interested in any goddess. He has his God, his church. He's happy. Please, please leave him alone." Frank was a decent, kind person, and Mama's

44

treatment of me had marked him too. He deserved to have the life *he* wanted.

"I won't trouble him, Lilly. It makes me sad that we lost him, but I understand."

I suddenly realized what she was talking about. I panicked. "Wait! So, you think…because I'm a memory freak…this historian should be me?"

I could not deal with that scenario. I'd battled for my sanity at times when memories escaped my tight control, cut loose, and mixed with reality. I wanted to jump out of the truck and run. "Lo, I can't do that. I'm not reliable. Not strong enough." Tears welled in my eyes. A high edge of fear cut into me like broken glass. "Please don't. Please, please!" I clamped my teeth and hunched tight in my seat. A glance in the mirror on the back of the visor reflected a pale face and wide manic gray eyes.

Lo reached over and rubbed my shoulder gently. "I'm so sorry. I didn't mean… Sweetheart, I promise, I won't ask anything of you that you can't or don't wish to do. I won't try to force you into anything, either. Please don't be frightened. Goddess knows, all I want is for you to learn the truth and understand our lives, the lives of your family."

She kept rubbing, and her touch did soothe me. I drew deep breaths. I rubbed my wet eyes and straightened. "Okay. Over that little break down. Is there more?"

"Yes. Much more."

Of course, there was.

We arrived at our next stop, a tightly stacked red and yellow stone house almost identical to my birthplace. Pretty as a postcard in a western tourist shop, at least it had a roof, wood frame, windows, and door. Smoke poured from the chimney. Expensive heat. They would have to haul wood in by the truckload since there was little here to burn. The sharp wind hit me when I climbed out of the truck. I shivered, but most of my chill came from inside.

Lo drew a deep breath, straightened, and formed a stern no-nonsense expression. Preparing for battle? She knocked at the door, waited for a moment, then opened it, and went in. I followed, careful, watchful as always. If she had to fight, I would be ready to aid her.

We entered a homey comfortable room that was not to my taste, but again, picture perfect. I liked my well-worn, mid-century modern, converted motel rooms better. This place had a living room, kitchen, and a door leading to what I assumed were bedrooms in the back. The air was so warm it suffocated me. A dense sugary odor of flowers assaulted me in an invisible cloud. They hung from the ceiling in profuse multi-color bunches, drying in the excess heat. My olfactory senses wouldn't function again for days. A tiny spiral headache formed right above my eyes. Eyes that immediately watered, adding to the discomfort of the tears I'd shed before we entered.

The woman who waited inside the door had to be at least six-three. Not an ounce of fat on her, but she was *big*. She had to be a Dusalte. She was a bigger, older, and taller version of me, Lo, and Mama. She wore slacks, a blouse, and several odd mixed bead necklaces. Dark hair, gray eyes, she looked to be in her early forties, except for the deep frown lines between her brows.

Lo nodded. "Goddess bless, Araun."

"Goddess bless, Luella," the woman's kitten soft, throaty voice didn't match her stature or expression.

Lo caught my arm and drew me forward. "I want you to see and talk to Lilly." Her words sounded like an apology.

Araun stared, narrow eyed, as if my every flaw had suddenly become visible and painted on my skin. She shook her head. The beads strung across her chest clicked and chattered. "Damaged." The soft voice hardened. "Goddess damn Louise."

Okay, that wouldn't work. I jerked my arm from Lo's grip. I drew myself up and stared straight at Araun. "You will not curse my mother."

As her primary victim, cursing my mother out loud was my deeply held and personal right. I stood there, feet planted, hands curled into fists. *Wait! Who was I going to fight?* A woman who said something I didn't like? This was not me, not my way. Better control, Lilly, you need better control.

Araun smiled. *A trying to be nice and hating every second of it smile.* "So, damaged…but not broken."

Damaged but not broken. At least that observation of me came close to the truth. My mother's abuse was brutal, both physical and emotional. Unfortunately, I carried a child's desperate contradictory need for an abusive parent's love. Nobody got to trash her but me.

Araun shrugged as if our words were nothing more than stray petals drifting from the dead and drying flowers above us. "Please sit. Let me make coffee."

She wanted to play hostess? Okay by me. Now I understood Lo's reluctance to come here. We sat at a table by the kitchen. Too cozy. Too crowded. And the air thickened with flower scented hostility.

Araun pulled out a coffee maker. The house might look crude on the outside, but inside had all the conveniences. The strain returned with Araun's next words. "Are you teaching her, Luella?"

Lo frowned. Obviously, she didn't appreciate Araun's question.

"I am," Lo said. "I had wanted...no, I'll go on."

Araun grunted. She stood by the kitchen counter, watching the dark coffee drain from the basket into the pot. She wouldn't look straight at me. *Okay woman, I don't like you either.*

Lo shifted in her seat like she was sitting on a rock and couldn't find a way that didn't hurt her ass. "Lilly, I told you we are the Bastet Tribe. And this land is our home."

I nodded. This discussion was not what I wanted, particularly in front of Araun. Her displeasure at my very being seemed obvious. I had to fight to sit immobile, too.

"Bastet and the other nine tribes came to America in the early 1800s and moved west—along with vast numbers of others, desperate for conquered and stolen native land to make a new life. We settled here in 1870. Other of our tribes moved elsewhere, some north to Oregon, one to Louisiana, all over the US."

"Settled? Why here?" Oh, hell, I meant to be truthful but sounded so rude. "Sorry, Lo. It's kind of majestic at times, sunset, dawn, but absolutely nowhere."

Araun busied herself with coffee mugs. Her face settled into a smug expression, the kind I wanted to wipe away.

Lo gave me a warm smile, but I could tell she

struggled. "Yes. It's isolated. The goddess led us here. There was—is—a reason. You'll learn later. Our people...we're...oh, how can I say it?"

"You use words, Lo. I'm confused. Our people? Tribe? You talk about a goddess, then in the next breath comes genetics, mutations. What is that?"

I leaned back and folded my arms under my breasts—and immediately dropped them. No, I would not be defensive. Better rude and ill-tempered than defensive.

"Lo, I'm a little touchy on the goddess issue. Do you remember the last time you tried to get custody of us? Right after Mama almost killed me—again. She played the religion card and swore you were all devil worshipers. Frank and I never thought that, but she was so adamant, so desperate, and the judge believed her. If I hadn't known her, I would have believed her. Can you see why I'm having a problem?"

"Devil...no. Worship? No. Lilly, if you understand nothing else, understand this one fact as you go forward and learn more. We *serve*. We do not *worship* the goddess."

"Goddess? Like Wiccans? You know, Mother Earth? The seasons and rituals?" A person could find anything on the internet, each described in a hundred different versions and interpretations.

"No, Lilly, not Wiccan. Their beliefs are fine, but more complex than ours. Our goddess is a single and specific entity. Specific, because every tribe sees and serves her in a unique way."

"Unique? How?"

"It depends on the situation."

"Whoa, now that's convenient." And I was a

facetious bitch. *But wasn't that the beauty and practicality of religion? Worshipers could twist and manipulate it to fit all occasions, rationale, and desires.* "Why haven't you told me this before?"

"Your mother refused to allow me. If I spoke of it, she would run away again. I thought I'd get you when you graduated from college. Then you connected with that man and shut me out completely."

McKay. I understood. When I was with McKay, beginning as a sweet lover and ending in disaster, he had consumed my life. But she could have told me all this back at the tavern, why come here? Oh, right, I had to see my abandoned birthplace. Make a sentimental connection.

Distress drew a line between her brows, and tears formed in her eyes. "I'm doing a poor job here. I've only confused you. I simply can't tell you everything at once. You're going to have to experience things to know and understand. I don't want you to go into shock when you see something...unusual. Or if something strange happens to you."

She reached out and grasped my hand and squeezed it tight. "Lilly, all I ask is that you be patient. If anything happens that you don't understand, come to me so I can explain."

"Okay, Lo. But...unusual? Strange? Those words are wide as a river during a flood."

How did I find or judge unusual when most aspects of life and a sense of place were so alien? I was a city girl, always, and I had loved it. This place and its inhabitants might be Mars for all I knew.

Eventually, I'd tell her about the strangeness of a knife that would come and go at convenient times and cut anything but me, but I'd kept it a secret—my secret—so long. I didn't want to speak of it in front of Araun, either.

The tears in Lo's eyes suddenly swelled and dripped down her face. Oh, no. My turn to hug her. "I love you and yes, I will trust you." The two people who would never intentionally hurt me, she and Frank, deserved my trust.

Araun made excellent coffee. I won't say the hostility ceased entirely, but it eased. We lingered around the table and they talked about a festival on the Autumnal Equinox. No pagan rituals, but a fun time. They laughed when I told them Frank's images of dancing naked in a meadow. That wasn't going to happen. Not sure if he would be disappointed or it was simply a running joke we shared.

Then Araun led us outside behind the house. She possessed a significant green house filled with masses of plants, half in full flower. We entered a smaller house sized building. A fragrant work shed, where Araun explained her lotion and essential oil business, all created from what she grew. I didn't ask and she didn't explain the smaller glass walled enclosure in the corner of the room. Yeah, it looked like a serious laboratory.

It was time to go. I had one question.

"Araun, are you a Dusalte?"

She stared a moment, studying me. "Yes, Lilly. I'm your grandmother. Luella and Louise's mother." She stated the words as simple unembellished facts.

Shocker. Not that we were related, anyone could see that, but a grandmother? Why hadn't Lo introduced her that way at first? I'm supposed to question Lo about anything strange, then she acts in an inexplicable way herself.

Araun didn't look old enough to be my grandmother. I'd thought she and Lo were the same age. I did ask the prime question. *Did Araun know my father*? No, she did not. She didn't know Frank's either. Frank and I were ten years apart, and we could easily see we had different fathers.

I didn't talk on the way back to the motel. Too much to think about. By the time we got there, I had my questions ready. We loitered in the truck in front of my apartment.

"Lo, let me see if I have your little story straight." *Try not to sound too inane, Lilly.* "All residents of Garnet are in a tribe, and that tribe is one of ten. It's named Bastet. It's a closed society of blood relatives but with a few outsiders to prevent…mutant…DNA. And you worship…serve a goddess."

"Correct."

I chuckled but then made myself stop. "And I'm related to everyone in Garnet by varying degrees."

"Yes. Some very distant, and others, like me, close. Several by marriage. Marriage and marital agreements are a vital part of our society." She stopped and appeared to be thinking so hard I easily understood that the lesson wasn't over. It didn't take long. "There is one other thing. Those of us with tribal blood and genetics are born with certain…talents. They are what we call the Gifts. Gifts from the goddess."

I bit my lip to keep my mouth shut.

Lo seemed more relaxed talking away from the tension that came with Araun. "The goddess blessed us, all the tribes, with natural abilities other human beings don't have. It makes us different as individuals and as a people."

My always articulate aunt was again fumbling for words. "Lilly, are you telling me that you never felt that way? Being different from others around you?"

And that went straight to the heart of my desperate life.

"Different?" I didn't hide the anger, the bitterness. "I've tried my best *not to* be different. I wanted to be normal, ordinary. I spent most of my childhood struggling for normalcy—or at least the appearance of it to let me fit in." I had to please Mama and keep her calm, so she wouldn't hurt me. I had failed, spectacularly and often. Why? Because I *was* different.

"Can you give me an example of those talents, Lo? The Gifts?"

From her tight frown, I'd say I'd asked an uncomfortable question. She answered anyway. "Most Gifts are very personal, very private. It's not considered polite to discuss or overtly display them in public. However, a few are obvious, but those are kept in the tribe." She flipped her hands up off the steering wheel. "Damn it all, your mother's Gift was her ability to tell any lie and people would believe it despite factual evidence to the contrary. You are familiar with that, aren't you?"

Familiar? Oh, shit. I didn't want to talk about how that gift hurt me several times. "Question. You must answer this one, no evasions."

"Very well. Ask." A wary reluctance filled her voice. I might get the truth—or I might not.

"Why am I here? It's supposed to be about protecting me from McKay, protecting my probation status, but I think there's something else."

"I love you Lilly. I want to protect you. I want you to have a better life. But if I tell you…"

"You think I'll run away?"

"Maybe." And another grand sigh. She was using up a lifetime of those in a few days. "I've wanted you here in Garnet, hoped you would come, for years after Louise was hospitalized. But I understood. You were an adult by then. There was nothing in this desert for you. Then I had a dream during the last months you were in rehab. The goddess sent a message. In the dream she instructed me to get you here as soon as possible, by any means necessary."

"She wanted me here? Your goddess? Why?"

"To save our tribe from extinction." She delivered those six words with a stoic neutrality that rivaled Sheriff Harrow's demeanor. "Something bad, something evil has happened or is going to happen. Lilly, you must fix it or change the outcome. The dream came, assaulted me, every night for months until you arrived." She breathed deeper. "Last night, for the first time, I slept soundly all night."

It took what seemed like a long time for her words to circle my brain. All rational thought ceased. When it returned, I laughed. It started as a choke, then bubbled up, roared. I sounded like a buffoon, a raucous blubbering fool. I loved Lo, but I couldn't help myself.

"The goddess said…oh, Lo. Oh shit."

Lilly Dusalte, go forth and save my people.

I wrapped my arms over my stomach. Laughing that hard hurt. "I'm sorry, I'm sorry. I love you, trust you but… Oh, Lo, do you know how that sounds? It's worse than a poorly written book. It's a myth, a plot for a fantasy novel." The mirth overtook again, and I lolled there, shaking with laughter.

She waited for me to settle down. "You're right, Lilly." No anger. She sounded resigned. "It is ridiculous. I was, and am, dumbfounded. But I believe in the goddess. I'm going to follow instructions. My job is to make sure you get information in increments, like steps, so you can progress safely, if not gracefully, into your place in Bastet."

She started the truck engine. My signal to get out. I was ready by then. She'd left me flabbergasted. And worried. Had my aunt, one of only two stable influences in my life, fallen prey to the mental illness of her identical twin? Oh, I was certain she believed every word of her extraordinary story. Because I loved her, I owed her so much, there was nothing I could do but go along and hope for the best. Yes, I had dealt with one facet of the supernatural with the knife, but this jumped a level above in bizarre. *Lilly, the goddess proclaimed, save my people—our people.* Snicker, snicker. Well, I asked, and Aunt Lo told me.

No problem residing in Garnet. I had no money and nowhere to go, anyway. I'd need major permission from probation and paperwork filed in order to leave, but I wanted to lay low and be calm. Might as well stay and see how the Garnet circus performed.

It was barely noon, so I decided to give myself an hour to meditate. First time since I'd arrived. The paramount lessons I learned in rehab—besides how to work through blinding pain—were yoga and meditation. Meditation was the next best thing to the true sleep denied me by McKay's fists.

Entering my new place of residence, I positioned

myself on the floor, closed my eyes, and relaxed—starting with my toes, then my feet, and on throughout my body. Practice made it easy to slip deeper, to shut off those stray thoughts and fall into what I call the *Void*. It's vast, pitch-black, hollow, and empty. People have told me the Void didn't happen to them when they meditated. Like my knife, it was mine alone. I'd been there before, often. It's a place where I can slow my mind and rest. I don't have to fight to keep my memories at a distance. When I'm there, they go away. Most of all, for a brief time, the constant, low level hum of fear in my mind eases.

This time, though, the Void was different. Way different. It was light, shifting, burning brilliant then dimming to barely visible. This time, my sanctuary felt almost alive. It whispered and flowed around me like the brush of air across leaves. Certainly not the familiar quiet, dark, peaceful place that allowed me to rest. Not bad different, though. No fear, no stress—until I wasn't alone. Something, someone, touched me. What? No! I popped my eyes open and shook myself. Was I in such bad shape that I was creating illusions *in* my mind? Had Lo's story of dreams, prophesy, and doom infected me? The essential rest in darkness had to be there. Without it, I might not survive. I went to shower and hopefully wash all the creepy ideas away.

Chapter Five

Later that afternoon I got through to Frank on the phone. I told him only the things that I thought wouldn't upset him. I did tell him about Lo's belief in the goddess though. I did not tell him about the assertion that her goddess ordered her to get me to Garnet as a savior. It would be too much. He'd be in a rental car following the next Road Rash bus to town, riding to my rescue. He'd had to rescue me too many times. I did, however, tell him about meeting Araun.

"Apparently, Araun is our grandmother," I said. "She looks like a Dusalte. And I don't think she likes me."

He chuckled. "I do remember Araun. Yes, our grandmother. But Mama didn't allow me to call her that. Araun made foul tasting medicines Mama would make me take. I finally ran away and hid for three days. It stopped then. I remember believing that Araun didn't like me either, but now I think she was upset because Mama was starting to…behave erratically." Frank would never call Mama crazy. But she never tried to kill him. "I heard the thousands of years history myth, too. Bastet, the tribe—and the other tribes. And that did originally spark my interest in ancient things. But they also believe…"

Uh, oh, Frank's worry for me rose in his voice. "Believe what? Come on, Frank."

"It's something, besides McKay, that has worried me about you going to Garnet, Lil. They believe this goddess gives them supernatural powers. I can't accept that." Frank had an understandable bias against all things that didn't fit in with his current beliefs.

He cleared his throat. "I don't think…" Frank the word master, struggled, much as Lo had with her story. "I remember. Araun, she handled snakes. She'd go out in the desert, find them, and bring them home. I was a kid but…that's not a typical grandmother phenomenon. She talked to them, too."

Well, that explained something I'd never understood about my brother. He'd never said much about Garnet. The place, people, and its peculiar religious dogma and practices had terrified or at least severely disturbed him. He was a child when he left, but it terrified him so much he had fled as far in the opposite direction as he could go.

"Wow! I didn't see any snakes." I wasn't particularly frightened of snakes. I'd worked in a reptile store in college and could deal with them. I knew how to spot and avoid the venomous kind. Not that I wanted to hang with any on a social basis.

Frank chuckled. "I remember the big parties, lots of excellent food, singing, a few fights." He was silent for a moment. "I've forgotten most of the details."

Uh, oh. That was bullshit. Like me, Frank never forgot anything. Unlike me, he had perfect memory control and never seemed to deal with my kind of mental turmoil.

He changed the subject. "So, the sheriff, why do you think he's so unfriendly? Pax? I vaguely remember him from school. He was big and tall for his age. He's younger than me, thirty-four, thirty-five."

"Frank, believe me, I understand the sheriff…mostly. This is his town to protect. I have a deadly predator chasing me. The sheriff identifies me with the killer. Odds are McKay knows exactly where I am, and he won't hesitate to kill anyone around me if they get in his way."

Frank let out a sharp breath. "Then why are you there? There's no one to protect *you*. It's not safe."

"No place is *safe* for me until McKay is dead. The sheriff says the FBI is using me as bait, to draw McKay out and capture or hopefully kill him."

"That's unconscionable, Lilly. It's wrong."

"Frank, I can't do anything about it, except go back to jail. I'm sure they'll find a reason to send me there if I don't cooperate. Probation is a bit of a joke. Except that I'm not sitting in a cell."

He didn't say anything. I guess that meant I was right. Knowing Frank, my being right wouldn't ease his concern. *I loved my big brother so much.* I didn't share his religion, but I had confessed all the dreadful things I'd done while with McKay. Frank forgave me, and his only concern was that I be remorseful and repentant. I most certainly lived with remorse every day.

Then I had to ask. I couldn't hang up without knowing. "How's Mama?"

"Better. At least this month. Lo had her moved to a new hospital. I guess she didn't tell you yet. It's as pretty and pleasant as any asylum can be. Excellent individual care, and they've developed a different drug plan. I went to see her last week. She seemed happy enough. Or the drugs are working better. She recognized me for a while."

Frank visited her when he could. I didn't. Frank and I arranged for a time to talk the next week, and he told me to call him any time if I needed him, and he would get to me as soon as he could.

Later I went to Lo's trailer for the blouses she promised me. I had gifts of attractive clothing when I walked out of rehab and was immediately scooped up and taken to jail. The clothes disappeared while they locked me up to remind me that they still owned me. My jeans were new, but the knit shirt had seen better days. I looked like what I was—a homeless person living on the kindness of decent people.

Lo lived in a doublewide trailer behind the bar. Not new, but comfortable and filled with an eclectic mix of furniture and objects that completely belied the plain outside. Crystals, larger and finer quality than I would ever find on the side of the road, decorated every available surface. Brightly woven blankets draped across the furniture, so beautiful you wouldn't want to sit on them. The paintings on the wall were incredible, too. Mostly wild birds rendered in such detail they almost came alive. Raptors, songbirds, all by the same artist, but all unsigned.

"Lo, who did these?" I pointed to a canvas of an eagle feeding its young.

Lo came and stood behind me. "Your mother. She was an artist like you. There were more, but she burned them before she left. I had to fight to save these."

My throat tightened. I couldn't breathe. This was not possible. My vile, angry mother never did anything so striking, so alive. She couldn't have. She'd dedicated her hands to hitting me. My memory boxes opened and released their contents. I plopped down on one of Lo's dining room chairs, wrapped my arms around my chest, and lowered my head. Those memories so vivid, hurt so bad, as if I lived them again—hate and absolute terror.

Mama? Why? But I love you, Mama. Stop. No memories, Lilly, shut them down. I drew deep breaths and silently relocked the doors of my memory boxes.

Lo set a glass of water down beside me. I could see it there in her eyes, the pity, the kindness. I couldn't speak, but I did drink the water. It eased the burning in my hollowed-out gut. Lo relaxed at the table with me.

"I'm sorry." She glanced at the paintings. "I need to be more careful about hitting you with things I take for granted. I think I've bruised your brain today."

"It's okay, Lo. Truly, it is. Nothing can be changed."

I remembered the speech a kind counselor had given me once about mental illness and what it could do. She'd tried to convince me that my mother was ill and loved me, despite the abuse. Understanding illness was okay, but love? No, Mama did not love me, but as I'd grown older, I'd realized that it was fear of me that drove her, not hate. Why was she afraid of me? I'll probably never know the truth.

Lo's voice softened as she explained. "Louise was talented, but she didn't value her talent. She had the Gift to manipulate people with her voice, but the goddess also blessed her with the Gift to truly see animals, and to render them on canvas. For some unfathomable reason, she came to hate and fear her own skill as an artist. She retained her persuading voice, but saw art as a weakness, a vulnerability. Or maybe she didn't like the tribe's demands that she produce something. We're taught that, always. No matter how humble the results, we allow no tribe member to be an idler or a freeloader. The tribe's pressure, the rules and constraints are things I want to talk about soon. Tribe members have left because of them."

I heard a tiny bit of bitterness in her voice. And the goddess blessed my mother? Sometimes I wished I could be like Frank. Frank had his perfect God. He believed and was at peace with conventional spirituality. All I had was the cynicism born from brutality. Mama made me stay out of churches. She called me a demon child and was afraid everything would burst into flame and burn everyone alive if I entered the doors.

Lo stood. "Come on. Let's get you those clothes. We can talk more later."

I followed her to her bedroom. I walked out with three sharp stylish western style shirts, perfect for the tavern. I hurried back to the motel and changed to one of the shirts. The visions of paintings so incredibly detailed they could have been photos I shoved into a new memory box in my mind, locked it, and hurried off to work.

The two different bars set end-to-end inside the tavern had indeed come from two different old west saloons. Both were over a hundred years old, which made sense, since Lo had picked them up at antique auctions. Deep, rich cherry wood and oak, carved with flowers and intricate designs only added to their allure. I wanted to demand that anyone who came in treat it like a treasure. Thick glass carefully preserved the tops where patrons had carved graffiti to immortalize themselves in time. T. J. S. Cummings, 1875, J. R. Barton, 1894, Ian McNalley, 1899, and most curious,

Lady Silverheart, 1901.

Mine was the shorter bar, and that suited me. I would have more time to bullshit and do the friendly service that brought more tips. Lo's other bartender, Kaya, eyed me with suspicion when I met her, but I gave her my best humble act of *I'm not a threat, only the new kid on the block and sure would benefit from her experience. Yes, I was Lo's niece, but I would get no special treatment.*

Nothing is worse than a war with your co-workers. Kaya, petite, dark haired, and pretty, had skin a shade darker than mine. She'd come from Texas, and her musical voice carried a pronounced drawl.

"She's a good girl," Lo told me. "Reliable bartender. She's not tribe." Tribe. Not tribe. When Lo said that, I felt a distinction, a classification between humans on either side of an invisible line drawn in the sand.

I figured that most patrons, even a few of Kaya's regulars, would come to my side of the bar to check out the new girl. Flirt and see if I was available and wonder if, and how fast, my jeans would come off. I wasn't interested in flirting. I shut it down immediately and made sure all received the *not available* message. Friendly, that was all I wanted. *Let me get you another drink. More beer? I'll listen while you tell me your wife/girlfriend doesn't understand you.*

Since it was Tuesday, the tavern never filled up completely. Mostly men, mostly locals. A few introduced themselves, telling me "*I live in the valley,*" again as if it were notable. I fit in nicely with their physical traits. Height, men and women—average pushed six feet for all. While eye color varied, most had darker skin and brown or black hair. My and Lo's gray eyes were not exceptional.

Most patrons accepted their beers in silence this night. No one put money in the jukebox, so the only music came from soft country music CDs Lo played. Tips were fair. The sheriff came in, relaxed at Kaya's side of the bar, and drank coffee. I didn't see if he looked in my direction. I noticed Lo sitting beside him once, but she didn't stay for long. Deputy Ben entered, and he came to my section. Kaya gave me the evil eye.

"Hi." I offered him my best smile. "How are you?"

"I'm fine. Doc Hardy fixed me up."

That fast! I would have sworn he at least had a fractured jaw. He returned my smile with that appealing boyish grin. "Hey, that carving, the owl...that's so fantastic. Thank you."

"A little get-well present. I feel a bit responsible for your injury."

"Why?"

"You were sweet enough to welcome me, carry my bag." I laid my hand over one of his on the bar. "And you got sucker punched for your kindness."

He grinned and winked at me. "That's law enforcement. It happens."

"I suppose, but I felt bad. You want something?"

"Just coffee. On duty until twelve. I'll come back later and get a beer. Unless I get a call from Sioux Crossing. There are two deputies, but they need more. Three bars in town instead of one."

I served him his coffee, then gently ignored him, despite him signaling that he'd like to talk. I wanted him to like me, but not get too friendly. The sheriff came to him, said something in his ear, then left. Ben followed him. He didn't return after midnight.

After closing I cleaned up my area and went outside to walk to the motel. As the door closed behind me, I noticed the sheriff by the picnic tables at the side of the tavern. A security light spread a weak yellowish glow for a hundred or so feet. He leaned against the table in a casual way, but somehow didn't look casual at all. He again had that remarkable stillness about him. For a moment I wished I could talk to him one person to another instead of cop and criminal. No, that wouldn't happen. How could I talk to a person who disliked me so much?

His gaze followed me as I used my pen light to walk across the rocky ground to my apartment. I was briefly concerned that he might approach, but he didn't. He seemed to respect Lo, but you never knew.

One problem of female parolees or probationers involved those who have power over them demanding sex. So far, mine had been okay, but the sheriff wasn't typical. McKay had put me in a high-profile situation. Everyone was wary after his merciless execution of the FBI agents guarding me. So, life as I knew it before McKay would never be the same.

Chapter Six

Wednesday morning, my fourth day in Garnet, Lo led me out of the tavern and down the road to a building that had to be older and more decrepit than the sheriff's office. She opened the door to an aging reception office with no receptionist. The odor of coffee immediately assailed me.

"Doc? You here?" Lo called in a voice that led me to believe the doctor might be slightly deaf.

A man came from a back room. Age? Somewhere between eighty-five and a hundred and ten. He might have been as tall as the rest of us once, but time had stooped and thinned his body. Bald head, two-day beard, he shuffled rather than walked. I'd bet Ronnie the storekeeper would look like him eventually.

Lo laid a hand on my shoulder. "Doc, this is Lilly, Louise's daughter. I told you she was coming. Lilly, this is Doctor Phillip R. Hardy, or Doc Hardy, or usually Doc since he's the only one in town. We used to have a stool reserved for him at the tavern, but I think he's finally accepted that his carousing days are over."

Doc's worn face broke into a smile so warm I wanted to hug him. Certain introductions I'd received had been less than welcoming. Clearly delighted to meet me, his eyes twinkled, and he held out a palsy-like shaking hand. I caught the hand in mine. My own hand warmed at his touch. It felt so lovely, I was disappointed when he released me.

Nothing wrong with his voice. Loud. Yes, a bit of hearing loss there. "I remember your mother. Beautiful woman. And your brother, Frank. Broke his leg once. And the arm the next day. Told him bicycles were dangerous contraptions. Great goddess. He had one leg in a cast."

How wonderful. I'd never seen Frank young and free enough to try to ride a bicycle with a broken leg. Frank gave up much of his youth to care for me.

Doc had a small, pristine, and fully equipped clinic in the building next door. He obviously enjoyed showing it off. He invited us to share his fragrant coffee, but Lo insisted we had places to go.

When we left, Lo gave me another inkling about my ancestry. "The tribe has a larger clinic and two doctors in Sioux Crossing. There are two fully equipped emergency ambulances and EMTs, too. We use the hospital in Las Vegas. Doc provides regular care for us here."

Valuable information, but I could tell from her face there was more. "He's a healer, Lilly. Doc passes out meds for infections, stitches up minor cuts, and sets broken bones. His most vital role in Garnet is to stabilize major incidents like heart attacks and serious injuries when we need time to get an ambulance here."

"Healer? You mean as faith healing? Laying on hands?" Another superstitious concept. What would come next? Did they have a rainmaker or alchemist turning lead into gold?

She cocked her head with a sly smile. "Yes, Lilly. The goddess has given him that power, the Gift of healing. One that everyone knows but doesn't discuss outside the tribe. There are only three healers among all the tribes. You'll understand one day."

"But he doesn't rely on that alone? Right?" I raised an eyebrow and watched her eyes.

"No. He has medical degrees. They're old, but he keeps up with things. I trust him." She led me back toward the tavern. "You know you shouldn't be alive, don't you?" She cleared her throat. Or was that a poorly disguised sob? "The doctors…they said…you were crushed. Your body…"

"Stop it, Lo. I survived. Look at me. I'm a medical wonder. A Frankenstein jigsaw puzzle."

We reached the tavern, and when we climbed the steps, I noticed she was crying. I grabbed her and held her. The hug came from me this time. I knew her tears were for me. She made no sound, but her body jerked with the sobs.

"Come on, Lo. I made it."

"The pain…hideous…how could you…?" Another sob shook her.

"Opiates, Lo. All the excellent derivatives of the big M."

I wouldn't speak of my time breaking my morphine addiction. Nothing intentional on the doctors' part, of course. They thought I was going to die so they kindly kept the pain beaten into submission with anything they could. Lo sniffed and pulled a wadded-up tissue from her pocket to wipe her eyes.

Right after that we climbed in her truck and headed what seemed like a long distance north west to St. George, Utah. Las Vegas was closer, but Lo liked the smaller town. Fewer tourists to deal with. I agreed. Lovely place, and it had a mall. Last night while I was busy, someone had folded up and dropped two hundred-dollar bills in my tip jar. Lo swore it wasn't her. It was okay, though. I had worked hard and could use the money.

Attractive clothes are enjoyable, but not an all-consuming passion for me. I wore rags as a kid and practiced caution as an adult, even when I had access to McKay's money. The *nothing but what you can carry* mantra still possessed me. Jeans were okay, so I bought two new pair. I also added a pair of dress pants just in case. I liked my shirts more tailored and conservative than the western style Lo gave me. I found three, simple enough for the tavern, but I could dress them up if I wanted to. As if I would be going anywhere to dress up any time soon. Two support tank tops and panties with lace trim made the trip perfect. We finished shopping by filling the van with supplies for the tavern and had lunch at an Italian café.

Wednesday night at the tavern brought a change. Most of last night's crowd had been men. This night brought more women. Waitresses only worked on Thursday, Friday, and Saturday. The rest of the time patrons came to the bar, ordered drinks, and took them back to their tables.

Four women at one table shot me hostile glares filled with recognizable malice. I'd received such attention often when I was with McKay. He was a fine-looking man and would flirt outrageously when I was at his side. He gave women the idea that if they could eliminate me, they could have him. The battle would begin, and he would sit back and laugh.

These women glaring at me had absolutely no reason to hate me. I wanted nothing of theirs. They lounged at a table on the side of the room and bought their drinks from Kaya. Jeans, pastel T-shirts with kittens or cats printed on the front, cowboy boots—a saccharine western chic I guess you could call their style. Every now and then, when the light was right, their eyes would have an odd gold shine. Only for an instant, but unmistakable. I should ask Lo about that. They flirted with all the men and sneered at me like I was a mangy stray begging for scraps of food. I simply didn't care. My experience had made most daily shit like that seemed petty. Important things? I had to watch for McKay, avoid our stern angry sheriff, and avoid interaction with the FBI chasing McKay. Four ridiculous women with pissy attitudes? No problem.

Lo went and huddled with the women once, and to my surprise their body language changed. It abruptly went from belligerent to wary. I couldn't hear, but whatever she said didn't make them happy. When she left the table, they focused their glares on her, too.

Ben came in a couple of times, drank a coke, then left. More patrons arrived, and I got too busy to pay attention to unpleasant females. When I did look again, they were gone.

I had an excellent night, tip wise. I snagged a few bills out of my jar but left enough that it didn't look empty and forlorn, then set it under the bar behind the bottles. At least I didn't have to wash glasses. I only had to empty and stack them in wire baskets for the dishwasher. Lo employed a young man who came in early each morning and had everything ready to go for the next night. All I had to do was keep my area clean.

I had a couple of aches and knew I needed to figure out an exercise program, so I wouldn't lose what I'd gained in rehab. My stitched together muscles had to keep moving or they would seize up like rubber bands stretched too far then released. Since the gym at rehab was open all the time and I didn't sleep, I went down there often. I could exercise a bit in jail, too. Of course, on occasion, those bones and muscles reminded me of their abuse. Mostly if I worked too hard—or it rained. The desert might be beneficial for me.

When I started out the back door after closing, Lo told me to wait and she'd walk me. I told her not to bother and went on. I didn't want her around if McKay did show up. The hard ass sheriff? He thought he was so cool. He could take his chances.

I knew the path back to my place by now. The security light gave some illumination, but pure darkness formed a couple of feet outside its dim cone. I used a small pen flashlight since Garnet had no ambient illumination.

Unfortunately, the few hundred feet to the safety of home can be problematic, particularly when four women step out of the darkness, ready to rumble. I couldn't outrun them, race off, blind and stumbling into the night. Too far to make it back to the tavern, too. I moved directly under the security light. At least I could see.

I should have expected something like this. One-on-one, I could defend myself. I couldn't take all four. They were going to pound me, and it was going to hurt like hell. I'd give a bunch of that hurt back. Acute damage if called for.

I held up my empty hands and willed my muscles to relax, to be ready. "Hey. You ladies want to tell me what the problem is? I'm not after anyone's boyfriend. I don't think I've done anything that would piss you off, but if I did, I'll apologize."

One, the biggest, six feet at least, a hundred and fifty pounds of solid muscle, stepped forward. Okay, the leader. She had a round face, small mouth, and wide ass—and spunky little kittens printed on her shirt. Not ugly, pretty if she'd smile—which she certainly wasn't right then.

"You don't belong here, whore." Her voice would crack glass.

"Why don't I belong?" Calm, asking for an explanation, not placating, but easy. Not that it mattered. She wanted combat—wanted blood.

"You're not one of us."

I wondered if Lo would be coming out of the tavern soon. The woman faced me with ruinous determination. *No getting out of this one, Lilly.*

She took one step forward.

I tried reason again. Or at least to anger her more so she'd make a mistake. "Look, whoever you are—"

"I'm Simone, bitch." How did she live with that voice?

"Okay, Simone. All four of you going to jump me at once? Is that how it works around here?"

Violence again. I had so hoped I'd finished with that shit until McKay eventually caught and killed me. Oddly enough, Simone's three buddies exchanged quick glances. I had no clue what it meant.

Simone spit on the ground. "I'm enough for you, whore. I'm alpha."

"Alpha? What's that? Like top bitch dog?"

Simone snarled. Literally snarled. A shallow vibration, like an animal, it ended on a high note. I'd never heard anyone, let alone a woman, make such a sound of territorial aggression.

The first time I had to fight another woman was one of McKay's former girlfriends. It was a regular bitch slapping, hair pulling, shredded clothes spectacle, egged on by a crowd of drunks and bullies. I won, barely. McKay was angry, disgusted. He called me a pussy girl, and I asked him how I could do better. He sent me to a man he called Gabe. He told Gabe to teach me how to fight—and win.

Now Gabe, he wasn't big. Shorter and thinner than me, but he had lightning speed. Lean, with dark skin and ropy muscles, he taught no fancy martial arts, no intricate steps. He taught me how my most probable attackers would behave. He taught me how to react instantly, never hesitate. He asserted that, even for me, a tall, strong woman, my first action should be to run. If forced to fight, a single first blow was where I would have my best chance. Then I should run.

Simone pushed off, two steps forward, then launched her hefty body off the ground and through the air at me. *What the hell!* I'd expected her to charge like a bulldozer. She should use her body mass as a ground weapon, but this…amazing? Impossible? *Her weight alone should have prevented her torpedo act.*

My surprise only lasted a fraction of a second. A shitty fighting tactic, that leap. Once she committed, Simone couldn't stop or change direction. And I was way faster than her.

Thank you, Gabe, thank you so very much.

I stepped away and slashed a hard blow across her face and eyes with the side of my hand. She folded and collapsed. Real fights are not like they show in the movies and TV. A brutal blow to the face, eyes, throat, it hurts. It shocks the mind. Especially someone untrained to receive those kinds of blows. I glanced at the other women. They stood back, watching. Fine by me.

Simone staggered to her feet, shaking her head. Temporary blindness. By Gabe's rules, once she went down, I should have either run or beat the living shit out of her. This wasn't a barroom brawl. This was where I had to live and work. Maybe she'd come to her senses. Or not. She growled. Again, literally, a sound that her throat shouldn't be able to make.

She charged again. On foot, no leap. Fists raised— but so slow. I stepped out of the way again and let her pass. I linked my fingers. Both hands, locked together hammered her spine and her kidneys with a single blow. She smacked face down in the dirt. I kicked her in the head. Heads are hard. So were the new boots I'd bought in St. George. Again, thanks to Gabe, I knew a place that would hopefully knock her out without killing her. My foot found the honey spot. She jerked, then relaxed.

Were the others going to jump me? No. They hunched together, staring at something behind me. I whirled. Sheriff Harrow stood there, locked in what seemed his eternal stillness. How much had he seen? Did he see her attack me? Would he blame me? Odds were decent on that one. He stared at the three cowering women.

"Take her home." He spoke softly to them. Power hummed deep and low in his voice. *Take her home. Like a bag of groceries.*

They instantly obeyed. I stepped back and out of

their way as they hurried to their fallen companion. They easily lifted her and carried her into the darkness.

"I didn't start that." I felt the need to speak. To defend myself.

"I saw."

"You saw? Why didn't you stop her?"

"Did you want me to?" His voice was casual, almost amused.

Damn it! I wasn't amused. "Well isn't that your job, Sheriff? I had to hurt her. She won't forget."

He shrugged. "She won't complain. She challenged you in front of witnesses. You won. She won't trouble you again." He turned and walked back toward the tavern.

Well damn. Other than the fight itself, I had no clue what had just happened. Had he approved of my victory? No way. I went to the apartment, restless, wound tight. I couldn't escape in sleep. I plopped down on the floor. I'd try meditation again. To my surprise, I achieved a deep state of consciousness and fell into the vast empty Void within seconds. I existed in another place, another cosmic plane or universe. Again, it was shifting light, not the usual darkness. At least I was alone. Was my last visit when I felt something my imagination? Suddenly, instead of peace, a memory, the thing I desperately fought, escaped and slapped me like a 3-D movie.

McKay's lead bully boy had stolen my knife. For the first time ever, the knife hadn't returned to me on its own. McKay had no sympathy. He wouldn't make the asshole give it back. Fury boiled until it drove me crazy. So stupid, so young, I'd hunted the bully and found him in a bar down by the harbor. I quietly sent him gifts of alcohol until he could barely stand, then paid one of the bar girls to lead him outside behind the bar. A smart one, she instantly left the scene. We were alone.

The knife, my knife, he'd hooked to his belt. Then it appeared in my hand. It had never done that before. Show up in my sock drawer yes, but never in my hand ready for action. I'd never used the blade to cause injury. I knew I should run away. Pure rage came in a flood, wiping out all rational thought. *The knife was mine! How dare he!* I couldn't stop myself. I cut him. It wasn't a fight. He could barely stand. I danced around him and cut him more. At last I came to my senses and ran away. I left him behind me, screaming, carved up like a piece of bloody meat. I lay in bed for a week, physically ill, out of my mind with guilt. I had a right to take my knife. But the rest? So wrong, so evil.

Oh, damn was McKay pissed. Someone had heard the thief's cries, called the cops, and after a trip to the ER, they arrested him for outstanding warrants. McKay had counted on the asshole for a job. Someone told him they thought I did it. *What? No, not his sweet Lilly.* Like all bullies, the man had enemies, and one of them must have taken the opportunity for revenge. I hid the knife and did my best never to let anyone see it again.

More memories came, more instant replay.

They were not my memories!

The knife. Scenes spread through my mind. I was suddenly living inside those scenes that went on and on. How much blood had this blade spilled? Roars of a mob demanding more, the sound of slashed flesh in a quiet assignation. More blood, battle sounds, metal against metal, screams, death cries.

I opened my eyes, stunned. I'd left the peaceful meditation, but I brought something back with me. Knowledge. And compulsion. Compulsion I couldn't deny. I knew the positions. The stance, foot placement, thrust, cuts, distance…what the hell?

It forced me to action. I rose and picked up the knife. Movements I'd never made before came with practiced ease. Lilly Dusalte didn't know shit about how to fight, but this knife knew. It forced my muscles through a specific routine. It owned me. My body cooperated like I'd been a fighter all my life. Finally, exhausted, my hand released the weapon. It bounced on a rug and landed like a hot coal I didn't dare touch.

What was happening to me? I was not a true fighter, a killer, no matter what the blade did. I'd had the knife for so long, and it felt right in my hand. But the desire for blood? Not mine ever. Even with McKay's bully, I'd only started with a need to reclaim my property. What was different? Did the fight with Simone trigger something?

The knife had taken control. My continuous terror of developing Mother's illness bubbled up like acid in my stomach. I picked it up and turned it in my hands. A knife. A blade. Still mine, now more than ever.

Chapter Seven

Friday, another busy night, nothing unusual until the sheriff came in accompanied by Special Agent Jacob Hart. The special agent had supervised the two young agents assigned to protect me before McKay went to trial. McKay had killed both. Slaughtered. That was the word that said it all. Hart blamed me. Not surprising. I blamed myself.

The agent had kept a professional distance at first. Then it became personal. His immense and boundless contempt for me added weight to the guilt I lived with. I truly believed he would kill me if he thought he could get away with the crime. McKay was a distant figure, the criminal fugitive. Substantial Lilly stood right before him. He didn't approach, but he wanted me to know he had followed me from Boston and was watching. Hart and the sheriff talked for what felt like a long time, then they both left. The sheriff stopped me later as I walked out to go home. He said nothing at first, then…

"Hart is…" he hesitated.

"I know Hart, Sheriff."

"He's not rational. He's dangerous."

What's this? He was concerned about me? Warning me against the FBI. Not that I needed warning that the FBI—at least Agent Hart—found me contemptable.

"Yes, Sheriff, Hart is dangerous. I'm sure he told you what happened in nightmare detail. Nothing I can do about him. He used to come and watch me in rehab, I guess to be sure I suffered enough."

"He's worried. He's afraid his superiors will reassign him."

"He won't go. He may resign, but he'll stick by me."

A tiny flicker of surprise flashed in his eyes, but he said nothing.

When we approached the motel I said, "I'm going to look for stones. The full moon shows them every so often." I had a small flashlight in my pocket, but the moonlight was usually enough.

He remained silent but followed me as I walked into the desert. Odd, but I'd stopped the useless exercise of wondering about his motives for anything. Waiting for me to make a mistake so he could bring out the cuffs? He made one of my token life pleasures, searching for stones, as uncomfortable as doing a strenuous workout with acute PMS.

The desert wind, usually restless as an insomniac at three a.m., lay silent, waiting. The chilly night made me wish I'd bought a better jacket when I had a chance. I faced the almost full moon where it burrowed into an ebony pool. It shoved the brilliant blanket of stars aside, just as the sun would in the morning. No ambient light here, only moon and glorious starlight, almost as clear as it had been before Europeans came, conquered the land, and built their steel and stone monuments.

A sound slid across the desert. A cough, then a high-pitched cry.

"What's that?" I asked because his silence

unnerved me, not the sound.

"A mountain lion."

"I heard coyotes last night." I'd been spending part of my sleepless nights out on my tiny porch. I'd carve, but when it was too cool, I'd wrap up in a blanket and try to become part of my surroundings.

A cloud drifted over the moon and left only the stars to light the way. I'd have to step carefully. I struggled in my effort, clumsily bumping rocks with my boots. The sheriff walked silent and sure footed behind me.

"Can you see in the dark?" His question surprised me.

"No. Can you?"

"Yes. You're walking toward a thirty-foot rain wash cliff."

I whirled to face him. Toward? I was already there. My heels slipped off the edge. I gasped, tried to step forward…too late. Over correction, balance gone…I fell. Strong arms wrapped around me, lifted, and dragged me back. He held me tight while I struggled to get my feet under me. He abruptly released me and stepped back. I dropped to my knees gasping. I squeezed my eyes shut and rubbed my hands over my face. Damn, I hadn't brushed the sand off my palms.

The sheriff stood and waited for me to get my breath. He didn't help me, didn't touch me, while I forced myself to my feet and straightened my clothes.

"Thank you, Sheriff. I see your point about the dark." Oh, hell. What next?

"Ben likes you. He likes you too much." That voice again, bleak, threatening.

"What's too much? He's friendly. And none of

your business."

"It is my business. You're on probation under the jurisdiction of the law in *my* town. You have nothing that's personal or private."

He was right. Every law enforcement professional I dealt with reiterated those facts. Still a prisoner, I had no *rights* to anything.

"Yes, of course, *Sheriff*. How stupid of me to forget my lowly status. I like Ben. I have no immoral plans for him. He's too young for me. Too…innocent? Not an appropriate word, but as close as I can come. Comparisons, I guess."

"Comparisons? You mean as opposed to the depraved asses you…" He stopped for long seconds before speaking again. "Ben. He can't have…"

His fingers suddenly bit into my arm. He dragged me close. I grabbed at his shirt to keep from falling again. His breath came hard, right by my ear. "There will be no collateral damage here. I will kill you first."

The ass held me for a moment, close, his cheek against mine. His abrupt release staggered me again. He walked away, graceful and silent across the rocky ground. Oh, yes. He could see in the dark.

The Sheriff of Garnet had threatened to kill me. But minutes ago, he'd dragged me back from a precipice. If he'd wanted me dead, he could have let me go. *Stupid woman, wandering around the desert in the dark.*

I raised my hands to my face. His scent lingered where I'd grabbed him to hold on. His personal essence, masculine, deep…something had happened. Something in my life had changed. I wish I knew what it was. Flashlight in hand, I carefully made my way back to the motel.

Later that night I lingered on my tiny porch. The moon had moved across the sky, heading west toward the horizon, but it still bathed the ground in cold white light. The temp had dropped from chilly to downright cold.

Regardless of the temperature, I longed for the taste of a beer. I abstained because I never knew who was watching. No alcohol consumption, no hanging out in dens of iniquity, no hanging out with disreputable people. The tavern was the only exception, and Lo was liable for my behavior.

The big cat walked out of the shadows ten feet from me. Mountain lion. I'd seen pictures, but the experience, the actual presence of the living creature…how captivating. Slender despite its size, a sleek lean body, the moonlight gave its gold coat a shine. So graceful, each silent step barely moved the sand. It stared straight at me for seconds, merely acknowledging my presence, then stepped back into the darkness.

****

A week passed, and I'd grown bored. Since I had no real life, the computer was a dud too. I had no one to communicate with and cared nothing for the news. My world had narrowed to a single paved road across the parched wilderness, with only lonesome buildings to break the monotony. I'd asked Lo about the possibility of a gym in Sioux Crossing and to my surprise she found one closer—sort of. I'd noticed the barn by the motel of course. It was too big not to. A side room held a treadmill, assorted weights, a bench, and a leg press.

A bit claustrophobic, but still enough room enough

for me. I also asked about running on the road early in the morning, but was intensely and frantically discouraged. Lo and Ben treated me to ever more sinister warnings of rattlesnakes, packs of coyotes, and wild mountain lions. Okay, so I'd use the treadmill for my running. The one plus? The big open hallway in the barn allowed me to collect and store pieces of wood to carve. Long unused, I claimed the spot, and it slowly became my place, my sanctuary.

The desert presented challenges to finding appropriate wood. I'd cut no living tree. Ben took me out in his truck one day to hunt more. We went too far but had a picnic in a pine forest close to the Utah border. I remembered the sheriff's so hateful warning about corrupting Ben, but my pleasurable days were so few I ignored his words.

I filled my long days and longer nights with bartending, exercise, and wood carving. I often had the peculiar sense that someone watched me from the darkness as I worked on the porch, but I refused to surrender to paranoia.

Meditation, entry into my special Void, remained my best resource for rest. Nervous about going there, I had no other experience like my forced knife lesson, and no visitation by something unfamiliar in my trance. However, I did retain a compulsion to regularly practice with the knife. No meditation required for that. The ability remained sharp in my mind and muscles. Movement, positions, thrusts burned in my brain, became more concise, more a part of me. Though I feared this new skill, feared what it could do, I feared McKay more. I didn't question the weirdness, just as I hadn't questioned the weirdness of the knife itself throughout my childhood. My greatest battle was with complacence. It nagged me, tempting me to dangerous relaxation.

I was falling into the rhythm of the town. I'd had no more run-ins with the sheriff or customers, nor had I seen anything else unusual or odd. I also knew the friendly crowd of regulars who walked into the tavern each night, at least by name. I'd thought Lo might give me more information about the so-called tribes, but she didn't. She'd stopped explaining anything else, too. I guess she didn't want me to laugh at her again. She'd never lie to me, but her fantasy story about her goddess' plans for me had pushed me to an edge. Was it to encourage me to…belong? Goddess. Save the tribes, Lilly. Too much, way too much.

I did have to discourage Ben when he asked me for a date. There was a dance hall in Sioux Crossing, and he wanted to go. Yeah, I saw it as innocent fun, but I didn't know how he—or the sheriff—would see me agreeing to go. Having warned me, Sheriff Pax would not likely find me so innocent. Ben accepted my rejection with grace and an air of inevitability, as if he knew it was useless to ask but wanted to anyway.

I would sit on my porch each night until the cold drove me in. I did see the sleek lion often. Twice, a larger heavier cat came. It would walk by, other times it would lie down, lay perfectly calm, and stare. If I stood, it would immediately leave.

One Sunday night, sitting on my little porch, I glanced up to see the sheriff standing not far away, watching me. I again noted his unnatural stillness, but something was different.

"May I help you, Sheriff?" I stood to face him.

He stepped forward, grabbed me by the shoulders, and shoved me back against the wall by the door. His hips jammed hard against mine. Oh, I understood that. His knee shoved between my legs, spreading them. I relaxed for the inevitable. I hadn't expected it from him. So stern, upright, professional. If he had asked...

His hands squeezed my shoulders in a brutal, bruising grip.

"You don't have to hurt me. I won't fight you, Sheriff. You're the top dog here."

"Dog? I'm a..." His words trailed off. He shuddered. Good thing I was standing against the wall. He threw himself away from me. He stood on the edge of the light, bent down, hugging his guts as if in deep tearing agony. I could hear his ragged breath.

"Go inside. Now!" Nothing wrong with his voice.

I obeyed. Not much point in arguing. I went in to wait. He'd follow. I wouldn't resist. Then I could officially hate him instead of looking at him as a fine specimen of a man.

After a while, I realized he wasn't coming. I peered out the window. Nothing. How utterly confusing. Strange, and hurtful at the same time. Yes, he'd stopped, but this was too personal.

The next day I only saw him once. He never glanced in my direction and I didn't try for eye contact. Lo, the master of observation, saw a change in me.

"What's wrong, Lilly?"

"Nothing. Well, the usual. What do you mean?" *Lie like hell, Lilly. Don't cause trouble.*

Suspicious, she eyed me like I'd grown horns or alien antennae. "Something happened."

"My life is full of *happenings,* Lo. I can't keep

track. They range from eating an enjoyable meal to lying broken and dying in an ambulance. I always rank them and let the minor ones go. If I have a *happening* that comes in the top quarter, third, or even half, I'll let you know."

She raised her eyebrows, but let it go.

****

The tavern served alcohol, and another clash was inevitable. It happened in all such places, but Garnet and my living arrangement seemed particularly suited for such. Friday night was a perfect time. Henry Holton, a.k.a. Henry the Horse, weighed an astonishing 350 pounds. Not a Garnet resident or tribe member, but a regular who drove from Sioux Crossing.

Big boned and fat, hard solid fat, not violent, but he could do damage by accident. Ben told me they called him the *horse* for his equipment, which ladies swore matched his impressive body size. A popular fellow among certain women.

A drunken Horse sprawled like a beached whale across my bar. His hands scrabbled, trying to get to me. It took Ben and Lo to haul him off and drag him back to a chair.

"But I want to fuck her," he kept whining over and over. I saw the guys standing around, grinning. I'd never hear the end of this. *But I want to fuck her.* A beer in their hands and they'd remind me forever, all the while producing manly chuckles to show they were teasing, not serious. For a bar, it was a surprisingly well-behaved crowd.

Ick! Henry had drooled all over the bar top. I put on rubber gloves and wiped the glass top and anything he touched down with bleach. I lost customers because the cleanup took time. No one wanted to sit where Henry slobbered anyway. Not that I could blame them. They'd come back after more beer.

Henry must have sobered up, because he disappeared while I was in the back cooler getting a bottle of wine. Most customers wanted beer or the hard stuff, but a few wanted Lo's cheap wine.

The evening ended, and I headed home. I'd become complacent, used to having Lo, the sheriff, or Ben watch me. Near the security light, a foul-smelling wall stepped out of the darkness and grabbed me. The wall brayed a disgusting laugh in my ear. Oh, hell. Henry. I twisted away easily enough. Ah, the stink. The man was toxic waste personified.

"Go away, Henry." Not another confrontation. I wanted to go home.

He grabbed at me. I dodged, but he was between me and my apartment. He stepped fast for a man his size. I dodged his tree trunk arms. I had to stay out of his reach.

"You too good for me, huh?" Henry belched. Downwind, I gagged.

"No, Henry, too sober. Please don't do this. Go on home."

In my limited experience, he'd never been violent. He stood there, swaying. Damn. I'd have to go get Lo or the sheriff when he passed out. I couldn't leave him out in the open for the cougars and coyotes.

Complacency, my nemesis, flourished. I misjudged his level of sobriety and intent. He seized one of my arms in a massive paw of a hand and clamped down hard. I cried out in surprise—and pain.

"On your knees, whore. You can suck."

Then he hit me. Thankfully, not with his fist. An open hand the size of a baseball mitt smashed against the side of my head. Light flashed for a brilliant instant.

Stunned, I fell back, and landed smack on my ass. My left elbow struck a rock hard, and pain spiked and radiated up my arm. Blood gushed from my nose, over my mouth, and down on my shirt. This was not going to happen. I fumbled in my jacket. The knife came to my hand.

I looked up, ready to kick out, then stab. The sheriff was facing off with Henry. Henry stood mumbling and shaking his head. And he stayed that way as the sheriff came and knelt beside me. He didn't touch me.

"Can you get up?" That same, deep voice, impassive, devoid of emotion. *Not are you hurt? Not can I help you. Just can you get up.*

"Yeah." I managed to stand with a less than graceful struggle. More blood ran from my nose. My elbow hurt like hell, I hoped not fractured. I had a tight grip on the knife. Damn, the sheriff had to have seen the blade.

The sheriff stood by Henry again. Henry saw the knife. He glanced down at his arm, the blood on his sleeve. He gave a petulant whine. "She cut me."

"That's my blood, asshole. You hit me." Then I forced myself to shut up.

The sheriff laid a hand on Henry's shoulder. He turned him around, then popped a ring of keys from Henry's belt. "Go to your truck and sleep it off. Come see me in the morning for your keys."

Henry, suddenly meek and obedient, staggered away.

The sheriff came back to me. "Let me see that knife."

I stood there, my nose trickling blood…and he wanted my only weapon.

"No. It's mine." I gripped the hilt tighter.

"I can charge you if you don't—"

"Charge me? Henry assaults me and gets to sleep it off like a bad little boy. Is that how you do things here? You're going to take the side of every man in town who tries to rape me? You didn't have a problem when you…" I stopped. He hadn't raped me. No matter what he wanted that night, or how much he'd wanted it, he'd stopped himself and left me alone.

"I simply want to see your knife." His voice suddenly filled with classic reason. He stood straight, everything about him still under tight control.

I yielded to my inevitable probation/law officer status and laid the knife across my palm and held it out. He didn't touch the blade. The stone on the hilt, the jet-black stone, flashed a tiny light. What the hell? No stone, let alone a black stone, could reflect the low security light. It got worse. He took a quick step back. "Put it away." The words came, tight, terse, between clenched teeth. Well, well. Something about the knife had disturbed him. I slipped it back in the sheath and into my coat.

"Why didn't you wait for someone to walk with you?" He almost spit the words at me. Would there ever come a day when he didn't hate me?

"I'm tired. I don't…shouldn't need an escort to cross a parking lot."

"Obviously, that's not true. Do you want to press charges against Henry? Someone put him up to that, but he had to know it was wrong."

"Who would want him to…?" Ah, probably Simone. I hadn't seen her, but I didn't know anyone else who hated me that much. "No, no charges." I shook my head. I did not want to get in the legal system any deeper than I was. But if I did find out who set him—and me—up, I'd take personal action.

More blood trickled from my nose and down my lip. I swiped it with my shirt sleeve. My face hurt like hell, and I couldn't escape into sleep until it felt better.

"Well, Sheriff, are you done with me?"

He looked away, then back with an expression I couldn't read. "Ms. Dusalte. I want to apologize for touching you the other night. I am ashamed to say I've broken tribal law. There are consequences. To file a complaint, talk to Lo. She'll show you how. I will accept the tribe's judgement."

The sheriff blurted out the words like skipping stones on a pond. Apologize? For the night he'd started to rape me, but forced himself back in time? I could feel the truth in his statement.

He turned and headed toward the parking lot, probably to check on Henry. What could I have said? *That's okay, a slight, misguided rape attempt happens all the time. I'm sure you didn't mean to. It's not like I never made a mistake. A serious mistake that damned me to relive memories of unforgivable acts.*

I'd read, and believed, that rape was about power, control over a woman. But he had power like that to begin with. He'd been reminding me of it ever since I arrived.

I walked on home, wondering why he had such an impact on me. I'd admit that I'd been thinking about him often. Wondering about him, watching for him. Looking to see if he was the next one to walk in the door.

The sky had the whitewash of false dawn when he returned and banged on my door. I'd been sitting for a couple of hours with a bag of ice on my face, off and on, trying to reduce the swelling and pain so I could get up the energy to climb in the shower and change bloody clothes.

The minute I opened the door he grabbed me by the arm and snatched me outside. He dragged me toward the parking lot. He held the arm with the banged-up elbow in a fierce grip and it hurt like hell. Oh, I wanted so badly to fight. *Don't do it, Lilly. Remember.* The sheriff, the law, probation—he towed me along like a naughty child.

A small crowd stood around a pickup truck, Deputy Ben and Clark, the part-time deputy, among them. The sheriff shoved me forward and the group parted so I could see. The pickup truck door stood open. Henry, sent to sleep off his alcoholic stupor, was now stuck behind the steering wheel, hanging down, halfway out. Blood drenched his clothes. Like a leaking faucet, gravity drew red liquid over his head and ears to puddle in a pool on the ground. The source, a single large darker blotch, covered his chest. A knife wound?

No blood on his pants, so the killer dragged him partially out of the truck. The big man's legs caught under the steering wheel and dash leaving him hanging. Whoever killed him was in a hurry.

Horrified, I fought the nausea bumping the back of my throat. I stared into the sheriff's wrathful face. Then it hit me. Did he think I killed the man?

"No. I didn't…I wouldn't…" I twisted, tried to get away but his fingers dug tighter.

I'd seen blood and torn bodies before. Far too many. When you live with brutal, violent people, the inevitable occurred. I'd watched McKay kill.

Suddenly pissed more than shocked, I gritted my teeth. "Damn you."

"That's enough." He cut me off in an instant. He released me, and I staggered before Ben caught me in his arms and held me steady.

"Go back to your room." Oh, the sheriff's merciless voice.

Ben carefully released me. "What are you doing, Pax?"

"Shut up." The sheriff cut him off. Then, to me, "I told you what to do."

I backed away. There was no point in arguing. I think he knew I hadn't killed Henry. He wouldn't have let me go if he believed I did. Someone had attacked the big man when he was vulnerable, drunk, or sleeping. Did he want to accuse me to humiliate me in front of bystanders? All Garnet locals, were they his audience?

I forced my body to stand straight. I couldn't give in and run away. Would this bizarre circus never end? Now, I'd have to build a new compartment in my mind and lock out the sight of Henry's torn, bloody body. Poor Henry. Not the best man in the world, but he hadn't deserved murder.

Once inside my apartment, I stripped off my clothes, stained with dried blood from the earlier confrontation. Oh damn, everyone out by the truck had seen them. I tossed them on the bed and headed for the bathroom. I'd finished with my shower when I heard banging at the door for the second time. I only had my robe over my wet body, but I knew I had to let him in.

The sheriff marched past me into my bedroom. I followed. "What are you doing?"

Oh, damn, the gory shirt and jeans lay on the bed.

"If this is a search, Sheriff, it's illegal." No, it wasn't. Not for me on probation. "What are you looking for?"

He spoke in a level voice, with no belligerence. "For some ungodly reason, Hart, your personal FBI agent/stalker has made a surprise appearance. He saw you. He wants your clothes tested. You're giving permission for me to take them. If you want to wait for a warrant, you'll do it in jail in Vegas. That's his idea, too. Did you get Henry's blood on you?"

"No. I never touched him. All the blood on my clothes is mine."

The sheriff grabbed the bloodstained shirt and pair of jeans I'd worn and stuffed them in a bag.

He scowled, and violent distaste marred his face. "What is it with you?"

Oh, hell, the hostility was back. "Henry's never gone after a woman like that. He has regulars, women who like him. They were there. He should have gone home with one. Damn these men, Henry, Hart, McKay, why are they obsessed with you?"

"Hart is obsessed with McKay, not me. I'm a convenient tool. You've already asked me about McKay's obsession, and I've told you I don't know. Henry? I have no clue."

I rubbed the back of my neck. Would he accept any kind of explanation? Would that soothe him, move him back from unnerving speculation?

"I loved McKay once, Sheriff. McKay hated to lose anything. His ego wouldn't tolerate rejection. His obsession is not wanting me, but that he lost me. I escaped him. At least for a while."

"And now? McKay? Do you still love him?" The question, the words, came at me with colder fury than before. Why did he care who I loved? Did he think I was a brainless masochist? A meek little creature devoted to a man who so cruelly broke her body and mind?

"Love him? No. He's an important figure in my life, though. You know that. I'm sure he has an obscene use for me."

"You're a beautiful woman. Does he still love you?"

I had to laugh. It was as hard and bitter as any sound that ever came out of my mouth. "Love? There's no love involved. McKay is a psychopath who demands *absolute perfection* in all things. Or as close as he can get. I'm no longer a serious contender." Ah, that wasn't enough. "I'm too far from perfect now."

I pulled the robe's tie, held back the material, and let him see my naked body. The scars. The thick ropy ridges, gouges, and burns from McKay, and the perfectly stitched surgeries the doctors performed to set my bones and piece my organs back together. From my neck to right above my knees, they created a horrific puzzle of my mutilated form. My back was as bad.

My sheriff's reaction? A widening of eyes, the quick draw of breath. Shock? Disgust? I went to him. Close, too close, I invaded his personal space to remind him how close he'd come that night on my porch.

"What man could possibly want this body?"

The next expression I'd seen on doctors and nurses so often.

"Oh, no. Don't you dare, Sheriff. You have no right to pity me." I put out my hand to shove him away.

The rock-hard sheriff didn't move. You're too close. *Back away, Lilly, back away.* I did and closed my robe.

"Lilly." He said my name. Not Ms. Dusalte. Lilly. His voice had deepened. Not soft but lacking the rage of moments ago. "There was a time when battle scars were celebrated, like medals of honor. They meant you'd taken solid hits and survived." He came closer but didn't touch me. "Scars marked a warrior as someone with strength and courage."

"Strength? Courage? You are so wrong."

"Wrong? So, what are you, then, if not a fighter? An abused child? A psychopath's play toy? A perpetual victim." This sheriff had spent an inordinate amount of time studying me and reading reports, some of which I knew were outright lies. And he accused others of obsession!

I'd had enough. "So, are you psychoanalyzing me now, Sheriff?"

He shook his head and left me there, wondering what the hell was happening.

****

Henry's death weighed on me all the next day. I learned his murderer used a knife to stab him in the heart. I knew I wasn't responsible, but somehow it felt connected to me. I didn't think the sheriff believed I'd killed him, but if I had, he seemed willing to cover for me with the FBI. For Lo's sake I suppose.

A warrior, he'd called me. How archaic. At the

same time, it warmed me. Gave me a tiny sense of pride. *How dare he? He had no business giving me anything. None.*

Things changed the following night. The sheriff came to my side of the bar twice and asked for coffee. I obliged. We didn't talk, but occasionally made eye contact. What did he want? A truce? I thought about the possibility. About him, and yes, about McKay. I'd long since realized that McKay would be on my mind, a part of my life until he died—or I died. But this sheriff, what was he? Was he my enemy? Did I think of him as a man? An attractive man? A difficult man to be sure. But he hadn't turned away in disgust when he saw my nightmare body.

One night when I left the Tavern, he was outside, on the usual guard duty. I walked over to him. Try for a truce. I could do that.

"Good evening, Sheriff."

He acknowledged me with a nod of his head.

"I know you have issues with me. Your concerns about McKay for the people here are rational and valid. I do want you to know that I appreciate you and Deputy Ben watching out for me." There, that was all he was going to get at that time. But did my thanks for his guarding me mean I forgave him for pushing me that night?

He must have thought so. He reached out and brushed his fingers down my arm. The first gentle touch I'd had from him. His deep voice slid over me like thick coffee cream over a spoon. "I wanted you to see Henry. To see there is danger here, not just from McKay. You're getting too complacent." I nodded my acceptance of his words, and then turned and went on home. Yes, it was home now.

Chapter Eight

Kaya arrived one Monday at noon to sign payroll papers for Lo. She had declared a truce with me. It was her truce because I didn't care. We weren't BFF's, but we got along in a friendly girl sort of way. We talked that day, and the next thing I knew, I'd robbed my tip jar and we headed to Sioux Crossing. She rode a medium-sized Italian bike, a pretty piece of equipment in red and silver. I guess we looked odd on the bike, me being over a foot taller than her, but what an exhilarating idea to get out of Garnet. She wore eye goggles and handed me an extra pair. I started to ask about helmets but rationalized that there were far greater dangers for me in the world than a bike crash. At least that's what I thought until I was sitting behind her doing 80 miles an hour down the rough two-lane road to the Crossing.

Sioux Crossing was Garnet on a modest dose of steroids. It had one traffic light flashing caution yellow and rolling-stop red. A minor collection of stores, restaurants, and services, some built of concrete, but most functioned in metal prefab buildings plopped down on hard flat desert land. I could see a couple of miniscule and unpretentious neighborhood subdivisions of mobile homes, a factory that made auto parts, and a sign pointing down a road to the Ingot Hole Copper Mine. Kaya waved toward a modern sheriff's office, school, and library. She informed me that the library had free internet and computers if I needed one, since Lo's wasn't exactly private.

I had to limit my shopping because of the bike and what we could carry, but I managed a couple of books and a package of panties. About five o'clock, we headed to the Poplar Hill Diner. Of course, Sioux Crossing had no hills, and like Garnet, a tree of any native hardwood species had not graced the land since prehistoric times.

"Hey, I know." Kaya, always restless, bounced in her seat while we waited for menus. She bounced often. Petite young girls could do that. I'd look like a spastic buffalo. "We can go to the Ballroom tonight. You can come home and stay with me, so we don't have to ride back in the dark."

"Ballroom. Is it a bar? I can't do that." No, I couldn't go into a bar except Lo's tavern. Probation, probation, what if Hart was watching?

"No bar. Just dancing. Well, no dirty dancing. No alcohol and no hanging around in the parking lot. It started out for teens, but now lots of people go."

"On a Monday night?"

She winced. "Yeah, we take what we can get. Television at home or drinks at a bar. That's it. The Crossing is not a snake pit of entertainment."

Snake pit? Right. Kaya was from Texas. Rattlesnake roundups.

It sounded like fun, so I called Lo and asked if it was okay.

"You don't need my permission, Lilly. I'm not your jailer."

"Sorry. Habit."

At the hospital, rehab, and jail, I'd asked for permission often. Asked for permission to move, to speak, to piss, and shit at times. I called and asked her because the FBI reminded me several times before I left Boston that Lo was taking responsibility for me and they would blame her if I failed at anything.

The crowded diner meant our waitress didn't get to us right away. Kaya knew her and told her to take her time. It wasn't long before Sheriff Pax and Deputy Ben walked in. They came straight toward us. Was Kaya waiting for them? Well shit. Didn't I get enough of them in Garnet?

Ben slid in the booth by Kaya, and the sheriff, of course, sat next to me. Close enough that his scent overrode the odors from the kitchen—not to mention what it did to me. What was there about this man that made me want to draw deep breaths like I was sniffing a bouquet of fragrant roses?

He seemed relaxed, sitting there ever so close. What a change. I did remember he'd seen me naked. My fault, but…oh, hell. I didn't care. I couldn't relax, but I could summon a little snark. "Did Lo call you? Are you checking up on me?"

The corners of his mouth turned up a tiny bit like he wanted to smile and fought the urge.

"No. We came for supper."

Ben flinched. So did Kaya. Both knew I'd had difficulties with Garnet's sheriff.

Ben and Kaya started and then kept a conversation going. The sheriff talked less than I did, and I wasn't about to speak. That left me time to be completely aware of his presence. So near if he were a tree, I could lean on him in a quiet forest. When he moved his arm, it brushed mine. His leg would touch me occasionally. I bit my tongue and held steady, but I found myself wishing he would do it again. How was I supposed to deal with this? Of course, I had no experience with what anyone would consider a *normal* relationship with another human being. Mama, Frank who saved me, McKay who almost destroyed me, and now this man followed another confusing path into my life.

The waitress finally came back for our orders. Restaurants hadn't been an element in my life for a long time. Most of the stuff on the diner menu had Spanish names, so I stuck with a burger and fries.

We barely made it through dinner when Ben and the sheriff got a call and had to rush off. The sheriff handed the waitress money as he went out the door. When we asked for our tickets, we found that he had paid for our dinners too. Kaya was pleased, but not me. I wasn't comfortable with things like that and might never be again.

The Ballroom turned out to be another metal warehouse building with a slick wood dance floor, snack bar, spectator seats, and weight-lifting female bouncers, who turned out to be the owners. Again, being the new kid on the block they checked me out. We had a pleasant talk, since both had lived in Boston, but thankfully not during the time I had my troubles. A former schoolteacher and an electrician, they'd retired to live with the teacher's mother in the Crossing. They'd opened the Ballroom for younger people since they had no recreation activities at all. To their surprise, entertainment-deprived adults also found pleasure in the setting.

When we'd arrived at eight, the music was loud

and fast, but as the night progressed the DJ slowed it down. No crowd. I didn't care. I danced. Between dances I ate cheese nachos and drank sodas. Like an ordinary person. Ordinary on the surface anyway. All that liquid had predictable results.

When I went into the restroom, one of the women from Simone's nighttime gang attack was standing at the mirror.

"Hi." She spoke softly, eyes downcast. So, no fight.

"Good evening." I acknowledged her greeting, then went into a stall. She was there when I came out to wash my hands.

"I'm sorry," she said.

"For what?"

"I followed Simone. Sometimes you're judged by who you follow more than what you do."

Oh, hell. The girl was a genius. "It's okay." I shrugged. "I've followed bad people before." Understatement, of course. This apology was easy to accept. "Not that I think Simone is bad, but what was she so pissed about? I never figured that out."

She glanced over her shoulder as if someone would sneak up on her in the three-stall bathroom. She leaned toward me and spoke in a whisper. "Right from the start, Simone was jealous about the attention Pax paid to you. Only a day or so after you arrived, she was following you, watching you. She can, you know…and she certainly wants him."

You know…? You know what?

"The sheriff's attention is on me because I'm an ex-con on probation. He thinks I'll cause trouble. There's nothing else."

She waved her hand in front of my face. "You're not blind, so you must be stupid." She giggled all the way out the door. She was right. I was stupid. The sheriff paid attention to me. From the moment Road Rash dropped me off. I paid attention to him. Not friendly, but certainly interested. Communication was better now, but so far, not a solution to the problem. Where was it all going? I had no idea.

"Last dance," the DJ called. It was only eleven o'clock, not a two-a.m. bar time. Half the lights went off leaving dark corners. A slow dance. Someone grasped my hand and pulled me onto the floor.

I thought at first it was Ben. Shocker, but the sheriff drew me close, and I slid my arm over his broad shoulders. He danced as gracefully as he moved, and I fell right in with his rhythm. No words, but his breath caressed the side of my face. His fingers pressed on my back at times as if he wanted me closer. When the dance ended, he released me and left. He left me. Alone. Standing there. What an ass. Or had he thought the situation required words, and he didn't have any? That I understood. I couldn't think of any right then either.

I went to find Kaya. When we arrived at her house, I met her mom and dad, then she put a blow-up air mattress on her bedroom floor. Kaya produced a bottle of vodka and a carton of orange juice. It'd been over two years since I'd had a drink, and it didn't take long to forget my troubles, including the lawman. I told Kaya a brief, sordid, almost true-life story, but I don't think she remembered much. A few drinks took care of me. No sleep, but I did maintain a pleasant alcoholic stupor for a while. When that wore off, I felt like I had a knife in my skull. I was better than my new drinking buddy who spent an hour in the bathroom dry heaving. Of course, the gruesome trip back to Garnet, at eighty miles an hour on a bike, was an insidious version of hell. We both had to work that night. We managed an acceptable level of service, though Lo eyed us skeptically at times. I took pity and let Kaya spend the night with me. As usual, I didn't need the bed. I felt sorry for her. She genuinely liked Ben. She was a decent girl, smart, funny, but I remembered how Lo spoke of her. "She's not tribe." I did remember Lo's speeches about marriages. Condemned by birth, it was unlikely she would have a deeper relationship.

Chapter Nine

Lo arrived at my door early on the following Monday after my dancing and hangover trip to Sioux Crossing. "Be ready to go at three o'clock. There's a new moon tonight, and the tribe is going to have a party in the valley."

"Party? Didn't get an invitation. Don't want to go." I didn't like the way the non-tavern-patron locals snubbed me. No one tried to provoke me as Simone had, but my tavern buddies didn't give me grief if I filled their ice-cold mugs and mixed excellent drinks.

Lo was adamant. "Nope, you gotta come. I have something to show you. Another lesson." It had been a while, and I'd hoped she'd given up on the goddess subject.

The sheriff hadn't spoken to me since he left me standing alone on the dance floor last week. I barely saw him. Not in the tavern or in the yard when I walked home. I'd made up my mind I'd talk to him, ask him straight out what was happening. Why he would cuddle close, then back away. Of course, Ben was gone too, so it could involve an unlikely outbreak of major criminal activity in the Crossing.

I tuned back into Lo. "Jeans and a warm shirt and jacket are fine for tonight." When she arrived, she presented me with a superb, butter-soft, brown leather jacket to replace my usual denim. Oh, it was perfect to cut the cool nights. Again, I wished she'd been my mother, or that Mama had abandoned me in her arms.

Although Lo owned the tavern, she worked nights right along with me and Kaya. I didn't mind earning my way here in Garnet. I'd held service jobs in college because my scholarships didn't pay for everything. In the city I had libraries, coffee shops, and two-dollar movies. If I didn't keep busy here, I'd break down under the weight of the desert's omnipresent silence. Was I happy? No, but at times, watching the sun rise over the dry hills or sitting out at night carving wood with my occasional big pussy cat audience, I managed hours of contentment.

"What's the significance of a new moon?" I asked later after we hit the road.

"Beginning and end, waxing and waning—mostly a damned fine excuse for a party. Happens once a month. Not that we party every month." She had a wide, playful grin on her face.

She drove into the valley, past the road to my birthplace, past Araun's house, and across the shallow creek. That's one feature I did like about this place. The contrast. Where there was a trickle of water, there was green. Instant green, not gradual. At a certain point, away from the life-giving source, the green stopped as if the desert had drawn an invisible line to halt the invasion.

A different route this time. We crossed another thin stream and drove through a narrow canyon between rock cliffs. Not soaring, but vertical and unclimbable. The road stretched on through the tight passage for a quarter of a mile. It ended in a small bowl with the same vertical walls. One rigidly constricted way into and out of a steep sided funnel. Not comfortable at all.

"This is Oro Canyon. It's a special place." Lo smiled like a kid at Christmas. Wow, she was in a fine mood today.

She parked in a flat space that had seen regular vehicle use. We walked along the creek bordered by willows and toward a high rock wall carved by ancient waters. The creek ended—or more likely began—in a wide shallow pool. A thin stream poured into the pool from an irregular shaped hole, a cave in the rock, twenty feet above us. Not a high volume of water, so it sounded more like a shower than a roaring waterfall. A place of remarkable, uncomplicated beauty made more remarkable by contrast to the arid earth.

Lo executed a vertical assent up the sheer rock cliff face toward the cave. There was a path of sorts. I followed her, slower, desperately clinging to any protrusion I thought might hold me. The pool, only inches deep, wouldn't cushion my fall if I slipped. Lo reached the cave and disappeared inside. I followed.

The cave itself was wider and taller than its opening, and the floor lay flat as if planed and sanded like wood. A deep, rich, earthy odor and moisture in the air gave a finger to the nose searing dryness outside. Lo waited for me about twenty feet in. A slight echo bounced back when she cleared her throat. She held out a hand, and I went to stand beside her. The only light came from the hole of daylight behind us. Enough to see, but not far.

I stared into the darkness where the shallow stream of water emerged. I could see another path, flat and well worn, leading deeper inside. "People come here much, Lo?" I pointed to the path.

"Not too often. There's a larger cavern below. It's beautiful. I'll take you there someday."

"Someday? Why did we come here, then?"

"You remember I told you about my dream?"

"Oh, yeah. That. Your ambiguous nightmare about me being a hero-slash-rescuer, etc." I watched her, hoping she wouldn't go off on that again. Believing in her goddess was one thing, but her expectation of my tribe-saving action was another.

As usual, she ignored my skepticism. "In the dream, I was standing here in this spot when she spoke to me. I wanted you to see it as I did."

"Ah…you're hoping I'll have an epiphany? See a manifestation of your goddess?" I wanted to leave. She didn't move. Frank and his rigid, multifaceted religious rules made me uncomfortable. Lo seemed to have rules that were more chaotic and complex, and equally disturbing.

I knelt by the stream and scooped up a handful of water, then let it glide through my fingers. I then inhaled the scent left behind. Clean, clear. Something flickered deeper in the cave. I stood. "Is someone back there. I thought I saw a light."

"It's not likely. Not today." She sounded so odd.

The light flashed again. Something in me demanded that I go and find the source. I took three steps in that direction.

"Lilly, there are holes back there." Lo's voice rose in alarm. "And bats."

That stopped me. It was insane. What was I doing, charging off into the dark?

Behind me, Lo gasped. "Your knife."

I'd started wearing the knife on my belt since I no

longer felt the need to hide it from anyone. It was easier to carry that way. Lo must have seen it by now, but not as it appeared in this cave. A glowing blue sheen seeped out of the knife sheath. I drew it and lifted it high. Brilliant blue-white radiance filled the cavern. It painted the blade's swirled rune patterns across a spreading pool of water and hanging spears of rock.

The earth around us suddenly hummed. It sang to me, a deep vibration through my body. Low notes as if they came from deep within the earth, then rose across a scale until it trilled like a flute.

I had heard this song before. When I was a child—and when I lay dying on a frozen Boston parking lot, clutching a handful of dirty soil.

The light faded. The song ceased. I glanced back at Lo. To my amazement, she was on her knees on the cavern floor, her face wet with tears.

"Lo?" Alarmed, I sheathed the knife and hurried to her. "What's wrong?"

She wouldn't speak, kept shaking her head. I lifted her to her feet and led her back out into the sunlight. No way was she capable of the climb down. I helped her sit and then rested with her on red earth at the cave's edge. At least we were in the sun. Tears continued to run down Lo's face, and her body trembled.

The knife's light show was new and surprising, as were its involuntary lessons on how to master cutting and killing. We sat there for a while, and she slowly calmed enough to speak.

"Where did you get that knife, Lilly?" Her question came out hushed, reverent as in a church—or a funeral home. *And just as uncomfortable*.

"I don't know. I was ten when it showed up. In my

underwear drawer of all places. Contrary to your belief about me, I don't remember everything. I guess I should have told you about it, but it's been a guarded secret for so long. Until I came here, it was just a knife." No. She deserved the truth. "Well, not exactly just a knife. No glowing blue light, but it would disappear when I was in a place where I couldn't keep a weapon. Like jail and rehab. Then it would show up when it was safe. It will cut anything. Almost anything. It won't cut me."

Incredibly, her rapturous expression transformed to something deeper. Shit! She's the one who had an epiphany.

"Lo, I'm sorry I didn't show it to you, but I thought you'd seen me wearing it at times. I'm sorry I laughed at your goddess story too. But you have to admit my being tribal savior…well, that's in another class altogether." I didn't know if I should say anything else. What could I say to someone who remained in the throes of a spiritual experience?

Lo sniffed and wiped her eyes. The smile I so loved reappeared. "I'll tell you a story, one of our legends. Have you ever read about objects of power, relics like the Spear of Destiny? The spear that pierced Christ's side on the cross. Holy chalices and crowns and scepters, all associated with significant religious events are common."

"Yeah, in lots of books and movies."

"Well, some of those relics do exist, though probably not in the form depicted in fiction. The goddess is our guardian, our protector. Long ago, in a time of war and major upheaval, she created three weapons, three blades. She forged them in the heart of the earth. She named them Bi'ar, Ben'zir and Ba'ran. She attached a stone to the hilt of each. Bi'ar has a black stone, Ben'zir a clear stone, and Ba'ran's stone is red. These weapons are not exactly alive, but they are sentient and do our goddess' bidding. Act by her will and her instructions."

"And you think my knife is Bi'ar? Out of a legend? How old?"

"At least 3,000 years. Our historian, a member of another tribe, has clay tablets with the story."

I glanced over my shoulder into the cave. "Lo, I have a problem. Not with supernatural. Hey, I've got the damned teleporting knife…that's supernatural, isn't it? Now it's decided to glow in the dark. But the goddess thing still troubles me. Serving, not worshiping. Is there that much difference? Serving how? What exactly is she? Do you know?"

She didn't answer for a moment, then she smiled. Contentment filled her voice. Yep, she'd accepted her visions, omens, whatever, as genuine and would plan her—and my—life around them.

"Lilly, I believe that there is an all-encompassing power that created our universe. Call it God if you will. But I also believe there are other powers involved, lesser powers. Powers far beyond human. Our goddess is one of them. I say one of them, because there may be others out there. There are stories in older texts, but only the goddess herself would know."

She licked her lips and shifted her body. "The debate over physical proof of God's existence is raging at times. But our goddess? In the cave, I again received physical proof of her existence."

"That's heavy-duty stuff, lady. Religion, ritual—"

"No rituals, Lilly. We celebrate celestial holidays, but that's more custom and tradition. Regardless of what you call our goddess, every pure-blood member of the tribe is connected to her. We're told—"

"Told by whom? Who tells you these things?" *That's it Lilly, be the skeptic.*

"Our histories, oral and written. Lilly, look at Frank. He rejects the goddess, but he studies the chronicles of history. He builds his faith on them."

She patted my hand as if comforting me. I think she needed that comfort more than I did. "This is what we're taught. While she's linked to us, the goddess won't interfere directly with our lives. I don't know if that's true. For a while, she had servants, one in each tribe. Even that stopped years ago. She does give us a single leader now. A man we call the Dominus. We presume she talks to him."

She stopped speaking, but silence carried an aura of deep contemplation. I waited until she spoke again. "Lilly, regardless of what we're told, I believe the goddess intervened, saved you that day you were injured. The fire, the one that killed all those men who hurt you? One man got out, burned...died the next day. He said the fire didn't start, didn't spread. It was everywhere, all at once. And then you lived when you truly should have died. I think she saved and sustained you."

"But you said she didn't interfere."

"I said that's what I was taught. What's happening now is as new and strange to me as it is to you."

I kicked at a rock, dislodged it, and watched it roll down and splash in the pool below. "It's about trust, Lilly. Your mother and others have horribly betrayed you. Asking you to trust a goddess, a being whose power and purpose you cannot fathom…I understand."

"Does she have a name?"

"No. Once she might have. Now she's just the goddess."

"I trust you, Lo. I trust Frank. I know the knife is real. The stone on the hilt did shine a bit when I showed it to the sheriff. He backed away like it was on fire. The light show in the cave? Never happened before. I can't explain what happened. It's easy isn't it, to assume all the objects and events you don't understand you attribute to a goddess."

"Oh, most certainly." She laughed. "I understand your skepticism. But I think it's a bit facetious."

Lo became silent, waiting on me to think it through. While I wasn't a scholar like Frank, I'd studied anthropology and the basics of religion. From the beginning of history and before, man needed to take control of the terror of the unknown by attributing it to the work of gods—and goddesses. Did that make them real? Then there's the theory that belief and worship give them life, and when the belief wanes, those gods die. I leaned against Lo, needing her warmth.

"I'm going to leave philosophy and religion to you and Frank. If you have any revelations, you can let me know." I drew the knife again. "This bitch? At least it's useful at times. I can peel an apple with it." I stuck it in the dirt like a dull, cast off kitchen knife. "Magic knife, sacred knife…bullshit. The damned thing has never saved me from one minute of pain, fear, or humiliation."

I jerked it out of the earth and slid the blade into its sheath. The knife, or something, had decided to train me to use it as a weapon. I'd stopped fighting the compulsion. I could concede that Lo's goddess, whatever she was or whatever her power or purpose, existed. And this goddess had plans for me. A captive of my own sins and how I would pay for them, she did not require my consent. *Bi'ar? Sacred? Since it wouldn't cut me, I couldn't even use it to kill myself.*

Chapter Ten

Descending the cliff path proved to be more challenging than climbing up. I managed but had to scoot on my ass across a wide rock I'd swear wasn't there before.

We went back to the truck and drove out the long rock-walled funnel to the main road. Another mile on, we reached rockier ground. Men and women, many I'd not met, awaited us. They unloaded the truck while Lo led me up another path, smoother this time. A striking circle built of sandstone, at least a hundred and fifty feet across, created an amphitheater with three levels of stone seating and a perfectly flat floor. What a sight.

Lo threw her hands wide, smiling with obvious pride. "This is the Mahakee. The people who built it were gone before we got here, but they graciously left it for us."

"That's pretty impressive." Impressive yes, and stone-ass uncomfortable if a person had to sit a long time.

Lo put me to work. I helped raise a large open sided tent, carried boxes of food and coolers of drinks. The sheriff was in uniform and on duty, so he wore his professional, impassive expression. I saw no sign of the man who'd paid for my dinner and danced with me last week. At least he'd stopped glaring like I shit on his doorstep. I did note that I'd never seen him in anything other than a uniform. The sheriff and the man fused into a single entity.

"How many people are coming?" I asked Lo. We were now setting up tables for the food.

"Well, it's usually a hundred. I think we may have one or two guests from another tribe."

More cars and trucks arrived, and wow. These Garnet people knew how to capital D, Drive. Mercedes, BMW, Porsches, tricked out mega trucks, I'd bet nothing in the field they used for a parking lot cost less than fifty thousand. Except for Lo's truck, that is. But that was her, unpretentious as always.

Huge chunks of meat roasted over beds of white-hot coals. Sweaty men tended the fires and looked as if they'd been at it all day. Ah, the sweet odor of food. Well, at least my tribe wasn't vegetarian. That would be a tragedy. *My tribe? Was I thinking of it that way now?*

By the time darkness fell, a hundred or more people had arrived, men, women, and children. Ben waved at me, and I waved back. I'd relaxed enough to enjoy myself a bit. Electricity, via a generator, provided superb lighting. The wind subsided when the sun fell, as if it had called a truce for the party.

Lo made a determined effort to introduce me to every person there. Several greeted me with warmth, others with cool politeness. A few refused to approach, including Simone and her girlfriends. The sheriff, still in uniform, waylaid Simone once and she hung her head, intent on what he was saying. Her hunched shoulders and down-tilted face made me wonder if he threatened her. I didn't like her, but I thought she should fight back, not let him treat her that way. At least hold her head up and face him. *How hypocritical.*

McKay had me like that often, bullied into submission.

At dinner I settled down at the children's table. Working in the tavern I'd had no opportunity to meet or interact with them. I liked kids, particularly those old enough to communicate, but young enough to retain innocence. These children were intelligent, well-loved, and brave. We carried on conversations at all age levels. If Frank and I had been able to stay with Lo…ah, no point in thinking about what might have been.

Eventually, stomachs full, everyone migrated to the amphitheater to sit on the tiers around the brilliantly lit flat floor. Then the fun started. To my surprise, not only did I love everything, but it felt like Saturday night at the Tavern—minus the drunks, arguments, and sexual games. Lilly the city girl, a former nightclub princess, would have turned her nose up. Another reminder of the girl who was gone forever.

They'd brought music, and everyone danced. I danced with Ben twice, including a slow dance where he was careful not to pull me too close. Off duty, he looked fine in jeans and a knit shirt that showed he used weights often.

One young woman, barely out of her teens, sang several songs, accompanied by a young man on a guitar. The amphitheater circled her brilliant voice around us and into the night in a way that no other venue could. When Lo introduced me earlier, Simone dragged the girl away, so I didn't know her name.

The music suddenly ceased. Every voice fell silent. In a single breath, tension filled the air much as song had blessed it moments ago. Lo and I sat on the lowest tier of the amphitheater, feet on the flat rock floor. I turned to her, but she held up a finger. Her hand slipped in mine, and she squeezed it hard, as if to force me into silence. Was she afraid? The floor cleared. What were we waiting for?

A sound drifted through the darkness. I'd heard it before. A mountain lion, calling in the night. We lived close to a zoo once, and I knew African Lions had deep, heavy, roars pulsing for miles. The mountain lion's cry is loud, but higher pitched and more like a tomcat challenging all others in a back alley—a massive tomcat. *And this was a challenge.* The air vibrated with the sound. Parents drew children closer but didn't rush them away. The night filled with expectation, like the moment before the start of a race.

"What's happening, Lo?" I whispered.

She held her finger to her lips again for silence.

I'd run and staggered down perilous paths numerous times in my life. I'd once called terrifying things like guns, dirty money, and blistering rage a part of living. This situation took everything down to a more elemental level.

Psychology 101? History? The word tribe implied a group of distinctive individuals with common psychological, social, and physical traits. Group dynamic, a cohesion that made those individuals act as one, transpired before me. Should they suddenly collectively consider me a stranger, an outsider, they could turn dangerous in an instant. Common sense suddenly leaped in and screamed in a shrill voice. *"Run like hell, Lilly. Go now!"*

Another sound. From a different direction this time. A different cat, one with a deeper, stronger voice.

A mountain lion stalked into the arena. For at the

moment, I could only describe the area around me as such. I'd never seen this lion before—he wasn't built like the male who hung around my place. This one had muscles and was pounds heavier, with longer legs and body. The lights gave its much darker coat a healthy sheen. He strutted and stalked in a circle. He stopped and cried out a challenge again. Again, came the roar of acceptance. Less distant, louder. Everyone flinched and drew closer.

A second cat silently entered the arena. This contender was another obvious male—a mature one with a light gold coat. Not bigger, but more heavily muscled than the first, and he didn't strut. He gracefully walked toward the first cat. They were going to fight, like gladiators before the roaring crowd. This crowd didn't roar. The residents of Garnet—the tribe—remained silent, watching the pair as they circled. I wanted to scream, but I had no voice. Arranged big cat fights? Like a horrendous dog-fighting ring where beasts tore each other apart.

Step after step, gliding, prowling, they sauntered with the grace given only to cats. The odds? Well, the dark challenger was slimmer, possibly faster, but his opponent had weight and powerful muscles. Those thick defined muscles moved under light golden fur. It could be an equal match.

At a silent signal, the cats flung themselves at each other. They met in a roaring, screaming brawl. Savage snarls, sharp tearing teeth. Killing claws unleashed, lodged in flesh, the big cat had his challenger down. He escaped, twisted away. His escape cost him more torn skin. They crashed together again. Fangs and claws locked, they rolled across the stone. The larger cat raked bloody furrows across his challenger's fur. Red sullied each animal and smeared the rock floor. Human witnesses remained silent, as if hypnotized by the violence.

The sound of deadly conflict shattered silence and echoed in the air as music had only minutes ago. Up on their back legs again, dancing, battling upright. It seemed forever. Back and forth, relentless savagery, tearing, biting. I'd seen nature shows where big cats fought, but only in short battles that rarely showed this much blood. Not a TV show, this was close, immediate, and in your face horrifying.

The heavier cat prevailed. The dark challenger went lax and submitted, his body a bloody dripping ruin. The victor had the loser's neck clamped in powerful jaws. He dragged him across the rock. Shook the limp cat like a piece of meat. Everything stopped. What? Why? Waiting for the kill? Like everyone else, I held my breath.

The victor released his opponent. The challenger didn't move. Then he twitched. Alive, but gravely wounded. The big cat circled him, roaring a primal message. *I won. Hear me, see me. I won.*

Then he stalked toward the spectators. Everyone remained frozen. Three feet in front of the first tier, the lion stopped. Blood smeared around his mouth and over his head. Torn skin across one injured shoulder, and one leg had multiple scarlet holes where fangs had punched deep into flesh. Yet, somehow, I knew he would never give in to pain. His masculinity alone wouldn't allow him that relief.

The big cat strutted slowly around the circle. He kept up a low rumbling growl. What was this?

Everyone lowered their heads as the victor passed. He stopped occasionally, stared up into the tiers and snarled. If he were a man, I'd swear he'd issued another challenge. "*Do you want some of me? You want to fight, too?*" Ah, no. He was coming around to my side. I wouldn't move. No challenge from me, buddy. But bow my head? I don't think so. *Wait. Was that my challenge?*

The cat stopped, directly in front of me. I could smell the blood, the musk of virility around him. Common sense, as it had earlier, said be afraid. It ordered me to draw my knife and hope a light show startled and frightened the danger away. I didn't listen. This cat was not my usual nightly feline visitor, but those visits had moderately inured me to such. I stared into shiny gold eyes. Cat's eyes, but different. Something else gleamed there.

"You're hurt," I spoke softly. *After all, I had an intimate relationship with pain.*

Closer now, inches away, his head by my knees. He sniffed. My boots, my pants, did I smell that bad— or that attractive? I had lots of time to read in rehab, and of course, remembered it all. When a cat wants to claim something, it will mark it with its scent. It will piss on or bump its head against its chosen object or person. That sparked the cat's scent from glands located on the side of its face. This monster cat stepped forward and did the head bumping and rubbing on my jeans. I froze, rigid in shock. My brand-new jeans that I bought with hard earned tip money. My jeans that cost me hours toting beers and listening to drunks babble. His thick, heavy skull rammed hard against me while he rubbed his bloody mouth and face across, up and down, leaving streaks, red stains soaked into the fabric.

What the hell?

"Really?" My shout came out high pitched and furious. The cat jumped back. He crouched. Shouting was never a smart idea with an uncaged wild animal. "These are brand new. I'll never get that shit out. Why couldn't you just piss on my boots? At least they're leather."

If I thought there was tension before the fight, this time it was a collective gasp from the crowd. The big cat froze, stayed motionless, as if he stalked wary prey. He suddenly relaxed. He made a coughing sound. Then another. He rose from the crouch, turned, and walked away into the darkness. I could have sworn he was laughing at me.

I turned to Lo. My voice crackled with hysteria. "That was about the weirdest thing I've ever seen in my life. You want to explain?"

She stood. "Later. Let's get cleaned up and go home."

I gave up. The defeated cat stood—barely. His face and neck smeared crimson, obvious gashes across his back. He fell once, rose, and went on. He limped away into the darkness, too. Would he live? I had no idea. No one around me seemed to care about the loser.

I received speculative and outright interested stares as we cleaned up our area of the party. No one asked a single question or made a single comment. No hostility, but no conversation either. And the kids? These people had brought their children to this bloody terrifying battle. None seemed traumatized like I would have been at that age.

Lo started talking as we rode back to the tavern.

"We own thousands of acres, square miles, around here."

"We. Residents of Garnet?"

"The tribe, yes. We don't allow hunting, so the lions and coyotes tend to come here for safety. There's not enough wild game to sustain them. People feed them. They've become semi-tame. You know, they have…habits. Routines…like people."

"Ah, hell, Lo. You and the people of Garnet have sent my bullshit meter past critical." What an utterly ridiculous explanation geared to keeping me from some secret she didn't want to reveal. I had to laugh. "What can I say, Lo? I have a knife that glows and one of the semi-tame lions comes and watches me at night when I'm on the porch. I'm not brave enough to feed him."

Lo drew a sharp breath. "Watches you?"

"Is that bad?"

"What does it look like?"

"Smaller, slimmer than the two tonight."

"You don't try to approach it, do you?"

"No. Lo, I'm not that stupid. I've listened to your ridiculous *feed the cats and coyotes* story. But someone orchestrated what happened tonight. I don't know how or why. And you know what? I don't care anymore."

I already had an overload of information for one day. Earth songs in a cave, glowing knife, serious philosophical religious discussion, I was tired. Meditate. I'd go meditate and find the Void and hope it was empty.

Chapter Eleven

No one spoke of the breathtaking cat fight out in the valley during the passing days. Oh, I got a few weird gazes, but I could deal. And something new had entered my life. I'd come to a point where I could feel the violence that lurked deep in the fabric of these people and place. *They were bound by a set of rules or laws, which I'd never seen, from a nameless goddess who, according to Lo, did not meddle in their lives.*

Ever since I could remember, from Mama's abuse to McKay's pure evil brutality, to this barren desert, I'd lived with violence. I wasn't inured, but I'd realized I'd become like my fellow tribe members. *So weird shit happens. Deal with it.* Fight or call a truce or leave. But I hated that poor Henry's murder had shrunk to a tiny wrinkle in the fabric of Garnet. Oh, they—we—tribesmen and women did go to his funeral, and we did mourn. He wasn't tribe, but he had no family. Bastet adopted him in death. They would never have allowed it in life.

I helped prepare for the Autumnal Equinox near the end of September. According to Lo, the event, and one like it in the spring, provided the revenue for other government administration. Government?

Not official, not incorporated. Lo did offer a semi-explanation. It was a strict facet of their, at least to me, elusive tribal law. Ronnie Valentine served as mayor, general manager, and treasurer, and had for years. The sheriff and deputies rounded things out. Lo had a place, a significant role, but she refused me an explanation. The trio was the extent of Garnet bureaucracy, and surprisingly they ruled Sioux Crossing, too. No elections ruled by consent. According to Lo, no one ever complained. I called BS and suggested that law enforcement needed serious review. She thought that was funny.

Lo explained the Summer and Winter Solstices were more important than the Equinox, but they were private, more formal. They, too, happened out in the *valley* like the little down-home barbecue/cat fight. I wasn't looking forward to something more *important.*

There'd been no sign or word of McKay. Hart stopped coming around. Had he gone to other places to check out sightings and rumors? That worried me. Every survival instinct I had nagged me. *McKay is coming, McKay is coming.* I tried to keep busy, not think about what could happen.

Ronnie contracted with a small carnival to set up for Autumnal Equinox festival week. There was also a mega craft and antique flea market covering a couple of acres. The event was first organized in the 1970s, and Lo said people came from all over the country to buy and sell stuff. The only campground would set up overflow sites since the nearest hotel was mega miles away. Private security, hired for the event, wandered around in a dazed stupor. Ben said he got the fun task of coordinating the hired help. Poor boy stayed stressed and sweating copiously most of the time.

Garnet, while surrounded by close mountains and mesas, was flat and level. Geography and serious advertising by the tribe guaranteed a successful festival outcome. Lo confiscated what I had come to consider *my* barn for extra supply storage. I had room to carve though, so it was okay.

I'd seen little of Sheriff Harrow, too. I'd swear he was avoiding me. So why did I find myself thinking about him so much? He wasn't my type of man. Too stiff, too formal, he might wear that uniform to bed. Why did I stealthily watch for him, trying to see him without him knowing I was looking? Why did the recall of the dance where he held me close remain so vivid? Him releasing me and walking away without a word… How did I deal with that?

I liked the way the man moved. The way he could be utterly immobile when he watched someone. When necessary, he could reach out and snatch something, an arm to stop someone or a bottle used as a weapon, faster than I could see. And I found myself wondering if he watched me when I wasn't looking. It made me so conscious of myself, how my own body moved.

I'd found an outsize piece of dead wood one time when I went to St. George with Lo. A purchase from a flea market since it was of wood I'd never seen before. A broken tree trunk, three-foot high, and far longer and thicker than anything I'd had before. Wide at the base, the branches extending twelve to eighteen inches, perfect for carving. Lo complained about sending big men and a trailer to pick it up, but she did it for me anyway. I'd again raided my tip jar and ordered new tools. It was going to be a challenge. I'd never created a piece this size. I'd blocked the table up, so it was the right height. I closed my eyes and laid my hands on the wood, gently feeling the shapes and contours. The images came, pictures in my mind, and I sorted them. And yes, there it was. I knew. I picked up my knife and made the first cut.

A mountain lion would be perfect. I'd had enough up-close encounters with the real thing to last a lifetime. The bigger lion, the victor at the battle would be my subject. I couldn't get the full lion out of the piece with its irregular shape. The head, shoulders, part of the body, front legs folded, the cat would leap from the base of the wood. As I worked, I felt something I wouldn't call peace. It was more a lessening of the turmoil inside. A kind of stasis that let me experience ordinary. In college, in the time before the troubles, after I'd escaped Mama and the time before McKay, it had sustained me.

The big cat carving occupied my free time from the tavern. It didn't tire me. Late one night, I reached the point where I turned off the lights and began finishing by touch, my fingers gliding along the lines and shapes. I'd barely started when the lights flashed on. Blinded. I slapped my hand over my face.

I knew by his scent that the sheriff approached me. I managed a squinty-eyed glare at him.

"What did you do that for? I was working."

"I thought you said you couldn't see in the dark."

"No, I can't see. But I can feel the wood." I opened my eyes a slit. I wanted to show him how pissed I was, but it's hard to glower with squinty eyes.

He didn't speak for a moment, then he said, "I'm sorry. I didn't know."

An apology? That made two now. What the hell was he doing? *What devious evil was he planning for helpless Lilly? Or if we had music, would he hold me close and slow dance with me?* The barn, the empty night, why did it seem so intimate with him there? My body wanted me to move closer.

He turned his attention to the piece. He reached out, then stopped. "May I touch it?"

I shrugged, surprised that he'd asked permission.

His fingers glided over the cat's rough image as mine had moments before. When I carved, I forced a part of myself into the image. This time more than others, I could feel that I was with the leaping cat.

"It's beautiful." His words sounded odd, almost breathless.

"You may have it when it's finished." I stared at the dirt floor and scuffed my foot like a shy kid. "If you want. I always give my carvings away."

"Why? This is excellent. You could sell it and make money."

"No. I give it all away. It's not finished unless I do. Maybe it's because I'd spent most of my life without…things." So true. Mama would destroy anything she thought I valued, and so would McKay. But I think my need to share my vision was something deeper, something more personal. More satisfying. He stared at it a moment longer.

"Lilly?" He raised his hand and offered me something. An uncut topaz the size of my thumb. A master jeweler had wrapped thin gold wire around it and attached it to a gold chain. "I thought…I know you like stones."

Oh, my God…or goddess…whatever, it was marvelous.

I was standing there, frozen, staring wide-eyed, and mouth open. He reached down, took my wrist, brought my hand up and placed the topaz in my palm. I closed my hand over the stone, brought it to my chest and held it tight.

The topaz sang to me, much as the earth had in Lo's cavern. The stone sang not in sound, but in perceptions. Beauty, splendor, depth, height, and oh, the loneliness and sorrow of life it could not know. This was easily as mystical an object as my knife. I clutched it tighter.

The sheriff gave me a rare and precious smile. "You do that all the time, don't you? Hold things you like close to your heart." Genuine pleasure filled his voice.

"Yes." I choked on the word. A single word and I could barely get it out.

"I'd very much like to have the carving when you finish." He walked away. Again, he left me speechless, confused, wondering what had happened.

I opened my hand to stare at the stone. Why did it seem so precious? Why did my body warm with desire and a heavy longing to be safe, lying in his arms? Desire? How many years had it been since a single thread of desire had touched me? Not since McKay had turned against me. I wanted this man, this stern lawman, wanted to kiss him, hold him, make love to him. My mind said I should reject my desire. I'd had too much emotional trauma to genuinely love a man. And there was the horrific appearance of my scarred body. He'd seen it, but...

Sheriff Pax, so forbidding, believed that I was a danger to his people. Right? *But he gave you a gift, Lilly, one you should cherish always.*

Now what do I do? How would I act around him? I

didn't know, but thinking about him suddenly became more important, more immediate.

****

The week of the Equinox began with the arrival of the carnival on Sunday night. Carnival rides, nothing death defying, were enhanced by assorted games no one could win. Come Monday morning, tent booths sprang up in careful rows at the arts and craft and flea market. The campground filled to overflowing with RVs and hardy souls in tents. A first-rate variety of food trucks made appearances, too. Staid, sleepy Garnet came alive with every new visitor.

Ronnie Valentine, proprietor of Garnet Mercantile, oversaw things, and the tavern became command central. Arguments abounded, and I carefully stayed out of the line of fire. I worked mornings too, helping Lo set up things. She did pay me extra. I reminded her I didn't need to sleep, and she reminded me that I did need to rest on occasion.

Lo had a five-year running battle with Ronnie over serving food. She wanted to add a kitchen for snack type foods at the tavern, wings, fries, etc., and Ronnie was adamant that she not run a *damned* restaurant. He told her the tavern alone brought in too many strangers. But people were taking their money to Sioux Crossing, Lo argued. That was a loud and unsettling conversation, and I skipped out as soon as possible.

At times Ronnie, Lo, and the sheriff huddled in a corner and whispered. It worried me because when I approached to bring them drinks, they stopped and resumed after I'd gone. Were they talking about me? Other people deciding my fate again. Irritating, but I reminded myself of the dreadful decisions I had made that got me into my current situation.

Lo wanted something, but the sheriff and Ronnie were reluctant. Finally, Lo prevailed. I could see it in her face. On Tuesday morning of the Equinox week, I took a walk through the craft tents. Crowds of people moved with me and purchased material goods. Pictures, art pieces, things they could hang on their walls, stack in their kitchens, add to their collections. Except for wood, I have poor taste in design. I would decorate a room with all the eclectic skill of a drunk chimpanzee. Frank and I learned to keep only what we could carry, because we never knew when Mama would think she saw a demon behind a bush, and we would have to run away. No, I didn't need any decorative object I couldn't use—except the exquisite topaz on its gold chain that I now wore, always.

To my surprise, I saw Araun in a tent selling scented candles, soaps, and assorted jars of powder and lotion. She had a crowd standing around, waiting for her. With her medieval style robe, her hair braided and wound around her head, she would have been perfect at a fair with knights on horses staging reenactments.

I squeezed my way into her tent.

"You look busy," I said. "May I help you?"

Her head jerked up. She gazed at me, expressionless, then nodded. She handed me a metal cash box and said, "Do the sales."

Okay, so no polite, *yes please.* Well-mannered behavior was certainly not mandatory for everyone in the hereditary, religious, or cultural traits of my tribe. *Did I think that again? My tribe?*

The crowd remained steady. I learned that the chattering customers were repeats from previous year's festivals. They sang the praises of Araun's products. My grandmother reigned as an accomplished purveyor of natural and homeopathic products.

Everyone paid with cash. Ronnie's rules for the event. A bank from Vegas sent an armored truck with a satellite dish on the roof and teller windows where people could take their credit cards and get advances. I had to laugh. McKay would snatch that baby in a heartbeat. Forget the armed guards standing around. He'd take the truck before it reached the Arizona border while it was still full. Most of his criminal activity was under the table and with electronic accounts, but he loved a flashy heist. Ah, I was thinking far too much about McKay.

A sullen, stringy haired, teenaged girl I hadn't met arrived after a couple of hours and relieved me of my cashier duties. Araun didn't introduce her and dismissed me with a silent nod of her head. She didn't offer me a miniscule bar of soap, which I could have used since she found me so unclean and odious. Ah, family. Maybe Mama had the right idea to leave here. No, she could leave, but she should have gone alone, leaving us with people I now know would have loved or at least tolerated us.

That evening Lo, Ronnie Valentine, and the sheriff huddled in a corner table and argued again. It carried a more serious note this time. Too far away for me to hear, but oh, boy, the body language. I did get close enough one time to hear the sheriff say, "Next year," punctuated with a fist slammed on the table. Lean, lanky Ronnie had lost weight, and fatigue showed in his eyes. His expression would have terrified children. Hell, it terrified me. Lo wagged her head back and forth. Whatever she wanted she wanted it now. Eventually, an exhausted Ronnie gave in. The sheriff hadn't, but the argument ceased. Efficient government in action. Three people, and if two agreed, shit happened. According to Lo, the parameters were transcribed in the mysterious tribal law—and a copy of that baby wasn't anywhere close to me.

About nine, Lo told me to go home and rest. "I want you to go with Pax to Las Vegas tomorrow. He has a delivery to make. Be ready to leave at five in the morning. You'll be back tomorrow night. I want you to start meeting members of other tribes. It will be brief, but that's best right now."

"Why? Lo, I don't want to go anywhere with your stick-up-his-butt sheriff. I mean, yes, he's a little nicer occasionally, but in a vehicle…"

He'd given me a lovely gift, but as usual, he'd completely ignored me in the following days. To ride that close to him, considering all my—our—unresolved issues, was a misstep of epic proportions.

"It's only one day. Do it for me, Lilly, please." She clasped her hands and smiled so sweetly it looked bizarre. Lo wasn't sweet. "Ronnie and I have agreed that Pax will tell you more things about the tribes on the way. The whole organization. It is important. He can explain things far better than I can."

Yes! Explanations, those rare creatures that surfaced sporadically. Since she put it that way, I agreed. He and I were as close to a truce as we were going to get. The topaz and the cat carving equaled a cease-fire. Didn't it? I'd sent word when I finished his sculpture. He sent Ben to pick it up. He didn't bother to come himself. Ben's comment? "His is bigger than mine." He grinned with that little boy look. "But I already knew that."

Smart mouth little shit. I punched him, but he laughed. He did stop and reach out to touch the topaz hanging on its chain. I couldn't read the expression on his face.

I'd been to Las Vegas a couple of times. McKay's business was on the east coast, not out west. He made me stay at the hotel. I didn't like the casinos because of all the cigarette smoke, so I ate a lot of room service food and watched television on a big screen TV. I could see all the brilliant lights out the window at night and wanted to go out and explore. I didn't. By that time, McKay had started to hurt me when I disobeyed him.

"Wear something proper," Lo instructed me. "Business professional. Trust me."

I nodded. *Trust me. Repetitious and annoying, it encouraged the opposite of the word's meaning.* At least I'd purchased decent clothes, some ordered online and another trip to St. George. At four a.m., I pulled out my brown dress pants, dressier boots, a tank top, and a soft white silky blouse. The tank had to serve as an undergarment because I couldn't wear bras. A couple of scars decorated critical locations. Bras chafed and drove me crazy. Thankfully, I wasn't so large it was immediately noticeable.

One expensive purchase in St. George was a beautiful, tailored, weightless wool jacket, perfect for inside where frigid air conditioning prevailed. Beige tweed, it went nicely with the pants. I'd start with my leather coat in case it got colder. And of course, the beautiful topaz at my throat. I was ready when the knock came at the door.

When I opened it, the sheriff, still in uniform, stepped in. His gaze went up and down my body.

He made me feel naked. He hadn't done that when I *was* naked. "That knife you carry. Can you use it?"

"What?"

"Can you?" His gaze met mine straight on.

"No comment. You see, I live in this tiny backwoods—make that back-desert—town. I'm on probation. It's big enough to be considered a real weapon."

The knife called Bi'ar would guide me, let me know when to draw. I was certain of that. I had it in my jacket pocket, and it gave off a tiny vibration that felt like excitement. I didn't have the nerve to explain my new more intimate connection to a blade. Let the knife take over and Lilly became an expert fighter—or a zombie knife fighter. How about a robot?

"Yes, Sheriff, I can."

"Excellent. Wear it today. Under your coat."

Oh, my, how remarkable. If my day started out this shocking, what would the passing hours bring?

I'd braided my hair into a single rope, and it hung to my waist. I needed to get it cut to a more manageable length. There was one beautician in town, and with my usual bad luck, that beautician was Simone. Let her get close to me with something sharp? No way. Make up? A little around my eyes and on my lips. I made a turn in front of him. "Is this satisfactory for our trip?"

He nodded, silent as usual. This was a man who could handle any situation unfazed, including a fashion critique. He'd come for me in a giant and obviously expensive SUV. It had to be his personal vehicle. I knew what they cost and wondered how much a small-town sheriff made. Of course, given all the high-end vehicles I'd seen at that party, he wasn't out of sync with the Garnet crowd. Nothing in this place was what it looked like on the surface. I had to climb up to get in, but the seat fit me comfortably. Black vehicle, black upholstery, dash with instruments like a jet plane, oh, it was fine. He started the vehicle, went to the highway, and turned west.

Right outside of town he turned again. He pulled up to a small ranch type house, the kind multiplied by the millions in subdivisions around the country. The only distinctive feature was two tall, brilliant green trees in the front. Such a staggering contrast to the surrounding desert. Irrigated, they had to have water, a constant drip.

He opened his door. "Come inside. I've been in the Crossing all night, and I need to shower and change."

I followed him as he opened the front door and ushered me in. No lock? Well, Lo had told me they had almost no crime. So, this was his home. *Make that his armory.* Firearms of every type decorated the walls and covered all available space. From black powder muzzle loaders to a pile of assault rifles in the corner, the sheer number staggered me. Were they confiscations? The only weapon free areas were a recliner in front of a big screen TV, a clear spot on the couch for one guest, and, oh, the sturdy dining table where he'd placed my mountain lion carving. I felt so honored that he'd moved precious weapons to make room.

"So, Sheriff. Like guns much?"

"Yes. Come here."

He stood by a peninsula separating the kitchen from the dining room. Semi-automatic pistols covered it, arranged in straight lines. He nodded at them. "Which of these can you use?"

"Most of them. I know the basics."

"Which would you *prefer* to use." Ah, impatient now.

"I would prefer to use none." I picked out two, both I'd used in target practice with McKay. "Either of these fit my hand." I laid the guns down. "You know I can't carry one. Probation, remember. And you are not the only law man out there. If I'm caught—"

"You *can* shoot?"

"I can shoot." A gun nut boyfriend in college delighted in teaching me—until he realized that I was the better marksman. "I don't want a gun." Panic edged my words, sharp as the blade sheathed under my arm. The image came again. McKay's boot on the FBI agent's neck when he pulled the trigger. He forced me to watch as he killed Julia next. She hadn't received a merciful bullet. "Too loud, too easy, too fast, no."

"Have you ever…?"

"No." The word came out in a soft breath. "I have never shot any living thing." I was the indirect cause of many dying, but I lived with it along with my other sins.

"Will you shoot if someone shoots at you?" He picked up the two I'd selected and thrust them toward me.

"I thought this was a business meeting." *Don't panic, Lilly*. "Will someone be shooting at us?"

"It's not likely. But if it happens, I'd like to know you have my back."

He'd pushed the collection of pistols aside with careless ease and placed two hard gun cases on the counter. The ones I'd said I was comfortable with went in each case with loaded clips. He raised his eyes to me. "Well? Will you back me up? Or will you turn and run?"

Was he asking me to fight for him? Me, the woman evading a seasoned killer? The sheriff's own words came back to me. The ones he'd thrown my way the night I showed him my scars. *"So, what are you? An abused child? A psychopath's play toy? A perpetual victim."* Damn my memory. It blasted me with images. The fists coming at me, bones breaking, the razor…. *"Damaged but not broken."* I'd accepted that judgement from Araun.

I gazed into his eyes. "I'll have your back, Sheriff. I swear, no one will touch you while I live." A firm oath and gut deep trouble. What would I do? How far would I go? He accepted my words with a single nod of his head. Then his shoulders slumped, and he seemed to give in to weariness. We hadn't started the day yet.

"I need to shower. Will you make coffee?"

His coffee maker was like mine, but his imported coffee far superior to anything in the Garnet grocery store. I made a full pot. It brewed, and I was pouring a second cup when he returned.

Oh, my. He was still straight and uptight, but in jeans and a button up shirt, a fresh shave, he was far more appealing. His skin, darker against a white shirt, hands far too slender for a man his size, that perfect male body…stop it, Lilly. Without the formal uniform, the symbol of control, I could detect a wildness, something less civilized, a rough untamed spirit. He walked past, and his now familiar scent wafted over me.

"You clean up pretty good, Sheriff."

He shrugged. "Uniforms are more practical. I rent them. Truck comes by here twice a month."

"Twice a month, once a week, everything in Garnet has its own pace—mostly slow."

"Or never." He eyed me as he lifted his coffee. A slight tilt of his mouth…oh, was that humor?

"You could call me Pax, if you wish."

"I'm not sure I know you well enough yet."

He turned away. Did that bother him? How well did he think he knew me? He'd read the reports and seen my naked pieced-together puzzle of a body. He had threatened me over possible collateral damage from McKay, but he'd also slow danced so close to me. He'd given me a beautiful stone on a gold chain that I wore every day. I had worked incredibly hard on his sculpture, committing far more of myself to the wood than I ever had before. This trip might sort us out, one way or another.

The sheriff stowed the two pistol cases in the heavily loaded SUV. All I had was a small pink tote, borrowed from Lo, with my hairbrush and other emergency supplies. No purse, only a small wallet in my pocket. I liked my hands free. He locked up and we were on our way.

Chapter Twelve

Las Vegas wasn't that far, a little over a hundred and fifty miles, but he stopped after a couple of hours for breakfast. We ate at a friend's restaurant, an old Army buddy, and yes, he had served for six years. I heard a couple of wild stories involving exploits where I couldn't imagine participation by our staid sheriff.

Once we were on our way again, I asked, "Will you tell me what's happening?"

"If you'll accept what I tell you without too many questions."

What a jerk! "Questions are the keys to understanding, Sheriff. We appear to be on an armed mission, hence my burning desire for information."

He didn't speak for a while, then he started. "Lo told you about our tribe, Bastet."

"Just that everyone in Garnet considers themselves a part of the tribe."

"No considering involved. You are a part too, Lilly. We are the Bastet Tribe. Did Lo tell you there were ten tribes?" My, my, was that frustration in his voice? Shocker.

"She mentioned it, yes. Ten connected tribes, but no details."

He frowned. "I don't understand why she hasn't explained more."

"Lo's been dancing around details of Garnet life

since I arrived. I believe she thinks that if she says too much, I'll run away, screaming in horror. You asked if I was a perpetual victim. That's how Lo sees me. But she did see the worst during my time in the hospital and rehab. To her, I'm fragile." Well, I had broken down over the paintings, Mama's precious art. But damn it all, I'd endured the weird, bloody cat fight without questions, hadn't I?

"How do *you* see me, Sheriff? Besides a threat to your town, your tribe?"

He didn't answer for a minute. Taking time to make up a lie?

"So far, you've played Lilly the victim, the artist, and the fighter."

"Played?" Damn what an ass. "You consider my life, events in my life, a role-playing game? An amusing performance?" My voice carried too much anger, too much resentment. How divine to release that jab of rage—I'd swallowed under threat of dire consequences too long. "What do you want from me?"

"Can you, will you, role play on behalf of Bastet in Vegas?"

"Yes, if required to do so. What's my part? Let me see. Ah, you're the stern forbidding cop and I'm your girlfriend. Your assistant? No, wait. I'm passive arm candy? I've done arm candy before."

"No, I'll play the stern cop and you my knife-wielding-warrior-girlfriend."

"You have a foolish amount of confidence in me." I clapped my hands to show sarcasm. "So, my role is girlfriend?"

"Yes. But my girlfriend would call me by my name."

"Okay. I'll take that under consideration. No promises. Sheriff." What if I failed? I had failed countless times.

We rode on in silence for a while. Silence has weight, a heaviness that can drive you batty if you don't break away. He broke first. Score one for me.

"Lo, Ronnie, and I are the Bastet tribal principals. Three individuals lead each tribe. I'm Commander, Ronnie is Accountant, Lo is…" He sighed. "Lo is Priestess. The Bastet tribe is officially and legally a corporation, and yourself and other tribe members are stockholders. We own land, businesses like the mine, factories in Sioux Crossing, and other interests, like stocks and bonds. We have capital assets and pay substantial dividends quarterly. The ten tribes, ten separate corporations, are also individual parts of a larger unit. The Ennead Corporation."

"Ennead? What is that?"

"It's a name, Lilly. There has to be a name and that was chosen. However, the Ennead were originally a group of nine deities in Egyptian mythology. You've seen our tendency to be superstitious and mystical. "

"Superstitious? Mystical? No, I'd never believe that." He grunted like I'd mightily vexed him. Another point for me in the game. I plunged into a pool of cynicism. "I agree that if you're going to tell a story it should have fascinating names and places. I mean, deities, gods, goddesses, and magic knives. Right out of a fantasy novel."

"Magic knife?" He sounded curious, not surprised.

"Talk about something else, Sheriff." I shifted, uncomfortable despite a seat that tightly conformed to my ass. I didn't like confinement, no matter how big the vehicle. "There is one thing I don't understand. Well, no, there's more than one, but this is really bugging me. Make that two things that bug me."

Get it together, Lilly.

"One, why do you live the way you do in Garnet? The whole semi-poverty, super private, keep all strangers out business. You've got to have money for all those luxurious cars. And two, what is, are, your primary tribal and individual goals. Are they religious, political, financial? Or all of the above." Oh, I was on a roll. "Okay, three things. What is the common denominator of the collection of all the tribes into the Ennead Corporation?"

He didn't answer.

"Hell, you're as bad as Lo." I gritted my teeth. He looked miserable. I loved it. Until he spoke again.

"Questions two and three first. Common denominator and goals of the tribal corporations and Ennead are the same. Secure, protect, and most of all, maintain the cohesion and continuation of all the tribes. That's part of the preamble to the Book of Tribal Law. I had to memorize it in school." He stopped talking to steer around a dangerously slow car. When the road before us cleared, he continued his lesson. "Basically, survival of our way of life to carry out our service to the goddess. Call that religion if you like. A few do."

I gave an exaggerated sigh. "Now that wasn't so hard was it?"

"There's more, Lilly. Much more."

"My brother—"

"The priest? I remember him. He was wild. All of us younger boys admired him."

"I have difficulty picturing Frank as wild." My

143

weekly talks with Frank had become so strained that I found myself saying less and less until it was now little more than a hasty, *"I'm okay, Frank. Just working and carving wood for fun."*

The sheriff's silence forced me to go on. "So, tell me if I'm wrong. This still…disturbs me. It's the thing Lo calls a Gift—as opposed to a birthday or Christmas gift. The one that everyone considers poor manners to discuss. Now, as I understand it, those Gifts are exceptional psychic talent or some mystical power that comes from the goddess. Frank would call it magic. Does that sound right? Can you do things? Are you like a witch? Or wizard, or sorcerer, a magician? Do you do tricks? Rabbit in the hat, ex cetera. I'm trying to be open minded."

He hit the steering wheel hard with one hand. A score for me. I'd pissed off the staid Sheriff of Garnet—again.

"You're not open minded, Lilly. You're damned offensive. A Gift is in the blood, our heritage. Magic is the wrong word. It would take a year to tell you specific facets of Gifts—even if I knew them all." He jerked the wheel, a quick whip and lane change to keep a truck from running us off the road. When he straightened the vehicle, he said, "You have Gifts, too, Lilly. I don't know the form or function of them, but they're in your blood."

"Why don't any of you talk about these Gifts?"

"It's considered personal. Talking about it is like boasting, bragging. It's vulgar and rude. We all serve and stand equal in tribal law and before the goddess."

Well, at least he matched Lo on that. However, I'd found that when people speak of equality, they believe others are more equal—like themselves. This was going to make for a deep soulful conversation with my brother. A light knob of a headache formed at the base of my skull.

I watched Pax's intensity, the way he gripped the steering wheel. Maybe he didn't like to drive.

"All right, Sheriff. Forget the mysticism. Gifts, magic, and religion, too. Exactly what do you want me to do in Vegas? Be specific."

"I want you to be watchful. Be calm, quiet, and learn. Like you did at the tavern when you first arrived. You watched, listened to get a sense of the strangers around you. And no, that is not specific. It's the best I can do right now. Accept things as they happen. It's important. If I say get down, or move, or run, do it. And yes, fight if you must, if you're attacked. Don't ask questions until later."

Wow, he sounded almost desperate.

"Ah, Sheriff. You think there might be a shoot-out on the strip? Showdown at the casino corral."

"That hasn't happened in years. We usually go outside of town to fight. And we try not to kill each other."

Shit! He was serious.

He went on. "Lo usually goes with me to these meetings, or she and Ronnie go together."

"And she insisted I go instead."

"Yes." An angry hiss came out with the word.

"And you didn't want to take me?" I laid my hand over my heart. "I'm so hurt."

"You should have more experience. We're going to meet the leaders of the other tribes, and possibly our primary leader. Think of him as the CEO of the Ennead

Corporation."

"Your leader? Who is he?"

"His name is Charles DeLeon. We refer to him as the Dominus and address him as sir. He's been running things successfully for about eighteen years. We've prospered during financial down times, too. He might attend. I'm not sure this time."

Lo had spoken of this Dominus. Neutral, not bad not good, but then Lo left out so many things in my tribal education.

Our vehicle slipped into a steel log jam of traffic, streaking along at eighty-five miles an hour. The sheriff stared straight ahead, silent, until the group of speeding daredevils went on—at a hundred miles an hour.

"Lilly?" My name sounded heavy coming from him right then. "Our Dominus is the strongest of us. The goddess chose him, gave him power. He's our physical conduit, our only direct connection to her. He's powerful and dangerous to cross. Things are better now, but when he came to power... I was young, and it was a troubled time. I don't know or understand his Gifts, but obviously they aided him. I know when he wants something done or something to go away, it happens."

"Oh, that's not hard to understand. Something done? Something to go away? Or someone? Piece of cake. That feels so much like McKay and his organization it's spooky."

I glanced over at him. I couldn't describe his expression right then. Appalled, shocked, my words had hit major nerves. Did he think my comparison of the tribes and McKay to be accurate? It took a while for him to speak again. When he did, he sounded kind of lame.

"The Dominus knows your story, I'm sure. Nothing happens in the tribes that he doesn't know. You will meet him if he's there. He can be abrasive. I know you're a fighter deep inside. It frightens me. You're not in his class."

I laughed, and it came out more of a giggle. "Yes, sir. You are saying I shouldn't run my mouth. Challenge him. Too dangerous. Okay, I'll cross my legs at the ankles, sit up straight, and smile like a painted doll."

"I understand the level of difficulty for you. You'd hate it, so that's why you have to be careful."

A challenge? I'd modestly kicked a little girl-fight ass once and faced down a freaky mountain lion slobbering and smearing blood on my pants. Certainly not spectacular. I had to stop talking and think. I couldn't quite grasp all of what he said. I still didn't see the need for *no discussion of the Gifts.* My primary gut reaction would remain skeptical of most everything I'm told. As for the Gifts, I think I had the concept down. Concept, not facts. My skill carving by touch, shaping things in the dark? Is that, as Lo said, a Gift? An unusual method, yes, but certainly not magic. Nothing special enough in terms of a goddess. Blind people had heightened senses in other areas like hearing and touch. They repeatedly created remarkable things.

The mountain lion who came to visit me at night? Lo had said wild animals had become too friendly with humans. Plausible. That situation was far more incredible and unbelievable when the two cats fought. Super mystery there.

My sheriff, vague as always, had asked me to

147

accept things as they were. And when the hell had he become *my sheriff* in my mind? *When he gave you the topaz, stupid girl. Or was it when he called you a warrior?*

Chapter Thirteen

The sheriff's phone rang, and he accepted a series of indecipherable calls, one sided conversations that seemed to leave him a tiny bit pleased, a little bit frustrated, and a whole lot angry. Concentrating on driving and talking, he'd forgotten I was there. It fascinated me. The neutral cop face mask had slipped a little in my mind. He now expressed a normal range of emotions. I'd bet he could turn those emotions off in a heartbeat. The unfeeling cop could reappear in an instant.

"Something wrong?" I asked when he'd finally finished.

"Yes. There are issues. We're going to have to stay overnight. Maybe tomorrow, too."

"I don't have any extra clothes."

"No problem. I have an expense account. You can go shopping."

"May I, will I, have time to go out and sightsee? Or will I have to keep my nose up your ass all the time."

Oh, now that jaw dropping was priceless. He stammered twice before he could go on.

"I know you've had a rough life, Lilly, but—"

"Do I have to be so crude? No, but it's fun when you need a reaction. Hey, I was always a proper lady around Mama and McKay. They'd hurt me if I violated their rules."

"You think I won't hurt you?" He glanced over and gave me a sly grin. I had amused him. How cute.

"No. You won't hurt me. You're scared of my Aunt Lo." He didn't answer so I knew it was true. Had I hoped that he'd say something? *No, Lilly. I won't hurt you because I care about you.*

We rode on in silence until finally we reached our destination. The Vegas Hierapolis. I leaned forward and gawked out the window. So not cool, but I couldn't help myself. I was suddenly a kid with an all-day pass to an Orlando theme park. I'd stayed in a few rich swanky hotels in my life. Nothing equaled this.

Magnificent gold and ivory colors, acres of glass, and a tropical forest lined the driveway. A true temple to Mammon, it stood as a testament to incredible wealth and avaricious consumption. Ten men and women in deep blue porter uniforms stood lined up at attention, waiting for our SUV to roll to a stop under the portico. When it did, they converged on us like sharks in a feeding frenzy. I jerked back when my door flew open. A stoic gray-haired man in a tailored suit worth more than the average person made in a month offered me his hand to exit.

"Welcome to the Hierapolis, ma'am." False smile, false greeting, but porters scurried around us like fiddler crabs on a beach, grabbing things out of the back hatch. *Good manners, Lilly.* I accepted the hand.

The porters loaded the entire contents of the SUV on luggage carts in less than a minute. One smaller box required two men to lift and set it on a separate sturdy conveyance. The body of our vehicle rose with a soft hiss when they removed that one. My little pink bag appeared pitiful and forlorn atop all those bulky black cases that contained things I didn't want to ask about.

The sheriff received the same false greeting from the tailored suit. With the suit leading the way and the army of porters following, our little parade entered the palace. A marble floor spread out over the expansive lobby. Strategically placed tables held monstrous fresh flower arrangements, and stylish furniture circled sitting areas. Yet it all seemed and felt gaudy and fake. Oh, the materials were genuine and costly, I had no doubt, but the atmosphere shouted insatiable indulgence, materialistic falsehood, and bleak desperation as people scampered in all directions.

The tailored suit pointed the way to the attached casino and three gourmet restaurants. Specifically, to me, he carefully noted the hallway that would lead to various designer shops. Paris, London, Italy. I'd have my choice. *Paris, London, Italy—how amusing.* All I had was my little stash of tip money. I had plans for my hard-earned cash. People passed by, staring. Some gazed at us through dead eyes as they plodded along. Others strutted like addicts on a brilliant high. We did not check in. That was for peasants and other low life. We went directly to private elevators.

The moment we'd left the SUV, the sheriff was by my side. He kept his hand in the small of my back. A feather's touch, but he leaned in closer for the appearance of intimacy. Amazing. He was silently telling the gawkers that I was with him. That I belonged to him. So sure, so confident, it had to be an act, a role like he wanted me to play here. So, I did play, for those few minutes, submissive and silent. The confusing and irritating man had brought guns and asked me to cover his back. Now he wanted to claim possession, protect me? Role playing indeed—nothing was real.

We had an impressive suite near the top on the thirty-eighth floor, way too high for me. I didn't look out the window. Despite lavish and obviously expensive materials in the suite, they'd hired a cut-rate interior designer. With blah colors of soft green, beige, and white, it consisted of a sitting room with couches, table, chairs, a bedroom with two king beds, and a spectacular spa bathroom bigger than my whole apartment in Garnet. In the bathroom, adding to the excessive spa ambience, more thick towels than I'd use in a year. A mammoth jetted soaker tub, big enough for two...oh, yes. I would take that baby for a ride. The constant rub of cloth over my scars irritated damaged skin, and a swirling bath in warm water did ease the chafing. Maybe I could persuade Lo to install one for us. I'd heard her complaints about aches and pains.

The sheriff had the porters put two cases to the side of the room, but most went downstairs. They didn't offer to open the remaining cases either. He didn't tip but accepted the service as his due. I checked out the fridge in the area behind a lovely decorative screen flanked by green plants. Soft drinks, juice, beer, wine, and there were other goodies in a cabinet, cookies and chips. None of those little counting racks that added to your bill, either. An extensive menu with the number for room service lay on the counter.

I plopped down on the couch. "So, Sheriff, I guess you're a big shot regular here. Are you a casino high roller?"

He sat in a chair across from me. His slightly squinted eyes were the only sign he'd been awake for too many hours. "This hotel is owned by the Ennead

Corporation. Management reserves the top five floors for tribal members. I'm the Commander in Garnet, so I get a suite. And they knew we were coming."

My mind jammed up on the site and the luxurious path I'd traversed. "You're telling me that the people of Garnet, including those living in doublewide mobile homes and rock houses, located in the most remote place in the country, watch animals fight like gladiators in the decadent, debauched Colosseum…" I was out of breath. But not for long. "They are part of a wealthy corporation, stockholders who own all of this." I threw my hands out to encompass not just the room, but the entire gaudy building.

"People live how they want to live, Lilly. Garnet residents want the simplicity. We don't flaunt our assets. Ten tribes, maybe 3,500 to 4,000 individuals." He rose and walked to the window. "We have a low birth rate. The Corporation is worth billions. There are dividends. Staying here free is one. There's a hotel in the Bahamas and suites of rooms at the hotels in Orlando." He sounded proud and genuine. "Besides, it's considered an absolute honor to belong to Bastet and live in Garnet. You've seen the cars, but not the size of their kids' college funds. And you've never been inside all those doublewide trailers. Or out back in their barns."

An honor to live in Garnet? I remembered the cavern. The way it sang such a personal song for me. Yes, if a person deeply believed in their goddess and being close to the earth, like Lo, Garnet would be a prime location. Pax came to sit on the couch beside me.

Then I thought of something else. I don't know why it hadn't occurred to me before. It took a minute before I could speak. "Dividends. You get dividends? Just for being in the tribe?"

"Yes. Substantial dividends."

"Sometimes Frank and I had to go beg food from the neighbors. Weren't we part of the tribe when she took us away?"

"Lilly…" He leaned forward, hands clasped, elbows on his knees. His expression? I knew pity when it stared me in the eyes. "Yes, you were always a part of the tribe. Your mother received her share. According to Lo, and I don't believe she would lie, Louise rejected all money offered and everything else Lo tried to do for her. Every time Lo would locate her, try to help her, she'd take you kids and run again."

Rejected money? Of course, she did. *My perfect all-encompassing mass of memories threatened escape. The carefully constructed and locked compartments held records of every scene I'd ever lived. My nightmares called them home.*

It had hurt so much when other children made fun of my rags. Frank risked everything to steal food and blankets when Mama had locked me in a building outside during the bitter winters. The humiliation, hunger, pain…and she refused money. We starved while she refused money. *Shut it down, Lilly, shut it down.*

"Lilly?"

What? Oh, the sheriff was kneeling beside me. Control, I had control. Yes, I did. Everything settled back in its place.

"I'm okay. Sorry." I went to rub my eyes when I realized he was holding my hands. I could look straight into those dark eyes. Beautiful eyes. Did getting out of the uniform do that? Make him more human?

"It will be okay, Lilly." He squeezed my hands. "Trust the goddess."

His sincerity, his plea for me to trust the least trustable of all things, an invisible specter, sounded so hollow. I heard the intensity of a zealot who had seen a miracle that reinforced his faith.

"Pax? You really believe in her. Like Lo."

"Yes, of course. I think you do, too. You've seen too much now. Admitting it is your problem."

I shook my head. This was getting too deep in spirituality. Gifts might be real, the goddess might be real, but that didn't mean I had to swim in a pool of dogma. Most of all, I wasn't sure I wanted her. I survived without her, without Garnet, without their precious corporate dividends. Yes, something powerful, something mysterious, kept me alive in that parking lot where McKay had tossed me away like human refuse. When I died, something brought me back, in the ambulance, on the operating table, too. I didn't ask to live. I remember praying as a child when it hurt so bad. I prayed to die. I prayed to die when McKay and his men raped and tortured me. *The goddess? If she had the power and wanted my respect, wanted me to serve her, she could have shown up sooner.*

I'd do what they wanted me to on this trip. I said I would, but I'd seriously consider trying to leave when I got back. Maybe I'd go find McKay, attack, and make him kill me.

The sheriff stood. "I have a, I hope, short meeting. Then I need to rest. I called and tried to get Lo to come because of the changes. She refused. She plays the mysterious far too often. I hate it when she does, but I can't stop her." He opened his wallet and offered me a credit card.

Oh, hell, it was one of those black ones with limits in the millions. The name Bastet Corporation embossed in the plastic made it official. "I added you to the list of signers. Here's what I need you to do. Go down and get a fancy dress for cocktails and dinner tonight, shoes, whatever you need. The women around you will be wearing what Lo refers to as '*haute couture designer rags.*' I don't know what that is, but you find someone who knows and buy the same. Pay whatever it takes. Look sharp. You're representing Bastet. Get something to wear for tomorrow and the next day, too. Can you do that and be back by four?"

Speechless, I nodded like a bird on a perch, pecking at seeds.

He reached out and tapped my chin. I guess my mouth was open. He grabbed my hand, laid the card on my palm, and closed my fingers around it, much as he had when he gave me the topaz necklace. I was careful not to hold it to my heart as he said I did with precious things. No credit card is precious.

He went to the door. "Your room entry card is on the table there, under the lamp. Don't forget it. You'll need it to access the private elevators, too. Regular ones don't come up here. Oh, and would you get me a tie? Something for a black suit?" He walked out.

I stared at the card, trying to let my mind settle. Then I stuck it and the room card in my wallet and headed out. Oh, I'd traveled before, and I knew the value of a concierge. This one, female, gave me vivid descriptions of what women would wear since she'd overseen various events. I didn't have to leave the hotel property. I squeezed in a splendid late lunch that cost as much as I made on a busy Saturday night at the tavern.

I could tell by the shop windows if a place was for me. I didn't look at price tags. Most didn't have price tags, anyway. Business outfits for the next day were easy. I chose simple tailored things, classics for most any daytime setting. No skirts. I didn't like them. Never had. The stores delivered to the room, so I didn't have to carry anything.

Then I saw it. Not in the window, but on a mannequin inside. The manager, a well-dressed man with thinning hair and a slightly British accent pounced on me when I walked in. He linked the fingers of his well-manicured hands across his chest. I guess he wanted to make sure I was creditable enough to shop at his store.

I started to wave the little black card at him, but it wasn't necessary. My attitude by then was high-dollar shopper, not a looker, so I passed whatever test he had. The dress? I wanted it. Nothing else would do. He volunteered information that they could tailor it to my body and deliver within a few hours. I guess a demand for instant, well fitted haute couture was common in the land of high rollers.

A magnificent copper color, not brash or shiny, but with a metallic sheen that changed shades when it moved. It completely covered my collarbone and rode down to slightly above my knees. Not too short so I'd be tugging it down constantly, but it did show my long legs. It covered my breasts because the big show was behind. Fabric came under the arms, barely skimming the sides of the breasts, and turned to end in a V below the waist on the base of my spine. The entire back gaped open. A crosshatch network of tiny, almost invisible copper chains held it together over the shoulders and back. The garment required dress tape. Lots of tape. No gaps allowed.

Biggest problem? Panties. Everything would show. For that dress, I'd go commando. It flaunted my back scars but covered the ugly doctor stitched incisions on the front. I'd had lots of internal organ damage from multiple boots. But the bare back... The gazes of the women in the fitting room held varying expressions when they saw the tormented skin. The lines on my back and shoulders so regular, so obvious, that they could only come from a whip, hot iron, or carefully applied knife. They were disturbing as the devil's mark on a witch. Anyone would know they epitomized evil. The manager came in, called by the concerned ladies. Would he refuse to sell it to me?

The tight British accented manager walked around me, fingers over his mouth, like judging a prize pup at a dog show. Finally, in a voice that could have only come from a man born and raised in the deep south, he said, "You should look hideous. But lady, you are sexy as hell. This is you."

He came closer, tugged at the hem, and gave directions for fitting. I'd never used tape before, and they had to show me how. I purchased everything right there, shoes and a small purse that I might or might not use. The high heels I took with me, so I could practice walking. I hadn't worn such in years.

Yes, they would deliver the dress before four. I did buy a short, light, collarless jacket close to the same color that would cover things up. The dress was for effect and might need an unveiling moment. I wasn't showing off. I'd use whatever I had for any required reason.

They put the card through and gave me the receipt in a gold embossed envelope. I didn't have to sign. When the manager handed it over, he said, "Make him pay, darlin', you're worth every cent."

Well, we'd see wouldn't we. Pay? Wait, did he think I was a prostitute? Oh, a hooker that specialized in scar fetishes. How fun was that? I peeked at the receipt when I was out of the shop. I cringed. The sheriff's head might explode. I arranged for a hairdresser to come to the room around five to do my hair. I wanted the hairdresser to cut and style the mess. I bought Sheriff Pax a conservative blue and gray tie for his black suit. It hadn't connected in my mind, but there were a couple of garment bags among his things. Were they just in case, or did he always travel expecting to need a formal suit? Who knew?

Pax lay asleep on the couch when I returned so I tried not to disturb him. I was comfortably relaxing in the frothy bubbling tub, sipping a glass of lemonade, when he opened the door and walked in.

"No privacy around here I guess?"

"I've seen you before."

Yeah, he had. "You should try this tub. Later, you should try it is what I meant. You still look tired. You might fall asleep and drown." I didn't want him to think I'd issued an invitation to join me, though the tub was big enough for two. "It has its own circulating hot water heater, and the jets are in perfect places."

He settled across the room on one of the long brocade upholstered benches. "You find something to wear? Tonight? Tomorrow?"

"Yes. It's all haute couture spectacular. And horribly expensive. I deserve it." I didn't say I'd spent fifteen thousand dollars of his money…well, he said buy nice. He kept staring, studying me.

"Okay, that's your bad ass sheriff face. Spit it out. Ghastly news, minor problem, catastrophe?"

"Could you deal with it if you see McKay?"

My body went cold, despite the warm water. The long awaited inevitable had arrived. I should have expected it the minute I left Garnet. Las Vegas. Perfect. I shut off the jets, climbed out, and ignored him while I picked up a hotel provided luxury robe. I slipped my arms in and tied the belt. *Calm, Lilly. Remain calm.* My scars ached.

Pax watched me, but he wouldn't meet my eyes. "He was in LA. He disappeared three days ago. I received the alert."

"So, he could be anywhere." Thick anger swelled in my guts. "You have people who can spot the bastard, but the FBI can't catch him. That's astounding. He killed two of their own." I fought for calm, but my voice betrayed me.

"You don't have to be afraid of him, Lilly. You're not alone, here." I could hear the urgency in his voice while he kept pleading. "You have Bastet, your tribe. We are not defenseless. You have the Ennead Corporation which the tribes formed to protect us from people like him. That's its purpose. Security in this hotel belongs to us."

For the last year I'd expected to turn a corner or open a door and McKay would be there. Painful muscles tightened, like they had in rehab when I forced them to move. That would happen again when I sighted him. Sharp memories would batter me, too. What if I couldn't control them? I went and sat on the bench beside the sheriff.

"You think he'll show up here, don't you? Is that what you're telling me?"

Both his hands curled into fists. "There's a possibility. This is an ideal place. You were in rehab, then safe in jail, and safer in Garnet. If he found you among all these people, he could think you're vulnerable. He'd be wrong. I'm telling you, you're safe with me…us."

Safe with him. I felt safe, but I'd been wrong before. "McKay's last words to me in that parking lot where he dumped me to die were, *'Well, baby, it's been fun. See you in another life.'* I died in the ambulance and again in the hospital. The doctors, paramedics, something, brought me back. Did that make this another life?"

"I don't know. Are you looking for vengeance? You have a right to that."

"I'm not sure. I thought about it often in rehab. Once I wanted him in jail, because locking him in a cage was the worst I could imagine. Then I realized that McKay always created his own world around him. He'd take over, make himself King of Incarceration, Lord of the Cell Block, and live as well as he could. Worse? Odds were excellent he might get out. If he lives, people will suffer. He needs to die."

He took my hand and squeezed it between his. "Will you try to kill him if you see him? Do you want me to kill him?"

"You'd do that. Kill for me?" Everything in me wanted to cry because I knew the answer to my question before it came. He was tribe. This sheriff was a true warrior, fighting his battles out of place and time.

"Yes, Lilly, I would kill for you."

"No thank you, Sheriff. I have some pride."

He gave a sharp snap of laughter. "Now that's my tribal warrior girlfriend."

Then he grabbed and dragged me to him and held on. Oh my, it felt so fine. His laughter and his arms around me. I wanted him to kiss me, but he only smoothed a strand of hair away from my face. "Hey, did you get my tie?"

We'd never spent time talking as we had on this journey. If he went back to being an ass when we arrived home….Garnet? Home? Yes, Garnet and my sheriff equaled home, my home. It was time to be rid of the shadow of McKay hanging over me. I would deal with McKay when I faced him.

Since he'd called me his girlfriend, I did something out of character for me. In a way, it would be a step toward an uncertain future. I'm not a showoff. I put on my panties, a tank top, and the high stiletto heels. I needed practice walking. There was more room in the living room, so I told him to sit on the couch. I drew the knife. The runes on the blade glowed like I turned on a switch. Oh, he'd seen it, but only once and not that way. I relaxed and let it take me through the moves. Slash and thrust, it flowed easier, I moved more gracefully since I'd practiced. The knife and I worked in sync. Or had it taken control and I was its puppet? Even in high sharp heels I moved with an elegance that would never be mine, not on my own. I finished in a low defensive crouch. My turn to laugh. I kept it to a little snicker. He had the most curious expression on his face—and a noticeable bulge in his pants. *Warrior girlfriend indeed.* "Are you okay, Sheriff? Pax?"

He gave me what I called a *shit-eating grin.* "Am I Pax now?"

"Until you act like an ass again. You didn't believe me when I said I had your back, did you?"

"I believed. I didn't think you'd be so…capable."

"Now you know. No guns." I held up both hands. "Please, no guns."

"Okay. With that blade…no guns."

With all my heart I hoped I would never have to follow practice with action, and I could ignore the violent urging of Bi'ar, my bloodthirsty magic knife. If legend said the goddess made Bi'ar, did it also say why? I'd asked Lo and she didn't know.

My little show made me sweaty, so I went in to take a shower. My dress and hairdresser would arrive soon.

Chapter Fourteen

Sheriff Pax and I had reached an odd level of intimacy that involved his personal observation of my body and one hug I didn't want to end. When I walked into the bedroom after the hairdresser finished with me, he stood there only in his slacks. Oh, yes, a fine-looking man. Not necessarily handsome, often too stern, but I liked looking at him. Solid chest, excellent muscles, yeah, I could see the girls in Garnet jealous. He did have scars. Strangely fresh scars, a telltale red instead of the hardened pink and brown of mine. No stitches had closed them.

He glanced up and saw me staring. "What?"

"Is your tie the right color?"

"I guess." He flashed a mocking smile. He knew his appeal. Surely a woman, or many women had enlightened him. His behavior since I arrived in Garnet ranged from tolerable to infuriating. He kept coming close then abruptly walking away. His original hostility, his threat to kill me, his precious gift of the topaz, I never knew what would come next.

"You do know that your hovering over me when we arrived this morning said you owned me, don't you? That we're sharing one bedroom, even if it does have two beds, denying an intimate relationship won't be believable. McKay, if he's around watching me, he'll consider it a challenge. He intended to kill me. He won't tolerate failure, even his own. There's a possibility he'll bring reinforcements."

Pax smiled. A knowing, deadly smile. Raw and imminent violence lay there. I'd seen his anger, but never that way.

"Lilly… Damn McKay. He certainly won't be here tonight. This is for tribe members only." He shrugged. "When I hovered over you this morning, I was warning that I, Commander of Bastet, protected you from any threat. Not just external threats. We are the tribes, united, but we're like a large dysfunctional family. We've lost so much of the true aspect of the goddess we serve. The only thing that holds us together in this modern age is greed. The money and the corporations. You understand, don't you? Money, greed." I looked away. I'd forgotten he'd diligently read all the reports on me before I arrived in Garnet. My acts of greed had frequently led to violence. I was a facilitator, not an actor, but guilty all the same. I shrugged, resigned to acceptance of my actions.

He brushed my chin with his fingers. "Okay. But there may…there will be hostility tonight. Verbal, but if anyone troubles you about your past, I'll deal with them."

"So, you don't think I can handle a little hostility? Word play?"

"This is hostility on a different level. You don't know the rules yet. And it's like the Christian bible quoters. We adhere to select parts of tribal law that match any point we want to make at the time. I warned Lo…never mind."

"Is there a hierarchy? How high are you? Here and Garnet."

"In Garnet I'm on top." No arrogance there, just

fact. "Here among the other tribes, I guess I'd say I'm in the top ten percent. We're measured by money and Gifts from the goddess. And the will, the readiness to fight. Bastet has money. We have Gifts. We do not retreat."

"You measure the Gifts you don't talk about?"

"Yes, but sensitive people know." He shrugged.

"So, who is on top? Under your oh so powerful Dominus."

"Right now, it's Simon Balance. He's leader of the Pallas tribe. After him it's Miriam Abba of Anzû. But things are changing. I could tell that by earlier phone conversations alone."

"Pallas, Anzû, do I need details?"

"Not now. Eventually. I suspect Lo knew about this delay and didn't tell me until it was too late. She sent you here to expose you. She's bad about that. Testing people. It's dangerous for you. The Bastet Priestess takes her position seriously."

"Her position?"

"The priestess is the arbiter, the negotiator of the tribe. And occasionally the judge."

My sweet Aunt Lo? "So, it's throw me into the fire and see if I jump out or burn."

He didn't say I was wrong. I knew so little about these tribes, dangerous tribes if I believed him. And Lo had deliberately withheld information. Again. I let it go for then. Time to get ready for the circus.

My dress hung in its protective covering in the bathroom. It was going to take a while to get into it. The dress shop manager said if I had a problem I could call, and they would send someone up to help me. Oh, hell! Yesterday, I was mopping vomit out of the men's bathroom wearing a hazmat suit. I could handle this.

After removing the beautiful topaz, so it wouldn't get entangled in the chains, I stepped into my wonderful dress. Now that was magic. It fit better than any garment I had ever owned. The dress shop had thoughtfully applied the double-sided tape for me so all I had to do was peel the cover strip and press down. Two intricate hooks held it across the shoulders, then tape down under my arms and down my sides to the V on the base of my spine. That kept me from flashing my breasts from the sides but allowed the skin and curve to show. I'd seen pictures of movie stars wearing breathtaking cleavage and wondered how their girls didn't fall out. Now I knew. They taped and glued those babies in.

The tiny copper chains across the back were visible up close, but not in the mirror. This dress wasn't about the breasts. The softly draped neckline covered them. A thin light jacket completed it but didn't have the spectacular look of the dress alone. The idea of putting on a show troubled me. Or was it secretly what I wanted?

The hairdresser had cut at least a foot of my thick hair to make it manageable. A true artist, she'd styled it perfectly on the back of my head in an intricate design. Pinned tight, sprayed, and coated with shine, that baby wasn't going anywhere. And she'd done my eyes perfectly. Smokey, but touched with a hint of copper, so exotic. All I needed was a little lipstick and I was ready.

What about my knife? I didn't want to leave it behind, but I didn't want to use a purse. My penchant for having my hands free made for inconvenient situations at times. The knife wasn't small. Even though it wouldn't cut me, what about my dress? I turned the blade point down and slid it between my breasts. Yes, there was enough folded material to cover it. And a strip of the dress tape held it in place. Perfect. It cooperated and if I kept my long waist body straight, it wouldn't show—or poke me in the navel. Could I draw it with the tape? I reached for it—it was in my hand.

"Bi'ar." I turned the blade slowly, and the etched designs glowed. Was arriving in Garnet what had drawn it from slumber? Did it know its time had come? I carefully returned it to its silken sheath.

I walked into the suite living room. "So, am I acceptably attired? I won't embarrass you. I've been to dinner parties before." In a past life, I played the part of McKay's arm candy, his prize for success. Two of those had ended in nasty bloody gun fights rather than meals. Pax was armed tonight, as usual, but didn't seem stressed.

He came to stand in front of me. "Lilly, you are so beautiful."

"As long as I'm dressed, I'm okay."

"No. The clothes…forget the clothes. Such courage…" He stopped. Oh, yeah, men weren't good at that kind of talk. But his eyes locked on me. Yes, I was beautiful to him, scars and all.

"Pax…" It was enough.

"We have to go now."

It was 7:45 when we left the room and stepped on the elevator to go up. Not far since we were near the top anyway. The doors silently slid open to a massive glass domed penthouse paradise. My heels made tiny clicks on a marble path bordered by resplendent orchids and ferns of every kind. Exotic tropical fish swam in seven-foot glass columns. Sandalwood and citrus perfumed the air.

We entered a lounge where men and women gathered in tight clusters, chatting in low murmurs. Luxurious chairs bordered the room. They remained empty, so I surmised no one felt relaxed enough to sit. That meant the level of tension filling the air had soared to critical levels. It would be like breathing under water. Well, Pax did warn me. Our dinner promised to be a stimulating exercise since the evening had barely begun.

Servants in black and white, carrying trays, glided around like the fish trapped in their tall glass bowls. They offered drinks and food that few seemed to want. Not much party spirit here. Someone should liven things up.

At least the dress shop had insured I looked acceptable. Most of the women wore black or jewel color dresses, and diamonds sparkled at necks and ears. I didn't want to maim Pax's black card with diamonds, so I'd purchased earrings to match the dress. Garnet's simple, humble lifestyle didn't stand a chance here. Silence fell as multiple faces turned to us, but I ignored them. My steps forward faltered, and then I stopped. Standing there, smiling, handsome as ever, was McKay.

Chapter Fifteen

Fate, that unholy bitch, wouldn't have it any other way. How perfectly orchestrated, she—or an evil minion—had perfected this scene like fine art. Thank God, or Lo's goddess, that McKay didn't see me first. I had time, only seconds, but I could do this. Memory consumed me, immediate, vivid. *Pain, raging pain, terror. Gunshots, screams, blood, copious amounts of blood. It hurt so much...let me die.* I fought, shoving those scenes of my life back in the compartment where they belonged. I exhaled, releasing the breath I'd held. I'd won my eternal memory battle—this time. The past under control, I turned my attention to the evolving calamity.

Pax's body stiffened into that incredible stillness that so fascinated me. Something had gone awry in his ordered world. He thought he had reliable sources of information. He'd called this gathering *tribe member only* with his usual absolute confidence. He relaxed as suddenly as he had frozen. My stern sheriff stood ready to face any challenge.

McKay always appeared perfect for any occasion. Impeccable, as if he stepped off the pages of a men's magazine—or when a dignitary would crown him King of the City. He wasn't a big man, certainly not like Pax. Handsome, graceful, with dark hair that curled a bit around his angelic face. His virile body tucked in a fabulous black suit, no god or goddess should bless a man with all those spectacular features. Bright blue eyes that softened when he had wanted me. Eyes that froze with arctic cold fury when he killed. Like the time he beat my 100-pound friend Julia to death with his fists.

I had to keep my mind clear. *Live in the moment, Lilly.* I cared nothing for the people in the room, but under no circumstances would I break in front of the Sheriff of Garnet. His hand lay against the small of my back, again claiming me. Why not? He'd become more important in my life than McKay. "I'm sorry, Lilly. This is wrong. It shouldn't be happening."

I managed a tiny smile for him. "I'm fine, Pax. It was inevitable. It has been from the moment the doctors said I'd live. Stand with me. Watch my back." I turned and laid my palm flat on his chest. I could feel his heartbeat, steady, strong. From the instant I met him, no matter how much he disliked me, hated me, I understood that he would give everything to protect me from McKay. I was tribe, and he'd accepted it as duty.

He caught my hand, lifted it to his lips, and smiled. That gesture wasn't duty at all. Like the hospital and nightmarish rehab, facing McKay was part of my penance, atonement for my first inexcusable blindness to his sins. I would stoically suffer many times for redemption.

McKay spotted me. Oh, how priceless. How utterly wonderful to behold the expression of shock on his face. Only a flash, a blink of the eye, but I'd watched him for hours when I was with him. I knew. He recovered instantly. He was too intelligent, too talented an actor not to.

I think he passively kept track of me but hadn't known I was in the hotel today. I didn't know I'd be here until late yesterday. What did he know about the tribes? Why was he at a tribe member only dinner?

I tried to force my face into the stern mask like Pax had when I first met him. *Nothing wrong with emotion, Lilly. Just don't let it control you.*

We marched forward into the fray. A man stepped out to meet us, offering his hand. Heading us off, keeping me from a showdown with McKay? *Presumptuous little prick.*

"Pax, it's good to see you."

Pax accepted his hand. He could play that game. He kept close by my side, so possessive, as he introduced me. "Lilly, this is Simon Balance, of Pallas."

"Ms. Dusalte. I've heard of you." Balance gave me a condescending smile. Small eyes, smaller nose, he oozed an aura of slime that most people would want to immediately wash away. A blessing—he hadn't offered *me* his hand. This man was a powerhouse of the tribes? How did they tell? Looks were deceiving here, as in the rest of the world.

Pax and Balance exchanged inane words at first, then Pax started a fight. I thought I knew all the sheriff's voices, but I was wrong. He heaped incredible scorn on the man, far more than his battering of me when I arrived in Garnet. "Tell me Simon, why do we have a stranger at a strictly tribal event?" Ah, the disdain, the scorn in his voice. Simon Balance was shit on his shoe. Wow!

Balance lifted his chin and stiffened. He looked like a wuss, but he wasn't backing down. "Well, Pax. Since I decided that we needed to be more inclusive."

Nose in the air, I'm superior voice. "That it could be beneficial to Ennead."

"You decided? Because those exercises in inclusion have worked so well in the past? In Atlanta? And Chicago?"

Balance flinched.

"Does the Dominus approve, Simon?"

"For tonight." Oh, a smug knowing smile. "He's here. I spoke with him."

Pax didn't move, but the air around us shifted. He had only mentioned the possibility of their leader's presence. Obviously, it changed things.

Balance turned. He avoided a true face off with Pax. McKay had come to stand behind him. "You should meet Mr. McKay. He has business propositions for the Ennead Corporation. He'll show them at the meeting tomorrow. I'm sure you'll be interested."

Mr. McKay? *On the FBI's most wanted list, and he hadn't bothered to use an alias.* Flaunting his omnipotence? Oh, yes, that was my personal psychopath in the flesh.

"Mr. McKay," Balance babbled on, "I'd like you to meet Pax Harrow and Lilly Dusalte of Bastet."

McKay stepped forward, a beatific smile on his face. He stretched a hand toward me, not Pax. A memory flashed again. Bloody, brutal, terrifying. I fought back, but a tiny choking sound escaped my throat.

Pax stepped forward slightly in front of me. "If you touch her, I will kill you." No emotion, no pressure in those words and yet they blasted out with strike-force power, a battering ram of truth. Would he kill for me? Right there on that beautiful marble floor? Absolutely.

"Pax, what are you doing?" Balance puffed up, a small man trying to project wrath. "My guest…"

McKay, the consummate player in his social life, prudently stepped back to save the situation. "It's fine, Simon. I'm the one who doesn't understand your customs." He smiled and nodded at Pax. "I apologize, sir."

Pax didn't reply. McKay backed away, the smile never leaving his face, sure Pax had accepted his apology. Well, there are diverse kinds of acceptance. Like forced and genuine.

I realized then that the room had fallen silent. Oh, yes, everyone had heard that little exchange. What a fun night we were going to have. Conversations resumed, and I'd bet they now had something new to huddle close for and to exchange vulgar gossip. Pax didn't leave my side as he introduced me to other guests. The tribes, Adapa, Nergal, Siris, Gaia, others, all named after ancient gods. I'd bet Frank could give a biography of each deity.

Finally, McKay approached again—cautiously. He kept a safe distance. "Mr. Harrow, may I speak with Lilly for a moment? We were friends, once. I won't…touch her."

Pax turned to me. I nodded. It had to happen sometime.

"Speak. But know if she gives me a word, I will bury you in the desert."

The original threat to kill him if he touched me shocked McKay. This one did not—or if it did, he hid any reaction. Pax was formidable, and McKay was always a superb judge of character and intent. He didn't think his little victim Lilly could or would harm him.

But the big man behind her, that was different. McKay leaned forward, hands out and open, in a slight bow. "I understand."

Pax moved away, but not far. He could hear our conversation. So could others around us listening intently for each word. *My turn. No more fear, no more waiting.*

Arrogance was always McKay's best presentation. Such a blissful smile on an angel face. His words didn't match his demeanor. "This is a violent bunch you've fallen in with, Lilly. I'd have thought you'd be more cautious by now."

I shrugged. "What can I say. They're family. We don't get to choose."

No reaction to my assertion of family. That meant he already knew. I wanted to ask what the hell he was doing here, but his presence had trapped me on an edge, hanging on by my fingers.

His curious gaze slid over me. "You look incredible."

"Thank you. First-class hospital, skilled surgeons, fantastic rehab, lots of screaming and crying. And drugs. They worked."

"I regret—"

"Don't lie to me."

He gave me what was once, in my mind, an endearing look. Like everything else, it was an illusion. He would not fool me. But he tried.

"I made a mistake, darling. That's the truth. I didn't realize your worth until you were gone." It sounded so soulful, so genuine.

I made a mistake, darling? Not I'm sorry I hurt you? Tortured you for days without mercy?

"McKay, you left me broken to pieces in a frozen parking lot. Mistake? Yes, it was. You failed to make certain I was dead before you ran away."

My former lover spared one glance at Pax as if expecting an attack. Pax only looked amused, not threatening.

McKay tried again. He gave me that lazy sensual smile I'd once loved. "Oh, Lilly, of all the women in this world, you know me, don't you?"

I knew McKay. I knew what it was like to love him more than life. I knew what he had done to make my body sing with passion. When I defied him, the man who gave me incredible joy had taken it back like a tiger devouring living prey. But pain, weeks, hours, minutes of agony had taught me something.

"Oh, yes, McKay, I know you. You're a psychopath. Every person you deal with—every person you use—you've chosen because they have something *you* want, or something they can do for *you*. What do you want now?"

"I'm trying to rebuild." His eyes narrowed. He would dare to reprimand me? Accuse me? *Yes, he would.* "You destroyed my previous business ventures, Lilly. My entire organization."

"Thank you. I did my best. The FBI helped, of course."

Okay, that brought a tiny reaction only I would notice. A sharp, thin breath in his throat. Pissed. Score one for me. His ego, the idea that he could make me care again forced him on.

He held out his hands again and pleaded. "You and I had something special between us once."

The room blurred, and I realized I was holding my

breath. *Breathe, Lilly, breathe.* Pax had spoken of role playing. My role with McKay? I had overlooked purest evil, made justifications for him, blamed his victims. *I accepted my guilt.* I was no longer the woman he knew.

"We do have something special between us, McKay. A body count. I remember every victim in bloody detail. I see them in nightmares. Shall I be specific? Little Julia whom you beat to death, two young FBI agents, ten people in the bank heist that went wrong. Your own men who died in that fire? Those sons of bitches rise up from hell and haunt me, too." After swallowing hard, I found more words.

"McKay, the fact that you're standing here, alive and free, is proof that there is no God in heaven and no justice in this world. I am not free to act as I wish right now, but if I ever am, I swear on my soul that I will spend the rest of my life organizing an army of decent people who loved your victims. Then we will hunt you down and tear you apart." Bi'ar hummed and vibrated between my breasts, reminding me it would accept blood offerings.

McKay always had excellent instincts. He quickly backed away.

Pax came to me. He gave me a uniquely beautiful open and honest smile. For me, that smile just for me. I returned the joy with exuberance. A victory. I'd turned anxiety and fear into anger.

"See. I had control. I didn't try to kill him or anything. Too many witnesses around."

"Lilly Dusalte, I'm proud you belong to my tribe."

"Well, damn, Pax. That's…disturbing." I leaned closer, my body against his. "When I arrived in Garnet you pawed through my bags, my thrift store clothes, looking for a way to get rid of me. Tonight, I'm standing here in an eight-thousand-dollar dress, taunting, threatening, one of the country's worst criminals. Where do we go from here?"

"It doesn't matter. It's bound to be interesting." He paused. "Eight thousand dollars?"

I grinned, then giggled like a little girl.

Chapter Sixteen

Pax stayed with me and we mingled. McKay kept his distance. I met polite people, curious people, hostile people. My feet, pinched toes, and throbbing arches threatened mutiny. Then someone new arrived. The room fell silent, as it had when Pax and I entered.

Garnet's sheriff had always impressed me with his solid determined strength, even when he disliked me. This new man's presence washed over me in invisible waves, like an unrelenting, incoming tide. Certainly, he was as powerful as Pax, but different in so many ways. How odd that I knew this about a stranger.

Six-five, a long lean body, not as muscular as Pax, but still a perfect masculine animal. He had the aura of a predator searching for quivering prey. Tiny prickles dashed up my spine. I shivered. *Be still, be silent, little girl. He might pass on by.*

He came closer, stepping with the light-footed grace of a sprinter. Black hair with a touch of silver at the temples, caramel colored skin, and eyes—were they gold? Sometimes Pax's eyes seemed gold, but this man's were pure and constant. And that face? Exquisite as a young god. He surpassed even McKay.

In terms of power and presence, though, he and Pax could be twins. There was nothing soft, nothing yielding in either man. What a spectacular head-on crash they would create if they were to battle.

Pax grasped my hand. Claiming possession again? He'd seen me staring.

"That's Garrett Dain, of Fenrir."

"Fenrir? As in the Norse god's pet wolf?"

"Yes, the wolf." Pax breathed the words like a whisper. He wasn't afraid, or uncomfortable, he was ready to fight. He released me and stood straighter.

Dain hadn't noticed me. He spoke only to one woman and three men. They gave him strained smiles—until he turned his back. He needed a Kevlar vest. Had he deliberately chosen to greet those who despised him, to show he didn't consider them worthy opponents? To show they didn't intimidate him. I knew this man was going to pay attention to me. With his looks he had to have a massive ego. I was something new in the game. He'd notice the new. What I hadn't expected was the connection when his eyes met mine. The dangerous animal stalking prey fled. Sharp interest, male to female grew.

What's this? He had considered my eyes first? Men never do that. They go for the breasts. He closed the distance. I felt his presence, his dominion over the room.

Oh, hell no. I'd already faced down my bogey man this night, my monster under the bed. This was nothing.

"Harrow." Dain greeted Pax with a nod of his head. He didn't hold out a hand. They wouldn't touch. Everyone observing us carefully backed away. Had these two met before?

"Dain." Pax had fallen into his no expression, no emotion mode.

Dain stared at me, then back at Pax. Wasn't Pax going to introduce me?

Pax laid a hand on my back again. Possession. Testosterone rising! Spines straight, utter stillness, body language in both men silently and forcefully proclaimed, *I'm ready, bring it on!*

Pax's turn. "This is Lilly Dusalte. Luella's niece. She's recently joined the tribe in Garnet." His hand moved from my back to my waist as if to pull me closer. I moved away a single step to prevent that.

Pax and I needed to have a talk. He'd actively offered to protect me from McKay, but this was different. He didn't own me, and I didn't want or need him challenging another alpha male in an awkward act of vanity and possession. Yeah, he might see a danger I couldn't, but I didn't think so.

My jaw tightened, and I clenched my hands.

Dain's eyes narrowed. A watchful man. He didn't miss my tiny bit of defiance. Perhaps his ego wasn't as big as his looks said it would be.

"Ms. Dusalte." Dain's voice was deep as a cavern and soft as fog on the ground. "Are you enjoying your stay in the desert?"

"Yes. It's a bit lonely, but I appreciate the solitude at times." Warm, friendly, and cautiously polite. *Take that, Mr. Pax.*

"My home is in Oregon." Dain smiled as if he knew all my secrets and could draw them out whenever he chose. "There are forests and mountains. And so much life. It's magnificent and hard to be lonely there." His expression, tone of voice, and body language said nothing more than a polite dinner table conversation. And yet I heard the invitation to join him at some fabulous locale.

Pax was intuitive, too. Testosterone reached critical

status. He urged me away. I didn't fight him. I gave myself points for that. He was my guide, like it or not.

Dain shrugged slightly. "Perhaps we can speak later, Lilly."

Yes, he had zeroed in on the emotional tug-of-war between Pax and me. More familiar, he'd called me Lilly.

"Yes, Mr. Dain, that would be fine." Mr. Dain. Not that familiar for me. Yet. Insipid, but I couldn't think of anything else that wouldn't sound like a babbling silly girl. If I did, it might come out like *I'll bet that hard body is magnificent under that suit. Sleek and lean and that mouth...whoa!* Was the testosterone affecting me, too? Demanding that I respond as a woman?

I hadn't had more than a tiny flash of desire in the last four years, until Pax hit me with it when he gave me the topaz in my work barn. If he hadn't run away that night something else might have been said—or done. Now this total stranger comes along and zaps me like a slap in the face. Oh, I could see myself and this Dain guy, naked and...shit! Like that would ever happen. My expensive fancy garments had made me forget for a moment. I'm a nightmare naked. No man would want that—except possibly the one holding on to me now. The one who considered my scars as valuable battle trophies.

Chapter Seventeen

I wasn't over or underdressed in my costly scrap of cloth. Of course, the jacket covered the most naked skin—and the scars. These people moved around the room, politely bounced off each other, then moved on. If these were my people, the collective tribes, I again noted a couple of things that did mark us as a group. Darker skin and height. There were no short people present, nor were there any shy introverts. All educated, articulate, they could, if they chose, verbally, emotionally, and physically shred me—or at least back me up against a wall. I'd already used most of my strength for the night in the battle with McKay. *Show no weakness, Lilly. Keep your mouth shut. A pinprick of blood in the water will bring out the fangs.*

Siris, Nergal, Talos, most representatives were cool but polite. Evelyn Marcos of Gaia, hostile, Marian Krantz from Siris, warm and friendly. A woman greeted Pax with a kiss on the cheek, and he hugged her with what seemed genuine pleasure.

"Lilly, this is Leslie Apros. Leslie is my mother's sister." Yes, he cared for her.

Leslie was a pleasantly attractive woman. Tall as the rest of us, her full-figured body made her seem almost motherly—almost. Pax bore no resemblance to her. Leslie's smile for me was genuine. I could take that. Her deep, almost masculine, voice surprised me.

"Luella was right. You are magnificent."

Lo had called me magnificent? I didn't know what to say.

Leslie laughed. She carefully guided me and Pax over toward a quieter corner. More serious conversation. I didn't mind with her. She had no problem with discussing the obvious. "So, who is this McKay fellow Simon is pushing on us?" She beamed a smile. "Obviously, neither of you are fans. You, Lilly, were exceptionally articulate." She lifted her glass in a toast to me. "And you," she nodded at Pax, "were exceptionally terrifying."

Pax glanced at me. I figured that meant he wanted me to speak. I'd stick with the uncolored if not complete truth. "McKay is a merciless killer. I lived with him for three years, then turned him over to the FBI. They let him escape. He's a psychopath." I glanced across the room at McKay. "But that's my personal opinion."

Leslie frowned with intensity. "Simon has made odd and ruinous decisions over the last five years. Financial and personal. Now, he's obviously making another. I've heard that Pallas is almost bankrupt. What's shocking is that the Dominus has allowed Simon's proposal and his *guest* to get this far into the tribe. The FBI, you say?"

Oh, no. I had to stop her. "Please don't go near him, Leslie. FBI be damned. The fact that he's here in a semi-public situation, without an alias, should tell you something. Call the FBI if you want—anonymously. With a throw-away phone."

Pax leaned forward, his voice strained. "She's right, Leslie. I don't know what's going on right now, but please don't put yourself in danger."

Leslie grimaced, but I could see in her eyes she didn't accept a request to not act. She was too strong. Pax called the tribe leaders predatory. She didn't seem like it, but neither did she seem weak. I was a lightweight drowning in a sea of type *A* personalities. How many of these people knew what McKay was? How many cared?

Pax glanced around the room. "Leslie, will you stay with Lilly for a few minutes?"

"Of course." Leslie seemed surprised. As he walked away, she cocked her head, and her mouth twisted into a wry grin. "Lilly, do you need protection?"

"No. I'm simply uneducated in the social rules of the tribes. I'm sure he thinks that in my ignorance, I'll create a monumental pile of shit for him to clean up. I'll embarrass him." I leaned closer for taunting subterfuge. "Or worse, I'll wander off to find that lovely, dark and dangerous man who was here only moments ago. He can't have gone far."

Leslie's long, loud peal of laughter drew stares. I loved it. "Oh, my dear. You are priceless. And so considerate of the Bastet Sheriff. Why is that?"

I shrugged and had to laugh too. "I guess I'm easy. He's been feeding me, and he bought me this pretty dress. Shoes, too."

She laughed again, but not so loud. "And shoes? Then it must be true love. I wish you were ours, but you're too strong. Most of the aggressive warrior traits go to Fenrir and Bastet. It's always been that way. As the goddess wills it to be." Leslie spoke of her goddess with a warm familiarity.

Pax had walked across the room to a man and a woman standing by the wall. He embraced the woman. Lighter hair, pretty, and easy to see it was friendly and not romantic.

"Rowena. His former wife." Leslie spoke quietly.

"Wife?" Now that was new.

"They were married for the requisite time a number of years ago."

"Requisite time?"

"Yes, five to seven years." She frowned. "You don't know...what is wrong with Luella? She should have taught you. Because our birthrates are so low, we regularly request that young fertile tribe members marry for a specific time. Hopefully to produce a child. It's an arrangement with strict rules. Every now and then a couple will remain together, but most partings are cordial. Pax and Rowena's certainly were."

Arranged marriages? Another aspect of tribal life Lo hadn't told me out of fear it would spook me, and I'd run away. Was that worse than Bi'ar or the fighting big cat performance? Yep. It was. Why? Because it involved a man with whom I'd developed a semi-relationship. Before I could ask for more info, Pax returned, and Leslie left.

Conversation stopped as if someone had sent a telepathic signal. Telepathy? Was that one of the Gifts people in the tribes were supposed to have? I planned serious harassment of my aunt until she broke down and talked.

As one, the group moved down a walkway toward the other side of the glass domed roof garden. Here lay another spectacular construction, filled with what had to be thousands of dollars in flowering plants and trees with fairy lights. I'd have enjoyed it on a different occasion.

Ah, the dinner table. More flowers, crystal, silver, the long narrow table would encourage conversation, at least with the people across and beside you. A millionaire's gourmet food fest had to be forthcoming.

Doublewide trailers and dirt roads in Garnet? No matter the riches hoarded on the inside of the tin boxes—or their mysterious barns—it was insane. I needed a better explanation of why they lived that way, one that didn't border on ludicrous.

Pax spoke in my ear. "There are name cards on the plates. Sit by your name. Please. I don't know who sets it up, but it gets tense at times."

"Don't worry. I did promise I'd be a polite, obedient little bartender on probation." For the briefest moments, I thought I saw an expression of fear flash across his face.

The narrow dining table had a low, but formidable, flower arrangement all down the center of its extended length. It left barely enough room for a dinner plate. And that plate would sit on a precarious edge, threatening to dump food in the diner's lap. It would certainly discourage fast extravagant actions.

One grand chair placed at the end must be where the exalted Dominus would...what? Give an audience? Or eat dinner with the rest of us? Oh, this would be entertaining. I wasn't a part of their game. I could observe and laugh at the inevitable discontent. I saw the alleged tribal power man, Simon Balance, standing near the middle of the table. His tight mouth and red-faced expression broadcast pure fury. This was getting better. The dinner might take on the spirit of a rousing bar fight. At least I wouldn't have to protect my bar. I didn't have to worry about a bully tossing his victim over and crushing my livelihood. Narrow table, but certainly sturdy. If they started throwing anything but verbal punches, I'd crawl under until it was over. A respectable plan—until I realized those in charge of such things designated me to sit in the prime guest chair, right next to their so-called Dominus.

The only sounds then were the rustle of fabric as everyone found their place. They might be unhappy with the seating arrangement, but no one would say so. Pax, certainly surprised, led me to my place and left me. Fingers brushed my arm. Oh, my, the charming Garrett Dain was pulling back my chair for me. Yes, his card was on the plate next to mine. *Like a lady, Lilly, do it right. You can handle the beautiful man. Pretend you're naked, showing the scars in all their glory. That would wipe the sexy smile from his face.*

I sat carefully, correctly. I glanced at Dain. Face serious like everyone else, then he winked at me. Where was Pax, anyway? He had moved in to sit directly across the table from me. A guest of honor, too. I had no clue what was happening, but his stiff body language said he wasn't having fun.

Everyone waited, silent, ladies seated, men standing, five minutes, ten, then, at an inscrutable magical signal, everyone stood. I did the same and Dain was there again, a gentleman to help with my chair.

So, the silent wait and standing must be a sign of respect, like a judge in a court room. Or a king on his throne. Then the *man* himself came in. He had the height associated with the tribes. A sharp chiseled face, a distinguished well-dressed gentleman—and a head full of pure white hair.

That bitch Fate had kicked me in the face again. I knew him. I'd only seen him one time in my life. No little box for that memory. He would stand like a monument, stark and raw forever. Eight years old and he had hovered over my bed. The Dominus of the tribes was my long missing father. How utterly perfect. How clichéd. Staged and performed.

My tribe, my family, could this whole incident be a setup for me? Was I egotistical enough to believe that?

The Dominus settled into his chair. Once he was down, everyone else sat, too. I guess I wasn't fast enough because Dain guided me into my seat. That was kind of him. I obviously wasn't functioning right then. Silence ruled the table. Not that I'd been able to form words if asked.

I fell into a silent crisis. At least I was sitting. My second worst nightmare had jumped me, fangs and claws, biting and tearing at my heart. How incredible. How intolerable. His presence triggered a total memory crash and burn. That catastrophe had come twice before in my life and never in public.

Scene after scene rolled across me like a tsunami over the sea. Lost and alone, I drowned in memories. The voices came. The ones I feared would eventually bring my mother's madness upon me.

Devil child! I love you Mama. Please don't hit me, Mama.

I'll teach you, bitch! Kill me, McKay. Not her. Please not her.

No collateral damage, I'll kill you first! Please don't hate me, Sheriff.

Frank? Help me Frank, please help me. *Hide Lilly.*

Hide. I'll distract her.

I fought. Survival demanded that I do so. I fought for Lo and Frank who loved me, wanted me to succeed, to rise above my grievous life. I fought to crush all memory and emotion, so I could perform and not act like an escapee from an asylum. It took years and years to earn those memories. My mind fought to lock them away again. *Push, shove, got it, now, on a roll. Concentrate.*

Finally, the flood subsided. Under control. A draw, not a win. I could function. My hands? Only shaking a little. Eyes? Perfectly dry. Pain? A little ache near my spine. My mind? Hey, anyone can fake sanity. Right? While it seemed forever, I could tell only seconds had passed while I battled my own nature.

The Dominus spoke. "Good evening, tribesmen and women. I apologize for my sudden appearance at this gathering. I know you like to schedule private meetings with me, and we will do so. Please, enjoy your dinner. We can talk tomorrow."

I stared down at my plate. I'd corralled my break-dancing mind. Now I had to keep it under control. Finally, I looked at him. Easy. After the big memory battle, I could do anything.

The Dominus smiled. Yes, he recognized me. Did I detect a hint of uncertainty there? I had my right hand on the table. He started to place one of his over mine. I jerked it back. No! He couldn't touch. I couldn't bear to feel his touch. My hand's movement clinked my glass against the plate on the cramped table. It sounded so loud in the quiet room.

That's when, thank God, goddess, or the chaotic universe at large, a kind soul sent a silent signal and the waiters poured in. Like I wanted to eat—ever again. However, it was something to concentrate on, so I didn't have to look at him. *McKay hadn't broken me. My long absent father would not.* I didn't dare look at Pax. I had no idea if Lo had told him the tale of my father.

A hum of quiet conversation began. Dain's fingers glided down my arm.

"Are you enjoying Las Vegas?" he asked. "Have you been here before?"

Yes, that's it. Calm and easy. Talk to him, Lilly, talk to him. Ordinary talk. Get it together. "I've been here twice. Haven't seen much of the place. I was always locked in my room." *Damn, damn, what did I say?*

Dain's eyes widened a bit, but he went on. "Then you should allow me to show you around tomorrow."

Your turn, Lilly. "That's kind of you to offer."

Thank you, Mr. Dain. Insipid conversation. He politely gave me a short verbal tour of attractive places we could go in Vegas. I'd grown calmer. I'd concentrated on trivial things, a single flower in the table centerpiece, the gold band on the plate edge. A waiter started to pour me a glass of wine and I waved him away. I'd managed something else ordinary. At least, that's what I thought. "Water, please."

Dain frowned. "It's excellent wine. You should try some."

"I can't. I'm on probation. Lots of rules. I don't want to go back to jail."

Oh hell, not again.

I slapped my fingers over my mouth. I glanced over at Pax. He was frowning, and that was too bad.

He'd brought me here. No, it was Lo who had insisted. I didn't dare look at the Dominus.

Dain laughed deep and soft. Sexy, so sexy, no one could miss him flirting with me. "Probation? So, you've been a bad girl. How exciting."

"Not really. It's more like sordid pulp fiction."

And where was McKay? There he was, across the table two seats down from Pax. He could hear our conversation. The woman between Pax and McKay, I hadn't met her, hunched down, obviously uncomfortable. Hell, everyone I could see looked uncomfortable. Except Dain. He appeared thoroughly relaxed and amused. Such confidence. I suspected it would take an all-out war to disturb him. Pax glared at Dain with undisguised hostility, probably making a silent demand that he *not* question me again.

Finally, I glanced at the Dominus. He didn't make eye contact. I did notice that no one addressed him, acknowledged him in any way. Conversation was his choice. Why would Mama... *Do not think about Mama, Lilly. Do not go there.*

A waiter set a lovely salad in front of me. Excellent. Something else to do to keep from engaging anyone in disastrous conversation. But after I ate a few bites I stopped. Given how my guts twisted like leftover spaghetti, anything that went down had to stay put until I could escape this bizarre circus. I couldn't taste it anyway.

Positioned there beside this formidable Dominus, despite the deference of others to his command, I realized something was missing. Pax had warned me not to challenge him. I'd met deadly men and women before. I'd learned how to sense them. They radiated fearful energy that would make a person lean away in unconscious dread. Criminal bosses, hitmen, snipers, all professional killers wore violence like an invisible overcoat. It came from inside, rising from the depths of Hell to consume a soul. The Dominus lacked all of those attributes.

I wanted to get in his face and demand why he left me to Mama's savagery. This night I was more afraid of my own actions than what the all-powerful Dominus could do. Bi'ar quivered between my breasts as if to agree with me.

Okay, time to confront the big bad one. I turned to face him. Let the battle begin. Battle? More like a firing squad. *Get over it, Lilly. You can do this.*

The Dominus smiled. Had he been waiting for me to get my mind and memory under control? How kind of him. Bullshit. When had he learned that I would attend this farce? He had to have known what his appearance might do to me. My place at the table, him reaching for me, wanting to observe my reaction. He wanted to play me, use me for a purpose of his own. He was not a beloved parent. The Dominus was a manipulator in the tribe's soap opera of life.

He spoke first. "Do you like Garnet, Lilly? Are you comfortable there?" His voice came in perfect measured tones. Measured specifically for me. Concerned, like I would jump up and run at any moment. I swallowed hard. "Garnet is lovely. I've learned new things. Met new people." Points for me. I could talk. *Keep it bland, Lilly, no more embarrassing utterances.*

"Tell me about them. The things you've learned." He leaned forward in interest.

I doubt he cared about me or what I was doing. He acted like a helpful host trying to draw out an introvert. Uhhh…what did I say? "I've learned how to be a bartender."

"Do you enjoy that? Bartending?"

I don't think my bar resume was what he wanted. It was all my barely functioning mind could do. "Most of the time I do. When there aren't too many drunks, or the FBI isn't hanging around." *The mouth! Not again.*

"I'm sure you can handle the drunks." He frowned. "Is the FBI troubling you?"

"No, not much. Pax usually chases them off when they get too obnoxious."

He glanced at Pax and smiled in what looked like approval. Dain sitting beside me, had his fingers over his mouth, fighting laughter. It got worse.

The woman between McKay and Pax, I had no idea who she was, had been conversing with others down the table. She suddenly stared directly at me. Wow, talk about evil smiles. She had plans to socially subvert me.

"Ms. Dusalte, we were discussing a comfortable personal space during conversations and other situations. Do you have a preference?"

Is that all they had to talk about. Okay, she could have the truth. "My personal space is straight arm's length plus eight inches."

She frowned. "Eight inches? Why?"

"That's for the knife blade."

Oh, Goddess strike me dead here and now. But my voice slid out like I'd oiled my tongue. Confident. I sounded confident. The Dominus laughed out loud. He was king of the hill—he could be as loud as he wanted.

Pax choked like he'd swallowed an orange whole. And Dain, he tried not to laugh but didn't quite make it. He held it to a few little jerks. Well, damn, people shouldn't ask questions they don't want answered.

The Dominus reached over and patted my hand. This time I let him. He approved of me? I amused him? Okay, I'd accept that for the moment.

We finished the main course, though I couldn't tell what it was. I ate half of it but didn't taste a bite. No one, including the Dominus, asked me questions again. I avoided eye contact with Dain.

The Dominus conversed with Pax and Dain, something about the stock market. I got the feeling the two men were important to him. He ignored everyone else.

It had to happen. The scene. I won't say it wasn't my fault, but I suppose I could have prevented it if I'd been in my right and controlled mind. My brain had, unfortunately, turned to oatmeal.

Faulty AC, or something, but the room temperature made a sudden, unexpected spike. Uncomfortably warm, certain of the other ladies with jackets and stoles removed them. Without a thought, I slipped off the jacket. I'm used to my scars. I see them every day and unless one is painful, I take them as a part of me. Of course, when I turned to fold my jacket, I flashed everyone seated near me. It took only seconds to realize what I'd done. Two people could see my back close-up. Garrett Dain and the Dominus.

The look on the Dominus face…oh, I can't describe it. I thought he knew about me. He placed me in a chair beside him. He might have known McKay hurt me, but not received details of my ordeal. This man, my father, had never cared about me. He wouldn't have abandoned me if he had. So, what was I? His child. A possession for his ego.

All conversation ceased. Even those down the table who couldn't see understood a significant drama had unfolded. They could see their leader's face.

I saw where the Dominus, my father, directed his eyes. He was going to try to kill McKay. Right then, at the dinner table. He would fail. McKay was never unprepared. Chaos and wicked disaster for the tribes would be the only outcome. I couldn't allow that to happen. For Lo's sake, for Pax, for Bastet. It would be too much to bear. This time it was I who touched his hand. "Sir. Please. I beg you. Let reprisal be mine."

I'm not sure why I spoke that way, or where those words came from. They had a definite effect. He froze. His face had a look I totally didn't understand. Then he smiled. Genuine.

"You are correct, daughter. Forgive me. Reprisal is indeed a warrior's right." He stood and spoke to his...what? Worshipers, devotees, groupies?

"Enjoy your evening, we will begin meetings tomorrow."

Daughter, the Dominus had named me in front of the leaders of the tribes. With a half bow to me, not the assembled dinner party, he left the room.

Damage control time. I looked straight at Pax. "I didn't know." I hissed the words through clenched teeth. "I swear I didn't know." I didn't want him to think I'd lied or kept something so important from him. He'd dumped me unprepared into a vicious situation, and I'd taken control and acted. Not acted well, but I hadn't fallen to pieces. I needed no acidic comment from him. He scowled and turned his head away.

Chapter Eighteen

The room slowly recovered from the Dominus' departure. The servants went on serving, but a few guests left. I saw them only peripherally but noted that those who hadn't seen my back made sure to get a look. I stared at McKay. If he was worried it didn't show. He'd had years of practice allowing people to see only what he wanted them to see.

Dain watched me closely. He had a gleam in his eye I didn't understand. It seemed part desire, part curiosity, and all amusement. And I was tired of not understanding.

"What?" I demanded. So far, I'd survived not one but two major emotional traumas this evening. I had a right to at least modest irritation.

Dain's eyes widened, followed by a raised eyebrow and another charming smile. "Oh, I'm just surprised. I wasn't aware that such an interesting and beautiful woman lived among the tribes."

I winced and shook my head. "Beautiful? I have no ego left for beauty. If I'm interesting, it's because I'm the new kid in town. Or you have a weird scar fetish."

I closed my eyes and groaned out loud. Could my mouth dig a hole any deeper? I wanted to crawl in that hole and bury myself.

Dain leaned closer. A little more serious. Soft voice, sincere tone. "Your scars are a part of you, brave lady. Do not demean them. Honor to the Tribe of Bastet."

Pax had said the same thing to me the first time he saw the scars.

Dain raised a hand to touch me. Pax growled. Literally growled like an animal. Deep and thick, no throat should have been able to make that sound. I'd heard it once before. Right. From Simone when she attacked me.

At that point, everyone who remained at the table immediately stood to leave. We hadn't had dessert. They jerked and fluttered, seeming disturbed. Dain, not disturbed at all, helped me with my chair again. He disregarded Pax's scorching gaze, but he was careful not to touch me. So, I touched him. Fingers on his hand, no more.

"Thank you." His presence, bringing me back to earth, had averted a nightmare. It was an unexpected lift in a night of revelations that could have crippled me.

"I'll see you again, Lilly." Yes, he would. I liked him. Liked his sense of humor. He'd make a respectable friend if friends were possible among these strange people.

I went to Pax. I left the jacket off and carried it. Let them stare. "Can we go now?"

The moment he said yes, I relaxed. Mistake. Emotions darted across my mind like kids playing tag. Tension created violent stomach cramps. I'd have to let something loose. My legs visibly trembled. Pax had his Sheriff Stone-Face expression, but he led me to the elevator. Down, down. Damn it. Hurry up and get the door open.

Straight to the bathroom, grab a towel to protect

the glorious dress. On my knees before the luxurious throne, I emptied my stomach several times, long after there was nothing left to come up. Dry heaves, stomach cramps, on and on. Oh, my head hurt, throbbing with each strained heartbeat. A quart of tears flooded from my eyes, and my nose dripped like a toddler with a cold.

It did stop. Every muscle I had was limp as a rope. Then Pax had me, lifted me to my feet, and carried me over to one of the benches. He unhooked the clasps that held up my dress and peeled the tape away. Bi'ar dropped to the floor. He kicked it aside. The goddess knife. Again, he wouldn't touch the blade with his hand. I'm not sure how he managed, but he got me into one of those fancy spa robes and sat me down. The bench had a side arm, so he leaned me against it. "Try to hold on, please."

I did, barely. The room came in and out of focus. Thoroughly detached, I watched as he picked up the dress, carefully at least, and placed it back on its hanger. He went out and came back with a glass with an inch of clear soda.

"Drink this. It will ease the taste in your mouth."

I managed that at least. He had a soft wet rag and tenderly washed my face and neck. Cool water spread over my skin, freshening, soothing. He stood behind me and tugged the pins out of my fancy coiffure. I sat there and focused on his fingers slowly drawing hair down to my shoulders. He had a brush ready to ease out the tangles. Why did it feel so delightful to have someone brush your hair? If anyone had suggested that the severe Sheriff of Garnet would be the one to do so, I would have rolled on the floor in deranged laughter.

My mind kept jumping back and forth from that first day when he rudely searched my bags. Wait! I'd just had two of my nightmares come to life, and I was thinking about the man gently brushing my hair. How he had changed. Or had I changed?

When he finished, he lifted me again and guided me to one of the beds. My robe came off, and he slipped a large T-shirt over my head. The stoic, angry man, the one who had threatened to kill me, was putting me to bed like a child. And I let him.

Oh, that bed felt sublime. I may not sleep, but I could rest in comfort. He sat in a chair beside me.

"I tried, Pax. I did. I'm sorry if I messed things up for you."

"You didn't mess things up." He tucked the covers around me. "I'm dense around people. Unless they're causing me law problems. McKay surprised me. The Dominus calling you daughter…it took a while to realize, but everything was staged for you tonight. The only time it wasn't set up was when you flashed your scars. Set up by whom? And why? I don't know. I expect we will find out eventually. You held your ground. Completely unprepared. I'm proud of you."

I let out a long sigh. "I wonder if the show planner got what he was looking for. You panicked McKay. I liked that. And the other, your Dominus, my so-called father. I've only seen him once when I was eight. He told me he was my father. Then he abandoned me, left me to a monster. A set up? Then it had to be him. McKay was surprised to see me at least."

"The Dominus makes it a practice to know everything. No one can predict what will happen around him. I won't call him a tyrant, but a few of us are uncomfortable with his methods. Certainly, he could have met you in private first." He stroked my hair. "As for McKay? No one knows what's up with him. Except Simon, and he's not talking. The Dominus can eliminate any McKay problem—if he chooses. I think he was going to tonight, right there in the dining room. Your scars shocked him. He may have known McKay hurt you—hell, I knew that. But until I saw... Why did you stop him?"

"He has no right. No right to any aspect of my life. Not for love or hate or revenge. He has no right to pretend, to play the protective father." I tried to rise and couldn't. My strength depleted, spent in an intense mind challenging dance with men I hated.

He frowned. "The Dominus is the tribe, all the tribes. In the end, that will count. The goddess chose him. We play his game."

"I don't want a father." I almost said, *but I want you.*

He reached over and dimmed the lamp by the bed. Try to sleep." He brushed the hair away from my face. His fingers lingered on my cheek.

"Pax? You don't know, do you?"

"Know what?"

"I don't sleep. I had a concussion, after McKay hit me in the temple with his fist. I stopped sleeping. I can lay down and rest. But no sleep. Doctors said brain injury."

Pax didn't react to what had to be an outrageous claim. I tried to meditate. It didn't work. He climbed into bed with me. "What are you doing?"

"I'm going to be here if you need anything." He moved his big hard body against mine. Oh, it felt so pleasant, so comforting. I wanted so much to draw him closer.

"Why are you being so considerate of me."

"Because it's my fault. I knew it was too soon, you shouldn't have come here. You need more time, more information. I should have fought harder to keep you away."

He wouldn't have won. Lo stood as an impenetrable wall—or Hurricane Lo, if required. He moved closer and wrapped an arm around me. Oh, he was wearing shorts, but I only had a long T-shirt, probably one of his. I was too exhausted to argue. And his body, warm, strong, offered comfort. This man and I had become intimate. No sex, at least not yet, but intimate all the same. After he went to sleep, I'd get up and do something, watch TV in the next room. I don't remember when I fell asleep. I woke sometime later, my face against his chest. Living, breathing, steeped in his clean scent, I slid my hand up to his cheek. He murmured something and tightened his arms around me. Yes. This was the place to be. When I woke again, the room was light. We'd never closed the curtains. It wasn't possible, but for the first time in three or so years, I'd slept. I didn't know whether to feel angry or elated.

Pax was still asleep, breathing softly. I watched him for a while as the sky grew lighter, then I slipped out of his arms and went to the window. I stretched his T-shirt until it covered the most intimate parts. Silly, since he'd snuggled up against them all night.

The window faced east, and the city lay below. I ignored my customary anxiety triggered by height and watched the sun edge over the horizon, dispersing shadows while it spread the coming day across the city. A new day, a different day.

"Come back to bed," Pax grumbled. "Not time yet."

I went to sit down beside him, as he had me the night before. He stretched, shoving the cover down to reveal that well-muscled chest I'd snuggled against in my sleep. I wanted to run my hands along the warm flesh.

"You do sleep." He grinned. "You even snore." He reached and his arm circled me, dragging me closer. "Well, it's more of a little snort than an all-out deep throated roar."

"I do not snore." I managed a little indignation. Snort? I snorted? I laid my hand over his heart. I loved feeling it beat. My mouth was hovering over his lips…oh, I shouldn't. I needed more time. But I wanted— The phone rang. Right by the bed, its speakers obviously set on high, too damned loud to ignore.

Yes, saved by…the goddess? I jumped up and escaped to the bathroom. Oh, I wanted to explore this new side of the Garnet sheriff, but not like that and not right now. Our time would come. I wanted to think about the fact that I'd truly slept beside him. While it wasn't the strangest in the string of recent traumatic events, I had to ask what happened and were the doctors wrong. Was this sleep because someone was there in the bed with me? Is that all it took? So, could it be anyone? Oh, I could find a big dog to sleep with me. A sudden image of Garrett Dain jumped up in my mind and shouted, *choose me, choose me.* What? I immediately shoved the thought down.

I showered and dressed in a pair of beige slacks, pale blue blouse, and a navy jacket I'd purchase to cover the knife. The topaz went around my neck again. When I finished, I went to a table in the sitting room with Pax. A massive breakfast, eggs, bacon, biscuits, fruit, and blessed coffee awaited me. After losing everything in my stomach last night, I needed fuel. The hotel kitchen provided it in appetizing abundance.

Pax grinned as he watched me eat. "I like a woman who appreciates food."

"I always appreciate anything that isn't peanut butter, oatmeal, or from an institutional kitchen. Are you a cook?"

He chuckled and shook his head. "You saw my place. Don't have time. Don't want to. Damn Ronnie for not allowing a real restaurant in Garnet. Why do you think I go to the Crossing so often?" He went on, using his neutral sheriff's voice. "I'd like you to come to the general meeting at two this afternoon. Meet me here at one-thirty, please. Until then, you're free. You can go sight-seeing, shopping, whatever you'd like. Check with the concierge. She can help you with places that might interest you."

I was ready for that. "There's a sizeable wood carving supply place down south of town. I checked it out on Lo's computer. I've saved enough tips to go get me a small set of real carving knives. You think I can get a cab to there?"

He didn't say anything for a moment. I waited for him to warn me McKay was out there. He watched me across the table and sipped his coffee. Then, "I want you to...please. Use a corporate car and driver. A trained driver will stay with you and take you where you want to go. It's one of the tribe's benefits. Call down to the desk and tell them when you're ready. It's safer, you can go to more places."

"You hesitated. Before you told me to take a car. Why?"

"I want to protect you. I can't help it myself. But I didn't want you to think I was…trying to control you."

"Thank you." Wow! I did not expect that.

"You may use the card I gave you if you want."

"No. I have enough." I'd spent my share of the tribe's money for the week—or year. I needed more time to think about the so-called tribal dividends. I needed to absorb the fact that Frank and I went hungry while Mama rejected money. That one might take a while—or not. Nothing could change what happened, and it might be best to keep those memories locked away. Garnet might be the ass bottom of the world, but I was growing used to the town. I liked my little apartment. I liked the lion who occasionally came to sit with me at night. I liked my better natured customers. I had a job that kept me busy and allowed me time to carve. Garnet had provided me with pleasure I never expected to achieve. For the moment, I had no need of tribal riches.

He stood and when he got to the door, he stopped.

"Lilly?"

"What?"

"That dress is worth every penny of eight-thousand dollars."

"Okay. I'll wear it again sometime. For you, Sheriff. I'll wear it for you." And I'd damned sure take it off for him, too.

Chapter Nineteen

The massive lobby surrounded me like a sparkling fantasyland of wonders as I walked through to ask for a car and driver. I passed the casino where lights flashed, and the noisy rattle and jangle slapped at the ears of entering and departing guests. A familiar voice called. Garrett Dain suddenly appeared at my side, hand on my arm, gracefully stopping all forward movement.

"Good morning." Dressed less formally, sports jacket and slacks, he still made an impression. The attention of two friendly and attractive men in one morning. How was I so lucky? I should hit the casino and see how far my fortune would roll.

Of course, I recognized that Dain didn't intercept me by chance. Stalking? Ah, yes, Pax had warned me about predators in the tribe. Dain's golden gaze measured me with interest. He flashed a leisurely smile. "Where are you off to so early?"

"A woodworking shop south of town. Pax wanted me to get a car and a guard…a driver."

Dain moved closer. He reminded me of the big cat in the arena that night, rubbing his bloody head on my legs to mark me with his scent. He wanted to mark me? I'd bet he would if I let him.

"I have a car, Lilly, and a driver." He also had a roguish smile on that beautiful face. That smile said, *I'm a bad boy and you gotta love me.* "Let me take you out. I know this town. I'll give you a guided tour along the way. I can protect you."

I knew I shouldn't. It would seriously piss off Pax.

"I'd love to go with you, Mr. Dain."

"Please call me Garrett."

This man was tribe. I might not be safe with *him*, but he'd defend me from any outside harm. I'd borne Pax's wrath multiple times for months. I could do it again.

He snatched out a phone and without identifying himself ordered his car. Must be nice. It was there when we reached the portico. A limo. Of course.

I slid across a smooth gray, butter-soft seat. Dain asked, and I supplied him the address of the wood working supply shop. He gave it to the driver, and we rolled out into the morning sunshine.

Dain sat close, his body slightly touching mine. Not presumptuous, but comfortable. The air around him drew images of his forest home into my mind. Cedar, pine, and a touch of summer rain.

He cocked his head. "Woodworking?"

"Yes. I carve." I pulled out my phone and showed him the photos of the owl, mountain lion, and the other pieces I had in progress.

"These are impressive."

I had to laugh. "No, they're not. They're fair, given my tools and the limited availability of suitable wood. I've been saving my tips, and I'm hoping I have enough to get a new set of carving tools."

He frowned. "Tips? You truly do work as a bartender?"

"Yes. I work as a lowly bartender. I live in a motel converted to apartments and tend bar for a living. It's a distinct perspective. But I'm okay. And it beats the hell out of a jail cell."

"I wasn't trying to demean you or your job, Lilly. And you'd be surprised at how I've lived at times." He reached for my hand and gently gripped it between his own. "Including jail cells."

I didn't want to talk about jail. "I'm surprised you haven't yet asked me about last night."

"I'm curious, but no I won't ask. I will note, however, I'm hearing outrageous rumors. It would be pleasant if I had a glimpse of the truth."

I had to laugh. How gratifying. This man made me feel so exceptional. "Okay. I don't know what you've heard, but I'll save you time pandering to gossips. Your Dominus? The man who called me daughter last night. Not much to say there. I've seen him once before in my life. McKay? I was a major player in his criminal organization. I ratted on him to the FBI. The scars? McKay caught me and paid me back. Hospital, surgery, rehab, then to Aunt Lo's tavern. That's about it." Las Vegas contained unusual architecture, hotels, and casinos, steeped in glamor and delight at nighttime, but seemed to drown in despair in the stark morning sun. Dain's fingers, long and beautiful for a man, tightened as if to comfort me.

"I spent the night researching Mr. McKay. I'm sure others did too. The depth of your courage is stunning."

"It's not courage. More like endurance." My mind flashed to Bi'ar. "It's about gaining strength. Fighting back." I pulled my hand from his, reached into my jacket, and drew out my knife. I wanted his reaction. Bi'ar's runes gave a brief glow. "This is 99 percent of my courage, Garrett. They call it Bi'ar."

He stilled, eyes wide, staring at the blade. Damn, why had I done that? Knowing Lo and Pax's reaction, it was not a wise move.

"Put it away, please."

I did so, and he visibly relaxed.

"How long have you had that weapon?"

"Most of my life. I didn't mean to surprise you. I don't understand your reaction. You and Lo and Pax are the only ones I've shown it to, but all of you recognized and accepted it as something significant."

"Lilly, they teach us the story of the three blades in childhood, along with so many incomprehensible histories. We're taught to revere them as true symbols of the goddess. I don't know of anyone in the last two generations who has truly seen them. Supposedly, they show up during times of intense turmoil."

"That's interesting. Lo and Pax treat me as if I embody that turmoil. Rightly so, I guess. Garnet's been kind of hectic since I arrived."

I sensed a change in him, from modest to intense interest. "You have an aura of distinction, an otherness around you. All the tribe members at the dinner last night sensed your difference."

"Okay. You got what you asked for. It's my turn. Your Dominus, what is he to you?"

"The one the goddess chose and expects us to obey."

I had to shake my head at that one. "Expects? I don't know you well, Garrett, but everything about you says you do not live by others' expectations."

He shrugged. "Let's say I'm cautious."

Pax seemed that way too. I had to wonder if a rebellion of leadership was in progress.

Garrett Dain and I had formed a connection of sorts. Not erotic or even romantic, at least on my part, but more than friends. He'd easily stepped past my defenses and into my personal life.

I tried to keep my voice level and unemotional. "The Dominus. He wants something from me. Or has plans for me—which isn't surprising. My life has been planned and controlled by others for some time now."

Garrett shook his head. "But you're breaking free. I saw that last night when you marched bravely into battle. Honest and true words offered with a threat. Arm's length plus eight inches for the blade. You were magnificent."

I grinned. "Walked bravely? Or blundered blindly? I had Bi'ar taped between my breasts. I should have flashed it, too."

He laughed out loud, a deep, jubilant sound that drew me out and forced me join him in mirth. He raised my hand and brushed it with his lips—his sumptuous lips. "And yet, despite your concerns about him, I honestly believe the Dominus was going to kill McKay last night. That would have been inconvenient. You stopped him. Why?"

"A simple truth. McKay's mine. I'll deal with him eventually."

"You're new. You don't know it, but personal battles, even ones deadly as yours, are common among us. Carefully concealed, but common. An entire chapter in the tribal law is devoted to the proper challenge to battle and the proper response. It amazes me. Why have they sent you here unprepared?"

"Amazes me, too." Lo withholding pertinent information could hurt me here. We rode in silence for a while. He kept a warm grip on my hand. When he turned his attention back to me, I had a question.

"Garrett, what does McKay want here? Do you know? Something that will eventually transfer all the tribe's money to him, I'm sure. If he can't make you give it to him, I'd bet he has a backup plan to somehow steal it away."

"I'm not sure. The whole situation is odd. Simon is attached to McKay like a leech. But then, Pallas needs money. I think McKay is offering that to Simon's tribe. That the Dominus allowed it to go so far is extraordinary. I think Simon sees McKay as a savior. What I don't understand is why the Dominus is entertaining the idea of someone from the outside. Controlling strangers among us is in the first commandments of tribal law. Archaic as the law is, we do try to follow."

"Where can I get a copy of that law. Amazon maybe?" *Change the subject, Lilly.* "What do you do for your tribe."

"I'm a corporate lawyer for Ennead."

"Really? You seem…" Oops, stuck my foot in it again.

"What?" His eyes sparkled. "You think I'm too handsome, charming, and witty to be an immoral barrister?"

"Well, sir, at least you are humble and unpretentious. Under the enchanting facade, I sense…restraint. Intense restraint. I feel something restless in you. It's not exactly consistent or compatible with a lawyer's image."

He didn't say anything. Had I offended him? But we had been discussing personal things in my life. It was only fair.

"Ah, we've reached our destination." He sounded relieved.

We'd reached paradise—at least for me. The business had hand carving tools, machine tools, including every saw or router imaginable. And the wood, a whole wall of boards, blocks, sheets, oak, ash, ebony, maple—ah, blissful day. Best of all, a sign pointing the way to the natural uncut pieces I favored.

"What are you looking for?" Dain asked.

"A set of knives. All I have is two multi-bladed knives, and I've worn them down to nothing. I did buy three new ones last month, but I want to look at and use fine tools." Unfortunately, the shop had a multitude of treasures. I wanted it all. Tool sets ranged in prices from one hundred to eight hundred dollars. I turned to him. "I need to bargain hunt. This may take a while."

"No problem. I've devoted my morning to you. I'll find a quiet spot and make a few calls. If you don't mind." He leaned close. Good thing Pax wasn't around.

"I don't mind your calls, Garrett. However, I'm a bit concerned about how I managed to get a *devoted morning* from such a *handsome, charming, and witty* man."

"You think I want to obligate you."

"Maybe. I'll apologize if I'm too suspicious. In my life, everything I gain, material or otherwise, I pay for eventually."

"You're right. We will always pay eventually. You're wise to be wary of strangers, Lilly. But I swear by my tribe and the goddess, I won't hurt you or make any claims on your body or life." That sounded so magnanimous, so noble. But that smile, the warmth. An act? It might be, but I certainly enjoyed it playing out.

I went to study the magnificent tools, a tiny fraction of which I could afford. I made my choice, a two-hundred and twenty-five-dollar, multi-sized tool set, then headed for the exhibition gallery. I fell in love. Sculptures, faces, figures, birds, animals, geometric patterns, and a section of perfect furniture. Every wood possible formed into magnificent art. My simple animal carvings on fallen branches seemed pitiful in comparison. Could I ever create such beauty?

I walked and eventually came across Dain, staring at a wood sculpture. A large piece, three feet high and twice as long. He had his hands in his pockets as if resisting the urge to touch. The look of longing on his face told a story, as did the *not for sale*, sign.

Two wolves raced across the rough ground in pursuit of prey. Exquisite detail and exceptionally fine wood gave it life. I could almost hear their sharp breath and the sound of paws thudding on the ground.

"Could you do this?" Garrett asked without looking at me.

"I don't know. It's more complex than anything I've ever tried. My work has always been smaller and more organic. Like that." I pointed out two nearby pieces where the images, a pair of herons followed the rough, natural shape of the wood.

"Would you try to do your version of this for me?" He reached out but pulled back before he touched the wolves.

"My version? Sure. If I can get the right piece of wood. We can look at what's here. If not, maybe you can find a piece in Oregon. I'll show you what shapes would be best." I held up a finger to warn him. "Don't cut any living trees, I only use fallen wood."

"Why?"

"Old wood has a feeling of time, and it talks to me." I flinched. After all the years of torment, my mind and body still cringed at how Mama would react to such talk. I hated that she retained that power over me. "I mean…I don't mean talk literally."

"Oh, I know exactly what you mean." He nodded at the wolves. "They're calling me." He lowered his voice to a whisper. "They're asking me to run with them. I walk through the forest at home, and the elder redwoods sigh and call for what they've lost since men came."

How utterly amazing. He understood an artist's mind. I started to hug him, but decided it wasn't the time or place.

I led him out where the natural pieces scattered across a massive lot. That wasn't necessarily bad in the dry climate. The weather aged the wood beautifully. Most pieces were junk, too small, too large, or a bad shape. Eventually, I found what I thought would work. I held Dain's jacket while he climbed over a dangerous pile of smaller wood, risking impalement like a vampire, to drag it out. It was too big and awkward for easy carry, so he arranged to have it shipped to Garnet. I did find five smaller pieces for my own collection, and he had them shipped too.

Garrett insisted on buying lunch, and since I'd spent most all my money, I agreed. Yummy food accompanied by laughter and no tension. By the time we were at the door of my suite, I felt relaxed and momentarily happy.

"I'll leave you here," he said. "There's an angry

sheriff inside waiting for you. I'm sure you can deal with him, but I don't want to cause more problems."

"How do you know he's there? And angry."

"Sensitive nose. I smell him."

He suddenly had my shoulders and pulled me close. I let him. When his mouth came down on mine it tasted fine, sweet, and warm. A jolt of desire hit me then. It filled me with sudden yearning for…someone who was not Garrett Dain. Garrett, for all his breathtaking looks and charm, for all his kindness, was not the man for me. Someone else had already claimed my heart.

He drew back and shook his head. "How sad. The most extraordinary woman I've met in years, and she's never going to be mine. But I will see you again, Lilly. I promise you that."

I gave him my best smile and hugged him. Yes, I would see him again.

I opened the door and walked in. Yep, there was an angry sheriff there. He had the stone face on, fists clenched. I'd seen it before. "Where have you been?" "To the woodshop." I held up my bag with the tool set. "Then to lunch. It's barely one o'clock. I'm not late."

"You went with Dain."

That of course was the issue. "Yes, he was downstairs when I went to get a car and offered to take me on a tour. Is that a problem? Do you think him incapable of protecting me?"

"He can protect you. But he's a criminal—an ex-con. You're not supposed to be with him. You're on probation, as you are so fond of reminding me." The accusation in his voice stung.

I shrugged, tossing away his complaint. "Come on,

Pax. It's not like I went out carousing, drinking, gambling. What is wrong with you? I had a perfectly innocent morning shopping, a fine lunch, and I come back to you acting like an ass." *The warm kiss was a sweet secret he should never know.*

He didn't say anything, so I went to the fridge behind the screen for a soft drink. When I came back, I sat on the couch across from him. I'd once dealt with thieves and murderers. I didn't know how to deal with a decent man, who sporadically had the disposition of a tomcat who suddenly realized his owners had neutered him.

"Pax—Sheriff—yes, I'm on probation. You're law enforcement. You brought me here to Sin City under your authority and supervision. You did not dictate any specific rules. Wait. I remember 'be watchful.' Okay, I'm your prisoner. I promise you I'll not make another move without your express and detailed permission."

"You shouldn't have gone with him." Ah, less anger, more petulance. How rare. Did I trouble him that much? I hoped so.

"Well, Sheriff, is there any other person here on your shit list? So I can avoid all contact with them."

"Did it occur to you I might be worried? I have to answer to Lo for you."

I shook my head with vehemence. "That kind of guilt trip doesn't work on me, Pax. *I've done nothing wrong. And you know it.*"

He jumped up and stalked out. Damn. We'd become so close last night and this morning. Now he was acting like a suspicious boyfriend. But he did come back, just before two.

217

Chapter Twenty

Meetings are usually boring. I hoped that after last night's dinner show things would calm down. The basement, a massive windowless square, had carpeted panels floating on wheels that ran in tracks across the ceiling. This divided the considerable space into separate rentable conference rooms. Our section, furnished with a rectangular table and chairs, would not hold the entire group from last night's dinner. I'd set up such for McKay at one time. Occasionally, they ended in violence. Only one door, but I could take out one of those movable carpet panels with a single kick.

The men and women that Pax had pointed out as tribal leaders appeared present. The Dominus hadn't arrived. While we waited for our super-duper leader to show up, I wandered around listening, but not engaging. It was better than standing or sitting in one spot waiting for something to happen. An event, disturbing, if not violent, was on its way. I could hear a familiar rumbling in my mind like an earthquake. I was trapped in a room filled with type A personalities, like Pax, most of whom would be armed. I rubbed Bi'ar in its sheath under my jacket. A single dark memory escaped its carefully locked box in my mind.

Trapped! I'd run to an abandoned factory to hide. I heard her coming. How did she always find me? I was thirteen. Strong enough to stand alone—but she had her vile boyfriend with her. Enough. I pushed him down a flight of stairs. I could have sent Mama after him, but I didn't. Why? Mama. Why? But I was no longer a child. She would never touch me again. A flight of stairs in an abandoned factory building led to my emancipation.

I shoved the memory back in its box. I did walk along that movable carpet wall, cautiously, pushing, testing solidity. Twice I heard, "Hasn't been addressed," and "Will not address," but I never caught the context, only that it seemed incredibly important.

The seating arrangement once again came across as seemed odd. As with dinner, there were markers. Pax and Garrett were seated side by side and me opposite them. Once more I held the honored seat beside the Dominus.

When I did sit, I moved my chair back as far as I could without being obvious. I didn't want my legs trapped under a table if I needed to act. I listened to intuition because it proved correct so regularly before today. The only time I ignored it was when I met McKay. Intuition screamed and danced around in my head that day, shouting danger, danger. Annoyed, I'd locked it in a soundproof box and ran headlong down the path to tragedy.

Everyone fell silent when the Dominus entered. At least he didn't focus any attention on me. He was neither tense nor relaxed, just a CEO at a meeting. First came status reports which were remarkable only because they showed me the breathtaking scope of national and multi-national interests of the Ennead Corporation. It bored everyone but me, and several nodded off only to jerk back to life before they started snoring. Imports, exports, shipping, trucking, manufacturing, all verified to be in the proper order by not one, but two separate reputable monetary management institutions. Talk about overkill. Someone believed in guarding the assets. Maybe they had a sticky-fingered embezzlement problem in the past. Revising security spurred the Dominus to request a report. That interested me. What was their physical security apparatus? Pax had reassured me the hotel was safe, but I'd seen nothing beyond service staff.

Then the Dominus asked if any of the tribes had anything outstanding before the December meeting. No, they did not. Finally, Simon Balance, Leader of the Pallas Tribe, brought in McKay. They hadn't allowed him to attend the regular meeting—unless he'd stood behind one of the flimsy panels.

As McKay's bookkeeper, I'd once plotted the route of stolen money and merchandise to secure warehouses and offshore banks. I'd purchased guns that killed police officers and monitored profits from women in the brutal sex trade. *God. Or goddess. I most humbly begged your forgiveness for those crimes.*

This McKay standing before this gathering, the businessman, I'd seen before. He gave an impressive performance. On a flat screen and computer set up against the far wall, McKay offered charts and reports of a shipping distribution conglomeration in the western states that he could join with one of the Pallas Tribe's businesses. It would provide lucrative profit once integrated with the Ennead corporate structure.

Simon Balance had done his homework, too. He backed up McKay with his own financial statements, everything to show a legitimate organization—on paper.

When he'd trusted me with his finances, McKay had delighted in showing me how he lied and cheated. Anyone paying attention to him in this meeting would have noted how his name did not appear on a single bit of the information he offered. McKay's greatest assets were his incredible intelligence and a psychopath's smooth ability to convince his victims he was on their side. This time, he considered the tribes his marks.

For the first time to my knowledge, his plans, his presentation, failed. I watched their faces, these tribal leaders. Calm, a few bored, a few annoyed, but none offering to commit to his scheme. They didn't ask questions. Had my speech, my performance last night contributed? That would please me. Poor Simon Balance. I could see comprehension of the rising possibility of failure had him emotionally crushed.

I knew the FBI took McKay's organization apart in the east. I knew how long it took him to originally build the business. He'd started years before he met me. How had he organized another one so quickly, one that would provide what he offered? I'd bet money that the whole business proposal was nothing but a scam.

My part, my role here, remained so uncertain. I doubted that anyone, least of all McKay, knew I would flash my scars and offer a terrifying personal glimpse of the monster inside him. Some wouldn't care. Others would have a higher moral standard. My treatment at his hands? All who were interested knew it by now and had likely demanded more information. Not necessarily with any sympathy for me but their Dominus' reaction to my scars had to create doubt. I realized something. The tribe, the goddess, superstition equaled what? A cult. Yep. And I was the newest member.

I'd told Leslie about McKay and the most wanted list, and I'm sure she verified and talked to others. I could tell by a few of the grim faces it troubled some of them. Would they require a vote, or did the big boss make the decision? And the financial details McKay offered? Enormous sums of money, yes, but in terms of the Ennead Corporation's worth, it simply didn't seem enough to take a chance on a man so obviously untrustworthy.

Simon might have pushed the deal through, if he had left out McKay, kept him in the background. But charismatic McKay was too pretty a picture for Simon not to flaunt, not to show off. And without my unexpected interference, McKay might have charmed them. Or would he? The extreme clannishness here had to be factored in. Such was certainly out of McKay's experience. Mine, too.

The Dominus held up a hand. All conversation ceased. He spoke, not loud, but he didn't have to. Everyone's attention was on him.

"Simon, I understand your issues." Balance turned pale and wilted in his chair.

The Dominus went on. "This proposal, on the surface seems legitimate. It would benefit Ennead and Pallas. It is the involvement of Mr. McKay that causes hesitation."

Hesitation? WTF. You don't hesitate with McKay. Not if you want to live. *Last night the Dominus was going to kill the man.* I believed that. Now? Let him sit in a board meeting? What game was this? And who was the referee?

The Dominus hadn't finished. "There are other considerations. Our focus, our goals, involve the welfare and security of the tribes and of the individual members. Then there is the world we live in, which is dangerous, volatile. I will admit we have occasionally stepped beyond certain boundaries in our need to secure our goals." He stopped and stared straight at McKay. "Mr. McKay, will you now, with all honesty, give us the true reason you wish this project to go forward?"

McKay might be a vile, evil man, but he was not a coward. He faced the Dominus. "Sir, should you currently have, or come upon an inordinate resource, one that needed to be concealed and converted, my proposal is a perfect vehicle to quickly and easily circumvent outrageous taxes this country and other countries impose. We will all benefit."

The Dominus touched his fingers to his mouth. Trying not to smile? "Thank you, Mr. McKay, for your honesty."

I wanted to howl with laughter. What a performance. McKay offered to clean the corporation's money to dodge the tax man. *Did I belong, by blood, to a billion-dollar crime family. The Goddess Gang? The Goddess Mafia?*

Bi'ar suddenly vibrated under my jacket. I laid my hand on the hilt and it jumped into my palm, ready to cut, ready to slash. Urgency rose like filling a glass of liquor. I leaped out of my seat and drew it in a swift, smooth motion the knife itself had taught me. One of the fabric-covered panels behind the Dominus burst out. A bulky brute of a man had shoved it aside. He gripped a small cannon in a thick fist. He pointed it straight between the Dominus' shoulder blades. So close, he could not miss.

I moved—or Bi'ar moved me. The gunman

stopped for a second to solidify his aim. My left hand gripped his gun wrist and shoved it aside. I wasn't strong enough to do that except by surprise. My right hand plunged the knife into his heart. It cut through fabric and protective ribs like cutting bread.

He did pull the trigger. Once. Hope no one was in the bullet's path because that size slug would punch through steel. I jerked the knife out. The would-be killer collapsed.

It wasn't over. Pax wrestled with another gunman to the side. Could I help him? No. Simon Balance suddenly stood. He too, had a gun. He pointed it straight at the Dominus. The barrel shook like a tree branch in a fierce wind. Pull the trigger and it could hit anyone.

Throwing a knife looks terrific in the movies. A showy toss and it goes in like poking butter. Courtesy of splendid scene editing. It's not that easy in real life. A human arm had to be exceptionally strong to throw that hard. Distance, balance, the weight of the knife—it all mattered. *Except when it was Bi'ar.*

I threw. Sloppy, like flinging a stick and hoping it would bounce off his head and distract him. A brilliant flash of blue from the runes on the blade, and Bi'ar's hilt stuck out of Balance's chest. The impact forced him to stagger backward. The gun dropped from his fingers. The tribal leader collapsed slowly to his knees. He fell sideways, and he disappeared under the table.

How utterly amazing. Did I do that? Bi'ar, the goddess weapon, killed. But it was Lilly who had wielded the blade. Justified? Two men dead. If I had hesitated to check out the morality of my actions before I struck, the Dominus would have died.

A gunshot, loud, immediate. I jerked my head in that direction. Pax stood over the assailant he'd wrestled down. His gunman lay crumpled at his feet, pulsing blood on the carpet from a large caliber bullet wound. Pax had taken the man's gun and used it against him. Garrett had a third man I hadn't seen arrive in a headlock. With infinite grace, he twisted. The sharp crack of the man's vertebrae snapping sounded louder to me than any gunshot.

Had we not stopped them they could have killed everyone in the room. Fierce, savage, it had only taken seconds for four men to die. What did Leslie say last night? *"All the aggressive warrior traits go to Fenrir and Bastet. It's always been that way. The goddess wills it so."*

Noise filled the room, but no angry shouts, no screams. *And where was the security that they discussed only an hour ago.* I walked to Balance. I had to drag his body from under the table where he'd fallen. Dull eyes, slack face, dead all right. I put my hand to the knife and, as always, it came to me. Blood bubbled up from the hole in his chest. No blood remained on Bi'ar's blade. The incised markings did glow blue for several seconds.

Two men. I'd killed two men. Not that I was a stranger to slaughter. I'd seen men and women die in brutal acts of violence. But only once in my life had I drawn blood myself, and I stopped before I killed. Was I now like…no, not like McKay. Not like McKay at all. Logic and reason shouted at me.

But was it Lilly who killed? Or Bi'ar? No. I wouldn't escape that way. Bi'ar required my hand. I'd accepted the weapon. What did I think would happen when I allowed it to teach me how to fight?

McKay had been sitting by Balance. He remained still, calm as a meditating yoga instructor. No surprise, no shock at what I'd done. Or it was effectively hidden. He smiled as if he could wallow in my success—as he'd wallowed in my agony when he hurt me.

"How does it feel, Lilly?" McKay chuckled. "If you were a man…"

If I were a man… No, not just a man. *If I were him.* I'd be sexually aroused. I'd watched him kill, then had him slam me against a wall, tear off my clothes, and take me while blood pooled around our shoes. I could kill McKay. The knife trembled in my hand. It knew. It wanted more blood. My heart raced, and adrenalin flooded my world.

"Stop it. Hold. Not time."

I heard the voice in my head and felt an unyielding hand clamped on my shoulder. No one was there. No doubt I'd gone as crazy as Mama.

McKay's smile grew wider. "My sweet Lilly."

I walked away. I had killed in defense. I was not a murderer. I sheathed the blade and went to where the Dominus and Pax stood talking. A hand caught my arm. A real hand this time, not imaginary. Dain. He jerked me close. He only offered a few words. "You did nothing wrong. You wielded Bi'ar, the goddess' true weapon, in defense of your tribe. You are a fearless warrior of Bastet." Did he always know the right thing to say? I managed a tiny smile.

"Thank you. My friend."

Pax watched like he wanted to come to me, take me in his arms, comfort me as he did last night. I shook my head. He could do that later.

The Dominus spoke. "Be quiet." He didn't shout but everyone froze, including me. How did he do that? He motioned me closer. He spoke softly, not a whisper, but personal words for me. "May I ask where you got that knife." His curiosity sounded genuine. And a little too intense.

"I don't know. I've had it all my life. I'd like to get rid of the thing. I can't. I throw it away, and it always comes back like a faithful dog. I doubt it will let go until it's finished with…whatever it wants. Or I'm dead. I'm told its name is—"

"Bi'ar. Its name is Bi'ar." His words came out curt and anything but fatherly. Something had changed. Bi'ar disturbed him. It would disturb any sane person. The Dominus knew the blade and its history. Was that a problem for him?

I wanted to go to the suite and soak in that beautiful tub, surrounded by sweet scents. It might take away the acrid, coppery smell of blood. One incontrovertible fact remained. I'd come to Garnet a stranger because of the debt I owed Lo. If not for her, I'd be a cripple—or dead—and Mama would have to live in a state asylum that was one step above hell. Now, I'd irrevocably committed myself to this collection of weird people, kith and kin, my relatives, my tribe. *I'd killed for them. I'd signed my name in the blood of their enemies.* Given the level of violence, I might die for them. There was Lo and Ben and yes, my charming Pax. And their goddess. Okay, I'd claim her too. I squeezed the knife hilt tight. It vibrated in my hand, as if acknowledging my acceptance of my new life—or begging me to kill again.

That's when the FBI troops arrived in force, along

with local police. Shouting, shoving, demanding. I glanced at McKay. Gone! *Yes, of course he was.*

Someone had alerted the FBI about McKay's presence, but the hotel's tribal security had held them back and ruined their grand entrance. And McKay escaped. Goddess, was there never going to be any justice? The Dominus had left us, too.

I spent the rest of that day and all the night in an FBI examination room. They handcuffed me, threatened me with every conceivable charge, and of course, revocation of my probation. In turn, I reminded them that I'd performed my agreed upon duty. *I'd led them to McKay. Twice, even if the second time was not my doing.* Both times, they'd allowed him to escape. Odd, they had no questions about the two men I'd killed. Did someone give them an alternate story of the event, trusting me to volunteer no information?

Ennead Corporation's lawyers arrived. They talked…and talked. Making noise accomplishes nothing.

And, of course, everyone at the meeting except me swore they had no idea of McKay's status on the most wanted list. My interrogators thought I had notified them of McKay. I left them to their beliefs. The feds had confiscated my knife, but that was okay. They couldn't contain it for long. Like my memories, it would eventually escape to haunt me.

When they released me, I rode with one of the lawyers back to the hotel. Marisa Trent, an extraordinarily stern, yet striking woman, didn't talk. I asked no questions. Nine a.m. and the sun, already bright, blinded me. Pax had not returned. He and Garrett had killed men, too.

The suite was empty when I arrived. I started to shower then changed my mind. I went down and bought a bathing suit, two expensive scraps of cloth that barely covered my maimed body. I charged it to Pax's card and went to the vast indoor pool area. Most midnight gamblers had passed out, and the kiddy pool was in a separate room. That suited me. I didn't want to frighten children with my scars. Screw the adults. Let them stare.

An attendant in the locker room graciously offered me a robe and a couple of big fluffy towels. Officially broke, I figured if Pax didn't return, I could rely on room service not to starve. At least until Aunt Lo retrieved me or they kicked me out.

When I stripped off the robe, the few people present stared wide-eyed at my scars and hastily cleared the area. Swimming was helpful in rehab, and I had frequently used it as therapy.

I dove in and swam slow laps in the cool water, until exhaustion satiated me and my legs cramped. I pretended I was swimming in a mountain lake surrounded by snowcapped peaks and green forests.

When I climbed out, Garrett Dain sat at a table not far away. The table sat back from the pool in a small garden area. I climbed out, dried off, slipped on the robe, and went to sit beside him.

He waved a hand at a goblet of a pink frothy liquid sitting on the table. "It's virgin and packed with restorative ingredients. I ordered food. It should be here soon." His own amber liquid drink looked more spirited.

"Thank you." I needed something. Swimming always burned calories, and it had been over eighteen hours since I'd last eaten. Sounds around us increased as more people came to the pool. Laughter, calling to friends, fun in Vegas.

I had questions for him. "Do you know how things are going with the feds? They kept me in a room all night, asked questions, then cut me loose."

"Lilly, don't trouble yourself. You did nothing wrong. Marisa, our extraordinary lawyer, will take care of everything."

I had to smile—in irony, not amusement. "But McKay escaped—again. They, the agents, acted like I was the one who let him go."

Dain shrugged. "Well, somebody has to be blamed. They arrived late for the party. You're convenient and already in the system."

The food arrived then. Small sandwiches of all kinds stacked on a plate, along with fruit and cheese. I dug in. A waiter replaced the sweet fruity drink each time the level fell to half-way.

I sat back, finally full, and sighed. I nodded at the empty plates. "Did you get anything, or did I pig out and eat it all?"

"Oh, I managed to sneak a few bites." He blessed me with a warm, generous smile, and his eyes sparkled with pleasure. I guess I was his entertainment for the day.

"Lilly, would you have dinner with me tonight? Then a show. Cirque du Soleil, Celine Dion, there are so many. It won't make you forget what's happened, but being around people enjoying themselves can be infectious. It might relieve the stress."

I wanted to go. So bad, I wanted to go.

I drew a breath to say yes when I realized Pax

stood behind me. Of course, by now I knew his scent. Sleeping in the bed with a man will do that.

"I don't think…" I let out a breath.

Dain's eyes narrowed. "You need permission. For dinner and a show? I'm not proposing a bacchanalian orgy." His words were for Pax, not me.

Pax growled. How did he make that sound? It came from deep in his chest and meant something. But what? It also drew something from deep inside me, something I couldn't define.

He laid a hand on my shoulder. "She's on probation, Dain. She's not supposed to associate with known felons. Yesterday she had to…"

Yesterday she had to kill two men.

Dain slapped a fist on the table so hard I flinched. "Is that how it is, Harrow? You brought her here, to a city full of lights and entertainment, and you won't allow her to touch what's within her reach? Are you any better than the man who locked her in a room on her last visit?"

Oh, I was happy Pax was behind me. I didn't want to see his face right then. Caught between two powerful men I froze, defenseless like a rabbit with a steel trap on one side and a fox on the other.

Pax broke. The hand that he'd clamped on my shoulder relaxed.

"Lilly can go where she wishes." Pax let out a long sigh. Had he been holding his breath—or holding his temper.

Dain wasn't buying the statement. "Go? Without consequence? Without reprisal?"

"Yes, of course. She's not a prisoner." Pax spoke neutral, measured words, then walked away.

I followed his progress across the room and out the door. He didn't look back.

Dain had his fist clenched on the table. I believe he wanted a fight. "Did I cause problems for you?"

"No." Pax wouldn't hurt me. I believed that.

"Lilly, if anything bad ever happens to you because of something I did, I won't let it stand. I promise you I will make things right." I could see how disturbed he felt by the look in his eyes and the way his other hand gripped his glass.

"I take responsibility for my own actions, Garrett. I can't accept any promises. I don't think I can give you anything in return."

"I require nothing. I think I told you that before. Now, will you go with me? I'll pick you up at seven."

I wanted to go. "Cirque du Soleil? But…how do I dress? I don't have the right clothes here."

"Wear what you wore the first night. You were magnificent."

"Okay. I promise I won't take the jacket off."

"Then I will be disappointed, I suppose."

"You actually do have a scar fetish, don't you?" In the bathing suit he'd seen that the scars on the front of my body equaled those on the back.

His laughter broke out and circled the room. Then I had to laugh, too. That was it, what I liked about him. I'd learned that Pax did have a sense of humor. But Dain? He recognized how an incredibly amusing life was the theater of the absurd. Tight ass Pax would never see it that way.

I did have one other question. "Before the meeting yesterday, people kept talking about something and why it wasn't being addressed. It seemed important.

Urgent. Do you know what it is?"

His lovely mouth pinched. "Yes. The ten tribes only had six children born last year. Something is wrong. And our leader, our direct connection to the goddess, refuses to discuss the issue."

"So, if the tribes don't have children…?"

"We will become extinct. We'll survive as human beings, but our uniqueness will be gone. Change, the thing our goddess has held at bay for thousands of years, will be upon us."

"Do you think that's bad?"

"Yes, Lilly. I'm her child, her servant. I want our people to survive."

I wouldn't speak of it to him, but the odds of my having children was miniscule. McKay's beatings robbed me of that, too.

Chapter Twenty-One

I didn't see Pax the rest of the day, and since I had no money of my own and needed the exercise, I walked. Several people followed me, of course. I don't know who set up my guard, Pax or the Dominus. Maybe the FBI, since there were a number of different faces among my shadows.

I pushed aside the fact that I'd killed two men yesterday. In rehab all the atrocious scenes of my life played out like movies in my mind. My constant efforts to control the memories paid off, even if a rare, but inevitable, crash and burn left me vulnerable on several levels.

I window shopped at a mall, spending time on the jewelry. Cut stones are beautiful, but I'd bet they wouldn't talk to me like those I pulled from the earth myself.

I didn't want to owe Pax or the tribe more money, but I did find an inexpensive little back street consignment shop. I purchased a simple hundred-dollar black dress and shawl for the evening. I could pay that back out of my tips. Oh, it was far less spectacular than my copper beauty. I'd paid for that dress, heart and soul. I didn't know if I could make myself wear it again.

Pax wasn't there when Garrett picked me up at the suite for a superb dinner. I followed his recommendations and tasted amazing edible things I would never otherwise consume. I broke cover and sipped a little wine. He was funny and told me wild stories of his hometown in the Oregon mountains.

The show? Spectacular. I'd never seen anything like it before. It impressed upon me how small my world was, and how little I knew except what I'd intermittently seen on television. Garrett and I talked but didn't discuss the tribes, the meetings, or the attack. He'd spent years overseas, and I wanted to hear about it all. I also wanted to know a little about his felonious adventures, too, but he wouldn't go there.

In the car on the way back to the hotel, Garrett lifted my hand and kissed my fingers.

"Lilly, if you ever have trouble, if you ever need me…"

"I have all your information, Garrett. I appreciate your kindness."

"I want your friendship. My intuition—or my desperate hope—tells me you are at the center of a momentous event in the story of the tribes. You will, somehow, bring change. I want to be there, to see it, to live through the coming days."

"So, are you a seer? A fortune teller?"

"No. But I'm not blind. That shiny knife you carry is one of the most precious relics of all the tribes. No one has seen it or the other two in my lifetime. I know it's goddess-given to one she finds worthy." As with Pax and Lo, Garrett held deep beliefs. He continued, "But I beg you, be cautious. What I'm hearing, facts and rumors, disturb me. I'm worried and suspicious—of everyone now. Simon was once a powerful tribal leader. What could McKay have done to influence him so?"

"McKay is charismatic, hypnotic. He draws people into his sphere of power, men and women, uses them, then tosses them away. When I first met him, he was like a demi-god who offered me a piece of his glory. He adored me. He was my perfect lover. Please. No more talk of him."

Garrett did kiss me again at the suite door. Lovely, but no fire, nothing thrilling.

Two a.m., and Pax waited up for me. From the number of empty bottles, he'd consumed a quantity of beer while I was gone. He didn't say anything. To my surprise, it made me a little sad.

The room phone rang. Pax answered and offered it to me. The Dominus wanted to see me in his penthouse suite. Well, it had to come sometime. Pax's mood went from annoyed to…what? Alarmed? Fearful? All sullen behavior vanished, and he wrapped his arms around me. "Please be careful."

"Pax. I'll be fine." He released me with a light kiss on my forehead. I went back out and headed for the elevator. A coldness overcame me and settled in my bones. My memory boxes containing all of Mama's abuse threatened me with hysteria. If my father keyed one open, they might all shatter and overwhelm me. I feared the contents of my own mind.

The Dominus, the powerful goddess chosen superior of the tribes, opened the door. He'd removed his suit jacket but didn't look relaxed. He reached out to embrace me. I stepped back. He winced and looked away. He was a handsome father figure and could benefit a child—if he'd stuck around. By unfortunate circumstance of birth, and my own actions, I somehow had become a player, a major player, in his tribal game. I had killed two men, one hired killer and one tribesman, so he could live. I owed him nothing, expected nothing, wanted nothing. The time he could provide for me had long passed.

The penthouse suite surrounded me like a lavish furniture store window. The luxury far outclassed my own rooms. Muted colors, every piece artfully arranged, but with absolutely no signs of life. A lazy housekeeper's paradise. The place was so sterile temptation rose to run my fingers across surfaces in search of stray dust particles. Glass walls did offer a magnificent view of the city. One glance, and I stared at the floor. No, I didn't like heights.

The Dominus offered refreshments. I refused all but the water he brought to me from a fully stocked bar. No mini fridge hidden behind a screen here. I sat on a lovely couch but had to squirm a bit to get moderately comfortable. Or the discomfort came from the situation and not the furniture. He sat on an identical couch across from me. He'd placed a bottle of amber liquid, an empty glass, and my water on a low table between us. A glass of water with ice. No plastic bottles for the penthouse.

He appeared warm, loving, and thoughtful, so perfectly paternal. He started talking, and that was best. I didn't know what to say.

"Lilly, I called and talked to Luella today. I'm sure someone already regaled her with the gossip of your stay here. I wanted to reassure her of your safety. I know she's denied you information. To me, that's unconscionable, but I'm sure she had her reasons."

"I love it when people talk about me when I'm not

around. But of course, Aunt Lo is my temporary probation officer and has the authority."

I'd disturbed him. Just a tiny twitch, but I think I punched a pin hole in his façade of calm fatherly presence. "Lilly, forgive me. I want to explain how this came to be. I do understand if you never wish to see me again. You have cause. Yesterday you learned how complex, how serious the tribes are. Aggressive by nature and culture, we have problems. One of those problems led to contact with Mr. McKay." His voice, low and deep, vibrated and swirled around me. Impressive—and calculated. I could pick out the distinct undertones meant to soothe and control me. I'd once practiced my listening skills to stay ahead of McKay. I had to anticipate when he was going to kiss me—or hit me.

"You must understand, Lilly. Around the time you were born our leader had set the tribes against one another. He was determined to control everything through chaos. I and others removed him."

He gave a wave of a well-manicured hand as if to dismiss the *removal*, the probable killing of a human being. I think he wanted me to accept the necessity and propriety of his actions. Fine. I had no right to judge him.

He went on. "I was born a member of the Siris Tribe, located in Florida. I met Louise when she came there for a vacation."

He kept his eyes on mine, and I did my best to imitate that blank expression Pax had perfected. I needed to determine what the Dominus wanted. And why Pax was worried about this meeting. No, I would not trust this man. It was personal, not objective, but I'd abandoned expecting anything from a stranger who had abandoned me.

Looking at him more closely, at his full square face and high cheekbones, I could see that all my physical features came from Mama.

His mouth pursed as if it didn't want to voice the words he desired. "Marriage among the tribes, because of our small numbers, is important. We no longer arrange mandatory marriages, although it was an excellent way of insuring our survival as a people in the past. Marriage is a major contractual event and sworn before the goddess. That doesn't mean we don't become estranged. I was married to a woman from another tribe when I met your mother."

He took a long swallow from his glass, then refilled it from the bottle in front of him. I picked up my glass and sipped the water. It tasted sweet for a moment, then cleared. Chemicals added to kill the taste of chlorine. Garnet's water, pure and precious, had no need of such treatment.

"Louise never told me she was pregnant. She left Florida and went home to Garnet where, I'm told, you were born. She refused to see me again. I did not know Louise had become so seriously ill. She seemed perfectly normal when I talked to her." He drained his glass—again.

"Tribal law gives mothers inordinate power over their children. Protective rules written in a time and place where women outside the tribe were nothing more than property. The law did not require her to name your father, but to only swear by the goddess you were pure tribe. I didn't learn of your existence for five years, and then only by accident."

Gave inordinate power. To me, inordinate usually reads as excessive, unwarranted, unreasonable. He drained and refilled another glass. What was he drinking? It did not seem to affect him, and he displayed no sense of pleasure in consumption.

"I don't know why Louise left Garnet, why she took you away. When I learned of you, I did contact her. She was in Chicago, and she allowed me to see you that one time. I wasn't supposed to tell you who I was, but I managed to get those words in. She demanded that I never speak of you or see you again. I offered her money, begged her to let me help. She refused. Since she'd never *officially* acknowledged me as your father before the tribe, I had no standing to act further."

Now that offended me. "Adherence to a rule, an ancient law, comes before the welfare of the children?"

"Unfortunately, yes. When you study our history, you will understand."

I remained silent, sipping my water. It was his scene, not mine. He continued. "About that time, things became more complicated and dangerous in the tribes. I realized that because only Louise knew I was your father, her silence might keep you safe from my…enemies. I walked away."

"Enemies? What the hell did you do that created enemies who would attack your children?"

He shrugged and smiled. Irony, not mirth. "Oh, my dear, while I am not the vile murderer that your McKay is, I am not a morally outstanding human being. I desperately wanted my people to survive with the tribal structure intact. Eighteen years ago, I seized complete control of the bankrupt, disarrayed Ennead Corporation. Many violently disagreed with that action. I have many faults, many weaknesses, but I am a superb businessman. I made it what it is today. Rich and powerful. During that time, the goddess chose me to be Dominus. I gained much, but I also lost. I had no thoughts of you, no thoughts of anything except surviving, achieving power, and saving the tribes from extinction.

"You didn't speak to Lo about me, ever, until now?"

"About you, no. Everything Luella and I have spoken of over the years involved tribe. I've made mistakes. I have regrets. All men do. I asked no questions. I never had or made the time to learn more about you, where you were or how you fared in life."

"Did the goddess tell you anything about me? I know I'm not important, but I'm curious."

He shook his head. Sympathetic, I think. Or agreeing that I'm not important. "It's not like that. I receive her messages when she needs me to act. No words. Just images. I wish she would be more concise, but I take what I get." He set his glass down, refilled it again, but this time didn't drink. "Thank you for stopping me from attacking McKay at the dinner. An attack on a guest would break tribal law and precipitate disaster. Even if, by that same law, he shouldn't have been there with us. And it certainly made me a hypocrite, suddenly defending you after my previous parental neglect."

A tiny swirl of dizziness clouded my eyes, then glided away. "McKay needs to be attacked. But not now, not by you acting as my father or the Dominus."

"I was told he hurt you, but only in a gossip kind of story. I didn't know you'd be here until hours before you arrived. I didn't make the connection, and I didn't know the extent of your injuries. I don't expect you to forgive me." His plea sounded sincere, but a broken piano could make music if you hit the right keys.

"My mother was…ill. My mother was the fiercest factor in my life. For me, a father didn't exist." Mama's illness focused on me. My focus was avoiding pain and surviving.

He held out his hands. "If you ever need me now, call, come to me. I will help you. It's not enough to wipe away my failure as a father, but it's what I have." He lowered his gaze and relaxed. Had telling me been that hard? Most of it sounded rehearsed.

What had I expected? He'd offered a warm daddy reception. I'd rejected the offer. Maybe he'd answer questions.

"When I arrived in Garnet, Lo told me to accept things as they happened and ask questions later. It hasn't exactly worked that way. Answers to questions from her are as vague as a parent's when a child asks about sex. Will you answer a question?"

"If I am able, yes."

"Are you my brother Frank's father?"

"No. He was nine years old when I met your mother."

Would that make Frank happy or sad? I didn't know.

My father/Dominus had more to tell me. "I am demanding that the FBI return your knife. Is it really…?"

I shrugged. "Bi'ar? It seems so, but I only heard that little myth about the knives and their purpose weeks ago. Don't worry about getting it back. The

242

damned thing comes and goes whenever and wherever it wants. I'm likely to go home and find it in my sock drawer."

He tensed. Only a moment, a miniscule twitch. I'd surprised him. Why? Had he been skeptical about the actual evidence of his goddess and Bi'ar suddenly proved it? No, that made no sense. Every person I'd met in Garnet seriously believed in the Gifts if not her. Why not him, her chosen conduit to her people?

He smiled then. I shivered because it was not a nice smile. "Lilly, we, the tribes, are not a peace-loving people. You belong to us. You are a most worthy member, and I'm proud of you."

I accepted his praise and carefully stowed it away in a memory box to take out and deal with another time. It did raise another specter. Violence as part of my genetic makeup? Is that what drew me to McKay in the first place.

No. Later. Think later.

A rumble of thunder shook the building. "It rains here?"

"Yes, it rains. Not often, so the ground doesn't absorb it all. It causes flash floods at times."

Another rumble, distant, but the flash of lightning brightened the windows for an instant.

Information had come to me in pieces. A problem because it often didn't exactly match what I'd learned or even my actual experiences. "One concept I don't quite understand are the Gifts. And why no one talks about them."

"No one talks about them because it's one of the goddess's most powerful laws. It's laid out and repeated in minute detail. Some Gifts are visible.

Healers and such. Other Gifts are powerful and incredibly dangerous. We couldn't function as a society if we were too fearful of each other. That has happened before. We don't brag, we don't use the Gifts as a conduit to power. Tribal law says *She* can withdraw them if she chooses."

"What makes you leader? Is it the mental images from the goddess? Or do you have unique or multiple Gifts?"

He watched me, more calculation, more manipulation. I didn't hate him, but I was getting closer. "Lilly, my original Gifts were withdrawn and replaced by my personal connection to the goddess. When I accepted her call to service, my hair, once dark as yours, turned white."

He brushed his hand over the side of his head. "It is a mark of my place in the tribe."

I remembered Lo's dreams. "Someone told me the goddess gives dreams. Communicates with tribe members at times."

For a fraction of a second, his face distorted, and I recognized absolute fury. Just as fast, it softened. "They are mistaken. Dreams? No. That's not the way it works. I alone receive commands and carry out her wishes."

I stared out the window. Distant flashes illuminated the night. Lo's dreams were real, not imaginings. She wouldn't lie. "The men, the ones Garrett, Pax, and I...killed. Hired guns. I've seen the type before. Rushing into a room...did they intend to take out the whole tribal leadership. Or was it something else?"

"I believe it was Simon's plan to take over if we rejected McKay. I think myself and other leaders were targets. I'm still investigating. I'm sorry you had to kill."

"Simon's plan? Not McKay's? He keeps hired hit men like that under contract all the time. Put them in a closet and pop one out when needed."

"No, my information said Simon, though the actual on the ground contract may have come through McKay, who seems to have disappeared. I know he's a threat to you, and I have allotted resources to find him. Please be careful until then."

McKay disappeared? Of course he had.

My father/Dominus' story seemed logical, plausible, covering most angles. Life was never that clean, never that easy. At least, mine never was. I could accept it for now. Acceptance. Not confidence. Yes, he abandoned me, but for what he considered valid reasons. Perhaps if I gave it time, I might even like him. He could not disappoint me more than I'd been disappointed in the past.

My father, the Dominus of ten so called tribes, left me with a phone number, told me to call any time if the FBI harassed me. FBI? I was sure it would only be Hart. Dogged, determined Hart, who had a virtuous reason to pursue me.

When I left the suite, I allowed my father to embrace me. Awkward and uncomfortable, for me, but he held on. "I'm sorry, Lilly. I'm so sorry." I could hear unshed tears in his voice. Genuine? Magnificent acting skill? I suspected I'd find out eventually.

Close in his arms, I noticed one detail. He'd said the goddess had turned his hair white when she chose him. I saw a tiny fraction of dark roots. His hair wasn't naturally white. It seemed important since he'd called it a symbol of his power. I filed the fact away to discuss with Lo later.

I returned to the suite at four a.m. I didn't go in the closed bedroom door. I felt no need to sleep, but a part of me wanted to go crawl in bed with Pax. Okay, so he was being an ass. I perused the room service menu and ordered many different items, just to try them out.

When Pax rose, he told me to pack to go home. It didn't take long to gather up our things and call the porters. There would be no more meetings until December.

Of course, Garrett was there when the valet brought our SUV. He locked me in a warm but chaste embrace and told me he'd come to see me, maybe for the Solstice.

The trip back to Garnet was, at first, remarkable for its palatable silence. Until Pax broke it.

"Did you enjoy your night?"

"What?" I jerked. The passing barren landscape had hypnotized me.

"Your dinner date."

"Oh, that. It was good not to think about... everything that happened. Terrific food. Garrett makes me laugh. And that show. Wow. Maybe I can go again someday."

Pax frowned. "And the Dominus?"

"Awkward. He made sorry, uncomfortable excuses." I burst out laughing. I tried to keep it to a tiny giggle, then it erupted into full blown mirth. Jealous. Pax was jealous of Dain and the time I spent with the Dominus. How could that be?

Mirth fled another mile down the road. My life, the sickening ride of highs and lows, suddenly backhanded me. For the third time, I completely crashed. A total wipeout, my so-called photographic memory let loose in a vicious flood. Memories of running in terror from Mama. Watching friends die, of fear, of pain, all burst out and assaulted me in waves. And I'd killed two men. The sound, blood…I did that, not McKay. Something dripped from my chin. What? Oh, I was crying.

My mind played back memories of watching McKay kill and my own sins, every single one. Over and over I could see it, feel it, in obscene detail. Screams, gunshots, and the grunts of big men as they crushed and raped me. Begging McKay to stop killing people around me. All the violence superimposed over a vision of burns and bloody slashes on my own body.

"Lilly! Lilly!" Someone shouted, shook me, hard. Pax? He'd parked the vehicle on the side of the road. When did that happen? Standing beside my open door, Pax shouted again over the roar of interstate traffic.

He climbed up to be closer. I stared into his eyes, gold now, not dark. He pulled me into his arms, and I hung on.

"It hurts. I can't. My fault. Mama…McKay. He killed because of me. Saw it in her eyes, the hate, why did she hate me so?" *Oh, now that made sense.*

Pax spoke into my ear. "Listen to me. Let go of the guilt. If you were the monster you think you are, I would despise you. I would drive you out of my home and protect my people. You're human, my love. I swear in the goddess' name I will never hurt you. I want to protect you, but you won't let me."

I couldn't speak. Couldn't think. He held me until the shaking eased. When he climbed back in the driver's seat, he produced a white handkerchief like the one he'd given me to carry my stones on that first day. I could see the wet spots on his shirt where I'd cried. The visor mirror stared back at me. Red eyes, wet, swollen, I cleaned up as best I could.

Pax carefully merged back into the line of vehicles. "I'll stop at the next exit and get you something to drink. We need to move. I don't want a trooper to come along and ask me what's in the back." Yes, he had a load again.

"I'm sorry. I didn't mean to delay you."

"No delay. What's a touch of PTSD among friends?"

Oh, what a marvelous man who had come into my life. Wait. Had I heard him call me *my love*? Relief struck me like a low note on a piano when we crossed back into Arizona.

As I predicted, I found my knife, Bi'ar, lying on the table when I arrived at the apartment. Magic Gifts indeed. I hated the weapon. I didn't want to touch it at all. I'm sure the FBI was frantic right then, too. Lost evidence? How careless.

I glared at it. "Leave me alone, damn you." Okay, now I was talking to a knife. "Go haunt someone else. Tell your goddess…tell her I can't keep doing this. I can't." I hid it in the back of my closet.

Chapter Twenty-Two

The Equinox festival had two more days to run, Saturday and Sunday, so I went straight back to work. That helped ease a degree of the pain and confusion. Pax and I had an understanding. Not sure where it would go. He was away for days after he dropped me off. I received an embrace and a sweet kiss, but his urgency to go was palatable. Not necessarily an escape from me though. He didn't want to talk, not yet. I understood. We both needed time to assess things.

I did have to take a couple of hours to tell Lo everything. We sat at a table in the empty barroom, and she served me made-from-scratch cheesecake with cherries and a perfect glass of wine. So delicious, so sweet. I think I could endure most anything with enough of Lo's cheesecake.

Once I started my story, I must have been clear and concise. She didn't interrupt, even when I told her about Pax in my bed and my sleeping when I huddled so close to him.

Shock was too small a word. The Dominus/father thing hit her hard. "I've known Charles for years. You told me about a white-haired man, but I never made a connection. Louise refused, absolutely refused to discuss anything. She swore you were tribe, but never more than that."

"Lo, he said he was appointed by the goddess. Is that important?"

"Yes, it means the goddess can deal directly with him, not just through dreams. He's the goddess conduit for all the tribes. Once, each tribe had a goddess-chosen. Something happened. We don't know what. He is the only one she speaks with now."

"But you had dreams. He told me that couldn't happen."

She stopped, and her eyes got that far away look that indicated deep thought. Finally, she shook her head. I didn't understand that.

"Everyone's nervous around him. Wary. Why?" I leaned forward and gripped her hand again.

Lo took a breath. I could tell she was prepared to dump a load of unbelievable on me.

"The goddess gave him the power to kill. He can, from a distance, with his mind, stop hearts. He can also cloud minds, force obedience. It's not…a Gift."

"And he does this…when?"

"In the early years, when we'd fallen into dangerous war, I believe he did. Never since we made peace and agreed to abide by the tribal law again. But he would certainly retain the ability."

"He hasn't killed? Not since the troubles?" I had to clarify. "That you know of?"

"That I know of." She shook her head.

I remembered my father's reasons he hadn't come for me. Tribal war? Yes. It could be. But the ability to do a *remote control kill?* Certain of the fantastical things I'd seen and heard were real. Humans sporadically fall dead for no apparent reason, but science usually sorts it out.

"Lilly? You had to kill men? Even a tribal leader?" She reached across the table and again caught my hands in a fierce grip. Tears formed in her eyes. "I'm so sorry. I didn't mean for that ever to happen."

I squeezed her hands in return. "You didn't know."

"You did right, protecting the Dominus, but oh, my sweet goddess, you shouldn't have to carry that burden. All I wanted was for you to meet other tribes, learn more about our structure."

"Sweet? Lo, she gave me the damned knife." My voice rose, and she winced. Control. I had to keep control. No more breakdowns. I released her and cut another piece of cheesecake. "Well, I won't carry it again. I'll throw it in the deepest hole I can find, and if it comes back, I'll do it again. Let's talk about something else."

Getting rid of Bi'ar was a lie, and I knew the minute I spoke the words. It had stayed with me most of my life. It remained irrevocably mine. One thing nagged me, just an idea. Should I ask? Yes. "Lo, you know I trust you."

"I do. That is so precious to me. For you, so betrayed, it's rare."

"I need information. Real answers, no more withholding. I wouldn't ask if I didn't feel it was vital. It's like a grain of sand in my eye or a pebble in my shoe."

She leaned forward. "Then ask, Lilly. The goddess has touched you as she never touched me." I didn't like that look of awe in her face.

"Yeah. I'm so blessed." She winced slightly at my sarcasm. "It's a puzzle I'm putting together. Talk more about the so-called Gifts."

Lo's fingers played with the ruts in the table carved by thousands of drunk and not so drunk patrons. "Lilly, your Gifts, memory, the ability to carve by touch, are benign. Healing like Doc's Gift is fantastic. There are a few though, that can turn to evil. I have one of those. I can control minds. I can force commands on people if I choose. Not on the Dominus' level. He's far higher than me. And not just tribe members. I used it—"

"On the guy that attacked Ben, my first day here."

"Yes. I sent a psychic command for him to stand motionless, then fall unconscious."

"Command. You demanded with force? Can you make them believe that a suggestion is their idea? What's your distance? How many can you do at one time?"

"Wait, wait." She jerked back. Maybe she wanted to escape.

Once I'd recovered from my outside Vegas breakdown, I'd spent hours in contemplation.

Lo gulped a whopping swallow of her wine. She set the glass on the table but gripped it in both hands as if it would escape should she relax. "Yes, Lilly. I'm strong enough to command certain people to do things, evil things, against their wills. And they won't know it didn't come from their own minds. But not everyone. Far from everyone. And there are degrees. Some I can't touch. I must be able to see the person. Only one person at a time." She chewed on her lip, obviously uneasy.

"Can you make a heart stop beating like you say the Dominus can?"

She gave a furious shake of her head. "No. I can only…no."

"Okay, now, I want you to try to force me to walk across the room. I want to know what it feels like."

"What? No. Why would…no." I think the look on

252

my face, whatever it was, convinced her.

Lo leaned back and relaxed. Her face went slack, trying to calm the turmoil, I'm sure. She drew a deep breath.

I felt nothing. I tried to open myself, as if I were going to relax and meditate. Still nothing.

Lo frowned. "That's odd. I can't seem to reach you."

I grasped her hand. "Try it now. With touch. Command, Lo. Put all your will into it. Make me do something."

She squeezed my fingers. She relaxed, then grunted and frowned. "Oh, there you are. But I can't. Let me in."

I relaxed too. Her warmth, her love, surging into my mind almost overwhelmed me. Oh, if only she'd been my mother. *No, Lilly. Accept what you've received. Don't fall into that fantasy.*

"Do it, Lo. Force me." Her eyes narrowed as she concentrated.

Her demand of me didn't come in the form of words. It came as a feeling. I wanted to go. I needed to leave the tavern. She pressed harder. Uncomfortable, but then I leaned into it—and shook it off. And I certainly knew it hadn't come from my own mind.

Her action had triggered something, though. An image of me, sitting with the Dominus, only he sat beside me, not across from me. He shouted ferocious words. *"Damn you, let me in!"*

I had remembered the most traumatic events in my life like staring through a sharp focused lens. Others, not so clear. But the memory of the Dominus' fury, demanding entry into my mind... Somehow, though, he'd made me forget. I remembered the slight sweet taste of the water. He'd drugged me. What else had he done?

A spasm of intolerable terror caused my stomach to tighten and threaten to reject the wonderful cheesecake. I shoved it aside. I would not give in.

Lo's voice softened with relief. "I cannot command you, Lilly. I expect that immunity to mental commands may be one of your Gifts. Your protection."

"Are there any others like you?"

"Possibly. Remember. We don't discuss the Gifts. And we only call upon them when needed. If I talked about my Gift of mind control, everyone would shun me. I learned early to keep my mouth shut."

I remembered Simon's desperate expression, his shaking hand, impossible aim. Was he fighting someone's command to kill? *Was I set up to kill Simon?*

I wanted more. "Lo, what if you tried to force someone who was resistant like me, to do something, using all your power?"

"I would never do it, can't conceive of it at all."

"Guess."

She frowned and swallowed another big gulp of wine. Was I driving her to drink?

Lo finally answered me. "It would, I suspect, depend on the person. A weak-willed person, one susceptible to suggestion, manipulation, would not think to resist. And there, it would depend on what I wanted that person to do. I'm not sure a weak-willed person would harm someone they loved."

"What if the person was strong?"

"They would fight. Maybe break down if I prevailed. Mind damaged, insane." She looked up sharply. "You don't think…Louise? Someone with the Gift forced or tried to force her to do something against her will. Maybe it broke her mind? But her decline began in puberty."

I leaned back and stretched. "I don't know. It's guesses, possibilities from an unknown. It's stupid, looking for excuses. Mama is mentally ill. Nothing will fix her."

"Welcome home, Lilly Dusalte, welcome home. As for Louise, the severity of her illness, there were other factors involved. We're twins. We have a connection. I would have known if someone tried that. I'd lived with her decline." She poured another glass of wine. "So, what about you and Pax?"

"Me and Pax. Is there a *me and Pax* equation here?"

"Darling, you've exchanged personal tokens. By long standing tribal custom, that means something serious."

My hand went to my chest where the topaz hung on its chain. "He gave me a pretty stone, and I gave him a piece of old wood I'd carved. It's no big deal." *Liar, liar.*

Lo laughed out loud. The wine was taking over. "That stone belonged to his mother, Lilly. She returned to the goddess when he was fifteen. He loved her and mourned for years. And that sculpture, you created it with your own hands. He called me, so excited, to come and see it. Both are deeply personal. And precious. I'd never seen him like that. You'll understand him better soon."

"I'm processing things. If you'd seen the way he acted with Dain. Oh, hell. The dense fog of maleness almost drowned me."

"Oh, yes. I know Garrett Dain. He might lead you astray, get you in trouble, but I don't think he'd hurt you."

Oh, yes. Garrett Dain would lead me wonderfully astray if I would allow him.

I rubbed the back of my neck. I needed more rest. "I think the sheriff was born in a starched uniform. I'm not sure how to deal with his stubborn maleness. I don't understand why I slept when he was in bed with me. I've been awake for three years."

"I don't understand that, either. Pax is…complex."

"I totally piss him off." I had to admit that. "Never intentionally. I'm just being me."

"And he'll accept you, eventually."

****

The official week ended on Saturday evening with a big barbecue cooking contest in the tavern's parking lot. I worked my ass off right along with Lo. They drafted me as a barbecue judge. I'm not a big eater, but yum. A spectacular firework display over the desert completed the day.

I didn't see much of Pax during that time. Pax and Deputy Ben had their share of toil, too. Private security plus the Arizona State Troopers racked up duty time. When I walked outside Sunday morning, most of Garnet's peace had returned. A couple of trucks and a clean-up crew were making the flat and empty carnival site barren desert again. Best yet, a line of RV's and trailers exited the campgrounds. I could walk in the quiet empty land looking for stones again.

My ecstatic aunt made money. Not that she needed it. I think she took pleasure in being productive. We hadn't discussed that yet. I realized that our hospital money probably came from my share of the corporate profits. I had no clue what they might be. I had to learn about Frank's share, too. With things so unsettled, I wouldn't ask. My salary and tips remained adequate.

Most appealing was the arrival of the crate containing the wood for Garrett's carving. The wolves. I had it blocked and steadied on my table. While I did do finish work in the dark, I needed light to begin. Ronnie griped about my ordering flood lights when he went to St. George on a supply run. Ronnie pretty much griped about everything. The crate with the wood also contained another set of tools—one I couldn't afford. There was a note from Garrett. *The owner of the shop recommended these for a larger piece.*

He'd also included an electric router and other small handy gadgets. I didn't need them, but they would make the work smoother, faster.

The next week things settled back into their usual routine. I worked and carved, and Pax had to resolve major issues in Sioux Crossing, so he stayed there. He ignored me and I ignored him. Sort of. Do surreptitious glances with lowered eyes count? Or the occasional brush of a shoulder or a hand. One night he walked me to my apartment and gave me a monumental kiss. Then left me to go do lawman stuff.

Lo's mind and energy turned to the major Winter Solstice. The weather remained warm for this time of year according to her. I know she hoped the moderate temps would hold. She and Ronnie had loud discussions about renting something the size of a circus tent for the big party.

Another unexpected event. The Dominus called.

"Lilly, how are you?"

"Comfortable. Cold sometimes."

"Yes, winter can be a challenge. You have relatives in Florida. I can arrange a visit if you like. There's the beach and theme parks."

Yeah, like I wanted to deal with more strangers. "Thanks. I'll think about it."

"I called to check on you and tell you I've had no success in finding McKay. I've notified Pax. I want you to be careful. I know you hate him, and I'm afraid you might take dangerous action if you see him. I don't want you hurt."

Wow! Dangerous action? What could I say? I'd live with the specter of McKay's violence for over three years. It didn't matter if I'd thwarted him two times or ten times. Oh, I'd fight, make him kill me if it came down to it. I wasn't afraid of the inevitable confrontation, but I dreaded the possibility. And the Dominus was wrong. I didn't hate McKay. I was beyond that. All I had left was the knowledge that McKay had to die, now more than ever.

We exchanged a few more words, he reiterated his concerns, and I promised to be cautious. He made me laugh a couple of times, and it was nice to think, for the first time in my life, that I did have a father. It was way too late, but it was nice. I'm not sure why, but after that call, despite my threat not to carry Bi'ar, I dug it out and kept it with me. Intuition? Hunch? It was not because of any threat from McKay.

****

I went to the bar as usual Tuesday afternoon and spied trouble at one of the bar tables. Lo, Pax, and Ronnie Valentine in a hushed conversation. Yes, the

Priestess, the Accountant, and the Commander, running things with their usual dictatorial efficiency. What had Pax told me? *The priestess is the arbiter, the negotiator of the tribe. And occasionally the judge.*

I whirled to go back out…too late.

"Please come sit, Lilly, we want to talk with you." Lo's voice carried a command.

Oh, no, I didn't like that. I plopped down and gave them my narrow eyed stubborn gaze. "Talk about what?"

"About you and the tribe. Your place here."

"My place? I'm a bartender and an amateur sculptor. If you love me, please don't plan my life."

"You carry Bi'ar, an ancient relic created and given power by the goddess. Except for the Dominus, you are closer to her than any tribe member. That is your place."

I had come to consider myself tribe. It was too late to run away. Pax had been inching closer, but we had not quite regained the pleasant and comfortable level of intimacy we'd had in Las Vegas.

Lo gave me a long, silent, but meaningful stare. "You have two more major things to learn about us and Garnet. We've kept them from you because—"

"More?" My voice hit a high note there. "You're not done with me yet?" I slumped in my chair. "You said you didn't tell me things because you were afraid I'd run away. I get that. But there's more?"

"Stop that, Lilly. Remember Las Vegas. You faced your personal demons—unprepared—and you prevailed. You also acted on behalf of all the tribes in a deadly situation. I assure you that you can deal with what's left."

My demons? McKay. The father who deserted me. Prevailed? Not so sure on that one. "Thank you for your confidence in me." I did sarcasm extremely well.

Lo went to the bar and brought back cold mugs of beer. She set one in front of me. Out of habit, I started to reject the offering.

"You need to get over that, girl. You're not a drunk or criminal," my aunt shot back.

I stared at the glass for a moment, then picked it up. My first swallow, oh, it was splendid. I glanced at Pax. He surprised me when he grinned and winked. "Gotcha now."

"Yeah, I guess you do." And he did have me. This had gone on too long. I wanted him, needed action—uninterrupted action.

Lo had a long swallow from her glass and set it gently on the table. "This is about the most immediate problem. Garnet and the land around it, is held as a collective. But members can legally lease where they live or have a business like this tavern. I have a hundred-year renewable lease, a dollar a year. You know Roger Barter?"

"I've seen him. I wouldn't say know him."

Barter had kept harassing me in the tavern until Pax put a stop to his pestering. Barter, a big hulking wrestler of a man with a seriously scarred face, did a Henry thing and met me one night on the way home. Pax, as usual, was there too. I didn't stay for the discussion, but Barter never came in the tavern again.

Lo looked as if all her face muscles had shortened and drawn tight. This was new. "Roger is a troublesome tribesman. Always has been. He has a lease on three acres close to Sioux Crossing. Activity began while you were gone. It's a compound. Self-contained. Temp steel buildings going up, equipment carefully covered, water holding tanks, composting waste facilities. Massive spools of electrical wire. Half of the carefully covered items look like military equipment. The other half looks like construction."

I was curious then. "And aren't there any zoning regs?"

"No. No zoning. We've never needed it before. The compound is fenced, topped with razor wire. Razor wire? That's never happened before. Others simply tell us what they want to do, and we agree or disagree. Not this time."

The words *razor wire* reminded me of several walls I'd been behind.

Lo stared at the table as if seeing the scarred wood for the first time. "This is unprecedented for the tribe."

Pax sitting beside me leaned closer. "Barter made a half-hearted attempt to take over leadership of the tribe ten years ago, and a more serious one recently. He was defeated both times."

Ronnie's mouth tightened, as if something tasted bad and he couldn't spit it out. "Something is coming. Here to Garnet."

Holy shit! That woke me up. "You're expecting an…invasion?"

Lo picked up. "Ronnie has visions. It's his Gift. Like your memory."

"Gift? Or curse?"

That brought the tiniest hint of a smile to Ronnie's face.

I took another swallow of liquid gold. "My question is why? What's of value that would require actual physical conflict?" I'd seen the fancy cars and heard of what members might hide in barns, but this was too much. The vastness of the land around Garnet, the distances, what's there to fight over?

"Pax." Lo stood. "Show her." She gave Pax a look so meaningful and deep I knew I was in for another mind blasting revelation. He silently agreed. I drained my beer and followed him out to his official police SUV. We headed to the valley.

Chapter Twenty-Three

Pax cleared his throat. "I apologize."

"What?" I stared at him. He wasn't looking at me.

"I apologize for how I acted in Vegas. For what I said. About Dain."

"Thank you. And it wasn't all bad. You were a hero when I had my memory crash on the way home." Oh, goddess, I knew how hard for guys like Pax to admit they were wrong.

"Memory crash. That's what you call…your little…"

"Yeah. I'll tell you about it sometime."

"Lilly, I was so amazed. Everything that hit you, you hit back. Not exactly like I wanted, but you never yielded."

Now where was this going? Where did I want it to go?

"Okay, to use a cliché, *who are you and what have you done with my sheriff?*"

"Am I yours?"

"Yes, Pax. You trusted me in Vegas. Grudgingly trusted me. Well, there was the ridiculous issue of Garrett."

He hesitated, then relaxed a bit. "I want…"

"Oh, I know what you want." Okay, this was getting too emotional for me. "You want me to strip down to my tank and panties and show you my knife fighting routine again." He'd had significant swelling of a body part when I'd performed before. I reached over and punched him in the arm. "I accept your apology. And I offer my own if I offended you. My little show was a bit risqué. How's that sound?"

"It sounds…agreeable. And yes, Lilly, I accept your offer to show me the knife fighting routine again."

"It wasn't an offer. It was a reminder that you appreciated my expertise."

"Oh. Sorry." He was grinning, so I laughed. I wanted this man, wanted to be with him. He hadn't pressured me—but really? This long?

He drove to the narrow rock-walled Oro canyon to the cave where Lo told me the story of Bi'ar and the other knives. Where my knife gave out its light show. Yep, we were climbing again. During our ascent to the cave, I managed to slip and smear dirt all over my clothes, so I'd have to change before I went to work.

Pax was silent, and I made myself useful by keeping up a litany of complaints. He carried a flashlight, but he went inside to a box on the wall. A panel box. One snap and the lights came on.

Electricity? In a cavern?

"Why…" I started to ask, but why bother? Weird, thy name is Garnet.

"We have…events here."

Events? What kind of events? The battle of the lions, the Equinox, journey to Vegas—yippee, another learning experience.

The air, warmer than outside, made the tiniest of low murmurs. The tunnel widened out to the cavern with the gorgeous stalactites and stalagmites I'd seen, then narrowed again, and sloped deeper. Tastefully and unobtrusively installed lights guided our way. The tunnel opened into a massive hollow cavern. The lights didn't go to the ceiling.

"Come here." He held out an arm, enfolded me, and drew me close, my back against his chest. Nice, comfortable. "Look there." He pointed the flashlight to the ceiling.

Holy shit!

Gold. Streaks, thick veins, three to four feet thick, unmistakable gold. I'm not an expert, but I'd seen photographs. I had a required geology class in college. The remarkable vein went on, deeper, farther than the light would carry. Oh, a person could find gold in the ground in certain locations in the world. Most of it was so expensive to get to, it wasn't worth the effort. I could dig this out with a tall ladder and a spoon.

Pax moved the light beam around the precious material. "It goes on. I've followed its trail. It's unimaginable, this close to the surface."

"Pax, there's enough here in this room alone…" If someone dumped it all on the market at once…devastation, riots. All in the name of the country's richest individuals to increase their hoards.

"Hey, Mr. Sheriff, I'm not an expert, but this hoard…do you have a magic dragon on hand to protect this much gold?"

He laughed and hugged me tighter. Oh, that felt fine. That ache of desire he started when he gave me the topaz came again. I turned, slipped my arm around him, and laid my head on his chest.

Would he kiss me? No. He wanted to talk. Damn.

"This place is sacred, Lilly. The goddess is here. No member of the tribe would come in here with a pickaxe or a shovel. But little bits of it break off and fall into the stream. There's a place downstream where we sift it out. It can be considerable at times. Eighty percent of the take goes to Bastet, and the rest to Ennead."

He released me. Well shit! He walked to the stream and scooped out a handful of sand. When he let the water leak through his fingers, several quite visible nuggets remained. "Every year during the Summer Solstice celebration, kids between eight and sixteen pan below the waterfall where it's concentrated. College funds."

"What do the other tribes think about this? Do they know?"

"Yes. It creates bitter resentment at times, harsh words. We were already on this land, owned it, when we discovered its treasure. We have legal mineral rights. Other tribes do have abundant resources, mostly business enterprises. It's not like ours. It appears to them that we don't toil for our money like they do.

"In the 1920s, my grandfather and others died protecting this stuff from a gang of rogue tribesmen. They died to keep it a secret. That's one of the reasons for our simple homes. We don't flaunt our blessings to the other tribes. More important, this tiny town doesn't attract outside attention."

He tossed the nuggets away and wiped his hand on his pants. Not like the fastidious man I knew. "I tried to get another twenty percent divided among the other tribes, but Ronnie and Lo won't agree. They think it will fuel more demands. I'd give it all away if it would bring peace."

Ronnie and Lo were right. Giving more would only

create more greed and resentment.

He put the light on the thick lines of gold again. "The corporations were formed in the 1930s. They settled on the financial structure we have today. Bastet held on to this, thousands of acres of desert. The gold is not the only beauty here, just the only thing of monetary value."

I could see it then. One tribe, Bastet, had a stable resource. The economy would rise and fall, but this bounty remained better than electronic or paper cash.

He lifted a hand toward the ceiling. "This is worthless. We won't touch it, other than what the goddess gives us in the stream. That can be bountiful when it rains in the mountains. It takes a while, but all that water funnels down here and blasts out the cave opening. It forces more nuggets out, and they wash down."

I knelt by the stream. The nuggets did shine in the limited light.

It became so clear then. "Oh, hell. So that's it. McKay's grand prize. My fault. He focused on me in the hospital and rehab. He found the tribes. He locked onto the weak link, Simon Balance, Simon's desperation, and wormed his way in. His so-called proposal? An offer to launder gold.

"Kill the Dominus, the stronger tribe leaders, you and Garrett, then Simon could take over. McKay owned Simon."

I rose without touching the shiny pebbles in the clear water. For the hell of it, I drew Bi'ar. No brilliant light show, but the markings on the blade glowed. Pax drew a deep breath, so I return the knife to its sheath.

"Now that last thing you need to know about." He

circled me with his arms again. Oh, boy, how enjoyable. He held me so close. His mouth…oh, I wanted to taste that. That's when his phone rang.

"Cell service? Down here in a cave?"

"Unfortunately, yes." He answered, listened, then, "I have to go to Sioux City."

"Of course, you do."

Chapter Twenty-Four

Pax dropped me off at the tavern after the golden cave visit and headed for Sioux Crossing, lights flashing. Sound and light are different in this desert. A sound can seem close and yet be far away. The same for light.

I walked through the tavern and checked to be sure my side of the bar was in decent shape for the night. I left by the back door to go get ready for work. Hart was waiting for me. I hate it when people sneak up on me.

Jacob Hart, respected FBI agent with a sterling reputation, had absolutely lost his mind. I understood. Guilt over his and others' suffering drove me close to suicide. His only daughter, a young, enthusiastic, newly minted agent, died with McKay's boot on her neck and his bullet in her brain.

Hart couldn't get to McKay but guess who was available. I think he'd received inside information because he arrived in Garnet before me. Not sure how he remained on the job. If he caught a psych exam, they'd have booted him out the day after his daughter died. Maybe he had dirt on someone with rank—or they felt sorry for him.

Hart grabbed me and shook me like a dog with his favorite chew toy. He twisted my arms behind my back and had cuffs on me in an instant. It hurt like hell. I didn't resist. I cried out, and he drew back a fist. I closed my eyes. It would hurt more.

"Hart!" Someone shouted.

Deekens was here. I might survive. Deekens had the misfortune of accompanying Hart these days. Deekens was young but had the makings of a capable agent. Once he outgrew, if he ever outgrew, his boyish college freshman face. He wasn't my friend, but he had ethical standards and was only moderately afraid of Hart.

"What the hell…" Deekens was there, ready to thrust his way between us.

Hart shoved me. Handcuffed, inevitable result, I went down. Hit both knees, tore my jeans—and the skin under them. My head hit the ground, narrowly missing one of the rocks so plentiful here. Ow, again. I closed my eyes and listened to the argument between them.

No warrant.

Don't need one. Probation.

Call probation officer.

No. Don't have to. Want her in jail.

Hart suddenly grabbed my arms to haul me to my feet. Okay, too much. I screamed. He was going to pull my arms out of the sockets.

"Stop it!" Deekens shouted. Hart released me. I dropped to my knees again. Rocks tore more thin skin from my kneecaps. Excruciating.

Stop, Lilly, stop, you're making it worse.

More argument from Deekens, more threats from Hart. Deekens lifted me into the back seat of their car. Tears streaked my face. Pain had me shaking, and I couldn't stop. I sensed Deekens' fury with each ragged breath he drew. A bad place for him. Hart could destroy his future if pissed off enough.

Deekens drove. He and Hart stared straight ahead, not speaking. My face wet with tears, my nose ran, and I wanted so badly to wipe it all away.

"What did I do, Hart?" I leaned forward, trying to keep from putting pressure on my arms. I was seriously scared by then. I'd stood up to McKay, but Hart frightened me? McKay was playing a game. For all I knew, Hart was going to drive me into the desert and kill me. Deekens would object, but would he prevent my death?

Hart growled, but it sounded nowhere as fierce as Pax or Simone.

"Vegas." He spit the word out. "Out of state. And this knife…" He'd taken Bi'ar, which had been in the sheath at my waist. He bent forward and dug around on the floor. "Must be under the seat." Bi'ar had performed its dependable magic disappearing trick.

"What did my probation officer say?" My mistake. I hadn't thought to call.

Hart didn't answer.

"Hart, Sheriff Harrow asked me to go to Vegas. I was in the presence of a sworn officer of the law the whole time. I was acting as his assistant for business meetings."

Deekens drew a breath to speak, glanced at Hart, then obviously decided he should keep his mouth shut.

There was no way I could sit that didn't hurt. Deekens watched in the mirror, and I could see his narrowed eyes. I hoped he was planning a mutiny.

Wait, which way were we going? Yes, toward Sioux Crossing. Pax should be there. Was there a chance he would see me when we went through? Had someone in Garnet seen and thought to call him? Not likely.

Pain, shoulders, wrists, knees, where was my so-called goddess? Had she helped me on that icy parking lot in Boston to only desert me now? What were my odds? So difficult, but I dropped into my meditative state. Ah, the Void, the vast empty Void.

Goddess? Help me? I need Pax. The Void shivered—and kicked me out. I wanted Pax right then so bad. With all my will, I called to him. *Pax, my love, my heart.*

A pulse, a beat, yes, a heartbeat. Was that him? Pax, where are you? I could sense him, experience his confusion. He had a flash of knowledge. He felt the connection.

I concentrated on my pain, my discomfort. Oh, he was listening, looking. He didn't understand. But I was there with him. What a strange mind he had, full of visions of rocks and sand and running. Running for joy, leaping, chasing something. And me. I was there too. He saw me, desired me. I concentrated on what I could see. The sign on the side of the road. *Sioux Crossing— One mile.* And I sent that image, desperate need for help until—

"Stop!" Hart yelled.

My eyes popped open. Hart reached back and smacked me across the face. A fierce blow...blinding light...pain. I slammed back on my arms. I cried out again, sharp and shrill. The blow left me stunned, blind. *Had Hart heard my cry for Pax? I had long passed calling anything impossible in the tribe.*

"Don't hit her. You know better," Deekens protested. His voice filled with incredulous fury.

"Don't tell me what to do, agent. Remember who I

am."

"I remember." Deekens, young and noble, reminded his superior. "You're the one who's forgotten."

We traveled on, and my vision cleared. I could see Pax's SUV ahead, parked by the Sioux Crossing sign. He'd received my message. The SUV had its flashing cop lights on.

"Keep going," Hart demanded.

Deekens obeyed and drove on.

Pax was right behind us, siren wailing. We'd be in Sioux Crossing in minutes. In a burst of speed, the SUV drew alongside and closed in. It would force Deekens off the road. No seat belt, hands behind my back...oh, shit. But I was ready. *Do it, Pax.*

Deekens slowed. He pulled to the side of the road and stopped. The SUV stopped behind us.

"What are you doing?" Hart yelled at him.

"He's going to run us off the road. You have to stop this." He leaned toward Hart, pleading. "Jacob, you're crazy. You can't do things this way."

Hart threw open the door and jumped out of the car. Pax did the same. Deekens stepped out but stood still and didn't go to the two men.

Deputy Ben climbed out the passenger side of the Garnet police SUV and slowly walked toward me. Deekens watched but didn't move. Hart's voice had stopped, or at least the loud tone.

"Will you unlock the back door?" Ben asked Deekens. "I need to get my girl."

Deekens stared at him a moment, then silently complied. The door locks clicked. Ben opened the door and helped me out. I almost jumped into his arms, but it hurt too much. He held me up as we walked back toward the SUV. When we got there, I leaned against the vehicle while he removed the cuffs. I was outright sobbing by then. Oh damn, my shoulders hurt, my wrists were raw and red, too. Blood stains surrounded the holes in my jeans. My tolerance for pain was incredibly high, but the emotional in a place I thought I was safe...my body shook again, fine tremors defying my will as I fought not to move.

Hart stood with Pax on the far side of the road. Hart's head hung down and his shoulders were slumped. Pax was still talking to him. Pax had won. Easy to see that. He reached out and laid a hand on Hart's shoulder. The agent bowed his head. Compassion, or something other than rage, had prevailed.

Ben stood behind me and carefully rubbed my shoulders. He held me close against his body, and I leaned back. I needed the support. Hart suddenly stalked back to his car and climbed in. He didn't look at me. They drove away. Poor Deekens. I'd bet he was having a learning experience. I knew how much fun those were.

Pax came to me. He laid a hand by my cheek but didn't touch.

"He hit you." Oh, oh, there was that growling voice again. I didn't want any more complications laid on me. I wanted Hart to go away, and he had.

"It's okay. Misunderstanding. I should have called my probation officer and told him I was going to Vegas."

Pax shook his head. "I called him, Lilly. I do things like that."

He did. Yes, he took care of things. How was that going to work between us. "Pax, I do understand why Hart is the way he is. His daughter—"

"I know. He's lost his way in sorrow. I've been there. But he shouldn't have hit you. Come on, let's get you to Doc. He'll fix you up."

Ben lifted me into the backseat and belted me down. I grabbed him and hugged him. Of course, since I was higher, I mashed his face into my breasts. Oh, such a big grin he had when I released him.

Lo met us when we returned to Garnet. They released me into her arms because guess what? Pax and Ben had to rush back to Sioux Crossing to deal with another crisis.

Chapter Twenty-Five

When I asked Lo why no one guarded the gold, she gave me the same answer as Pax. *The goddess dwells there. She'd take care of the resource she'd given the tribe.*

Pax showed up again two days after the Hart incident. I worked in my barn as I did most nights. The chilly night had descended on the desert, but the barn would hold the day's heat a little longer. Flood lights provided a bit of warmth as they illuminated the carving. Dain's wolves required a bit of work on the base and my signature stone. He'd said he'd be coming down for the Winter Solstice celebration, so I had time. My work had gone faster thanks to the extra tools he'd included when he shipped the wood. I looked forward to seeing him again, my friend, that lovely smiling man from Oregon.

The smaller barn door opened, and Pax came in. He went to sit on the tall bench near the wall. Silent. Ten minutes, twenty...

"You need something?" I snapped the words. Yes, his sudden attention and equally sudden departures were getting on my nerves.

"No. Just watching you."

"Why?" I stopped, curious then.

"I like your intensity—the way you focus on details."

Suddenly, I was cold and tired. I wanted…what did I want? I remembered Las Vegas, how warm he felt in my bed. How I slept. I went to him, close, but not intimate. It would end in disaster—or an interruption—but, "Hey, you want to come stay with me tonight?"

He raised an eyebrow. "So you can sleep?"

"You can keep me warm." I stepped closer and lowered my gaze. "You can brush my hair again. I liked that."

"I didn't believe Lo." He slid off the bench. "When she told me you never slept. Then you did. With me."

"A brain injury. From…" He knew what it was from.

I turned to go, and he caught my arm. "I need a shower."

"I've got one of those." He grabbed me and drew me close.

I stared straight into his eyes. "Do my scars trouble you? We can turn the light off." Oops, remembered something. "But you can see in the dark, can't you?"

"I told you what I thought of scars. Your scars."

"I know. But they're hideous." He responded by surrounding me with his arms and giving me the most fantastic kiss of my life. It was one that washed away all doubts, all fears. I felt so empty, so lost when it ended.

I cut the lights, and we went out into the chill moonless night. I'd forgotten my flashlight, so he led me, holding me close. When we reached the door to my apartment, he turned, lifted his head, and gazed into the darkness beyond the security lights. A low rumbling sound started, then stopped.

"That's the mountain lion. He comes at night.

When I sit outside, he keeps me company. He watches me, too."

"I know. You don't need him tonight."

"I don't need him any night. I like knowing he's there occasionally." And I finally admitted to myself that I was so lonely I'd accept a wild animal audience as company.

I wasn't exactly pristine myself, so while he showered, I washed in the kitchen sink and went to lie on the bed wearing panties and a tank top. He'd dispensed with all clothing when he came out. Oh, my…Goddess. I stared. Beautiful man, but he had scars too.

Across his shoulder, ragged lines like claw marks, his chest, what had happened there? He stretched easily, so smoothly, so economically, not a single move wasted. "Pax, you are so beautiful, so strong, how could you possibly want…"

"Want what?" He came to sit beside me.

"Want me. I am…damaged. Physically, emotionally. High maintenance, trouble. I know it's just sex, but…"

"Is that all it is? Just sex?" The dismay on his face stunned me. He shook his head as if incredulous at my assertion. "Lilly, I wanted to grab you and drag you home with me the minute you stepped off that bus. You stood there, waiting for your bag…I wanted to shout look at me, woman, see me. It pissed me off that I felt that way. I liked my life, my town, my place. And right then, I knew you'd change everything. Is that just sex?"

Amazingly, he wanted to talk. After months of silence. He must have saved it up.

"You remember when you brought that owl

carving for Ben? I wanted to crawl into a hole. All I could think was, *I wish she'd made this for me.* Then I kept saying stupid things."

So, he'd covered his attraction with nasty words and rude actions? He'd lost control of his emotions? "Pax, I understood you wanted to protect Garnet from trouble following me. That night…"

He had the grace to look embarrassed, contrite. "The night I was going to force you? I lost my mind. The very scent of you, your voice… No." He shook his head. "I will not make excuses. It was wrong. Foul, evil. I never in my life want to be that kind of man." His shoulders slumped. "Lilly, please forgive me."

Forgive him. He'd stepped back from wrongdoing. Many times, I had not. "Should I confess my sins to you, Sheriff? Let you in on the guilt I bear for things I've done? But I thought you hated me."

"Hate? Not you. I hate what's been done to you." His voice went hard with real fury. "I hate whoever threw McKay at you in Vegas. Why? To shock you. To see if they could break you. And our so-called tribe leader? Our Dominus? He should beg you to forgive him for abandoning you as a child and what he allowed to happen in Vegas."

Yes, the Dominus had pleaded with me for forgiveness, but I couldn't accept it as genuine.

I scooted closer to my love. "You said the whole thing in Vegas was about me. I think you're right. At least some part. We don't know why. So many things are out of our control. I also think we'll be forced to battle their schemes."

While I didn't exactly understand the true extent of the Dominus' power, I feared Pax was no match for him. Remembering Lo's words, *he can kill a tribe member with a thought*. I wasn't going to take a chance.

He reached out and tugged at a strand of my hair. "Are you afraid of him? The Dominus."

"I'm afraid he has plans for me. Like everyone else. Him, your goddess, McKay…even Lo in her own loving way."

He laid a hand on my cheek. "Hear this, Lilly Dusalte. I swear on my life I will protect you. I will stand between you—"

"No. You will not." Damn him. He dropped his hand. His eyes were gold again. How did he do that?

"Stand beside me, Pax. Not in front. Beside."

Then he nodded. "I'll try."

Trying was okay. It was the nature of decent humans to protect the ones they love. Stiff as a board, Pax lived and breathed protection. His warm smile, the loving expression on his face…this was right. This was perfect.

I had to clarify something. "And that is all I need. Your love. Love. I'll say it. You have mine. That doesn't mean I haven't been or won't be mightily pissed at you."

He grabbed me and rolled me over on the bed. Those beautiful eyes were pure gold now. His voice was husky and soft as a cloud of smoke. "Okay, declarations of devotion are done."

Oh, we kissed and fondled, his hands, his mouth…then, after all wakeful hours, I relaxed for only seconds while he was rubbing my shoulders—and fell asleep.

Damn it, I fell asleep. Years of insomnia, and now the love of my life in my arms and I fell asleep. I woke up when first light peeped through the curtains and I had my face buried in a fur pillow.

What? A fur pillow? I pushed up on my elbows. A massive mountain lion lay beside me, his thick heavy head resting on the pillow. The long, muscular body, russet and gold as the desert outside, stretched down the bed. Yeah, his back feet stuck out over the edge. A lengthy tail lay across my feet and dropped to the floor.

This was not my occasional visitor who sat at a distance outside and watched me carve in the chill night. No, this cat had marked me by rubbing his bloody scent glands on my pants after the fight in the arena at the party.

I had a lion in my bed.

Surprise is too trivial a word to describe what happened next. I yelped and threw myself to the floor. Awkward as a newborn giraffe, I slammed into the nightstand. The lamp crashed against the wall. I scooted back on my butt to the pile of clothes I'd discarded in anticipation of…lovemaking. I frantically pawed through them for my phone. Got it. Wait. Who should I call? Where the hell was Bi'ar? I glanced back at the bed, expecting to see the lion crouched, ready to pounce, to bite, to claw. He was between me and the door. The big cat raised his head and stared at me. Like saying, *what the hell*? His eyes closed. He dropped his head back on the pillow. Stunned, I sat there on the floor like an idiot. What should I do? My mind had turned to cat food. So, I called Aunt Lo.

Ring. Ring again, no answer. I scrunched up against the wall, as if becoming smaller would make a difference. Finally, right before it went to voice mail, she picked up.

"Lo?" Was that squeaky sound my voice?

"What…what time…Lilly?" Something crashed in the background. "Lilly? What's wrong?"

I cupped my hand over the phone, so I could speak softly. I didn't want a hysterical screech to upset the cat. "Lo, there's a mountain lion in my bed."

Silence. Then, "Well, about that…you know that second important thing we had to tell you?"

Babbling. She was babbling. "What do I do?"

"What's *he* doing?"

"He's lying down. Oh, hell, now he's sitting up and…staring at me."

"Well, Lilly, I suggest you open the door and see if he wants out. If not, you can cook him breakfast, or do what I'm going to do. Go back to bed.

"Out? Outside? Breakfast?" My throat seized and I choked on those three words.

The cat sat there, seeming interested, cocking his head occasionally. Those eyes. Bright gold, and…aware. Not animal eyes. He stepped gracefully off the bed and padded toward me. Thick, corded muscles in his heavy shoulders flexed under his skin. I dropped the phone.

Face to face, staring into his eyes, I knew. Impossibly, I knew. This was his magic. His Gift from the goddess. *The last secret of Garnet.*

If it hadn't been for my time here in the desert, I would have doubted my sanity. I'd feared that all my life, that I would be like Mama. This cat would be an illusion. But Bi'ar was tangible. It moved through space and time, a feat worthy of a science fiction movie. Physics, biology…goddess. Ancient, unknowable, a part of our blood. Gifts? What other miracles could she perform?

I laid my hand on the side of his face. "You could have told me, Pax. You could have trusted me." My voice splintered like a piece of wood I had carelessly broken. It hurt. That he couldn't be honest. Not at first…but when he'd given me the stone and in Las Vegas…yes, it hurt like hell.

I felt uncomfortably naked then. I grabbed my panties and tank and rushed to get them on. The big cat silently padded into the living room. He looked back at me. I did what I thought he wanted. He stepped out of the way when I opened the front door.

What a chill clear morning. Soft pre-dawn light surrounded us, and the scent of nearby juniper filled the air. The cat stopped on the porch. Head up, he sniffed. Looking, smelling for danger. With a single leap, a golden streak raced away.

In my scanty clothes, I ignored the cold and stepped outside to stare after him. I heard a soft sigh. Lo, dressed in a bathrobe, stood watching me. "Lilly, I—"

"No." I held up my hand to stop her. "Enough." She could have trusted me too. I went back inside. I plopped down on the bed. It smelled of him. The cat, the man. I'd offered him everything, from my hideous body to baring my soul. He'd held back.

The topaz he'd given me rolled across my skin as I moved. Desperate to clear my mind, I moved to sit on a rug in the living room and closed my eyes. I immediately fell into the Void. Yes, here I could ease the ache. Unbelievably, I was not alone. A voice snapped loud and quite clear.

"He has accepted you. Can you not accept him?"

I knew who had spoken. Only one thing remained. After living and working with Bi'ar, after proof that a man could change into a mountain lion, it had to be her.

A vision of the mountain lion—Pax—racing across the desert played out in my mind. The vicious battle in the arena. Clawing, biting, roaring rage. That was him, too. An impossible transformation. This was not a movie, a book, a story. This was my life. The one I'd battled and suffered through, Mama and McKay—

"Warrior! Cease your cowardly wail! Be worthy of him."

The words sliced like a sharp wind. Silence returned. The now empty Void remained but brought me no peace.

Damn her. How dare she call me a coward. I had fought. I'd been battered to near death. My Dusalte grandmother's words? *"Damaged, but not broken."* No, I was not broken. I was most certainly pissed. This wrinkle in my life would not take me down, though. This miserable bitch of a goddess could call me names, but she would not break me.

I woke from the Void, showered, dressed, and walked to Lo's trailer. She opened the door at the first knock. I sat at the table with a pot of coffee, cups, and a significant plate of pastries that tempted me. Yes, sugar was temptation on the highest level. She stared at me for a moment, then began.

"Lilly, I told you about my dreams. The goddess haunting me until I got you here. I knew how hurt you were, the horrific things you suffered, I was terrified. I didn't know about Bi'ar, what it did for you. I was afraid if I tossed you into complex tribal life you would leave. I had a plan. Ease you in, show you things." She poured coffee and shoved the pastry plate toward me. "It all fell apart. I sent Pax to meet you at the bus. Be kind, I told him. He was supposed to welcome you, not treat you like a criminal." She ran her finger over the rim of her coffee cup while her face produced most every expression I'd ever known. I said nothing and let her talk.

"I took you to the cave. I was going to show you the gold. What did you do? You pulled a knife, an incredible long-lost relic of the goddess. And the earth, her song, responded. Stories, legends, thousands of years, and it shows up here. With you." She rubbed her hands over her face. "The heart of why we didn't tell you? Knowing your history, we were desperately afraid you would be too frightened to stay. I sent you a bus ticket instead of an airline ticket hoping to slowly integrate you into our lives. Yes, it seems irresponsible and shortsighted—now. So, I beg your pardon. And I ask the goddess to forgive me. I should have trusted her."

Oh, my dearest aunt, at least you acted with love where others acted with malice.

"Lo, Mama tried to drown me twice, set me on fire once. And McKay? You know that, too. You think I'm so fragile a pussy cat on steroids is going to send me screeching down the road?"

Her eyes widened. She drew a breath to speak but I wasn't finished. "My life, except for Bi'ar, has been mostly rational. Violent, miserable—but rational. I know you love me. In rehab you held my hand while I begged you to let me die. And your goddess? The bitch popped in thirty minutes ago. She called me names and vanished before I could ask questions."

Lo's eyes opened so wide it scared me. *Please don't let her faint!* I hadn't meant to let her know I'd heard from her benefactor personally. She started to speak, but a violent shake of my head shut her up. It wasn't time to talk of that yet. She placed her hands over her face and cried. I went to hold her and tell her it was okay. And truly, at that moment, life was better than any I had lived in years. Oh, it wouldn't last, but right then was perfect.

****

I didn't see Pax again until early evening. He was in the back hallway of the tavern. I went to him, leaned close, touching him...almost.

He sighed. "I'm sorry. That little involuntary shifting mistake hasn't happened since I was a teenager. Stress. Exhaustion. Last night I wanted to tell you about it, show you."

"And I fell asleep. It's okay." He opened his arms. I was ready. We did have to talk, though. A corner table in the tavern was fine.

"Tell me about the lion. That's a pretty important level of annoying."

More annoying was that *I should have* figured it out. After the cat fight, after he marked me—was I that dense? No. Such an impossible phenomenon. Bi'ar came to me in childhood. Familiarity allowed me to accept its spectacular nature, moving through the world on its own. I'd known the blade most of my life.

"Lilly, it's an overwhelming complexity. I've lived with it my whole life. Only thirty of us can shift, now. Birth rates keep falling, fewer are born with the Gift."

"The other tribes?"

"The others do have Gifts. I don't know all of them. We don't communicate like we should." He lowered his voice. "The Dominus prefers that everything go through him."

"You don't trust him, do you?"

He slowly shook his head. "Once I did, but now I've heard too many things. Questions I can't get answered."

"Yeah, I have suspicions, too. Hey, I can't change shape. Can I? What about Frank?"

Pax shook his head. "The change arrives at puberty. If not then, never. What's the matter? Lilly? You're so pale." He reached over and grabbed me, holding me tight, safe. I needed it right then. A memory had escaped its prison.

"When I...had my first menstrual period, Mama kept watch on me. Every second she had a gun in her pocket. Not surprising. We lived in a slum. But she mostly stayed far from guns. She was going to kill me if..."

Mama tried to kill me various times in her bouts of madness. Why was that attempt different? Because at that time, for a brief period, she'd been rational. I'd escaped because certain Bastet genes turned in a different direction.

"Talk to me," I said. "Tell me more."

"Okay. Being a lion shifter is my only Gift. Unless you count the fact that I'm stronger than most men. I work out, but I'm way stronger. I see things, smell things better. Those of us who don't shift have other Gifts." He laughed softly. "We look like mountain lions now, but the histories say we were different long ago. Fun to think about. We had spots like a leopard once.

You're Bastet and your—our—children will have the same odds."

I hugged him. "That is so wonderful." *You have to tell him, Lilly. You have to. He might accept the scars, but the other?*

"Pax, so you know…my injuries…from McKay…I may not be able to have kids. I had damage all around that area, and I only have one ovary now. The doctors said the odds weren't in my favor. Possible but not likely."

He didn't say anything, but he didn't push me away. Then he spoke softly in my ear. "I want you. No matter what. I must have you, my mate, for the rest of my life."

I thought of something. I should have guessed. "Dain? Fenrir?"

"They're the wolves, yes. We're the only two tribes that have the ability to shift."

Oh, my witty, charming friend. I'd bet he raced through the mountains as Pax did his desert. I so wanted to talk to Garrett Dain again.

Chapter Twenty-Six

I'd thought we might be together that night, but a call came in from Sioux Crossing. *Get used to it, Lilly.* Lawmen worked all hours. I did ask him if he would show me how he changed shape, as if I could somehow touch that magic. "I will. When it's time." *Oh, we wanted to be enigmatic, did we?*

Three days later he stepped out of the dark and met me on the way to my apartment. He wrapped an arm around me and dragged me close.

"Pax?" Deputy Ben called out. "The Crossing—"

"Deal with it, Deputy!" he shouted over his shoulder. "You're a big boy now."

Okay, then.

Once inside my apartment, he pushed me into the bedroom. He stripped me down quickly, but apparently that starched uniform had a million buttons and his boots had five feet of laces that were tortuously slow to loosen before they would come off.

"I should shower." He tossed the last boot away.

"Later, we'll do it later. I'm not letting you get away this time." I grabbed him, and we fell across the bed. A sturdy bed thankfully, since we were by no means small people.

The full moon outside the window cast a white sheet of light over us, over the bed, leaving the rest of the room in darkness. He traced the pattern of scars across my chest and stomach with his tongue. I pulled him to me, wanting all that hard, lean muscle close. I wanted no separation between us. He sighed and whispered my name as if I were a secret he kept in his heart. This was pure pleasure, pure love we poured into the empty vessels of our hearts.

We lay there, body to body, mouth to mouth. His hands glided up and down, and my skin warmed beneath his touch. His earthy male scent filled the air I breathed. He was so gentle when he skimmed over my scars, several of which were sensitive and still painful to touch.

His eyes flashed gold. Cat's eyes. My lion. My love. We lay there in the silence of the night, in the silence of the desert around us. The goddess cast a spell that was ours alone. And yet, my love and I were a part of a magic that was not hers. A human magic that rose when two of the species joined, a connection that might last moments—or a lifetime.

I couldn't touch him enough. Couldn't get close enough to him. I tasted him, the salt on his skin, locked my hands in his hair, wherever I put my hands smooth muscles would contract.

Then a raw wild need arose in me. I wanted more. I wanted this man in me and over me, and I wanted to hold him, never release him. His heartbeat, the heat of his skin, the same need rose in him. We didn't need words.

I suddenly felt greedy, brazen, demanding. I opened and let him glide in me, wrapped my legs around him so I could hold him tight.

His strength…he had his arms around my back. He suddenly lifted me until he held me tight against him.

He wanted me to move at my own pace, not his.

Once upon a time, I had starved to be thinner. I had hated my body for being less than perfect for a vile man whose desire was not to love me, but to possess. Mama taught me that I was evil body and soul. Her devil child. I'd believed her. This most remarkable man in my arms this night wanted me unconditionally as I came to him.

We went on, slowly moving in a gentle wave, then faster and finally crashing. Or I crashed. He'd waited on me. In my euphoria I could hear his breath, could hear him calling my name.

Everything felt perfect. Not just tolerable, not just acceptable, but perfect. I belonged to him, to his tribe, to this desert world of Garnet. And his goddess, who was unfortunately, quite existent. Here we would make a home, defend that home, and we would live, not a flawless life, but a shared life. Oh, I had doubts. I'm sure he did too. But later, when the day turned bright again, we would deal with them.

Chapter Twenty-Seven

Another day, another meeting. I had no official role in the tribe hierarchy, but somehow the Bastet leaders felt I had to be part of loud discussions about the mysterious equipment stored in Sioux Crossing. Yes, those were armored cars, but there were only three of them. Troop carriers, only two. Mechanical equipment? Definitely. But old and well used.

Since I didn't sleep without Pax in my bed, I stayed out in the cold, dark hours and carved while he was working. I'd eventually adjust to a lawman's odd hours. Yes, it was cold outside, but I had warm clothes. I was sitting on my little porch one night, carving, when McKay stepped out of the shadows. He held a set of night vision goggles in his hand so he could sneak around in the dark.

He gracefully lowered himself into the chair on the other side of the little table. Perfectly dressed, he made a black leather jacket and riding pants look magazine model sharp. I hadn't heard, but he would have a motorcycle somewhere. A sporadic heavy truck had passed through town not long ago, and if he followed it, the sounds could blend. I used to ride behind him, loving that illusory feeling of freedom.

I had a knife in my hand, one I used for carving. Pitiful, not possible as a weapon. I laid it on the table. Bi'ar was sheathed at my side. My knife should have moved to warn me of danger.

I placed the carving on the table beside the knife. McKay lifted it. "Still cutting wood."

"Yes." Oh, but the months when I was sure I'd never create anything again. He'd done that personally, broken my fingers, one at a time. I immediately shut that memory down. I had to function here.

He turned the piece in his hands then set it down— carefully, as if it were fine art. I think he always respected me more as an artist than a woman.

McKay leaned forward, elbows on his knees. "Lilly, it doesn't have to be this way. These people, what do you owe them? You call them family, but they're strangers. And now you've killed for them. I don't understand. My sweet Lilly. I remembered how you suffered when others were hurt."

"You mean when *you* hurt others, McKay." I wasn't going to let him get away with pushing that on me. I could manufacture my own guilt, thank you. "How did you manage to get away? At the hotel."

"Come on, Lilly, when have I not had multiple escape plans?" He leaned back and linked his hands across his stomach, a man perfectly at ease. What was that? His fingers twitched with tiny jerks, as if desperate to break free of bonds. Not like the McKay I knew, who remained steady.

"The Dominus said he was looking for you. I think he's a little pissed."

He chuckled softly. "Yeah, crazy fucker, thinks he's a god. Or at least some magic chosen leader. Believe me Lilly, these superstitious fools are not as smart or frightening as they think they are."

Ah, but you haven't seen my lion, have you

McKay?

He didn't speak for a minute. You'd think we were a couple enjoying a companionable silence. "There's this place in Switzerland. Expensive place. They say they can remove scars. I think they use a laser."

Bullshit and more bullshit. "And?"

"I could pay for you to go there."

"No."

"Why not? I want to show I'm sorry." He sounded surprised. No doubt, McKay was off his game, off schedule, off plan—whatever. Or he was giving the performance of a lifetime.

"You can show me you're sorry by putting a bullet in your brain. You can save other lives. I've accepted my scars." I laid a hand against my chest. The worst, that cross stitching and the burns lay there. "My scars are medals of honor. They're awards for surviving you." *For taking you down, I wanted to say.* That might push him too far.

He chuckled, low and deep. Once upon a time I loved to hear that laugh.

"I meant what I said, Lilly. I love you. I truly didn't value you until you were gone. But I want to know. When did I finally lose you? What was the proverbial last straw?"

"That June you set up the armored car heist and killed ten people in a coffee shop. Killed them for a distraction from a crime committed a mile away. The Eckert family…"

"They weren't supposed to kill the kids, Lilly."

Not supposed to kill the kids. Give violent men guns, tell them to wipe out a whole family, but don't kill the kids?

I needed him to know something, I had to say the words, even if he wouldn't understand. "McKay, my scars are a part of my penance for sins of complicity, my participation in evil. Each one marks the times I turned away. When I pretended all that money, all that fun, didn't come at the cost of human lives. I could have gone to the FBI on my own at any time. I could have saved lives. But I didn't. I wallowed in a morass of self-pity while more suffered, more died."

He sighed, deep and slow. "You mean if I'd kept treating you like you were my one and only love you would have stayed loyal?"

He'd turned my guilt and into his own personal thing. He would see things that way. It was about him, always.

"Loyal, McKay? At first, I tried to think an internal moral imperative would have driven me away from you. I don't pretend anymore. The fact is, I absolutely ignored your brutality until you laid hands on me."

He laughed again, but it didn't sound like amusement this time. "What's with your sheriff? Never seen a man so hot for you. Of course, no man was hot for you when I was around. Cowards."

Oh, no, we weren't going there. "McKay, there's one thing I haven't figured out—"

"There are a bunch of things you haven't figured out, baby."

Whoa! That was sharp and rang with the truth.

I tried something different. "How did all this come about? I know you've tracked me. I've never hidden. How did you get to Simon Balance and the tribes?"

"Easy enough. I kept watch after you left the hospital. I found you in rehab. Hadn't made up my mind on what to do. One day, your aunt brought someone with her to visit you. A lonely lady who liked my eyes and wanted to talk while she waited outside. Got her phone number, called her, fucked her. She kept talking. Couldn't shut her up." He sighed, shaking his head. Always egotistical, he delighted in his own prowess. "Now, here's my Lilly connected to a bunch of violent, superstitious cultists with money. Then I learned about the gold. Poor needy Simon was the easiest way in. I had everything else under control until Vegas. Then you crashed my party."

McKay laid his arm on the table, his fingers tracing the contours of my carving. "Tell me, Lilly, have you truly joined their cult? Been redeemed? Saved by the magnificent white light?"

"The light is blue, McKay. And yes, I've become a believer."

He could not perceive the true nature of the superstitious cultists. He would not consider their blood related families, their goddess, and their magic.

"That is truly a disaster. I only wanted to give you the opportunity to change your mind." He slowly stood. To grab me, he'd have to bend over a bit. Hopefully, Bi'ar would come to my hand. He'd kill me, but my killing blade had struck true each time I'd wielded it before.

He suddenly straightened, went tight and alert. He drew a gun from under his jacket. Someone was coming. *Please, please goddess don't let it be Aunt Lo.*

To my surprise he slipped on the night vision goggles and raced away into the darkness. Then Pax walked out of the shadows.

I jerked up straight. "Didn't you see him? Why

didn't you shoot him?"

Pax moved closer. "Patience, please. I want more information. Then I'll kill him. I don't think he's going far."

A motorcycle started out by the asphalt. The sound moved away, leaving Garnet. It slowed.

Then stopped. Pax whirled and dashed toward the road. I kept my flashlight at hand, so I was right behind him.

Two shots. Two sharp, loud cracks. Echoes reverberated the sound of death from the desert hills around us. The motorcycle roared, then sped away.

No, no, no. Who challenged him? Who tried to take him?

Deputy Ben lay sprawled on the dirt in front of the tavern, his shirt steeped in blood. Pax knelt beside him. Terror grew, a living thing inside me. If I lost another soul to McKay, I would go insane as my mother. Ben, my wonderful young Ben could not die.

Two bullet wounds, one in his chest and one in his guts. I dropped to my knees. I laid my hand on his throat. Yes, there was a thread of a heartbeat.

Pax was on his phone, shouting, demanding an ambulance.

It had to come from Sioux Crossing.

Old Doc Hardy staggered up in his pajamas and robe. His bare feet slapped on the pavement when he crossed the road. He shoved Pax to the side and took his place. The old man breathed hard, gasped, muttered. On his knees, he laid both hands on the chest wound. Close to the heart. The killing wound.

"Doc?" Pax remained beside us. I could hear others come running. "Doc, are you, can you…?"

Doc didn't answer. The healer moaned, low and deep. I could hear the struggle in his voice. He couldn't do it—Ben was going to die.

With no warning, on my knees beside a dying man, something dragged me into my meditative Void. It shocked me so much I almost jerked out. Then I did something I hadn't done since I was a child. I prayed. Not to God as I would have in other times. That one never answered my prayers, even when a child begged him to spare her more pain. I cried out to the strange goddess of my people. I begged, pleading for Ben's life. My fault, my fault. If I hadn't come here… *The fireflies came first, those dancing lights. So, she was the one who kept my broken body alive in Chicago.*

Ah, she was there. I could sense her. I couldn't see her, but her presence weighed on me. And I groveled. I will do anything, take me, not him. Please, please.

Her voice echoed like a drum in my head. "I can give strength to heal. I aided your survival, your healing, once. There is a price. A sacrifice required this time."

"Anything. I'll pay. My sacrifice, mine alone."

Then she told me what she wanted. She told me what had happened that brought us to this point. Not in words, but like an instant memory in my mind.

She spoke one word. Âthrava. I wanted to cry, to rage. With boundless sorrow, but no hesitation, I agreed. From that day on I would do her bidding. My life would be hers and not my own. For a moment she possessed me, possessed my body. She suffocated me with her presence. She infused me with her extraordinary magic. I could not define that magic—I only knew it existed. I changed. I didn't have time to

298

catalog or examine those changes. I had to go on to save Ben's life.

I slowly woke. A pale blue glow shimmered around me—and Doc. Others had come, but they all stood back—except for Pax. He would not leave me. No, Pax would never leave me. The light around us faded.

Ben drew steadier, stronger breaths. Not conscious, not fully healed, blood trickled from his mouth, but he lived. The gut wound bleeding had slowed. The siren of the tribe's fully equipped ambulance transport wailed as it raced toward us.

Doc, the healer, collapsed and lay motionless on the pavement. Shallow breathing, eyes closed, he'd given all he could—but he too would live. Because I accepted her, agreed to be her servant, her healing power had temporally become my Gift. I shared it with Doc, and he saved Ben.

I gazed at Pax. He had tears in his eyes. "I should have stayed with him." But I could feel something else. Awe. He'd beheld a lifesaving wonder.

I countered his words. "We all should have done something different in our lives. I should have stayed away from this place."

McKay found the tribes while searching for me. He also found a prize beyond belief to claim.

The ambulance arrived. Staffed by highly trained paramedics, all tribesmen and women, they had Ben stabilized and on oxygen in minutes. They'd take him to the hospital in Las Vegas. I don't know what they would tell the police whom the doctors would automatically summon for a gunshot wound.

Pax and I followed the SUV, lights flashing. Doc

refused to go. Said all he needed was a cup of coffee, a satisfactory meal, and twenty or so hours of sleep. He had muttered something about a Fountain of Youth as he wobbled away.

I hadn't realized how utterly miserable it was to sit and wait while doctors struggled to save the life of someone you loved. Poor Frank. He'd done that for me that night in the hospital after they scraped me off the pavement in Boston. And Lo, she arrived the next day to stand what everyone believed was a death watch.

The goddess had given the power, through me, for Doc to save Ben. Part of her resided deep in me now. I didn't know everything, but she let me see a significant part of her history. She wasn't omnipotent. She had limits. She had rules. An ancient being, presence, power—whatever—she'd held the tribes as her own for thousands of years. Binding them with Gifts, the tribal law, genetics, we were hers. Something had happened, a disastrous cultural breakdown, and she'd lost control. With me, she'd regained some small measure of herself. Eventually others would join me.

"What did you see?" I asked Pax as he brought me coffee. "Before the ambulance came?" He sat back, fatigue winning a small battle with his desire to remain alert.

"The light surrounded us, bright, blue, clear. You knelt there with your eyes closed. Twenty or thirty seconds, then everything was back to normal. Well, as normal as Garnet ever is." He drew me closer. "I should have, could have, killed McKay."

I shrugged. "I missed opportunities, too. But we want him to suffer before he dies." Pax kissed me. Then he fell asleep on my shoulder. Only thirty seconds? It seemed as if she spoke with me over an hour.

By morning Ben was critical, but things looked better. Surgery removed the bullet near his heart. The gut shot went all the way through. It would be painful but Doc, with the goddess' help, channeled through me, had partially healed that, too. I kept hearing the word *amazing* tossed around. The truth was far more amazing than they would ever know. Ben would be in the hospital a long time. Then there'd be rehab. Poor boy.

Lo arrived, and we found a private corner to talk. Pax lay across a couch, sound asleep.

Lo leaned close. We weren't the only people in the room standing watch for a loved one. "Can you tell us anything, Lilly? What's happened."

She didn't mean what happened to Ben. How much could or should I tell her. Not much. Not yet. "I have…accepted the goddess' governance. It means she can speak directly into my mind, not in dreams as she did you. I'm doomed. But I had to save Ben."

Lo raised an eyebrow. "She used Ben as a pawn? To claim you?"

I nodded my head. "She comes off as a bit of a bitch. And never speak it, but she sounds a little desperate."

"But what about the Dominus?"

Okay. I had to lie there. "I'm waiting on orders. She contacts me, I don't contact her. Something huge is going to happen, Lo. I think we have a little time. But it's on its way."

I used my fingernail to scratch a spot on my head. My long hair, twisted in a bun for over 24 hours, demanded a brush. Lo gave me an odd look. She took my hand and led me into the women's restroom. It was certainly empty that time of night. She turned me away from the mirror, popped the clip that held my, hair and fluffed it out.

"Now look." She turned me around.

I can't say it shocked me. No woman could go through the ordeal of having their mind and body hijacked by a goddess and remain unchanged. Unlike my father, my hair was not pure white. There are words, beige, gray, brassy blond, my dark brown had morphed to motley piebald streaks. I shouted my displeasure. "What the hell? Goddess...whatever you are. What the..."

Lo cringed.

My once gray eyes had turned sky blue. Odd, Pax had said nothing, but he was so tired and worried.

Lo grabbed a handful of strands on each side of my head. She flipped them out and released them.

Faint blue light flashed through them. I slid my fingers in and brushed it back from my face. A deeper blue light glowed. Subtle, softer this time. Then it faded.

Completely confused, I said the first thing that came to mind. "How cool. Red and green highlights, and I can be a Christmas tree. Wait. Don't we have a Solstice tree? What does it mean to you? To the tribes?"

"The goddess touched you. Chose you to be her...surrogate. Your hair is a symbol. And it may get whiter over time. What will the Dominus say? I'm frightened. He's so powerful. He's supposed to be..." She hunched against the sink.

I hoped she wouldn't cry. She's my anchor, and if she cried I would too. I wanted to avoid that. "Don't worry about the Dominus. I'll deal with that one. Please go somewhere and get me a hat or scarf. I'll be damned if I'll flash this mess for everyone." *I did hope my bizarre hair transformation and blue eyes were the smallest of changes she'd made in me.*

Chapter Twenty-Eight

We waited until we could see and touch a seriously drugged Ben. Then Lo, Pax, and I returned to Garnet to rest. At least I hoped they rested. Instead of joining Pax while he lay on my bed sleeping, I meditated. Sure enough, she popped in. I was ready.

"What is Âthrava? What does it mean?"

"Âthrava is the true title for those with whom I can communicate directly."

"Are you really a goddess? Are you female?"

"You define goddess. Believe what you wish. The female spirit...the female nature, draws me. You must understand one critical thing. I am powerful compared to humans, but I am not all-knowing and seeing. Otherwise, I would not have embarked on this outrageous plan to regain power so my tribes and I will survive.

"Why me? Why make me your... Âthrava?"

"You are tribe. A part of me resides in you. Your mother was supposed to raise you outside the tribe. I urged her to do that when you were born. There were problems. Times when I couldn't find you. I love Louise, but I have lost her, much as you lost a mother."

"Why outside the tribe?"

"Had you been raised inside you would have fallen prey to culture. You, because of your experience...there is a modern phrase...think outside the box."

"Experience. Is that what you call it?"

"I kept you alive, Lilly, when he hurt you. I didn't have the strength to do more."

"I won't thank you for that. I desperately wanted to die at times."

"I know. But I needed you and could not release you. Understand this, the earth upon which each tribe lives, what they call home right now, is the source of my power. You were so far away. I beg your pardon for your suffering. I beg your pardon for allowing you to fall into evil."

"Stop that shit, goddess. I survived Mama. Fall into evil? Bullshit. I did not 'fall' into anything. I jumped. I'll pay for my decision. Your coercion, using Ben's life, was shitty. But I gave into it. Another mark toward redemption. I hope. Getting McKay out of this life before he harms more people, will be another. I swear, I don't want to kill. Bi'ar—"

"Bi'ar is not under my control. I created the weapon and then lost it. Your actions with Bi'ar so far are acceptable. Bi'ar's actions are unfathomable. Now we must speak of action. Our enemies are gathering and will strike soon."

And speak she did. She gave orders, and she answered questions.

Me? Her Âthrava? A lifetime job. The only way out is to die. Having found the first bit of true happiness in my life made me disinclined to pursue that option.

****

I gulped a few more mouthfuls of beer and gave the Priestess, Commander, and Accountant of Bastet the unwelcome news. "Approximately two-hundred extremely well-armed men are coming for the gold. Their goal is to take over and destroy the town. She's given me a plan to save us."

They didn't speak for a while. They didn't question me or my authority to guide them. I did speak of her actual power limitations and the grave outcome if we failed.

Lo spoke first after the blistering shock passed. "The tribes haven't been attacked from the outside in three hundred years. The history books…that's why we immigrated to America and the goddess directed us where to buy land she could control."

The goddess had told me that. How certain land was important, not just for its riches. If only the rest of it was so easy, so clear. I got the feeling that she was holding back information. I just hoped that didn't destroy us. My impression of her? She was sincere, but I'd bet she'd tell a lie in a heartbeat—if she had a heart. I had to go on. "Basically, we'll face a small well-equipped private army. She described it in detail. It's not far from here. I wish we could go take it out before they strike, but it's too well guarded." I could see disappointment on Pax's face. He would be ready to fight.

I kept the goddess' words foremost in my mind. "Our event starts at daylight three days from now. This is the difficult part. By *her* will, this battle is ours alone. Involve no other tribes so there are no obligations. I'll tell you exactly what she wants. I'm not leading a fight. And, as I told you, you don't have to accept what I say. But if you do not, Bastet may be destroyed."

I could see the dismay in Ronnie and Lo as they exchanged looks across the table. Pax spoke for the first time. "That's our duty, Lilly. We govern Bastet. We will listen to your words. We will be ready to defend."

I gave them more details about their actions, and with that, the leaders of Bastet dutifully went out and obeyed the instructions from their goddess.

I had another task. I had to deal with my hair. I visited Simone the hostile beautician. I needed her too. She'd never be a friend, but we could work with that. My hair had to be white, pure white, not striped like a mutant blonde zebra. Simone told me that all my roots had the purity I desired and assured me my tresses would grow. Cautiously, she let strands drift through her fingers. She jumped back when the blue flashed. I needed to find a way to kill the light show. She, like Pax, could change shape, so she accepted strange things better than most. She picked up her scissors.

Other than wielding Bi'ar, I had no true battle power. As her Âthrava, I could not be a ruler. I'd be her messenger or a knife fighter. Nothing more. The tribe listened to me now, but I didn't know about the future. The goddess said she'd give me lessons on how to control them. Lessons for a job I most certainly did not desire.

We, members of Bastet, were indeed a superstitious bunch—for solid reasons. The Gifts made us a people filled with mysticism and unworldly lives. People who lived and obeyed a tribal law written thousands of years ago.

Well before daybreak on our enemies' chosen day, Lo drove me up a hill and left me on a moderate rocky cliff that overlooked the long passage to Oro Canyon and the cave of gold. The sacred cave. She hugged me and kissed me, crying. Then she left me in the pre-dawn darkness and went to join the others and wait.

Cold, so cold, but at least no wind. Not long after

Lo left, Araun walked out of the darkness. She carried a small light. Even with all that I'd seen, all that happened, she shocked me. The goddess had spoken not a word about her.

Araun, my grandmother, sat cross legged on the ground, surrounded by at least five rattlesnakes. Reptiles, they coiled about her for warmth in the chill morning. Her Gift. Snakes. Oh, boy. I sat beside her, a distance, carefully avoiding her pets.

It was about to begin. My goddess came to me. I felt her inside, burning, not demanding anything, but waiting. Watching.

I had to make one silent comment to her. "We are trivial things in the desert, aren't we?" I didn't expect an answer, but she spoke.

"Trivial things indeed. And smaller things in the world. And yet, we, the tribes, have endured for thousands of years. We will continue to fight until the last of us has left this world. The last will be me.

You are the first of the modern leaders. There are others. Now I will be able to contact them. As I persuade each to accept me, my power will grow. Like you, your sisters will be tempered by fire and remade into something new.

We waited in silence, the only sound distant thunder to the southwest.

Light grew, as did the anticipation. From my perch, I could see the canyon. The slender opening in the rock that allowed long, narrow, steep-sided entry to the rock bowl and small pond. A clear path to the goddess' sanctuary—and the gold. Welcome, thieves. I knew Pax, Ronnie, Lo, and other men and women watched, armed and ready, from their assigned positions.

Two sounds came in the distance. More thunder from the mountains to the southwest and mechanical engines moving toward us. Our enemy had arrived. Armed men and their machines, a line of vehicles sped down the highway from the east, not west from Sioux Crossing. I did wonder where they'd kept them hidden. Out in the open people would notice and word would have spread. They turned and roared into the valley, tearing up the dirt road. Profuse clouds of dust roiled behind them. They made straight for the canyon. The Sioux Crossing Compound was, of course, a diversion.

I counted eighteen vehicles. Varied sizes, but I'd say enough to carry at least the two hundred men, possibly more. Men I could see in open carriers resplendent in their body armor. Each carried a rifle capable of spreading deadly little missiles without prejudice. Bastet, fully armed, would not be able to resist them if it came to a face to face. The vehicles poured into the valley. They approached the rock canyon where they could only pass through in single file. They slowed. Not all of them would fit the rock bowl, but within minutes, they filled it to capacity. The others stopped and lined up bumper to bumper along the long entrance road beneath the cliffs where Araun and I watched. Whoever led them had not known the limited size of the bowl. The men below were mercenaries, paid to use weapons that only had one purpose—kill people. I could hear them laughing and calling to comrades. They woke this morning with the knowledge that they might kill for money. They did not care about those who died. That was evil enough to condemn them.

Pax was out there somewhere, carefully hidden.

"Please be safe, Pax. My love, don't leave me." I tossed the words out into the dawn, hoping he would hear.

And the snakes. Multiple snakes slithered out of the rocks and holes around us. Cold blooded reptiles. I'm sure they'd hidden from the chill night there. I sat beside Araun waiting for the light while hundreds of them, large, small, went past. Finally, most disappeared below.

Several remained, coiling in the low, sparse bushes around us. There are snakes in the desert, countless numbers, but resources kept them spread far apart. Araun had to have called these for days. Her body shook.

"Araun? What are you doing?"

A look of surprise crossed her face. Only an instant, but I knew there was more Lo hadn't told me. It would take a hundred years to pry all that information from her.

Araun's voice had the sound of fatalism. "I am, Granddaughter, keeping my servants warm. And paying for my sins."

"Sins?" Oh, hell. Tribal mysticism and declared nobility. I'd fallen prey to those flaws myself.

Araun didn't look at me. "Ask Luella when you finish here."

I stood then, on the cliff overlooking the canyon, so any who wished could see me. The sun, now near the horizon of an open sky, offered plenty of light. I needed the confrontation. It didn't take long. A massive SUV with darkened windows headed up the hill straight for me.

I had covered my hair, packed it under a hat. I prepared, but the fact was, from this point, I didn't know what the hell was going to happen. The SUV stopped twenty feet from me, and two men climbed out. McKay, I had expected. The other, our esteemed leader, my father, the Dominus, well, I didn't exactly expect him, but was not surprised.

"Hello, Lilly," he gave me a warm smile.

I hadn't thought about him too much since Vegas, but he was family, he was tribe. He'd called to check on my welfare. To tell me he was looking for McKay. Of course, he'd lied.

I looked down and kicked the dirt with my boot, angry, yes, and disappointed. "The saddest thing about betrayal is that it comes not from your enemies, but from friends. Saw that perky little clichéd zinger on the internet somewhere. You're new to me, so I have low expectations. The people of the tribes, your people, they respected and trusted you."

"They may do so. I don't want to hurt any member of the tribe. I merely want to control the gold and make better use of the ore. Bastet has been sitting on this holy resource too long." He held out a hand, as if making an offering to soothe me. "You are right about Mr. McKay, in all things. He's not an innocent man. He's simply been too helpful to reject his services. He's provided a method to make use of the gold without interference. He provided the guards you see below."

"Provided, as in he's in charge of them? He gives the orders?"

"Yes. He's agreed not to touch you." His eyes narrowed. I could almost hear his unspoken words. *I'm going to rid myself of him very soon and I will make him pay for your suffering.*

McKay, standing slightly behind him, arms

crossed, feet apart, and goddess help us...his killing face on. His interest seemed to be on the narrow canyon below. I knew McKay. He had realized what was missing. Surprise from the locals. The noise at least should have called them out. I could see a group of men at canyon's entrance, standing guard to repel them. He'd seen the mistake, too. Jamming all those vehicles into an enclosed space.

I had more I wanted to say. "McKay? Him I understand. Greed, murder, that's his life. But you? You have so much. You want more? Stinking greed? That's what this is about?"

He gave me a beneficent smile. "There is power, too. I'm sure you don't understand. You've never felt the glory of such things."

Is that what he thought? The glory? He was as delusional as McKay believing he loved me. But he was giving me information. "Why the charade with poor Simon?"

His face took on a grim expression. "Poor Simon indeed. Another useful tool. Until you eliminated him. You know, I had wanted to be subtler. Unfortunately, certain influential tribe leaders needed to be removed." He chuckled. Not funny, daddy dear, you don't know it, but you aren't directing this play. He went on. "Whomever alerted the FBI about McKay being in Las Vegas ruined that. You complicated my plan, too. You shouldn't have been there."

"Tribe members removed! You mean murdered...for a pile of gold." My voice rose to a shout.

What the hell had McKay told him? Was he that dense? "Dominus, are you delusional? Stop and think.

312

Men with guns burst into a room. Three guns, one for you, one for Pax, one for Garrett Dain."

I struggled for control, but my mouth kept working. "That was McKay's plan, Dominus. Use you. Kill you. Then Simon, his personal tribe member, could take charge during the confusion."

McKay didn't respond. He focused his attention on his army below. He could see no danger from the actors around him.

The Dominus prattled on. "Lilly, the gunmen were to escort certain tribal leaders out of the building, not kill them. Only those who were powerful enough to object to my plans and influence others. They wouldn't have harmed me or you. Simon, in the mêlée, went mad and tried to kill me."

"So, you believe that Pax Harrow and Garrett Dain could be escorted out peacefully. Think about it for a moment. They would just walk out and go away? That's insane."

McKay turned back to us. He grinned. Still silent, but very joyful.

The Dominus frowned. Confused? I'll bet. I knew something else about him. *Distance killing with his mind alone.* What a crock. Oh, he had certain mind control power. He tried to take over my mind when he drugged me. I resisted him, but with drugs, he was able to manipulate me to forget. His was a pitiful Gift indeed.

The Dominus straightened, preparing himself for action.

Sounds came from below, metal banging against metal, voices shouting about setting up positions.

"Do you now truly believe in the goddess, Lilly?"

The Dominus grinned. "How did they convince you. I wouldn't have thought you so gullible."

McKay, standing behind him, simply shook his head.

My turn to laugh. "The goddess? Don't you believe, Dominus? Aren't you her representative? You know, white hair, direct communication."

"I am aware of certain special abilities given to the tribes, Lilly. They are genetically inherited. They're not magical or given by a mystical being. There is no goddess."

He had not only rejected her authority but fallen into disbelief.

I needed to move forward. "I get it, Dominus. She won't talk to you anymore. She left you, stopped talking to you when you started shitting on her people. That's why you dye your hair white. How long has it been, now? How long since you heard her voice?"

The Dominus' mouth worked a little, but nothing came out.

Rifle shots rang out in the distance. It sounded like it came from the highway, but in an area so vast, open, and silent, it was hard to discern direction or distance.

McKay twisted and searched the area around us. How fun, seeing him suddenly uneasy. He always had things under control. Powerfully intuitive, he felt that something was wrong, things were going sideways. He just couldn't figure out what it was.

The Dominus didn't seem to notice or care. He jerked and made one step forward.

Araun suddenly stood beside me. She'd been behind me all along, but neither of the men had focused on her. A pickup truck raced up the hill and skidded on the loose dirt before the drive stopped. Roger Barter jumped out. Not unexpected. He headed straight for us, waving his arms as if he had special news, something important—something that would change things.

Foolish man. The goddess had staged an event. She would not allow Roger to interrupt. He passed one of the low scrub bushes, and multiple snakes flung their bodies up and struck at the same time. Legs, hands bitten, and when he fell, screaming, his face. He continued to scream when he made a long bumpy roll down the rough hill. Each turn puffed up dust like a smoke signal.

I shivered. Any ambivalence I had about snakes and Araun evaporated.

The Dominus had come back into focus. His mouth open in shock. McKay's face turned white as bleached bones. I certainly enjoyed his terror. "Don't worry, McKay. The snakes aren't for you. Too easy. Way too easy."

Araun suddenly knelt by my feet again and lowered her head.

"By your will, goddess. I am ready." She spoke so softly I think I was the only one who heard her. Ready for what?

"What the hell is that doing here now?" The Dominus turned to stare back toward the road. "Where's the God dammed escort?"

A massive truck bearing giant wide load warning signs rumbled down the narrow dirt road into the valley. Too fast, way too fast. Not an expert, but its load looked like a dragline. The boom was carefully folded, but it weighed hundreds of tons. Mining equipment to help dig out the gold. Hadn't it been in

Sioux Crossing? Yes. Tribesmen had been busy last night. I bet they'd liberated the vehicle. I knew they couldn't stand back and let an invasion happen without participation. McKay whipped out his phone.

"No service, McKay. I'll bet some ignorant tribesman killed the local tower. Not for too long, I hope."

"Lilly, call them off!" The Dominus' voice rose, demanding. "You'll get them killed. They're no match for the weapons down there. There's no need."

I shrugged. "Sorry, Daddy Dear. Are you under the illusion that I'm in charge? I'm not. I'm just on top of the hill bearing witness. You've forgotten, I guess. This little part of the earth belongs to the goddess. To Bastet, too. It's their home you're planning to destroy. I know they think it's worth dying for."

I snatched my hat off my head. "I'm just following orders."

My pure white hair tumbled out like a flag in the morning sun. I couldn't see the flashing blue highlights, but I'd bet they made an impression.

"How? You…" He knew what my hair meant.

"Yeah, Dominus. You've been fired. Dismissed, canned, sacked. Yes, it happened years ago, but you've been coloring yours, pretending, keeping control. Now she's picked a new sucker to do her dirty work."

The wide load truck had reached the place where there was a traffic jam at the end of the road leading to the canyon. The men below were shooting at it, but it kept barreling on. It slowed, and the driver jumped out and raced away.

Thump! The ground shook. A hole, not an exceptionally large one, opened under the wheels of the trailer carrying the dragline. It teetered, swayed, and toppled over on its side. I'd bet they felt that earthquake shaking in Sioux Crossing.

I winced. My opinion? Poor planning on my tribesmen's part. Everything was set up and would work without it. Oh, well, they were the ones who would have to move it out of the way. Nothing more than foot traffic was going in or out of the canyon for a while.

Then I had to speak to the person in charge, the leader, the commander of the invaders.

"McKay! Call off your men. Get them out of there. They can't ride, but tell them to walk, to run away. You leave now, too. I'll meet you later. You and I can discuss our grievances then. You truly don't know what you're dealing with here."

McKay grinned, his eyes bright, because I'd recognized he was in charge, no matter what the Dominus thought or said. Once he had men on the ground, he'd hold the Dominus, and there would be no sharing with the tribe. McKay would be hauling out the gold.

The Dominus, under a delusion of power, spoke to me. "What do you think you're going to do, little girl?" He'd drawn a pistol. McKay had one in hand too. They could kill me. They might very well kill me. Yes, my goddess had warned me. It was one of several outcomes of the battle.

"Listen, both of you. Again. Nothing here is in my control." I pointed to the canyon. "And killing me won't stop anything." So much death, so much pain, all because of greed and desire to rule over others.

Screams came from the canyon below. *Snakes!*

317

Followed by gunshots. The reptiles had attacked, and countless were giving up their slithery lives—but not before releasing a massive amount of venom. They'd crawled into small crevices, under bushes and fallen willows, lain hidden, invisible, until Araun ordered them to attack. Armor covered those men, but they hadn't expected this. Many had faces and hands exposed, and other areas were covered only with cloth.

Shots, multiple shots, screams, chaos. From the night I committed to my goddess, I had begun to understand her nature—and the fierceness of her tribes. Raised on Mama's brutality, no wonder I'd fallen in with McKay. Never an excuse, but violence in my blood.

The event I dreaded most happened. The Dominus, my father, screamed at me. "Damn you, this is all your fault." He lifted his gun. He pointed it at me and pulled the trigger. Araun leaped up between us. The bullet slammed into her. High caliber, it punched clear through flesh and bone. It hit me in the side. She collapsed at my feet.

I screamed. Two things surprised me. The bright, burning pain, acid agony from my waist to my knees— and the fact that I remained on my feet. I grabbed the wound with my hands. Hot blood poured through my fingers. Oh, shit. The world went blurry. Down to my knees, then, try to breathe fighting the massive pressure on my chest.

Don't pass out, Lilly, don't pass out. You need to see.

"Lilly!" McKay cried out in despair. Despair? How obscene.

He acted, too. He shot the Dominus, my father, in

the back. The man went stiff. His eyes popped open, his mouth…he toppled flat on his face. McKay stood over him pulling the trigger. Repeatedly the Dominus' body jerked with each of McKay's shots. The sharp cracks cut through the air, each signaling death to the world. McKay's gun magazine clicked as it finally emptied.

My snake charming grandmother lay twitching and dying before me, and my former lover and torturer stood blasting holes in my father. When I started this morning, I'd known I would be facing a deadly challenge. But this? It was not one of the possibilities my goddess mentioned. I was alive…so far. How utterly outrageous.

The ground rumbled. I felt more subtle vibrations under my knees.

McKay came to me. Blood soaked my clothes. Was I bleeding inside, too? He lifted me to my feet.

"Lilly! Lilly, I'll save you, honey. Please don't die."

It was official. McKay had gone nuts. Or had the man with mind control powers driven him mad? I'd never know.

Pain savaged me. It spread down my side into my leg, and my right arm wouldn't move. I was going down soon. I begged. *Goddess, let me at least see what I'm dying for*.

I hit McKay with a weak, ineffectual fist. "No, no. I have to see."

The entrance to the cave, that monstrous black hole leading to the treasure men had killed and died for, blasted out a solid stream of muddy red water. Oh, goddess, the sheer thrust and volume. What a flood. How many days had it rained in the mountains to accumulate that much water? And she who was indeed goddess of this piece of earth held it back. Waiting. The stream quickly turned into a geyser.

The rock bowl filled in seconds. Water headed in the only direction it could. Down the narrow canyon. The flood slammed men and vehicles as it rushed on between the high rock walls. It lifted lighter vehicles and swept them away. They all crashed into the dragline where it backed up against a nightmare of crushed steel. The deluge carried living and dead alike over the blockade. No longer constricted by rock walls, water spread over the flat desert. The living were met by well-armed tribesmen and women. Men that escaped the tribesmen ran to where the mountain lions waited to drive them back. Now that was cool. I just hurt too much to appreciate it all.

In minutes, the battering ram, the grand slam torrent, drained to where only inches of water remained to be absorbed by dry sand. I had pledged my life to a drama queen goddess. I was so screwed. If I lived, that is.

Chapter Twenty-Nine

McKay went crazy. Make that crazier. He'd lost his army and killed his own patron in the tribe. Shock and pain drew me into a barely conscious state. Not unconscious as I wished, because I remained in agony. McKay dragged me away from the drama stage below toward the SUV. He lifted and shoved me in the seat. How thoughtful. He belted me in. I moaned, barely able to see. So close, I heard rather than saw him reload his gun.

The engine roared, and he headed across the rough desert. With the 4-wheel drive he didn't need the road, but oh the pain to me. I blacked out and came to, my head hanging down between my knees. There'd been no impact to tighten the strap over my shoulder, so I'd fallen forward. I grabbed my wound. My hand came away with fresh blood.

Asphalt! He'd made it to the road. McKay cursed as he drove. To say my mind wasn't functioning right was an understatement. I grabbed the handle above the door and managed to sit. I giggled.

"Screwed you up again, didn't I, McKay?" I took credit for the goddess' spectacular final act. He would never believe in her anyway.

McKay replied by hitting me. My head bounced off

the side glass. That was the old McKay, the bully I once loved. My mouth propelled me toward complete disaster. "Stop it, asshole. What happened to, *I'll save you Lilly?*" He hit me again. I yelped, tried to laugh at him, but couldn't. Wait, where were we headed? No matter, I didn't want to go.

"No. No. No." I reached over, stretched over, forcing my way through the raging fire consuming my body. I grabbed the steering wheel and, with my puny bit of remaining strength, jerked it down. With speed, it didn't take much. The vehicle lurched. Thankfully, I blacked out again.

I woke with McKay dragging me out the window of a smoking car. It burst into flames. Smoke rolled skyward in billowing black plumes. Oh goody, a beacon.

I blacked out again. Why couldn't I stay that way?

McKay had me over his shoulder, but then threw me down on the desert. Sandy landing, though multiple rocks surrounded us. Things were looking up. Oh, pain existed, but in the distance. My little bit of logical mind told me I was in shock. I'd die soon. The column of black smoke would mark our location, but I doubted anyone would arrive in time to save me. McKay would shoot me before that. Or more likely, I'd plain old die from blood loss.

I raised my head. McKay sat on a rock, heaving and trying to catch his breath. Not sure about time, but I managed to roll to another rock and drag myself into a semi sitting position. I checked my side. The bleeding had stopped at least. McKay had managed to get us part way up a small hill before he gave out.

And what was that? The roar of a mountain lion.

Distant, racing across the desert, but close enough. Soundless laughter filled me. Too late. But McKay wouldn't escape.

"What's so fucking funny." McKay pointed his gun at me. "Suppose I shoot you in the leg. Would you laugh?"

Oops, had to stall him. It took a couple of tries. "Water?"

"There's no fucking water, no fucking car, no fucking anything."

Yes, that's good old Garnet. How utterly amusing. I couldn't laugh anymore. I was having too much trouble breathing.

The lion roared again. Closer now. My hero, coming to save me. He would miss me, and the goddess would have to find someone else to be her puppet.

McKay heard it this time. "What's that?"

"Mountain lion."

He glared at me. "We're only a few miles from Sioux Crossing."

We couldn't be. I wasn't exactly keeping time, but we weren't on the road that long. McKay rocked back and forth. "I have men there. We're going to walk."

We? Was he blind? Delusional? I couldn't stand, even if he held me up. I'd be dead before we went a hundred feet. I was cold. And hot. I desperately needed water. McKay kept staring at me. He held his gun loosely in his hand. Had he realized that the whole game was over? He could kill me at any time.

He focused on me. "What happened to your hair? It's white."

I didn't have the strength to tell him. I couldn't say that happens when a goddess picks you out from all her people and talks to you in your mind. When she changes you. I could barely hold my head up. McKay suddenly stood. A low rumble came from the rocks around us. He whirled, unable to pinpoint the sound.

Pax stepped out from between two rocks behind him. Head low, shoulders hunched, attack position. McKay whirled to face a two hundred forty-pound cat. He had the pistol in his hand. He turned to me. Stupid, so stupid. I'd bet the Dominus had explained certain aspects of the Bastet Tribe to him. He hadn't believed—then. Now, after what had happened, he'd kill me if Pax attacked.

But turning his back on a cat? A cat that could pounce in less than a second. A gold streak and McKay tumbled down. Pax latched onto McKay's wrist and crunched down, teeth sinking easily into flesh, breaking and separating bones.

It was all over then—except for the pain. McKay's pain.

Pax's claws tore through cloth and flesh. Not deep, no, just enough to damage him. Again, shred his clothes. His knee? Oh, a big bite. Long sharp teeth. More bones crushed. McKay kept screaming. With one paw Pax flipped him over. He stood on him and raked his back in a crude approximation of the scars on mine. Flip over again and…emasculate. Oh, dear. That took more than one swipe.

McKay passed out.

Pax stood over him, breathing hard, but he'd run across the desert to get here. I heard another sound. FBI Agent Hart stood watching the scene. He must have followed us. Or Pax had him standing by. He had his gun out but didn't seem to be anxious to shoot. Finally, he sat on a rock and stared at McKay.

Pax came to me. I tried to touch him, but I couldn't lift my arm.

"Love you…" All I could manage.

The lion roared. Right in my face. Oh boy. That'll wake a person up.

All at once Hart was there with a bottle of water at my lips. Better. Did I see Hart and Pax talking, and Pax was naked? Had he shifted shape in front of Hart? Shown him a tribal secret?

McKay had regained consciousness. He moaned, coughed, and made inarticulate little sounds. Only grunting noises, but constant. Oh, goody. He was awake and hurting again.

Julia? Are you watching us from Heaven, honey? Can you see? Can you hear him crying?

More noise. More people. "No!" Hart shouted. "Take her first. Send another bus for him. They don't go together. He's under arrest, and I haven't read him the shit yet."

I remember pieces of the ambulance ride. Stabilized, hydrated, and on my way to the hospital in Vegas, I demanded several times that we stop at a store and buy hair dye. I specified the shade, too. Pax hadn't come with me. Sheriff Pax had his duty. That was going to be an inevitable facet of my life. Oh, I did remember grabbing one of the paramedics by the arm and telling him I had to go shopping for an eight-thousand-dollar dress.

Chapter Thirty

I survived. Seems I was first-rate at that—surviving. Medicated and when I wasn't asleep, I could function. Lo surged into my room. She hovered over me, crying. "Look at you, awake."

"Yeah. I didn't have to have surgery this time. A straight through wound. Hurts like hell, though. And I'll have a brand-new scar. This one will be round. All the others are straight—sort of." Had the goddess helped me, healed me a bit? Maybe a little. I don't know how much strength that flood cost her.

Lo had been into see me before, but I wasn't able to talk, only drugged babble.

I held her tight this time. "How long has it been? How is everyone? No one's come but you. I understand. I guess."

"I'm sorry, sweetheart. Pax and Ronnie had to deal with things. It's a mess and way too much attention on us. We buried bodies fast and deep. We couldn't get rid of all the equipment before the FBI came. Hart confused and delayed them for a while. Not sure how effective that will be. He's not high in rank. And there are other…agencies. I'm sure there are reports making their way up the chain of command. An armed invasion in the desert, taken out by a flood, doesn't happen every day. If satellites were recording, I'm sure we'd make a real show. Unless she could have covered us."

"I'll ask but I feel so raw, I don't want to talk to her right now."

Lo frowned, but she went on. "In better news. We had an emergency tribal meeting by phone and computer. Garrett Dain has agreed to temporarily take over as CEO at Ennead, smoothing things from that end. You're the Bastet Âthrava. It's been a long time, but the oldest tribe members remember what that was like. You are going to have to talk to them. It will settle down eventually."

"I'm *not* the Dominus. Just because my hair is white and flashy blue. Absolutely not. Retire that title. I'm the goddess' rep for Bastet. I hope they don't think I have a hotline to her. She comes and goes when she wants."

Lo just hung her head. It reminded me. "Araun. Did you find…"

Lo squeezed me tight. I heard the sorrow in her voice. "We found her. And him. We buried them. Will you tell me what happened?"

"The Dominus shot at me when he saw my hair. Araun jumped in front, took the major impact. The bullet went through her and wounded me. Then McKay shot the Dominus, grabbed me, and ran away. I wrecked the car, and Pax came. Now you tell me about Araun."

Lo wiped her eyes. "I'll try. Your mother's illness started to show when she was about six years old. No healer could touch the madness. Araun drugged her with…oh, goddess, potion after potion trying to find an impossible cure. Those drugs destroyed Louise. She suffered, Lilly. She ran away. She had no other defense, no escape. She came back when you were born but didn't stay."

I waited on her while she covered her face with her hands and sobbed. She slowed, and I handed her a washcloth from the small stack on the console by my bed.

"Please finish, Lo."

She nodded and sniffed. "When you came, Araun finally accepted responsibility for what she'd done. I know it was traumatic. I couldn't forgive her. Maybe the goddess offered her a way out."

"So, she sacrificed her life for redemption? To ease her guilt. I wouldn't have asked her to do that."

"It wasn't your decision, Lilly. I know it affected you, but there was nothing you could do or should have done."

"No, no, no!" Someone yelled from the hall. I knew that voice. "Hurry up. Hurry up. Don't let them catch us."

A wheelchair rounded the door on two wheels. It surged into the room at a dangerous speed. Deputy Ben pushed by a laughing Doc Hardy. Doc had retired from healing. The next one might kill him and the person he wanted to save.

The chair rammed into my bed. Doc stopped at the door and held up his hands, barring a couple of nurses from entry. "I tell you, I'm a medical doctor. Got a diploma...license." He broke into a coughing spasm that totally ruined his brilliant last stand.

Then Ben was beside me, half out of the chair and trying to hug me. He couldn't. We were both in too much pain. Finally, he settled for lying half on my bed and half in the wheelchair. His arms were around me, and it felt fine.

"I want to go home!" Ben pleaded, but he was laughing. "Take me home with you! Please, I'll be good. I'll take my medicine. I promise."

Laughing hurts like hell when you've been shot. And probably worse when you've been gut shot, like Ben. It got a little noisy then, so he and I hung on to each other while Lo got Doc settled down and the nurses pacified. She treated them all like drunks in the bar. She told Doc if he had a heart attack, he would be banned from the tavern forever. Part persuasion and part stern inducement. Exhaustion overcame me by the time everyone finished. I fell asleep.

I woke with Pax sitting beside me, holding my hand.

"Hi, sleeping beauty." He lifted my hand and kissed my palm. "Sorry I couldn't get here sooner. Big fuss."

"Excuses, excuses." Oh, I was so glad to see him. "I don't need details, but what's happening?"

"There are problems. We couldn't clean everything up in time, and the government's poking around. Everyone's curious. What were we fighting over? We've kept them out so far. The holy site, home of the goddess, religion card is playing well. Unfortunately, we're not an official religion. Someone suggested that we consecrate Ennead as a church. Become a religious nonprofit."

"And McKay?"

"One leg amputated at the knee. Hand is pretty messed up. He'll recover from most of his other injuries. He's missing certain personal body parts, too. They stuck him in a federal prison hospital. Hart tells me he jabbers insane stories about snakes and wild animals and seems to have lost his persuasive charm. Unfortunately, he's also jabbering about the gold, trying to buy himself out of trouble. I don't know who's listening. Thank the goddess we have complete mineral rights on the land."

"I'll bet Hart checks on him from time to time to be sure he's suffering appropriately."

"I expect so. Hart's been hanging around Garnet too long. He knows too much about us now. That day we rescued you on the road, I promised to let him in on the action when we took McKay down if he'd leave you alone. I kind of like his tenacity." He shook his head and chuckled. "I think he's in love with Lo. It's doomed, but stranger things have happened."

I moved over so he could sit on the bed and hold me in his arms. Something occurred to me.

"Did you ever find out who killed poor Henry?"

"Yes. Roger Barter. Finally got the DNA tests back on Henry's clothes. Those take months.

"Henry managed to get one solid lick in, and Barter bled on him. I suspected. I had to break up a fight between them earlier that evening. Barter…" He looked around to be sure no one was listening. "Barter was the cat you saw me fight that night. He challenged me. I should have killed him. For Henry."

I punched him. Not hard. I didn't have the strength. "And you dragged me out there that night, practically accused me of killing Henry…what an ass!"

He laid his head on mine. "I plead insanity. You were screwing my mind up so bad right then. I wasn't accusing you. I wanted to show you how dangerous things could be. I had to keep Barter calm until I had proof, too. Keep him from running. I wanted to show you…but you showed me. Your warrior's courage."

Okay, I couldn't stay too mad. "I do have another question. Who was the lion that came to sit and watch me carve at night? Did you send him?"

He frowned. "Send? Ben and I watched most nights, but not as cats. Ben and I would have instantly smelled him."

"Well, I don't sleep when I'm out on the porch, so I didn't dream. Do I have a genuine lion stalker?"

"Maybe. It's Garnet. Remember?" He shrugged, but I knew it troubled him. Yes, Garnet personified weird. But a strange unidentified lion on his turf? Sniffing around his woman? Genuine or shifter, no way would he allow that to go on.

Pax spoke softly in my ear. "Lilly, what's going to happen now? With you, with the goddess?"

"I don't know. So far, all she wants me to do is keep peace in the tribe." Personally, I hoped she'd leave me alone. I hope I'm strong enough to hold things together. Of course, she wasn't finished with me. "I told Lo, I'm not a Dominus. Forget that form of government."

Pax rubbed his face in my hair. "Will you marry me at the Summer Solstice?"

"Yes, I will marry you. I need you so much."

We kissed a while, made promises, talked of better days. It was cool until Pax gave that deep, impossible cat growl. Garrett Dain swept in, bringing laughter with his wonderful smile. Oh, dear, but what fun. The oh, so charming wolf had arrived.

Epilogue

I walked down the path to a place where the scent and color of roses reigned. She liked the rose garden best, they told me. She sat perfectly calm on a bench by a small fountain that subdued extraneous noise. Frank said the new antipsychotic meds worked better than others had. A young man in scrubs sat not far away. Ah, the benefits of wealth. Each patient had their own private keeper in this glorious garden.

She stared at the flowers, a blank drawing pad on her lap. She didn't move as I sat beside her. "Hello, Mama."

She turned to face me. Still so beautiful. I'd thought her an angel once.

A light frown crossed her brow, then recognition. "Luella?"

"No Mama. I'm Lilly."

She shook her head. "Lilly is my pretty little baby." She frowned. "My mother wanted to kill her, but I saved her. I ran away." She sat straighter and stared around. "Where is she? My baby?"

"Lilly is safe, Mama. She's safe and loved."

Mama relaxed. "I adore her, my precious little Lilly. Frank takes care of her. He stays home from school to watch her when I work."

I could not bear this. "Yeah, Frank's wonderful. He's a good son." I stood. I bent over and kissed her on the cheek. She gave me a placid, uninvolved smile.

"Goddess bless you, Mama."

I left her there sitting quietly among the fragrant roses. My mother had gone where no one in this world could reach her. I had feared her, hated her, loved her, and desperately longed for her love in return. Maybe we'd have a chance again in another lifetime.

Pax and Frank waited for me by the whispering courtyard fountain. Pax had the unfortunate duty of explaining about the money my brother and I had amassed over the years. We'd paid for Mama's care, my hospital and rehab, and had a decent sum left over. Frank hugged me. I missed him so much. He gazed out at a garden that bordered on spectacular. "Lilly, I know she's safe and comfortable, but I wish we could give her a better life."

Pax handed me his always available handkerchief. I accepted it and wiped at the profuse tears on my face. "She seems happy, Frank. At peace anyway. I realize you gave up most of your childhood to help me survive. There's nothing I can do to give that back to you."

"It's okay, Lilly. I enjoy my life now." Frank's expression gave me a glimpse of his true happiness. Just a glimpse, but oh, he so deserved to be blessed that way.

He hugged me again. "Come on, girl. Taking care of my baby sister kept me out of trouble, anyway. If not for you, I'd probably have been running with the gangs by the time I was thirteen."

I glanced at Pax. "I'm okay now. Someone is protecting me. Will you hold your nose and attend our very pagan wedding in the summer? I promise, no naked meadow dancing. Unless you want me to arrange a show."

"On the Solstice, of course. Yes, I'll be there." He brushed his fingers over my hair. He hadn't asked why it made the drastic leap from deep brown to pure white since he'd bid me goodbye at the bus station for my trip to Garnet. To my utter amazement, he hadn't spoken of it at all. At least I'd managed to get control of the magic light flashes. He also did not mention my eyes changing from gray to blue. I'd bet Frank knew and remembered more about Garnet than he said. It was okay, though. Certain memories were best locked away.

Another thing kept locked away. *Bi'ar, the cursed knife.* I keep hoping it will disappear, but it remains. It's still mine. It haunts me and joyfully reminds me of the ease of killing. Should the need arise, I will find it in my hand.

And my goddess? She's surprisingly reserved. She whispers in my mind and offers advice. Other times she tells me stories I don't understand. As I learn about the tribes, their history, their tribal law, one idea has become certain. This is not the end of her plans for us. She has a larger scheme in the works. I hope we survive. I will live in the desert, on her earth, and serve. I looked at Pax. He smiled back. There should be a few compensations along the way.

Addendum: The Goddess and the Tribes

The Tribes and names.

The tribes arrived in America in 1890 and migrated to locations chosen by their goddess. It was a long, arduous journey and a challenging settlement process, but by 1910, they'd purchased the goddess blessed land (Initially stolen from native Americans). Records created and necessary bribes paid, they settled in.

In a 1925 meeting, the tribal leaders felt a burning need to update their thousand-year-old multisyllable, difficult to pronounce tribal names. In keeping with tenets of modernization, and after countless exhausting meetings, they formed a committee. Decisions of the committee were to be final, with no appeal or challenges. The Historians would then record them in tribal law.

No one noticed that the naming committee consisted mostly of deep-seated traditionalists. They did shorten the names, which made them marginally easier to pronounce. Unfortunately, for tribal names they went to the history books and searched for names of ancient gods, goddesses, and mythical heroes. The tribal leaders were so tired of the battle, they allowed it to stand.

Tribe	Primary Home
Adapa	Colorado
Anzu	New York
Bastet	Arizona
Fenrir	Oregon
Gaia	Louisiana
Maris	Kentucky
Nyx	Virginia
Siris	Florida
Summanus	New Mexico
Talos	Oklahoma

Section One

A compilation of tribal histories because even the historians disagree.

About 3,000 to 4,000 BCE, a group of humans lived in an area east of the Black Sea. A tribe of hunter/gatherers, nomads, they roamed while people to the south were developing civilizations, temples, and establishing trade routes. They called themselves Ha'urva, a word that simply meant *"all of us"* in their language.

One day, a powerful supernatural being came to live with them. The Ha'urva didn't note her arrival. She was simply there, and they accepted her. For a thousand years she lived among them, joining their ceremonies, taking lovers, and yes, producing the occasional child that would mix her supernatural blood with theirs. She provided instruction and used her power judiciously so they would survive.

The Ha'urva prospered with her guidance until about 1,000 BCE. Then they grew too large as a group to be cohesive without a greater governmental structure. She gave it to them. Two tribes, then six, and eventually ten, all slightly different, but with her at their center. They came to perceive of her as their goddess.

For an unknown reason, the goddess and her tribes slowly grew weaker. To keep her beloved Ha'urva, she made a sacrifice. She irrevocably changed their DNA structure so that particular parts of it matched her own. She gave up her body, her physical presence in the world, to bind every tribesman and woman to her genetically, to give them certain traits, and the unalterable desire to cling to others of their kind. They grew taller and stronger physically, were less susceptible to disease, and lived longer lives.

One unforeseeable consequence of her sacrifice was that she could no longer walk among them and directly communicate with them at will. She had to create intermediaries. She called them her Âthrava, one for each tribe. The designation of the individual gave their goddess' culture a renewed formality. She could only speak to the regular tribe members through dreams. The Âthrava she could speak to and command.

As time passed each tribe developed a structure of tribal laws that kept the fundamental culture but allowed them differences. Wide differences at times. The goddess' DNA gave individual tribe members varied and uncertain extrasensory powers. Physical powers, psychic powers, and for a very few, the ability to change shape. They called these powers Gifts.

The tribes left their homelands and traveled, moving ever west with the boundless migrations. Each country they passed through brushed them with a bit of history, custom, languages. *Serve but not worship,* they would say of their goddess. She and the tribal laws were the center of their lives. Most tribe members believe there is a distant all-knowing God, a Master of the Universe. However, their immediate focus belonged to their unnamed goddess, who is their earthly guardian.

All ten tribes eventually settled in the United States after the Revolutionary War. Each found a niche, a location, and over the years, settled in. After much struggle and strife, early in the 20th Century, they developed the Ennead. Ennead was a desperate central binding corporation dedicated to the protection and preservation of their way of life.

Fragmented with internal dissention, the future looked bleak. Dissolution after 5,000 years, the progression from mud huts to doublewide trailers, seems unthinkable. Most tribe members cling to the idea that the goddess will show up and save them. She's been out of touch for at least 30 years.

Internal squabbles abounded, but the worst trouble began when all but one of her Âthrava died. The one remaining Âthrava was so dangerously flawed the goddess rejected him and gave up all direct communication with her people. An evil man, he continued to control the tribes as their leader, pretending that he was still her chosen. The only thing she retained in full measure was control of the earth where each tribe called home.

She realized she, too, was dying. Her people's beliefs, their cohesiveness, kept her alive, and it slowly drained away. She communicated by dreams, and nothing went the way planned. The women and men of the tribes were failing, or worse, betraying their own in the name of money and power. The goddess knew, if she didn't act everything would fall apart. Only something radical would save them.

Her plan? It would take 30 years and be fraught with complications. Failure would mean her end. She needed to choose new special servants to pull things together. The next group would be raised outside the structure of the tribe and all would be women. She would watch, and when an acceptable set of traits arrived in an infant, she would use dreams and what tiny bit of power that remained to move that infant out of the tribe. The girl would be raised to maturity by another culture. That distance gave each woman a distinct perspective. It would allow them to act when a woman born inside the tribal culture would hesitate and fail. The first complication? Finding the strength and have the cunning to somehow pry an infant girl away from the tribe. Tribal mothers could be savage when protecting their young. The second complication? Finding that Âthrava when the appropriate time arrived.

Then she had to draw each of her Âthrava in and convince her to take her place and dedicate her life to the goddess. The third complication? A strong-willed woman with extrasensory powers, most with abundant moral flaws, required shrewd coercion. She developed a plan to control that. It involved a certain degree of erratic moves and deception, but if humans could lie, so could a goddess.

Section Two

Cultural Development

The deepest, fiercest instinct of the human species is survival. It is so intrinsic, so desperate, that humans must by nature battle to the last desperate gasp of breath. Once the primitive human brain evolved sufficiently to comprehend and learn to fear the finality of death, it rebelled. That rebellion led to the invention of religion. It started with nature worship, the sun, moon, and earth, and steadily trudged on to the invention of gods. Virtually all those invented gods offered a version of life after death. The fact that none of them blessed worshipers with their physical presence in any demonstrable manner dissuaded no one.

Humans are clever, if not sensible. They realized that, since their deities refused them a physical manifestation, they had to make do with human representatives. Priests and priestesses. The chosen individuals strived for millennia to guide or compel worshipers to a specific version of their deity. Of course, they also required complete control of a human's life. Then came the demand for hard currency to fund temples and the holy hot line to…whomever.

And yet, for a few humans blessed—or cursed— there is direct evidence of powerful supernatural beings in the world. Those few humans rarely know the true nature of those beings. Gods? Goddesses? Angels? Demons? Really, a certain *look the other way* mindset is required.

Section Three

The Blades

In the early days, the war times, everyone fought with bladed weapons. The goddess, livid at the loss of her people to marauders, went to the deep molten earth and forged three blades. She named them Bi'ar, Ben'zir, and Ba'ran. She considered them her supernatural children, created to aid her human brood.

She imbued the knives with certain attributes. As with all complex supernatural objects, it went a bit awry. Each blade became semi-sentient and developed certain powers of its own. The blades, able to come and go as they pleased, chose their carriers. They chose, but (seemingly) only among what they considered warriors. They thirsted with a deep abiding will to draw blood. Rather than mere tools, they became players in tribal games. It was up to the individual chosen to control them. The color of runes incised on each blade and a stone on the hilt distinguished them. Bi'ar's runes glow blue and its stone is black. Ben'zir glows gold and its stone is green. Ba'ran has silver runes with a red stone.

A word about the author…

Lee Roland is a writer of urban fantasy and paranormal romance. She lives in Florida with her family. http://leeroland.com

Other books from Lee Roland and TWRP

Bone Dance

Thank you for purchasing
this publication of The Wild Rose Press, Inc.

For questions or more information
contact us at
info@thewildrosepress.com.

The Wild Rose Press, Inc.
www.thewildrosepress.com

www.ingramcontent.com/pod-product-compliance
Lightning Source LLC
Chambersburg PA
CBHW050031030726
47506CB00001B/227